With slow, assured arrogance, Lachlan lowered his mouth to hers. His strong fingers stroked her jaw, and their scorching heat sent sparks of longing across her throat, down her spine, over her breasts. *Mon Dieu,* what was she doing? Lachlan Maclean was a married man, and she was a proper widow in mourning for her father-in-law.

"Och, are ye a changeling, then?" Lachlan whispered, lips hovering like butterfly wings against her mouth. He gazed deep into her eyes, then brushed his lips over hers—light, deft, teasing, seductive. "A druid sent to bewitch me?"

Bewitch? That was all it took. Fiona lurched backward, breaking Lachlan's intimate grip on her jaw. To cover her agitation and hide her flaming cheeks, she bent and snatched up the puppy, then took three deep breaths, counted to five and stood. Her perfectly schooled, drilled and false features were serene once more.

"Is that what you think of me, my lord?" she said demurely. "If so, I'm amazed that you would trust me to serve your tea. What if I put eye of newt or tongue of frog in it?"

Lachlan stepped to the side, so the corner of the table over him between them. A veil of nonchalance descended challenging smoldering eyes, leaving the cool and distantly I call you Fiona? Aye? Weel now, since ye dinna fancy a *personal* reward"—he arched a dark brow—"perhaps I can make ye a present from here." He gestured to the jumble of items spread across the table. "A box of almond comfits, perhaps? Or a blue silk ribbon?" His intent gaze never left her face, and Fiona felt as if her fluttering heart must at any moment careen from her breast. . . .

Dear Romance Reader,

In July last year, we launched the Ballad line with four new series, and each month we'll present both new and continuing stories set everywhere from medieval England to the American West—the kind of passionate, romantic stories you love best, written by the most gifted authors. At the back of each book, we'll tell you when you can find subsequent books in the series that have captured your heart.

First up is the second entry in Lori Handeland and Linda Devlin's wonderful *Rock Creek Six* series. This month Linda Devlin introduces **Sullivan**, a half-breed bastard with no place in the world—until he finds his fate in a special woman's arms. Next, Maura McKenzie continues the *Hope Chest* series with **At Midnight**, as a modern-day newspaper reporter tracks a murderer into the past, where she meets a Pinkerton agent determined not only to solve the case, but to steal her heart.

The passioante men of the *Clan Maclean* return in Lynne Hayworth's spectacularly atmospheric **Winter Fire**, as a widow with a special gift meets the laird of the proud but doomed clan. Will her love bring about his salvation? Finally, Kelly McClymer offers the fourth book in the charming *Once Upon a Wedding* series, introducing **The Infamous Bride** who begins her marriage on a rash wager—and finds that her husband's love is the only wedding gift she wants. Enjoy!

Kate Duffy
Editorial Director

The Clan Maclean

WINTER FIRE

Lynne Hayworth

ZEBRA BOOKS
Kensington Publishing Corp.
http://www.zebrabooks.com

Prologue

Drumossie Moor, Scotland
April 16, 1746

Tiny grains of sleet spit from the twilight sky and skittered in the rising wind, then bit like cruel, icy teeth into Lachlan Maclean's freezing cheeks. Ragged patches of snow had accumulated in the battlefield's cannon-gouged hollows, and with each frigid gust, white crystals whirled and raced across the blood-soaked ground as if chased by unseen demons. The snow settled against the crumpled shoulders and mangled limbs of dead and dying Highlanders, cloaking them in a transient shroud of pure, gleaming white before swirling away into the gathering darkness.

Lachlan let his eyelids drift shut, then opened his mouth and thrust out his tongue, savoring the sizzle of snow crystals against his fevered flesh. *Och, thank God for wee mercies.* Unlike many of the wounded, he had managed to roll onto his back before passing out from pain and dizziness, and if, upon awakening, he found that the falling snow wasn't enough to quench his raging thirst, at least he had a diversion to pass the time until he died.

He noted with a dull, hollow curiosity that all sensation—the bone-twisting shafts of pain, the sickening waves of nausea, the deep, wracking chills that engulfed his body like the ice-rimed waters of Loch Linnhe—all had leached away. Not bit by bit, as a warrior would expect when his heart had pumped what surely must be a bucketful of blood onto the muddy battlefield, but all at once, in one slick, head-to-toe movement—rather like stripping the skin from a rabbit.

He attempted a rueful smile, but his lips had gone numb.

So this was how it felt to die. How very odd.

He shook his head in an attempt to clear his mind, then forced his thoughts back to Castle Taigh, standing like a fortress at the edge of the sea, rising like a sentinel from the mists and moors and mountains. Dear God in heaven, how he longed for the old days, when missing a clean shot at a rabbit had been his biggest regret.

Och, but what was he thinking about? St. Ninian, he was dying. 'Twas no time for maudlin memories.

"Sir?"

Lachlan flinched, startled by the aberration of a sweet, lilting voice at the gates of hell.

"Is the pain very bad, sir?"

Could it be an angel's voice? Nay, surely not. Father Stephen had said that heavenly messengers spoke in tones of sounding brass. This voice had been so low he scarce could credit that he had heard it over the sobs of the women who had come to claim their dead and over the curses of the Sassenachs who roamed the battlefield like carrion-glutted vultures. Damn their bloody souls to hell!

Lachlan shuddered and clenched his eyes tighter. St. Ninian, how had he gotten ensnared in such a hopeless, foolish battle? He should have stayed on Mull, stayed and ensured that Catriona and their bairn were safe. But nay, he was laird and eldest brother, so he *would* fight. Well, he had gotten his punishment. Since the Duke of Cumberland's victory over Prince Charles Edward Stuart earlier that day, he had watched in horror as British soldiers ruthlessly bayoneted the wounded and dying Jacobites. He had roared and cursed the gash in this thigh that prevented him from rising to defend his comrades. But as the hours had worn on, his rage had dissolved into despair, then into blank-eyed numbness.

He swallowed, hard. Such was the way of life. But, och, God help him, what if Jamie and Diarmid were among the fallen?

"Sir?"

Lachlan struggled to open his eyes, but the lids seemed weighted down by an icy crust of snow. He was so cold, so cold. The life was draining out of him, draining down a cool, smooth tunnel of ebony toward endless peace and rest. How delicious to slip away, empty of all sensation save gratitude—gratitude that even after all his wretched sins, God had allowed him to die in the arms of an angel.

A small, warm hand cupped his cheek, and feeling surged back into his body. He felt a jolt of raw energy, followed instantly by a delicious, shimmering warmth that flowed through his veins like honeyed mead. Impenetrable black shadows fled from his mind, and he saw a blinding bolt of light that dazzled, yet did not burn. It was as if he were looking straight into the face of the sun. He dragged a chill gasp into his lungs and tasted the icy tang of heather, the green sharpness of fir and the rich, mineral essence of the earth itself.

"Ye've an awful gash on your hand, sir. 'Tis bleedin' somethin' fierce."

The warm hand trailed from Lachlan's cheek down to his right arm, which lay in a useless, twisted heap across his chest. He had lost all feeling in it hours earlier, but not before realizing with a surge of dread that the tendons were severed—a tragedy for a Highland warrior. But what did that matter now? King George had won, and there would be no more Highland warriors.

He felt the angel lift his mangled hand and clasp it gently between hers. Blissful warmth melted through him until he felt he surely must dissolve and float to heaven. "Did God send ye?" he croaked.

"Nay, me mother did."

With monumental force of will, Lachlan opened his eyes, then blinked in utter astonishment. His rescuer wasn't an angel—she was a scrawny, wee, redheaded lassie with freckles and a runny nose.

"Good—ye're no' dead after all." She smiled shyly and ventured a sidelong glance from beneath lowered dark lashes. She had lost her two front teeth, and her eyes were the exact shade of the twilight sky—deep, peaceful violet. Eyes of wisdom and serenity, they were—not the eyes of a child. And what on earth was a lassie doing on Culloden battlefield?

He scarcely had time to gather a quick impression of long auburn braids, a woefully thin face and a ragged tartan shawl—he didn't recognize the sett, for it was far too faded—before she sat back on her heels and said, "Does it hurt very bad?"

He opened his mouth to reply, and a dizzying wave of pain crashed over him. He grimaced, and the wee lass clasped his hand tighter. Instantly, the ache vanished; then he was astonished to feel a hot, tingling sensation in his fingertips. Och, praise St. Ninian. Perhaps he hadn't severed the nerves to his hand.

The girl frowned into his eyes, and he decided he had never seen such a sad expression on such a young child. Clearly the waif was half starved, and shamefully neglected. Could she be a tinker's child, wandered onto the battlefield? Nay, surely not, for her voice held the cadences of an upper-class education.

Lachlan clenched his jaw and suppressed a sigh. The poor creature wasn't the first Scot plunged into poverty because of a father's allegiance to the Jacobites—and things would only get worse for the wee mite now.

The lass's frown deepened as she stroked a finger down his cheek, her touch as quick and delicate as butterfly wings. "I was standing across the field," she murmured, so softly he scarce could hear. "I thought ye were me father. He's tall and dark-haired like ye and as handsome . . . though you look a more braw warrior." She paused, and her finely shaped lips trembled. "But . . . but I'm afraid he must be dead."

Ah, that was it, then. Lachlan dragged in another breath—definitely easier this time—and gazed muzzily up at her. Tears mingled with her freckles, and her eyes sparkled like twin amethysts in the gathering dark. She and her mother must be from Inverness. Many of the townsfolk had crept onto the battlefield under the cover of twilight, and more than a few humpbacked crones and weeping young matrons had hurried past him, determined to save a fallen son or husband before the Sassenachs could slit him open. Most of the women had been too late, and there was nothing left for them to do but drag home their dead for a decent kirk burial. The duke's butchers didn't mind. It saved them the trouble of digging yet another mass grave.

"I . . . I'm sorry, lass," he managed to choke out. "For your sake, I wish I were your *athair*."

She chewed her lower lip and studied him anxiously

for several long moments. Her frown deepened until he
doubted her brows would ever come unknit; then all at
once she slanted him a dazzling smile, lifted his mangled hand and clutched it between her own. A golden
surge of warmth flooded up his arm, whisking away all
pain, numbness and despair.

"Thank ye for your sympathy, sir," she said, smiling
deep into his eyes. "I shouldna be doin' this, but ye've
a kind heart—"

"Fiona!"

The little girl blanched, then dropped his hand as if
it were a burning coal. His arm crumpled onto his
blood-soaked plaid, and agonizing claws of pain tore
through his flesh. He felt a swirl of icy air and heard
the rustle of petticoats; then a woolen skirt brushed
against his ear. A large, beringed hand closed around
Fiona's thin arm and jerked her to her feet.

"Mama—" Fiona gasped.

A dark-haired woman lowered her flushed face to the
child. "Och, ye wretched, headstrong girl!" she hissed.
"Havena I told ye never—*never*—to do that—"

"But he needs help—"

The woman shot Lachlan a scathing glance, then
spat on the frozen ground, inches from his face. "Can
ye no' see, ye fey, addle-witted changeling?" She vi-
ciously kicked her booted toe into Lachlan's side. He
groaned, then felt himself being sucked into a maelstrom of nausea. "He's a bloody Campbell—a bloody
traitor to the cause!" She shook the little girl until the
child's teeth chattered. "Look there." She jabbed a finger at the cockade pinned to Lachlan's bonnet. " 'Tis
the Campbell badge. He's the enemy, and he likely
killed your pure father."

The child's angelic face crumpled, but her eyes

sparked with a single, quick flash of defiance. "But he's hurt. I can heal him—"

"Hush!" With the speed of a striking snake, the dark-haired woman drew back her arm and slapped Fiona's cheek. The sound cracked through the air like musket fire; Lachlan gritted this teeth and choked back a wave of bile. "Never, ever say that again, ye vile, wicked child!" The woman spun Fiona around, and her black woolen cloak swirled like raven's wings against the snow-filled sky. "Look." She stabbed her finger at the endless piles of bloody, mud-splattered corpses crumpled in the drifting snow. "Sure and your father's dead and I'm all ye've got. Ye'll do as I tell ye, or by God, ye'll have us both hanged for witches and heretics."

Tears slipped silently down Fiona's pale cheeks, and her mother dropped to her knees before her. She stroked the child's gleaming auburn braids, then spit on her hand and wiped a smudge from the little girl's cheek. "There now, dinna fash, lass. I ken ye've the call to heal. But I've told ye once if I've told ye a million times—"

She shot Lachlan a venomous look, black eyes blazing with hatred. He turned his head away, too ashamed to speak out, to try and set things straight. A stifling black cloud of despair settled on his chest—dense, cold, crushing the life from him—and all at once he realized he truly was dying. He clenched his eyes shut and grimaced in agony, longing for the solace of tears, the refuge of understanding, the comfort of knowing that his clansmen forgave him, that his brothers forgave him.

The last words he heard came from the hissing, dark-haired woman. " 'Tis a cruel, ignorant world, luv. And if ye wish to survive, ye *must* hide the truth."

One

Fiona woke with a start. The dream clung to her mind with the chill, tenacious fingers of the dead, and her heart fluttered against her stays like the beating wings of a canary she had seen long ago in a shop on the Rue de Bussy. The tiny, bright-eyed creature had longed to escape its wicker cage, and Fiona had burst into tears and begged her mama to buy it so she might set it free. But Mama had laughed and dragged Fiona back among the barrows of onions crowding the bustling marketplace. "Silly, soft-hearted fool," she had scoffed. "The wee thing would likely be killed by some predatory cat. Nay, 'tis safer where it is."

Blearily, Fiona dragged her head from her father-in-law's frail shoulder, then glanced at the bare transom window. Outside, rain poured down in drenching sheets and drummed in the gutters with a theatrical flair that she concluded must be inherently French. Indeed, she had decided long ago that God Himself must be French, for surely only a Gallic deity would make the November skies weep until rain cascaded in pewter waterfalls from narrow eaves, and the sewers overflowed down the streets, washing away all sin—and garbage—before tumbling into the Seine. What could be more artistic and more practical, all at once?

She sat up and automatically tucked her errant auburn curls into a demure bun. *Mon Dieu,* how long had she been asleep? She frowned and glanced at her mother-in-law's prized gold pocket watch, which was prized not so much because it had been a gift from Bonnie Prince Charlie, but because it was the only valuable the family had never pawned. Fiona's feckless husband Harry—she crossed herself and muttered a prayer for his soul—had lost the watch in a game of baccarat a few years earlier, but his opponent's wife sentimentally had returned it to him as a love token when she and Harry had tumbled from bed and parted ways for the last time.

Fiona's brow furrowed, and she appraised Sir Hector's shrunken chest for signs of life. His hands lay curled over his collarbone like two moles burrowing into the dirt, the skin was yellow and shot with bulging blue veins, and the nails needed cutting. Although it was only four o'clock on the afternoon of All Saints' Day, the chill garret room lay in shadow so deep Fiona scarce could discern the old man's labored gasps. She gently pressed her hand against his haggard cheek, then breathed a sigh, reassured by a slight warmth and the unmistakable liquid shimmer of life beneath the bristly, black-and-white stubble peppering his jaw.

All at once, another feeling tingled up her icy fingers. Her eyes floated shut, and she allowed herself to enjoy it—just for a moment, just this once. In truth, the energy surging up her arm wasn't a feeling so much as an image—a glorious image of molten golden sunlight, tiny blue butterflies, and warm, drowsing summer fields that smelled of heather and dust and the tang of salt sea air. *Mon Dieu,* she could nearly taste that air: strong, vibrant, thrumming with the muted, joyous hymn of life that lay just below the hearing of human ears. She smiled. *Most* human ears.

She took a deep breath and allowed herself to relax. Leaning forward, she hovered a few inches above Sir Hector's bluish lips and whispered, "Where are we, *mon père?* Scotland? The Isle of Mull? *Oui,* but of course."

Sir Hector's eyelids rippled, mimicking the erratic movement of the eyes beneath; then he mumbled something in Gaelic. Instantly, the image in Fiona's mind changed. The golden light blurred and melted like sun-shot ice on a windowpane; then it split apart and ground together again in a wild, tortured black-and-red shriek of regret. She jumped and snatched her hand away. Sir Hector's lids flew up.

"Lass," he croaked. Confusion cleared from his rheumy eyes, and he coughed weakly. "Och, are ye all that's left to watch me to me grave?"

Fiona bit her lip, then leaned forward, smoothing the old man's pillow along with her agitated expression. Better that he not see the truth. Maeve had taught her that trick long ago.

Sir Hector bared his false teeth in a shaky grimace that passed for a smile. "Arrrh, I ken what ye're thinkin', lass. Have I no' heard me wife drum it into your head for years now?" His voice rose in a rusty falsetto. " 'A tranquil expression is a lady's best defense against the troubles o' this world.' " He snorted. "Bugger it! Madam Maclean turned to stone long before ye were born, and I wilna stand to see your pure heart follow suit. If I'm to die, ye'll do me the favor o' followin' your own wits, no' her blather. Logic and reason, lass. They'll show ye the truth—"

"Hush, *mon père*. You're not dying."

"Aye, lass, I am." His palsied, wrinkle-shrouded hand beckoned her closer. "But before I go, ye must promise me. . . ." His troubled voice trailed away.

"Oui?" Fiona tenderly brushed her lips across his forehead. "Tell me, *mon père*. You know I'll promise you any—"

The garret door flew open and banged against the crumbling plaster wall; then Maeve Maclean strode in. A sopping, gray-wool shawl covered her grizzled coronet of braids, her broad cheeks were ruddy with cold, and rivulets of water streamed from her sensible black-serge skirts onto the plank floor. A sturdy willow basket hung from her arm, and Fiona's stomach rumbled as the aroma of fresh brioche perfumed the stale air.

"Good. Ye're awake." Maeve stripped off her sodden shawl and hung it purposefully on one of the pegs that served as her armoire; then she crossed to her husband's bedside and lifted a darned linen napkin from the basket of warm pastry. "I had to queue up in that miserable rain for an hour to get these, so dinna bother to tell me ye've no appetite."

Sir Hector turned his face to the wall; then his eyelids—as thin and transparent as blue tissue-crepe—fluttered shut.

Fiona's heart did a sickening little flip. Sir Hector *lived* to argue with his wife. If the venerable Maeve Maclean wished to walk, he hailed a carriage. If she expressed a hankering for gateau au chocolat, he demanded blanc mange. If she announced her plans to stroll in the Bois, he settled in by their meager fire with a forbidden stack of salacious political pamphlets. This refusal—or worse—inability to rise to his wife's challenge could mean only one thing: Sir Hector

Maclean, exiled Jacobite chieftain of a once-mighty Highland clan, truly was dying.

This same thought must have struck Maeve, for her stout shoulders froze. Then she dropped the worn basket onto the bedside table, where it clinked against a half dozen bottles of apothecaries' remedies. She snatched up a green-glass vial and waved it under her husband's nose. "Hector. Hector! Wake up at once. I'll no' have ye dyin' on me like this. I havena had time to make any arrangements, and the money—"

"Hush." Fiona anxiously scanned her father-in-law's gaunt face and trembling lips. "He's trying to say something."

Maeve cast Fiona a basilisk glare, then dropped the vial of medicine and sat on the bed, her broad hips inches from her husband's icy hand. "What is it, Hector? Tell me, my dear."

Fiona blinked in surprise, then scanned Maeve's broad, determined face. Not once since the day Fiona had married the Macleans' only son had she heard her mother-in-law use a term of endearment. Oh, it wasn't that Maeve was cruel, or even particularly cold; it was the destruction of the Maclean clan and the loss of their lands, fortune, and country that had forced her into a protective fortress of impenetrable strength. And such strength could not allow even the tiniest fissure of tenderness.

Sir Hector's skin paled to the shade of poisonous mushrooms. Then he dragged in a stertorous gasp and mumbled, "Ye must go back. Promise me."

"Back? Ye mean to Scotland? Nay, Hector—"

"Aye, ye will," he croaked. "I am The Maclean, and our son—such as he was—is dead. Ye must go back. Tell . . . tell the next in line that 'tis his duty now. . . ."

His attention seemed to drift, like a dead leaf floating down into a pool of dark water.

Maeve dropped her husband's hand and gaped at Fiona. "He's stark, starin' mad. We canna return to Scotland. We've been banished for life, thanks to Hector's foolish allegiance to Prince Charles. Huh! Some allegiance, that—swearin' to serve a charmin', pretty lad who's drunk half the time and gaddin' aboot after wild dreams the other."

Fiona smothered a wry smile. Maeve could have been describing her gadabout son Harry as well as Bonnie Prince Charlie, and despite Maeve's frequent grousing, Fiona knew she still cherished a soft spot for them both.

"Besides," Maeve protested, "we've no money for the journey. Och, we've barely enough money for bread." She knotted her chapped hands in her lap and glared down at them as if they had drained away the Maclean fortune. "And how would we live? At least here we've your income from the patisserie—"

"There is money."

Fiona and Maeve jumped up and stared down at Sir Hector. His eyes were open, and for the first time in weeks, Fiona detected a hint of the wolfish cunning for which The Maclean had been famous. " 'Tis a fortune," he wheezed, growing blue about the lips. "A verra great treasure. I hid it on the Isle . . . a few months after the prince raised his standard at Glenfinnan. I kent we'd have rough times when I declared wi' the Jacobites. Better to hold a wee bit back than to let it fall into the wrong hands, aye?"

He shot Fiona a shrewd look, and she realized the wrong hands he referred to belonged to Prince Charles Edward Stuart.

Maeve opened her mouth to argue, but Sir Hector

cut her off. "Dinna fash, woman. 'Tis there . . . the answer to everythin'."

"But, Hector—"

"Nay, ye must listen. It's weighed heavy on me soul these long, bitter years." His voice quavered, and his expression grew agitated. "The new chieftain . . . 'tis Lachlan . . . Lachlan Maclean. Ye must find him, find out the truth. Promise me. Promise me ye'll find—" He gasped desperately; then his eyes fluttered shut, and his face sagged into the slackness of death.

Maeve shrieked, snatched up his hand and clutched it to her cheek. "Och, Holy Mary . . . he's like ice. Och, he canna be dead, he canna—" She rounded on Fiona, ample bosom heaving, gray eyes blazing. "Do somethin'. Ye can save him, I know ye can." She broke into great, wrenching sobs and grabbed Fiona's elbow. "Touch him. Heal him!"

Fiona's heart lurched into her throat, and she scanned her mother-in-law's stricken face. *"Ma mère, I cannot do it*—you know that. It's been years since I've so much as tried, and I had no success then—"

"Then what good are ye!" Maeve snapped. "Ye wicked, selfish girl. Hector loved ye like his own flesh. We gave ye a home, welcomed ye like a true daughter . . ." Her voice broke, and she slumped forward over her husband's still body.

Fiona folded her hands in her lap, then struggled to hold back a wave of sudden, choking tears. *Mon Dieu,* but this was unfair. And if there was one thing in life she hated, it was unfairness—although it often confounded her why that should be so, since life seemed made up in sum total of that self-same condition.

"Ma mère, you know the Church would find me a heretic if they knew. And you've told me always to hide my . . . my ability." She faltered, and her pulse

sprinted like a frightened rabbit. "So did my mother, many times. When she and Papa died of the fever, those were her parting words—"

"I care no' what Deirdre Fraser told ye! I care no' what *I* told ye. I care no' whether ye be witch or changeling or holy saint sent by God Himself." Maeve pressed Fiona's hand to Sir Hector's cold and silent heart. No feeling or image flowed up into Fiona's fingers, for there was nothing left in Sir Hector's earthly shell but a dull, echoing emptiness. "Och, I beg ye. Please, *please* heal him."

Before Fiona could stop it, her panicked mind darted back to the day seventeen years earlier when she and her parents had landed in France. They had fled Scotland after Bonnie Prince Charlie's appalling defeat at Culloden, and her father—a light-hearted rogue with a taste for claret and gambling, rather like Harry, actually—hadn't been the least dismayed with the prospect of a life of exile on the Continent. As the prince's most junior aide-de-camp, he had heard much about France's lax morals and loose women, and like a greedy child at a confectioner's, he was primed to sample them.

Recalling that wretched day, Fiona shivered and shut her eyes. She and her parents had disembarked at Calais on a foggy and fishy September afternoon, and her six-year-old's curiosity instantly led her from the bustling docks to a wide, cobbled square where a shouting mob of townspeople clustered around a leaping bonfire. She was cold and hungry, and when she caught the smoky smell of scorching meat, she thought perhaps the crowd was roasting tatties and neeps—a favorite with the Scottish peasantry, and with her. With the agile determination of a starving cat, she wound her way through the ragged Frenchmen, stoutly ignoring the shouts, curses and raucous laughter swirling above her head.

Then she reached the edge of the crowd, and her heart froze in her chest.

The bonfire had been roaring for some time, and the piled-up logs, leaping flames and glowing orange-white coals sent shimmering billows of heat over her face and hands. A tall, rough-hewn timber rose vertically from the conflagration. Tied to the pole was a charred, blackened, flaming *thing*.

Fiona opened her mouth and shrieked.

Her mother's steely hand bit into her shoulder and yanked her back into the bellowing, fetid mob.

"Och, lass, ye scared me half to death!" Mama gasped.

They stumbled away from the crowd and halted outside a dockside ordinary, which lay across the garbage-strewn square from the bonfire and the unspeakable thing. Mama bent and scanned Fiona's face, her dark eyes wide and anxious. "What were ye thinkin' of, dartin' off like that?"

Fiona swallowed, then swallowed again. Her stomach heaved in a way it never had during the rough Channel crossing. "Mama . . . w-what was that they were burnin'?"

Mama shot a scathing glance at the tight knot of people, then glared at her daughter and huffed out a sigh. " 'Tis best that ye ken, lass. 'Tis a lass they're burnin'. The townsfolk are yellin' that she was a witch." She stood and listened to the hoarse French shouts a moment longer. "She's a poisoner, they say, a child of the devil who masqueraded as a healer."

She grasped Fiona's clammy hand and dragged her back toward the dock. A few rods in front of them,

Papa lounged against a hogshead of mackerel, smoking a long-stemmed Dutch pipe.

"They havena burned a witch in Scotland for forty years or more," Mama scoffed, thrusting out her chin. "The Frogs—och, a barbaric people. A barbaric country. Ye best watch yourself here, missy." She bent and pinched Fiona's cheek. "Don't *ever* let me catch ye talkin' to your invisible friends, do ye hear me? And don't ye ever, *ever* dare try to heal anyone."

She spun Fiona around and jabbed a finger at the bonfire. Black smoke billowed over the crowd, and Fiona inhaled the greasy-sweet smell of roasting meat. Her stomach roiled. "Remember that, lassie," Mama rasped. "If they ever learn what ye are, they'll burn ye here as soon as look at ye."

Fiona's father ambled toward them, smiling and drawing nonchalantly on his pipe. "Say, what's all that?" He nodded at the choking black smoke and sniffed. "I'm rather hungry. Are they roastin' a pig?"

Fiona bent and vomited into the gutter.

The sound of Maeve's broken sobs dragged Fiona's attention back to Sir Hector's bedside. She shuddered, then forced all horrible memories from her mind. France had changed; they no longer burned suspected witches here. In truth, the French, with their unwavering devotion to the Catholic Church, had been most sympathetic to Fiona's eccentricities—certainly more than the commonsensical Protestant Scots would have been. If Jacques, who owned Les Trois Oeufs patisserie, heard Fiona addressing an unseen presence now and again, he raised no eyebrows. Jacques himself often spoke to St. Honoratus, the patron saint of bakers, and to the Holy Mother, of course. So what did it matter if la belle petite Madame Maclean did the same? *Mais certainment,* it did not affect her cooking.

Maeve resolutely wiped her tears, then gently folded Sir Hector's hands over his chest. Fiona sniffed and crossed herself. 'Twas too late to heal the poor old curmudgeon, but she still could pray for his immortal soul. She would get in no trouble for that, and it *was* All Saints' Day. She blinked back tears and struggled to recall to whom she should pray. Jacques had said that there was a patron saint for everyone. St. Joseph was for the dying, but Sir Hector was already dead. Would St. Joseph still count?

"Pay attention, missy. 'Tis no time for your fey wool-gatherin'."

Fiona snapped from her reverie and met Maeve's watery, red-eyed gaze.

Maeve patted her hand—once, awkwardly—and said, "Forgive me outburst. I was overcome. I ken ye canna help me poor husband. Only God could do that, and He's seen fit to take him, although why He would want an old goat like Hector, I canna say."

She stood, snapped the rough cambric sheet over Sir Hector's shrunken face, then strode to the door. "I'll go for the undertaker, though no doubt he'll charge us double for bringin' him out in this rain, and on a feast day. Money-grubbin' French." She snatched up her wet shawl and attempted to knot it under her mulish chin. "Keep watch, lass. And think ye on this mad idea of his. If there *is* a treasure buried on the Isle—and Hector surely never told me aboot any such thing—we need it somethin' desperate. Hector left nary a sou, and I dinna fancy the poorhouse."

Fiona jumped up and lifted her own blue-wool cloak from its peg. "Here, *ma mère,* wear mine. Yours is soaked." She settled the soft fabric over her mother-in-law's stiff shoulders, then stepped back, folded her hands behind her and gazed down at her threadbare slippers. "May . . . may I ask a favor, madame?"

"Aye."

"When . . . *If* you go to Scotland, may I come, too?"

Maeve flipped the cloak's hood over her head. "But, lass, ye love France. Sure and ye're half French yourself by now. Ye parley like a Parisian, ye've embraced the Popish faith, ye've got your fancy cookin'. Why would ye want to leave?"

Why, indeed? For an instant, Fiona let her mind drift, as she often did to lull herself to sleep at night. With a shiver of longing, she imagined the perfume of lilacs floating from the walled garden of Les Petits-Jacobins on a May evening. She tasted the garlic, rosemary, chèvre and roasted Provençal tomatoes atop Jacques's crisp baguettes. She heard the coo of pigeons drowsing high atop the sunset-shot gargoyles of Notre Dame and felt the icy crunch of frost beneath her slippers as she strolled the crystalline moonlit terraces of Versailles on Christmas Eve.

C'est vrai, she loved France. For her, every forgotten alley and hidden courtyard of Paris held unrivaled beauty, mystery and fascination. But, contrary to its much-vaunted reputation, Paris hadn't brought her love. Nor had it offered her respite from the recurring dream that she was suffocating and freezing to death all alone on a snow-shrouded moor. From time to time the dream altered shape, and she felt as if someone lay beside her in the blackness—someone suffering and in great pain. Night after night she would reach out her hand, but as she touched the dark, faceless stranger, he disappeared and she awoke—gasping, heart pounding, desperate to escape.

Then, always, came the loneliness. Marriage to wayward, philandering Harry hadn't eased it, nor, to her great shame, had widowhood worsened it. Her loneliness merely was, like the air that filled her lungs or the ground beneath her feet. Now and again she entertained the fancy that if she returned to Scotland, she might find happiness—or at least a few solid answers about her past. Years ago, Deirdre and Ian Fraser accidentally had let it slip that they had adopted her, and beyond that maddening threshold they had refused to go.

Fiona wiped her damp palms on her medicine-splattered apron. *Mon Dieu,* what good were her hopes? The cold fact remained that other than Maeve, she was entirely alone in the world.

"*Ma mère,* you're the only family I have left," Fiona said. "You know my background is . . . well, 'tis a bit of a mystery, and with my parents and Harry dead, there's no one else but you."

Maeve arched a sardonic brow. "Thank ye for the compliment."

"I didn't mean it that way. Please, *ma mère.* I . . . I just want to stay with you."

"And who says we're goin' anywhere?"

"But we have to. Sir Hector said we must find the new chieftain and inform him of his inheritance—"

"Ha! Some inheritance. A title that canna be used, lands that are no longer ours and a purse as empty as Madame du Barry's head."

Fiona blushed at the mention of King Louis' new mistress, who had managed to supplant the dazzlingly popular Madame de Pompadour in the affections of the monarch, if not of the people. Madame du Barry had once fleeced Harry of five gold livres, and neither Maeve nor Fiona had forgotten.

"But we must tell this gentleman that he's the new chieftain. 'Tis our duty. 'Tis a death-bed promise."

Fiona frowned absent-mindedly. "What was his name again?"

"Lachlan Maclean. And he's the best reason I can think of *not* to go to Scotland." Maeve's peaked brows lowered ominously, and her face turned a startling shade of red. "The mon's a traitor, lass—a two-faced dog in the manger who licks Campbell arse—"

Fiona began to giggle. Astonished, she clapped a hand over her mouth, then said, *"Ma mère!* You shock me—"

" 'Tis no laughin' matter, missy. Lachlan is Sir Hector's third cousin. Broodin' and black-hearted as the devil, he is—and just as handsome, if memory serves. But he's a Campbell through and through. He fought for Butcher Cumberland, ye ken—and likely shot his own flesh and blood."

Fiona lowered her voice to the calm, soothing tone she reserved for barking dogs and peevish children. "But Sir Hector begged us to find out the truth. Something weighed heavy on him all these years. Don't you think we owe him that much? Surely we must carry out his final request."

Maeve thrust out her pugnacious jaw. "I havena seen Lachlan since before the Risin', but I can tell ye this— the Clan Maclean would be better off wi' no chieftain at all than wi' the likes o' him. If he was on fire, I wouldna cross the room to spit on him, and I'm sure no' plannin' on crossin' the Channel to hand him me husband's title."

She snatched Sir Hector's pocketbook from the bedside table, then flipped it open. Her face paled, and her jaw dropped. Then she turned the leather pouch upside down and shook it. Out fell a twist of tobacco, a dogeared playbill announcing Monsieur Voltaire's latest offering, and an almond comfit coated with dirt and lint.

"Good God," Maeve blurted, "it really *is* empty."

Laughter bubbled like champagne in Fiona's belly, but she kept her face serene. "I beg pardon, *ma mère,* but since we're flat broke, it looks as if we might have to reconsider your plans after all."

Maeve snorted, threw down the purse and strode from the chamber, banging the door behind her. Fiona turned, then trailed across the room to Sir Hector's bedside. Desperately stifled sobs clogged her throat, and tears welled in her eyes, then slid down her cheeks. *Mon Dieu,* she would miss him so much, for he had shown her the only real love she had ever known. She reached for a soft cloth and a basin of water.

"Whatever it is that you wanted, I will find it," she murmured, choking back a torrent of tears. "I swear to you I'll find it." Then, as the cold Parisian rain poured down, she leaned forward and kissed Sir Hector's shrunken cheek.

Two

Castle Taigh
Isle of Mull, Scotland

Intricate feathers of frost covered the bedchamber windows and refracted the morning sun, dazzling Lachlan's eyes with a thousand glittering rays of silver and gold. The sunlight streamed across the cold flagstone floor and outshone the crackling hearth fire, and although Lachlan couldn't see beyond the ice-covered panes of glass, he knew that the fields and hills of Taigh Samhraidh would be cloaked in a shimmering mantle of frost. This was prime hunting weather, and he had risen early to snatch a few hours' freedom before facing the troubles of the day. But Sorcha had woken with other ideas.

His mistress pulled off his hunting boots, and he leaned back in the hearthside wing chair, then beckoned her to him. The sunlight warming his face was a rare treat in the Highlands this time of year, although not nearly as rare as Sorcha's sudden willingness to pleasure him in the French manner. He sighed, then lifted his hips a fraction so she could ease his jutting manhood from his breeks. Her long black hair brushed like silk against his bare skin, and he gently caught her head and urged her forward, eager to escape the chill air into the warmth and wetness of her sensuous mouth.

All at once, Sorcha pulled away and sat back on the moth-eaten Turkey carpet. With a tiny shiver, she twitched her nightshift over her knees and gazed up at the diamond pattern dancing across Lachlan's lean, tanned cheek. His peaked dark brows drew together in a brooding frown; then he nonchalantly reached for the pewter tankard on the breakfast tray beside him. Auburn highlights gleamed in his long, tousled hair, and for the first time since becoming his lover, Sorcha noticed that his hair wasn't black at all; it was very dark brown.

He tipped his head back and swallowed a draught of ale, Adam's apple moving up and down, sunlight limning his granite jaw and blade-straight, aristocratic nose. Tiny laugh lines radiated from the corners of his wide-set eyes, and she decided the time had come to voice her demand.

She rose and snuggled into his lap, then relished the sculpted perfection of his chest and the hardness of his impertinent manhood against her bottom. She snatched away the ale and set it on the table, then ran a finger down his nose, over the slight bump where he had broken it, to its elegant, slightly drooping tip.

"Why will ye never tell me how ye broke your nose?" she asked, pouting.

Lachlan arched a wicked brow, then wriggled his hips. She ignored his blatant invitation, and he heaved a long-suffering sigh. Then his wide, mobile mouth quirked into a smile. Deep, masculine dimples scored his freshly shaven cheeks, and she silently congratulated herself on lulling him into a rare good mood.

"Weel, lassie, every Highland rogue must maintain his air o' mystery," he declared, rolling his *r*'s devilishly. "Would ye fancy me if ye kent I'd broken me nose chasin' Rinalda's terrier out o' the pig sty?"

"Ye never. Me da says ye broke it at Culloden—"

To her astonishment, Lachlan stood and abruptly deposited her on the icy flagstone floor. His rakish smile vanished with the swiftness of the winter sun, and he decisively buttoned his breeks with one deft hand. He towered over her, shirtless and scowling in the chill air, and she instantly regretted breaking his playful mood.

Lachlan was a stunning man—tall and heavily muscled, with the narrow waist and massive shoulders of a hardened warrior. If that wasn't blessing enough, he was the most brazen, imaginative and insatiable lover she had ever bedded—and she had bedded many. Unfortunately, his flaws were as glaring as his attributes.

Her gaze flicked to his right hand. The long, sensitive fingers were stiff and curled inward, and a webbing of scars marred the smooth brown skin. Lachlan caught her gaze and turned away, then shrugged into his white linen sark. All Lachlan's shirts had flowing sleeves and long ruffles at the cuffs—the better, Sorcha knew, to hide what he considered an appalling defect.

Shivering, although more from the chill in Lachlan's steel-gray eyes than from the nip in the chamber's air, Sorcha retrieved her dressing gown from the foot of the carved-oak bed, then wrapped it around her nightshift. She shoved her feet into sheepskin slippers and strolled to the fire.

"Lachlan, we must talk. Me da wants to ken when ye plan to wed me."

Lachlan let his lids drift shut, took a deep breath, then downed another swig of ale. The peaty liquid flowed down his throat, chilling his belly and leaving a rank, sour taste in his mouth. He banged the tankard on the table and silently cursed his foolishness for allowing poor lame Rinalda to continue her duties as housekeeper. Och, but what could he do? The canny old healer had been with his family since before his birth. She had been his beloved nanny and had cared for Diarmid and Jamie, as well.

Lachlan clenched his jaw and fiercely quelled a bitter memory of his two younger brothers, irretrievably lost to him these many years. He couldn't sack Rinalda, for she was all he had left from the old days, when the Maclean clan had ruled all of Mull and he truly had been the laird of Taigh Samhraidh. His lips quirked sardonically. Nay, he wouldn't shear her dignity to suit his belly.

"Lachlan—" Sorcha whined.

He shot her a warning glare. "Dinna start, lass. I made it plain from the beginnin' that I had no plans to wed ye. Ye kent me intentions—or lack o' them—and ye lay wi' me all the same. We agreed 'twas all harmless fun, and Angus is a fool to be fillin' your head with false hopes—"

"Me da's no fool. He's a fine man, finer than the likes o' ye. Didna he march off to fight with The Maclean while ye stayed home to nurse your Campbell wife—"

"Enough." Lachlan closed the space between them in one swift stride. "I've told ye never to speak o' Catriona."

Sorcha thrust her face inches from his, and Lachlan wondered how he ever had thought her beautiful. Her olive skin was flushed with mottled red, and her lush breasts heaved with each agitated breath. Months ago Lachlan would have found her passion arousing; now it merely wearied him.

She thrust her hands on her narrow hips and cried,

"There's too damn much I canna speak of. Your past, your dead wife—"

He grasped her wrist. "Shout all ye want, lass. 'Twill do ye no good. I'll no' marry ye—"

"Get your vile hand off me!" Sorcha broke free, then swiped at her arm as if she had been burned. "Ye should be glad any lass hereabouts wants to wed ye. Och, ye might be Milord Charm and the handsomest rogue in the Isles, but we all ken the truth. Ye're nothin' but Duncan Campbell's lackey—a pawn to the Sassenachs, a traitor to your clan, and a beggar in the castle that once was yours." She whirled and strode toward the chamber door, dressing gown swirling like a snowstorm around her legs. "Play high-and-mighty laird o' the manor all ye want, but dinna come crawlin' to me when your cock's achin' for release!"

She grasped the iron door handle and yanked. "I'm glad ye dinna want to marry me. Aye, glad. Who would want to marry a cold-hearted cripple like ye?" Head high, she sailed through the open door and plowed straight into Rinalda. She shoved the housekeeper aside and hissed, "Get out o' me way. And I better no' hear ye gossipin' aboot your gleanin's at the keyhole."

Sorcha disappeared down the dim, tapestry-hung hallway. Rinalda shook her head, then stumped into the bedchamber. The old wisewoman's back was more stooped than usual, and weary purplish circles underscored the wrinkles around her eyes. Lachlan was about to inquire into the state of her rheumatism when she thrust out a chapped, birdlike hand. In it she clutched a heavy sheet of parchment that was folded and sealed with brilliant blue wax. Lachlan's lips thinned into a taut line. There was no mistaking the elaborately engraved *C* sealing the letter.

"This come for ye last night," Rinalda said, Highland accent thick with disapproval. She cast a sharp-eyed glare at the disheveled bed littered with empty whisky bottles. "But since ye was drownin' your sorrows wi' that hussy o' yours, I thought 'twould wait 'til mornin'. 'Tis from Duncan Cambell," she added, not bothering to curtsey. "And when ye've read it, I want to talk to ye."

Lachlan made a sound of aggravation, then snatched the letter and broke the seal. Striding to the cavernous stone hearth, he silently ordered himself to hold his temper, for Duncan's letter could mean only one thing: his greedy and careless brother-in-law required more money.

Doubtless the little weasel had frittered away the Michaelmas rent on silks and velvets to rival those of London's most foppish dandies. Then there was the appalling expense of entertaining the few members of society willing to associate with an untitled Scottish upstart. Aye, the Honorables and the baronets must have their picnics, their boating parties, their intimate little suppers, their evenings at Vauxhall Gardens and the theater. Och, and he mustn't forget the memberships in various clubs, the gambling debts, the coach and four, and the truly outrageous bills racked up by Duncan's mistress—an actress with a prodigious appetite for emeralds and penniless playwrights.

Lachlan threw himself into the hearthside wing chair, stretched out his long legs and forced himself to read Duncan's missive. Muttering an oath, he balled up the parchment and hurled it into the fire, where it curled, blackened and smoked.

"I take it from that scowl on your face 'tis no' good news," Rinalda remarked. She hobbled toward him, her movements still quick and alert despite the ravages of rheumatism. Lachlan had bought her a mahogany walking stick on a trip to Edinburgh five years earlier, but she adamantly refused to use it. Instead, she clutched at furniture or walls to keep her balance, and the stick lay wrapped in fine muslin in the pine chest at the foot of her bed.

Lachlan glowered into the fire. "Ye're right, *mo druidh*. And to think I've scoffed at your second sight."

Rinalda latched onto his shoulder, then patted his cheek with a palm as dry and rough as an insect's carapace. *"Hunh,* enough o' your sarcasm. I've no need for second sight wi' the likes o' Duncan Campbell. Sure and he's demandin' ye raise the rent—"

"Aye, damn him. That mon's no' just stubborn, he's stupid—and that's a bad combination. Winter's comin' on, and there's no' a farthin' to be had amongst the crofters. Michaelmas has always been the last rent day 'til spring, and by St. Ninian, I'll no' let him—"

"Aye, but what can ye do, laddie? The estate is yours no longer—"

"Dinna remind me." Lachlan shot up and paced to the frost-covered windows. Fury surged through his veins like a flooding tide, and he longed to be out on the hills, thundering his horse though the frigid air until all feeling left his frozen hands and burning cheeks.

Och, damn Duncan, damn the Sassenachs, and damn his own wretched folly.

"Duncan is demandin' another hundred pound, and I canna give it to him," he snapped.

"But ye always keep money back, to tide folk through the winter," Rinalda declared. "The old master taught ye weel."

"That was before Duncan decided he must buy his way into a title." Lachlan dragged a hand down over his face. "Aye, 'tis Duncan's money now, but what o'

Maire Rankin? Should I let her die o' the consumption because that bastard wilna let me fix the filthy drains and rotted roofs?" He braced his hands against the window frame and leaned his head on one arm. "Last week I spent the money on repairs on the worst o' the cottages," he confessed.

"Och, lad, ye've a pure heart—even if the tenants wilna thank ye for it." Rinalda stretched out her hands to the peat fire's meager warmth, then tossed him an anxious look. "Sure and I wish ye'd tell 'em the truth, lad."

The sun filtered through the frosty windowpanes and shone like heaven's blessing on her withered cheeks and soft white hair. A frayed and stained work apron covered her black woolen dress from collarbone to ankles, and Lachlan noted that the ties were wrapped twice around her thin waist.

"Have ye lost weight?" he blurted, determined to change the subject. "Och, *mo druidh,* ye're no' sick, are ye?"

She wagged a finger at him. "Havena I told ye a million times to stop callin' me that? I'm no' a witch and ye ken it. And I'm no' ill, either." She sighed, and her face seemed to sink into itself like a dried and wizened apple. "I just be worn out, lad. Ye've been a luv to humor me this long, but I canna run the castle on me own. That's what I come to talk to ye aboot."

Lachlan detected a flicker of cunning in her faded blue eyes. Rinalda might be tired, but she hadn't lost her wits. He folded his arms across his chest and glared down his nose in his most imperious fashion. "Why do I get the feelin' ye're aboot to pull another one o' your tricks? I recall all too weel the time I was five and ye persuaded me to eat tripe by tellin' me 'twas stewed honeycomb."

She chuckled. "Och, laddie, ye're too handsome to be so jaded and stone-hearted. Everythin' I do, I do for your own good. Now come wi' me. There's someone I want ye to meet." She stumped through the door, then turned down the hallway.

Lachlan caught up, offered her his arm and quelled an affectionate smile. "What are ye up to, *mo druidh?* I dinna like the impish gleam in your eye." Och, but who was he fooling? She could set the castle afire and he would welcome the distraction from Duncan's—and Sorcha's—demands.

Rinalda slanted him a toothless grin, and he reminded himself to tell her to wear her false teeth when strangers were in the house. "I found us a cook," she crowed.

"But we dinna need a—"

"Hush, lad. I seen ye sneakin' me bridies under the table to those hounds o' yours, and ye've cut back on your drinkin' so much I can only blame me sour ale. I never could brew strong and clear like your poor dead mother—God rest her soul." Rinalda crossed herself, and Lachlan blinked. To his knowledge, Rinalda followed no religion other than the ancient pagan beliefs that still flourished in remote, forgotten corners of the Isles.

He stooped to pass under the back stairway's low lintel, then glanced down the icy stone passage toward the kitchen. "We've been over this before—there's no one on Mull fit to cook at Castle Taigh." Och, and where were his dogs this morning? Usually they swarmed him the moment he left his chamber.

"The lass and her mama come over from the mainland wi' Two-Pack Ian," Rinalda said, referring to the chandler who brought their mail. "And ye wilna believe it. Guess where she's from."

Lachlan arched a brow. "Banbury Cross?"

Rinalda jabbed a sharp elbow in his ribs. "Nay. France! She's a proper French chef."

He was about to inquire why a Frenchwoman should travel to an isolated Scottish isle to further her culinary career when Rinalda flung open the kitchen door. Warmth enveloped him, and as always, he reflected that the kitchen was his favorite spot in the castle. His father had added the wing to the keep's original stone structure, and while the kitchen was bright even on the darkest days, on this sunny morning the large south- and east-facing windows dazzled his eyes. The view outside was breathtaking, with frost-covered herb gardens, ancient stone walls and sun-spangled grass that sloped down to basalt cliffs lapped by a sapphire sea.

With a glance of pride, he took in the kitchen's beamed ceiling, whitewashed walls and brick floor, which always seemed warm in comparison to the stone used in the rest of the castle. Wooden shelves rose to the ceiling, brimming with blue-and-white china, common redware, polished maple trenchers, softly gleaming pewter and wine goblets in both clear and green Venetian glass. A massive stone fireplace—large enough for the cook to walk in and arrange cast-iron pots over the coals—filled one end of the room, and nets of onions, shiny copper pots and bunches of aromatic herbs hung from the ceiling.

In the center of the kitchen, a sturdy oak worktable held pride of place. Beneath it, in easy reach of the cook, squatted several casks of ale and two unwieldy barrels of flour and oats. He couldn't make out what lay beyond the barrels, but he knew instantly that something was amiss; for instead of tearing up to greet him with excited barks and whines and howls, all six of his dogs clustered at the opposite end of the table, bodies hidden from view. Six madly wagging tails was all he could see.

He shot Rinalda a warning look, then walked silently toward the enthralled animals.

Three

Suddenly, a low, deliciously teasing voice said, *"Vous êtes des petits chiens avides. J'ai fait ceci pour impressionner votre maître et ce n'est pas assez."* The dogs' tails whipped ecstatically.

Lachlan smothered a smile. So, this French cook had baked some goodies to impress him, eh? He had better step lively then, or, as she said, his naughty dogs would get them all. He assumed his most lordly, forbidding air and rounded the corner of the table.

Before him knelt a slender young woman. Her hair was rich, gleaming auburn—the color favored by Titian, the shade of his brother Jamie's hair—and she clasped the head of his most ferocious wolfhound in her pale, slender hands. A sharp exclamation of warning formed on his lips, then died away as she kissed Fergus's cold, wet nose. The dog sighed blissfully and thumped his tail against the bricks.

"Votre maître est méchant, n'est-ce pas?" she said. *"Peut-être que mes pâtisseries l'adouciront."*

Lachlan cleared his throat. Really, this was too much. He wasn't stingy, and he wasn't about to let her pastries sweeten him up. "Pardon me, mademoiselle—"

The woman leaped to her feet and whirled to face him, dogs skittering in all directions. Lachlan caught his breath, then sharply reminded himself that the woman standing before him was nothing more than a penniless French cook in sore need of a job. Och, but he had never seen such a lass. She was beautiful enough, he supposed, but he had possessed half a hundred beauties over the years. Nay, there was something more to her than fine-looking flesh.

"I . . . I beg your pardon, monsieur." She raised her long, dark lashes and shyly met his gaze. "I didn't hear you come in."

Her pale, translucent skin gave her the look of a Celtic princess, not the coarse and tanned Frenchwoman he had expected, and she blushed deliciously under his stern scrutiny. Her eyes were an astonishing shade of violet—like autumn twilight over the sea—and for a moment, memory tugged at his brain. Had he seen such eyes before? Aye, perhaps, but only in his dreams.

A demure black-velvet ribbon bound her glorious hair close to her head, and disheveled curls crept enticingly from her chignon. Let loose, those gleaming red locks would flow past her waist in long, silken ripples—ripples he would love to stroke. His fingers twitched. Och, since when did penniless domestic servants possess such hair?

"I hope you don't mind me playing with your dogs," she added hurriedly. "They're so sweet, and they said they were hungry—"

Her voice—perhaps that was what drew him to her like a siren's song. Her low, husky tones would have seduced a priest, but it was her accent that charmed him. Not precisely French, yet certainly not English, it possessed an enchantment all its own.

He smiled quizzically. "Allow me to compliment ye on your English, mademoiselle. 'Tis excellent, indeed.

Were ye employed by an English family in your native country?"

She smiled, and a tiny sunburst of laugh lines appeared around her eyes. Stepping closer, he noticed an entrancing smatter of freckles across her nose. He lowered his gaze to her breasts and ardently wished she wasn't bundled to the gills in that heavy and all-too-proper cloak she clasped tight to her throat. His experience was that freckles on the nose meant freckles all over. His lips quirked at the corners. Och, and how he would love to connect the dots.

She caught up her plain, black woolen skirts and curtseyed. "I thank you for the compliment, my lord, but I'm afraid I'm not French. I'm Scottish. I was born not far from here, in Argyll. My name is Fraser. Madam Fiona Fraser."

She had removed her gloves—doubtless to keep his dogs from slobbering all over them—and her hands, though slender and elegant, bore the unmistakable roughness of a woman who worked for her living. A plain gold wedding band adorned the third finger of her left hand. He inclined his head, intrigued. Madam Fraser's graceful demeanor matched that of Queen Charlotte herself, and her voice held the cultured stamp of the upper class, yet her hands were as chapped as Rinalda's. Surely there was some mystery here.

"I beg your pardon, madam." He arched a brow at her left hand, then glanced pointedly at her dreary black garb. "Ye are, um . . ."

Rinalda, who had been watching them like a hungry fox watches a chicken, hobbled up beside him. "Madam Fraser is a widow, milord, and from a fine, respectable family. But she's in mournin' for her father-in-law, poor lass. He was her only support, and now she must make her way the best she can."

Lachlan cast a wry glance at his dogs, who had settled into a worshipful circle around Fiona's skirts. Clearly, he wasn't the only one interested in this beguiling redhead. "I'm verra sorry for your loss, madam. But I must confess to a wee bit o' confusion. How did ye get from Argyll to France? And what brought ye back? Surely, if ye're as talented a cook as Rinalda says, ye'd have fared better in Paris."

She dropped her violet gaze in apparent confusion, then bit her lush lower lip, barely revealing two tantalizing white teeth. "I hesitate to burden you with a story you must have heard a dozen times, monsieur."

Lachlan caught the uneasiness in her tone and immediately decided she was about to lie to him. So she *was* a servant on the make. He felt an unreasonable stab of disappointment, then realized that doubtless she had been sacked from her last position for dallying with the master. That delightful thought cheered him considerably.

He lounged against the worktable, nonchalantly crossed his arms over his chest, then arched a sardonic brow. "Burden away, madam. I'm verra possessive wi' me house staff, and I couldna possibly take ye on without hearin' all the particulars."

She raised her chin and calmly met his gaze. Her nose was small and straight, and her face was perfectly oval. Without sharp planes or harsh angles, it gave an impression of sweetness and harmony, like paintings of the Madonna he had seen in Edinburg Castle.

"My father was a Jacobite, monsieur," she said, her tone just a wee bit haughty. "When I was a lass, he joined Prince Charles and eventually rose to a position as his aide-de-camp. Needless to say, after Culloden he was forced to flee to France with the prince, and my mother and I fled with him. We lived in exile there for seventeen years."

Her luscious, Cupid's-bow mouth curved in a smile that would have been rueful, had it not been for the distinct gleam of challenge in her cool eyes. "As a Loyalist, perhaps you have the impression, so popular in the English press, that we Jacobite exiles led a merry life—rubbing elbows with King Louis, attending salons at Versailles, eating foie gras from gold plates. But I assure you, the truth is quite another matter." She took a deep breath, then reached down and patted Fergus's grizzled head. "Although raised a lady, I had to work or we all would have starved. My husband died young, and my father-in-law was too ill and broken a man to provide. So, if it bothers you, sir, to employ a gentlewoman who has had to earn her way in life—and whose family were avowed Jacobites—I will wish you good day and take my leave."

She turned, caught up her gloves and gracefully reached for a willow basket covered with a napkin. Suddenly, Fergus reared up. His clumsy paws knocked the basket from Fiona's grasp. It tumbled to the floor, and fragrant, crisp-gold madeleines flew in all directions, followed by snapping, snarling, snatching dogs.

To Lachlan's astonishment, Fiona darted into the melee and grabbed Fergus by his studded leather collar. *"Oh, vous êtes de mauvais chiens."* she cried. *"Est-ce que je ne vous ai pas dit d'attendre?"*

Lachlan caught her arm. "Careful. He'll bite—"

"J'ai honte de vous. Maintenant asseoir et attendre votre virage," Fiona admonished, shaking her finger inches from the enormous dog's wolflike nose. To Lachlan's astonishment, Fergus sat, then hung his head in shame.

"I apologize, monsieur," Fiona said, turning back to him. Two spots of red rode high on her satin cheeks, and her amethyst eyes sparkled with amusement and exasperation. "I baked the madeleines for you so you could assess my abilities. But when I got here, the dogs—"

"Told ye they were hungry. Aye, I heard," Lachlan said dryly. He picked up the basket, pried the rough-woven napkin from Rinalda's terrier's jaws, then handed both to Fiona. "And may I inquire"—he arched a brow—"do ye always converse wi' dogs? And did *they* tell ye I was stingy, or did ye deduce that yourself?"

To his delight, she blushed from the collar of her prim gown to the enchantingly disheveled curls of her hair. "I . . . I didn't realize you spoke French, monsieur."

"Thought I was an ignorant Highland savage, eh?"

"Oh, *non*, monsieur. I . . . well . . ." She gazed down at her scuffed traveling boots and fidgeted with her gloves.

"Never mind." He chuckled, then waved his good hand at his traitorous hounds, who were greedily licking the last crumbs of madeleine from the brick floor. "Clearly, ye're an excellent cook, and I find meself rather unexpectedly"—he shot Rinalda an eloquent glare—"in need o' one. Have ye any references?"

"Oui, monsieur." She scrabbled in the pocket of her skirt and drew out several letters. "From the Marquise de Villiers, who was a family friend. I assisted when her pastry chef came down with the grippe. Then there's one—"

Lachlan took the letters and tossed them to Rinalda. "Verra weel. I'm sure your qualifications are excellent. If ye're good enough for a marquise, ye're good enough for me, and me dogs." He flashed her a teasing smile, then stepped so close he could smell the scent of fresh herbs clinging to her hair. She stiffened and tried to draw back, but the heat of the hearth fire prevented escape. Och, she was so tempting, yet so innocent. Sorcha and her coarse demands were already a dim memory.

"Now, madam, let us talk seriously," he murmured, languidly studying the exquisite curve of her lips.

She gazed up at him, wide-eyed and startled. For an instant she reminded him of a doe caught in his musket sights—lovely, slender, graceful. Och, if he had any heart left at all, he would scare her away before he did her any permanent injury. He stepped back and scowled. "Ye're a Jacobite—"

"I hardly had a choice, sir. I was six at the time—"

"And it seems ye've heard of my, ah . . . loyalties."

He halted abruptly. The room fell silent but for the pop of the fire and the snuffling of the dogs browsing for stray crumbs. Fiona's beautiful violet eyes never left his face, and he felt the tension rise between them, like a spun-silver thread that grows stronger as it's stretched thinner. He wanted to toss out a witticism, tell the lass she was hired, then stroll away and tease himself with images of seducing her from her widow's virtue. But he couldn't.

Och, why the devil did God tempt him this way? Tantalizing, beguiling Fiona Fraser was a Jacobite, and her husband, father, and father-in-law had fought and paid a terrible price for their loyalty to Prince Charles. Resentment seared like shrapnel to Lachlan's heart. Why must it always come down to this? Whenever a man who would be his friend or woman who would be his lover heard the tale that he had betrayed his clan and fought for the British under Butcher Cumberland, all hope of understanding and forgiveness flew out the window. 'Twas bitterly unfair.

Aye, but then, what about life was fair?

As if moving of its own accord, his hand made an involuntary movement toward her his—*right* hand, the cursed, vile, crippled one. Och, St. Ninian, why did she have to be a Jacobite? Sure and she would never let him touch her, for he had been branded a traitor, and her enemy.

And he could never tell her the truth, no matter how his body ached for her.

She glanced down and, for the first time, saw the grotesque flaw beneath the flowing ruffles of his shirt. He dropped his hand to his side and forced an impenetrable mask of ice over his features. To his astonishment, instead of turning away in disgust, she bent down, snatched up Rinalda's terrier and cuddled it to her cheek.

"Monsieur, I care nothing about your loyalties," she said. "I care about securing a good job and a dry place for my mother-in-law and me to sleep." She cast him a virtuous smile, then turned and kissed the terrier's pointy snout. "Remember, I was raised in France, and the French are a most pragmatic people. The Hundred Years' War notwithstanding, they rarely let politics get in the way of practicalities." The terrier squirmed madly, and she set him down, then held out her right hand. "Monsieur, I'll be the best cook you have ever had, I guarantee. So, shall I start right away?"

Lachlan hesitated. Manners required that he take her hand, bow and lift it to his lips, but doing so would expose his crippled arm once more to her steady violet gaze. After Sorcha's vicious comments an hour ago, he wasn't about to endure more pity and disgust. He bowed stiffly, then turned and stalked toward the garden door.

Just before he stepped into the icy morning air, he turned. "Ye're hired, Madam Fraser. Just dinna keep feedin' all me victuals to the dogs."

Four

Fiona thunked her spade into the half-frozen earth, then tucked her hands to the small of her back and bent backward, sighing in relief. *"Mon Dieu,"* she called to Maeve. "At last I know why the Scots drink so much whisky. Never in my life have I worked so hard." She brushed dirt from her bare palms and noted with dismay that a blister was forming at the base of her ring finger.

Maeve paused in her efforts to wrest a mottled, purplish-white turnip from the ice-stiffened mud. "And whose bright idea was this, missy? Ye could be in the kitchen o' the castle now, sittin' by the fire and brewin' up a nice Scotch broth. But nay, ye've got to play at bein' a peasant." She wiped a hand across her bulbous nose, leaving a streak of grayish muck in its wake. The knifing sea wind had reddened her cheeks, and with her grizzled hair whipping loose from its braid and a gray woolen shawl knotted over her head, Maeve resembled nothing so much as a stout gnome tunneled from the bowels of the earth to give her daughter-in-law a good scolding.

"But I thought these turnips would add just the right piquant touch to a ragout," Fiona said.

"Hunh. That aloof devil ye're working for is more likely to live on bannock and cow's blood."

Fiona turned away to hide her smile, then leaned on the spade's handle and gazed in awe at the harsh beauty of Taigh Samhraidh. Rinalda had told her that the estate had been a reward to an earlier Maclean for his devotion to the chieftain of the clan, and that the Gaelic words meant "summer place." Fiona had smiled at the name, for it was impossible to imagine the land in any season but winter. The stark, barren slope of the stone-girdled mountains, the endless sere sweep of the tan and brown fields, the surging gray thunder of waves on the ocean—all were winter's adornments, austere and remote in their enigmatic grandeur.

" 'Tis bonnie, aye?" Maeve said in a proud tone. She tossed the turnip into a burlap sack and joined Fiona. "I told ye the Isles were magical." She pointed to an imposing, cloud-shadowed hill rising up to the north and west of the field where they worked. "That's Ben More. On the other side are the most spectacular cliffs ye'd ever hope to lay eyes on—all jagged black rock plungin' straight into the sea. Och, and ye should see the water, all foamy white, poundin' and swirlin' aboot the rocks. Right before the Risin', Hector took me on a tour o' Mull, and I remember him tellin' me there were sea caves all through those cliffs and around the sea lochs as weel. The Macleans once used them for smugglin'. He promised to take me to one, but never did. Och, that man was full o' hot air." She snorted and tugged at her shawl until her face was nearly hidden. "Treasure, indeed. I'm thinkin' we're two idjits on a fool's errand."

Fiona bit her lip and prayed that Maeve was wrong. They had spent the last of their money on the trip from France, and if it weren't for Fiona's astonishing good luck in landing a job at Castle Taigh, they would likely be starving by now. But, thanks be to St. Christopher, the patron saint of travelers, they now had food, a sod-roofed stone cottage built into the side of a low hill and the promise of Fiona's wages at the end of a fortnight.

The sea wind whistled through her dirt-caked skirts, and Fiona restlessly wrapped her cloak tight around her shoulders. Obtaining the cottage had been a bit of a problem, for yesterday morning, after the mysterious and dangerously handsome Lachlan Maclean had hired her as cook, his old housekeeper had said, "Ye'll be havin' a room next to mine in the servants' quarters, o' course."

Fiona had quelled a moment's panic, then called up the story she and Maeve had rehearsed on the boat from Calais. "I thank you, madam," she said. "But as I mentioned, my mother-in-law is all alone in the world and requires my care. I couldn't possibly impose on your hospitality and expect you to house her here in the castle. Is there an empty crofter's hut somewhere on the estate where we could live?"

Rinalda had folded her birdlike arms across her narrow bosom and appraised Fiona from top to toe. Her faded blue eyes were as keen as the knives on the table beside her, and for an instant, Fiona detected a flicker of shock in her gaze. The old woman blinked twice, then said, "Aye, there be a cottage, but 'tis a fair hike from here. Will ye no' be lonely so far from folk?"

Fiona smiled and shook her head. *"Non,* madam. Unfortunately, *ma mère*—my mother-in-law—was injured in a fire shortly before we left France. She was burned over much of her face and is quite terribly scarred. As you can imagine, she cannot bear people to see her in such a state, so an isolated spot would be perfect for us."

Rinalda had made sympathetic clucking sounds,

then bustled about the kitchen, putting together a basket of herbs and ointments to help heal Maeve's supposed scars. Fiona had knotted her gloves in her hands and burned with shame at telling such a lie.

But Maeve had insisted on the tale—and that they both use Fiona's maiden name. In truth, 'twas likely Maeve was right, for how could they assess Lachlan's character if he knew who they were? If he discovered that Maeve was the widow and Fiona the daughter-in-law of The Maclean himself, he would doubtless go out of his way to charm them and fool them into believing he was honest and selfless and worthy of the title of clan chieftain. And although the title was his by right of blood, such an honor could never be bestowed on a traitor.

So Fiona had accepted Rinalda's basket of simples, then spent the next day cleaning birds' nests and mouse droppings from the abandoned cottage that was now their home. Several of the estate's tenants had dropped by, either out of friendliness or curiosity, and with each visitor Fiona had repeated her tale: Madam Fraser was recovering from terrible burns and was not yet ready to receive company. A few of the crofters had caught a glimpse of Maeve, bundled in a shawl that hid her face from prying eyes, and by now, 'twas sure that all the estate tenants had heard about the newcomers. Although pitying, they would not be suspicious.

Fiona doubted the same could be said for the laird himself. She shut her eyes, and although the late-afternoon air was icy, the thought of Lachlan Maclean kindled a delicious, forbidden heat in her belly. It radiated to her extremities and left her feeling weak and giddy—rather like the flush she got after drinking too much brandy. She dimpled, then sighed. Harry had never made her feel that way. He had elicited a response more like porridge.

She gave herself a stern shake, then caught up the sack of turnips. *Mon Dieu,* what was she thinking? She was a modest and proper widow in her mid-twenties; she couldn't moon after the first handsome man she met. But what a man! Unbidden, Lachlan Maclean's lazy smile melted through her mind. 'Twas knowing, teasing, arrogant—as if he could see through her puny defenses into her very soul.

"And what are ye smilin' about, missy?" Maeve's voice knifed like the winter wind through her daydreams.

"Lachlan Maclean. I . . . I was wondering what sort of man he is."

Maeve's gray eyes, barely visible in the folds of her shawl, took on a jaded expression. "I ken what he is." She jerked her chin at a dry brown leaf darting past in the wind. "He's like that—blowin' hither and yon wi' whatever breeze takes him. 'Twas no' in his selfish nature to stand firm and fight wi' the Jacobites. Nay, he must needs bow down to that Campbell wife o' his—"

"He's married?" Fiona blurted.

Maeve swung around to face her, brows lowered in a belligerent frown. "Aye, married to a whey-skinned, half-English beauty. Half English and half *Campbell.*" She snorted again, disgust riddling the sound. "I met her at their weddin'—och, it must have been nearly eighteen years ago. She was a sly boots, all blond hair and languid eyes. The type who leads men around by the nose by playin' sweet and helpless. Fah! Helpless as a viper, I say." She paused and assessed the leaden sky for several long moments. "Rain's comin', missy.

Ye best be gettin' along to the castle. Your arrogant laird'll be grumplin' for his tea."

Fiona frowned, unaccountably ruffled by Maeve's bit of news. *Mon Dieu,* why should it concern her? Of course her new employer was married; how could such a virile man not be? She kicked at a frozen root and envisioned Lachlan's broad shoulders and devilishly long legs, all chiseled muscle beneath his snug, black-suede breeks. How would it feel for him to mold her to his slim hips—

"Quit yer dreamin', lassie. Och, you're worse than a convent-bred virgin—droolin' over a mon when ye should be findin' me treasure."

Fiona jumped and clapped a hand to her heart. *Mon Dieu,* was she going mad? 'Twas Sir Hector Maclean's voice she had heard, as real as if he stood beside her. She whirled and gazed around. Nay, there was nothing there, just the frozen fields, wind-bent heather and Maeve's startled face.

"What's amiss?" Maeve asked. "Ye look like ye've seen a ghost."

Fiona clutched her cloak to her throat. St. Joan, this was all she needed. Didn't she have enough worries without Sir Hector popping into her head at all hours of the day and night?

With a monumental effort, she smoothed her face into its usual tranquil lines, then turned to Maeve. "I'm just tired, *ma mère.* I've been having dreams. . . ." Sweet St. Joan, should she tell? "I . . . I've dreamed of Sir Hector every night since he died." Maeve's eyes narrowed, and Fiona rushed on. "He seems to be trying to tell me something, but then he starts grousing and gets distracted and can't remember what it is."

Maeve grasped Fiona's arm and strode toward the castle. "Och, that sounds like Hector, all right. Imag-

ine the idiocy o' that man, leavin' a treasure somewhere on the Isle, and no record o' where. No will, no
papers, nothin'!" She shook her head ominously. "
'Tis overwell hoarded that canna be found."

Fiona suppressed a chuckle, remembering their frantic and futile search through Sir Hector's effects for
some clue as to the treasure's whereabouts. They had
discovered that the old chieftain had possessed a clandestine passion for scurrilous broadsides, which revealed, in salacious detail, who at court was a witch
and who was a poisoner, who was a pederast and who
was impotent, and how the king was, ah . . . *ravishing*
the people for his own selfish ends. They also had
discovered a hoard of bitten-into chocolates and a
cache of laudanum, but no indication of where the
treasure might be. Or what, exactly, it was.

Fiona smoothed her hands over her skirts and chose
her words carefully. *"Ma mère,* I understand that we
need money most desperately, but I'm beginning to
think that perhaps there is no treasure. Perhaps Sir
Hector's mind was disordered toward the end—"

"Dinna even think that. I wilna be made the fool,
even by me own husband. Especially by me own husband." Maeve stopped and pressed a hand to her well-
padded ribs, then bent slightly, breathing hard. "Ye've
had strange dreams before, missy, and they've always
come true. Remember the time ye saw Mademoiselle
Pelletier down wi' the fever, and the verra next day she
fell ill?" She eyed Fiona dubiously, clearly torn between avarice for the treasure and uneasiness over her
daughter-in-law's strange talents. "Mayhap Hector is
tryin' to tell ye somethin'. If so, ye should listen."

Fiona cast her mother-in-law a hopeful smile. "Perhaps 'tis not about the treasure, *ma mère.* Perhaps 'tis

about Monsieur Maclean. We did promise to find the truth—"

"Nay, lass. Forget aboot that two-faced charmer and concentrate on findin' the treasure. Wild goose chase or no', *that* venture is more likely to have a favorable outcome." She took the bulging burlap sack and waved Fiona away. "Now, missy, back to the castle wi' ye."

Lachlan stood under the shelter of a carved and arched doorway that opened onto the steps to the courtyard. The rain that had threatened all afternoon had begun to fall in a mournful, desultory fashion, and water dripped in a semicircle from the eaves above him onto the slick gray cobblestones below. As the first icy drops had blossomed on the rotted straw and slimy potato peelings the scullion had tossed from the kitchen window, the servants loitering outside had scuttled to shelter. A stable lad had been playing in the center of the courtyard with a litter of pups, and Lachlan watched as the brat ducked into the shelter of the tack room, leaving the pups behind in the chilling rain.

They began to cry with high, pitiful little whines, and Lachlan's mouth hardened into a grim slash. He had bred the wee creatures himself, and although he would have taken a bayonet in the gut before admitting it, they had tumbled and chewed and wriggled their way into his heart.

Two-Pack Ian held out a hand to test the rain, then jutted his chin toward the pups and said, "Fine lookin' creatures, milord. Ye wouldna be up for sellin' one, would ye? Or mayhap a trade?"

Lachlan turned to the spry little man on the steps beside him. He and Two-Pack had spent a pleasant afternoon with Rinalda in the great hall, bargaining over the wares in the chapman's pack. To Lachlan's mild surprise, Sorcha had not shown up to pout and demand a length of silk or a bag of toffee. To his much greater surprise, he had found himself truly irritated that his new cook hadn't been available to help him decide on the freshness of the Flemish aniseed oil or the suitability of the red-wine vinegar from Italy.

Rinalda, instantly divining the cause of his irritation, smugly had explained that Madam Fraser was still getting settled in her cottage.

"St. Ninian," Lachlan had muttered, slamming a pair of shoe buckles onto the refectory table. Rinalda and Two-Pack Ian arched their brows.

"What's eatin' ye, milord?" For once, since they were in company, Rinalda used his erstwhile title.

"What to call her—that's what's eatin' me."

"Call who?"

"Madam Fraser—the cook—*Fiona*," Lachlan ground out. "What do ye call a servant who is a lady, who has had a fine education, and who clearly deserves respect?"

Och, he was a fine one to talk of respect, when his body burned with desire at the mere brush of her name on his lips. He glowered at the greenish window glass and wished the great hall wasn't so dreary. No one had cleaned in here for weeks, and he detected the stale scent of mildew, wet dogs and rancid beef.

Rinalda's moth-eaten brows crooked higher. "It matters no' to me, milord. I call her madam, for she's me superior in breedin', if no' in the peckin' order backstairs."

Lachlan threw himself into a carved Jacobean chair and heaved a sigh. "Weel, I canna call her madam. She's me cook, for pity's sake."

Two-Pack winked and said, "This new lassie—she wouldna be surpassin' fair, now would she?"

Lachlan glowered down his nose—rather hard to do, since he was sitting and the chapman was standing. "I canna say that I noticed."

Rinalda began to cackle, and he lunged to his feet and stalked out. She cried after him, "Call her Fiona, milord. 'Tis a bonnie name, to match a bonnie lass!"

Recalling the scene, Lachlan's brows knit in a thunderous frown. Fiona. The name tugged at his memory like a sublime and long-forgotten melody, although for the life of him he couldn't say why. Och, and he wouldn't admit it any more than he would admit a soft spot for those blasted pups, but Fiona Fraser had haunted his thoughts since the moment he had hired her.

He shook his head ruefully. St. Ninian, perhaps he ought to have a chat with Rinalda. The troublesome crone had, upon occasion, tried out various charms and herbs on him, but always with his laughing consent. The powder warranted to spice a flagging libido hadn't altered his brazen appetites one way or the other, and the ointment to ward off ague had made him break out in hives. Perhaps the old bat was testing some daft love potion on him without his knowledge. Either that or he was in grave danger of losing his wits. Or his heart. Och, indeed, indeed . . . and which would be the worse?

"Ye wilna sell, then?" Two-Pack queried, clapping his blue Highland bonnet atop his bald head.

Lachlan glanced down, scowling. "Sell what?"

Two-Pack pointed to the slick, rain-soaked courtyard. "The pups. They're right bonnie, wi' them fluffy gold coats. And such pure faces." He dropped his gaze and looked flustered at having shown such interest. A sharp trader never showed interest.

"Nay. I'm breedin' 'em special," Lachlan said. "I've always wanted the perfect huntin' dog to retrieve fowl from the iciest water or flush birds from the thickest cover. I started with a Tweed water spaniel and crossed her wi' a setter, then crossed the best o' their offspring wi' a water retriever that came off a fishin' boat from the Colonies. This is the third litter, and I think I've got it right at last." He gazed proudly at the pups, then started down the steps. "Help me get the wee beasties out o' the rain, then I'll see ye off."

He heard the clop of hooves and rattle of wheels as a lackey led Two-Pack's horse and cart from the shelter of the stable into the icy drizzle of the yard. Just then, Fiona walked through the gate, head bent, the hood of her Madonna-blue cloak hiding her gleaming hair. The puppies' whines turned to exultant barks; then Fiona glanced up and saw Lachlan. For a long moment, they stared across the cobbles into each other's eyes, and Lachlan felt a voluptuous shimmer of warmth pass over his skin, despite the icy drizzle trickling down his neck.

The frantic, joyous barks grew louder; then all five puppies erupted from their wooden box and hurtled pell-mell toward Fiona. Unnerved by the shrill noise and abrupt motion, the chapman's horse neighed and reared—front hooves slicing through the misty air, eyes rolling white with fear. Suddenly the animal broke free and charged. Before Lachlan could move, sharp, iron-shod hooves and crushing wheels thundered over the wee pups. Fiona screamed, and the liquid air rang with the piercing, frightened squeals of wounded animals.

Lachlan dove forward, Two-Pack at his heels. The

chapman caught the horse by the bridle and dragged it to a shuddering halt while Lachlan assessed the scene with one quick glance. Three of the pups had escaped harm and were pressed—wide-eyed, whimpering and shivering—to Fiona's mud-caked skirts. She bent and scooped all three little bodies to her bosom, then hurried toward him.

He reached the spot first, then knelt. One of the puppies—a sturdy little male he had named Roane—was frantically licking what clearly was a broken leg. With sure, gentle movements, Lachlan ran his hands over the animal's trembling body, checking for gashes or other breaks. Thank St. Ninian, this wee beastie would be fine. He turned to the other pup, and his heart went cold. Och, 'twas too late.

Fiona flung herself down beside him on the wet cobbles, then leaned over him, reaching for the crumpled, still puppy. He felt the warmth and weight of her breasts press against his thigh, felt the softness of her hood brush against his cheek. The wet wool fell away from her face, and he inhaled the intoxicating aroma of her hair, all hay and fresh herbs and some indefinable sweetness, like French fields under the summer sun.

She gently lifted the pup's limp and lifeless body, then cradled it to her face. *"Oh, vous êtes le pauvre petit bébé,"* she whispered. *"Oh, Dieu vous aide, mon pauvre petit."* Tears mingled with the raindrops glistening on her cheeks, and her stricken violet gaze met Lachlan's. "Her neck is broken, I think." Her eyes never left his.

Lachlan's jaw clenched; then he reached out his good hand and stroked one finger down the puppy's soft face, over the odd little cowlick along its nose. "Poor wee bairn. She was me favorite." His throat closed up, and he scowled, then looked away.

He stood, hands trembling, then bellowed at the careless lackey, "Get out o' me sight! And dinna let me see ye handlin' horses again, or by God, I'll horsewhip ye to within an inch o' your life." He hardened his face into impassive lines, then turned to bid farewell to the chapman. To his surprise, Two-Pack stood frozen to the cobbles, jaw hanging in astonishment, gaping down at Fiona.

Lachlan turned and found her sitting in a hay-clogged puddle with her knees drawn up to her chin and the pup cradled in her lap. Her eyes were closed, her head was bowed, and her slender hands pressed against the animal's limp little body. The delicate skin of her brow was furrowed in concentration, her lips were clamped and pale, and the mournful gray rain had darkened her glorious red hair to the shade of dead leaves.

All at once, just for an instant, Lachlan thought he saw a shimmering aura of golden light surround her head, then run down her delicate fingers into the pup's still form.

"Did ye see that?" Two-Pack whispered, eyes wide.

Lachlan stepped closer, convinced that the flash of gold light—if he indeed had seen such a thing—was a trick of the setting sun refracting through the rain. He ignored the fact that the sky was as dark as a bruise and there was no sunset.

Fiona's delicate features relaxed suddenly, as if she had been released from a crushing pain. Then she turned and smiled up at Lachlan. Her eyes glowed like fire-shot amethysts, and a radiant, breathtaking beauty shone from her upturned face.

"I think we were wrong," she said hesitantly, holding out the pup for his inspection. "She was just stunned, perhaps."

Heart thundering against his ribs, Lachlan dragged his gaze from Fiona's demure face and glanced down at the puppy. Its sides moved as if it was breathing; then it wriggled, opened its dark eyes and gave a tiny whine. Lachlan blinked in bewilderment. St. Ninian— the wee creature had been dead! He was sure of it, and he had seen more than enough death to know.

He glared down at Fiona. "What did ye just do?"

"Why, nothing, monsieur." She stood with lithe grace, then brushed hay from her sopping skirts. Her enchanting eyes were downcast, but Lachlan detected a dimple hovering at one corner of her mouth. "Perhaps his lordship needs spectacles."

"Dinna trifle wi' me, madam. I saw what I saw."

Her smile vanished; she paled and swallowed convulsively. "I-I'm sure the pup was fine. I just warmed it. Please, monsieur, let us not speak of it again."

Lachlan's wits returned, along with a jolt of angry pride. "Aye, weel," he muttered. "And what are ye doin' out in the rain? I'll expect ye in the great hall in half an hour, *after* ye've cleaned off some o' that muck. And dinna forget to bring me tea." Then he cast her a scathing glare, snatched the squirming puppy from her grasp and stalked away.

Five

Fiona balanced the tea tray on her hip and stepped into the great hall. Candlelight dazzled her eyes after the chill darkness of the stone passageway, and as her sight slowly adjusted, she silently berated herself for her idiocy at leaving France. *Mon Dieu,* she was a fool! She could be at the patisserie right now, happily laving puff pastry with creamery butter, serenely grinding cinnamon and nutmeg into sweet-roll batter, peacefully whipping eggs into a lemony froth while the warm, yeasty air grew fragrant with spice.

But no, her ridiculous dream of love, of freedom, of learning the truth about her past had lured her into this dismal castle, and into a snare set by her own pride. What had she been thinking of, healing that puppy like that? *Idiot, idiot!*

She suppressed a giddy shiver. In truth, she had been astonished that she still could heal. Then, the moment she had handed the dazed pup back to Lachlan, she had seen that her employer's probing silver eyes had ferreted out her secret. And now she must face him.

She took a deep breath, assumed her most serene expression, then glided toward the enormous stone fireplace at the opposite end of the room. Space stretched away above her head, echoing and cold, and massive hewn beams arched across the expanse,

painted with primitive Celtic designs, hunting scenes
and the Maclean clan motto: *Virtue Mine Honor.* Blue-
and-green embroidered banners hung from the beams,
and a cumbersome, carved-oak refectory table filled
the center of the room, its surface black and velvety
with age—and with a century's accumulation of grease
and smoke.

Scattered across the table were all manner of fascinating things, doubtless purchased on credit from Two-
Pack Ian. Fiona noted a pile of leather-bound books,
flagons of olive and sweet almond oil, bolts of un-
bleached muslin and smooth black broadcloth, glittering white cones of sugar, a small chest of tea, a pouch
of tobacco from the Virginia colony, several round maple boxes and a wire birdcage.

She paused, unsure where to set the tea. The lord of
the manor was nowhere to be seen, so she bent and set
the tray on the table next to an array of iron hand tools,
then straightened and glanced around the room. A
crackling peat fire lit the far side of the hall, and smoking tallow candles cast eerie shadows on the oak paneling and reflected from windows intricately set with
diamond-shaped panes of stained glass. A delicate,
carved-oak screen occupied the space behind the table,
and its fanciful design drew her gaze upward. Her
heart thundered to life, and she gasped.

Ranged on the opposite wall high above her, staring
glassily down through the murky shadows into her
eyes, hung the stuffed heads of half a dozen dead animals. Fiona caught her breath, then pressed a hand to
her damp bodice and counted. There was a deer, a stag,
a boar, a wildcat, a bear and a fox.

"You poor things," she said, studying them pityingly. Cobwebs interlaced the stag's antlers, and soot
encased the boar's curved yellow tusks. "I suppose

my lord Maclean shot you to prove his masculine prowess."

"Actually, me father and Sir Hector Maclean shot them."

Fiona whirled, then stared in dismay as Lachlan unfolded himself from a high-backed tapestry wing chair hidden in the shadows beyond the fireplace. He arched a mocking black brow at the stuffed boar. "Sir Hector got that one on his last visit here, right before the Risin'. I always thought it resembled the old curmudgeon."

Fiona gaped at the beast's reddish bristles, then swallowed. It *did* rather look like Sir Hector.

Lachlan sauntered toward her, smiling lazily. A letter dangled from the long ruffles hiding his bad right hand, he clenched a whisky glass in the other, and the gold-colored puppy whose life she had restored trotted at his heels. It gave one short bark and raced toward Fiona, then jumped and twirled and joyously begged to be petted.

Lachlan pinned her with a challenging smile and drawled, "Ye had me goin' for a minute, there, outside. I could have sworn ye snatched yon wee imp back from the jaws o' death."

She calmly met his searing gaze and didn't reply. His face grew tense and brooding; then he pocketed the letter, tossed back the whisky and dropped the glass on the table. The candlelight softened the planes of his lean, dangerously handsome face, and he stepped so close she felt the warmth emanating from his body and inhaled the masculine scent of his skin. Suddenly his hand shot out. He caught her chin in two steely fingers, raised her face and forced her to meet his eyes. Firelight flickered in their cold gray depths, like torch flame reflecting off an ice-covered pond. She shivered.

He eased closer, and his eyes darkened with blatant desire, then glittered with a thousand shards of silver. "I must reward ye for savin' me property," he murmured, voice low and husky—a languorous voice, calculated to weaken a woman's knees and sweep away her defenses. She had heard Harry use just such a tone on one of his mistresses. *Mon Dieu,* it had worked on Madam du Barry then, and it was working on her now.

With slow, assured arrogance, her employer lowered his mouth to hers. His strong fingers stroked her jaw, and their scorching heat sent sparks of longing across her throat, down her spine, over her breasts. She inhaled his whisky-scented breath and, to her utter mortification, felt her belly go liquid with desire. Her legs seemed ready to slither out from under her, and for a mad split second, she prayed he would press his sculpted body into her softness and relieve the aching passion welling up in her core.

The puppy began gnawing at the toe of her boot, and a tiny mote of reason drifted through her addled brain. *Mon Dieu,* what was she doing? Lachlan Maclean was a married man, and she was a proper widow in mourning for her father-in-law. St. Genevieve, she was no better than philandering Harry—or his mistresses! And just how did she expect to draw a rational, objective conclusion about this bold Highlander's fitness to be clan chieftain if she melted into a pool of lust—yes, lust!—every time he came near her?

"Och, are ye a changeling, then?" Lachlan whispered, lips hovering like butterfly wings against her mouth. He gazed deep into her eyes, then brushed his lips over hers—light, deft, teasing, seductive. "A *druidh* sent to bewitch me?"

Bewitch? That was all it took. Fiona lurched backward, breaking Lachlan's intimate grip on her jaw. To cover her agitation and hide her flaming cheeks, she bent and snatched up the puppy, then took three deep breaths, counted to five and straightened. Her perfectly schooled, drilled and *false* features were serene once more.

"*Mon Dieu,* is that what you think of me, my lord?" she said demurely. "If so, I'm amazed that you would trust me to serve your tea. What if I put eye of newt or tongue of frog in it?"

Lachlan stepped to the side, so the corner of the table stood between them. A veil of nonchalance descended over his smoldering eyes, leaving them cool and challenging once more. "Weel now, madam—or should I call you Fiona? Aye? Weel now, since ye dinna fancy a *personal* reward"—he arched a dark brow—"perhaps I can make ye a present from here." He gestured to the jumble of items spread across the table. "A box of almond comfits, perhaps? Or a blue silk ribbon?" His intent gaze never left her face, and Fiona felt as if her fluttering heart must at any moment careen from her breast.

As if he sensed her panic, his lips quirked into a roguish smile, and laugh lines radiated from the corners of his wide-set eyes. He caught up a hairbrush of smooth, polished maple and soft boar's bristles. "How aboot this? With bonnie red hair like yours—"

"My lord, I begin to apprehend that you like to tease, rather like a court jester." Fiona raised her chin and struggled to find just the right tone. *Mon Dieu,* what good were her years as a silent, cool-eyed observer gliding about the fringes of the French court if she couldn't best this maddening Highlander at drawing-room repartee? "If you insist on giving me a present for merely pointing out that your *pauvre petite chien* had been stunned, then perhaps I may make a suggestion."

Lachlan lounged against the table, devilishly long legs crossed nonchalantly in front of him. He tossed a comfit in the air and caught it in his mouth. "And what might your suggestion be?"

Fiona slanted him a shy smile and held up the puppy. "That you give me this troublesome little charmer, of course, monsieur."

Lachlan's black brows slammed down. "What the devil do ye want wi' a dog?"

"I love animals, monsieur."

"Aye, that's apparent," he remarked, one side of his sensual mouth quirking up. "Every time I turn around, I find ye talkin' to beasts—dead *and* alive."

Fiona set down the pup and toyed with the sugar tongs on the tea tray. She must steer this conversation out of dangerous waters. "Monsieur, if you have no intention of giving me the gift I want, why offer me a gift at all?"

Lachlan made a sound that was half chuckle and half snort. "Och, there's the French talkin'. Ye're always practical, aye? And just a wee bit selfish?"

Fiona fixed him with a guileless gaze, then handed him a blue-and-white china tea cup. "I don't know what you mean, monsieur. Sugar?"

Lachlan waved away the proffered sugar, then glowered into the fire. "How would ye care for a puppy? Rinalda tells me ye've insisted on livin' in that hovel near Ben More. That's no place for a highbred dog. Nay, I canna allow it."

"You've allowed me to live there. Am I no better than a dog?"

A muscle jumped in Lachlan's adamantine cheek. "Och, I dinna mean it that way, lass." He turned and looked at her—really looked at her for the very first time. No more seductive glances, no more teasing winks, no more challenging glares. Just honest gray eyes levely meeting hers. "Why do ye want a pet?"

Fiona glanced down, then nervously moved a blue-and-white china plate of pâté. Her father-in-law had been a great one for logic, rationality, and honest dealing, when he hadn't been blustering and baiting his wife. Maeve always had lamented that Sir Hector's honesty had prevented him from recovering his land and title, and from advancing at court. Now here it was again: that same direct honesty she had never found in Harry, but often had seen in Sir Hector. She smiled wanly. Perhaps 'twas something in the Scottish air—or in a Maclean chieftain's blood.

Well, an honest question deserved an honest answer. She raised her head and handed Lachlan the plate. "I'm lonely, my lord. That's why I want a pet."

Lachlan studied her face for several long minutes, then dropped his gaze to his plate. His long, black lashes cast crescent shadows on his chiseled cheekbones, and all amusement had vanished from his aristocratic features. "Aye, lass," he said. "I ken what ye mean. Loneliness is a terrible cross to bear." Distractedly, he took a bite of food, then choked, swallowed hard, and slammed down his plate. "St. Ninian, what was that?"

"Pâté, monsieur."

"Pâté? Och, I *hate* pâté. Where in hell did ye get it?"

Fiona smothered a smile and answered sweetly, "I made it, monsieur."

He glared down his sharp nose at the brownish paste spread daintily atop crisp-crusted, chewy French bread. "Made it? Wi' what? Toads?"

He looked so outraged Fiona began to giggle. *"Mon
Dieu,* you should see your face. You look as if you'd
just bitten into horse sh—"

She clapped a hand over her mouth, and Lachlan
broke into a wide, wicked grin. Hard, masculine dimples bracketed his lips; then he stepped close and
caught her forearm. Fiona noted that he never reached
out with his stiff, twisted hand; it was deftly hidden in
the full, graceful sleeves of his white linen shirt. "Och,
such language. And to think I believed ye a prim,
proper and much too virtuous widow."

She gazed coolly up at him, then dissolved into a
naughty smile. "Well, admit it. Pâté *does* rather resem-
ble, ah . . . *fumier de cheval.*" Lachlan chuckled softly,
then drew her toward him. Honesty and amusement
had vanished from his eyes, replaced by raw masculine
desire. Fiona thrust out her hands and warded him off.
"Monsieur, as I've said, there's only one present I want
from you."

Lachlan dropped her wrist, then shrugged, as if to
say, *Ye canna blame a mon for tryin'.* He bent, gently
lifted the pup from the Turkey carpet it was industri-
ously gnawing, then popped the little animal into her
arms. "Here, she's yours. Wi' me compliments." He
bowed with a graceful flourish. "What will ye name
her?"

Fiona nuzzled the puppy's musky golden fur. "An-
gelique, perhaps?"

Lachlan cast an eloquent look at the damp, chewed
carpet. "Nay, I think no'." Suddenly, he turned, caught
up his whisky glass, then strode back to the shelter of
his tapestry chair. In the orange glow of the firelight,
she saw him fish the letter from his shirt pocket, then
scowl blackly. "Ye may go now, Fiona. I've work to
do."

She caught up the tea tray and called the pup to heel, unaccountably disappointed with his sudden dismissal. As she left the hall, Lachlan called after her, "Och, and lassie? Call the pup Lazarus—for sure and I saw ye raise it from the dead."

Fiona poured a kettle of warm water over Lachlan's favorite puppy and rinsed all trace of rose-scented French soap from its thick golden fur. The little dog— now officially named Lazarus—ducked its head pitifully, squinted its eyes shut and shivered from black-tipped nose to woebegone, drooping tail.

"There *bébé*," Fiona crooned, wrapping the pup in a threadbare towel, then briskly rubbed it dry. "Now you won't smell so much like the stable." She turned and shook her head at Maeve, who sat peeling turnips on the bench next to their crumbling stone hearth. *"Mon Dieu, ma mère,* you would not believe it. That castle is little better than a pigsty. The rooms haven't been aired in months, dust and soot cover everything, the ale has gone sour, and the flour was full of weevils. I wanted to make *palmiers* for the master's tea, but had to settle on bannocks. Ugh. Jacques would have been scandalized."

"All those years in France have turned ye into a petite bourgeoise," Maeve remarked, not unkindly. "Ye'd rather cook and garden than dance. No wonder the Comte du Maine didn't press his suit."

Fiona wrinkled her nose, then wrapped the puppy in an old shawl and cuddled it to her bosom. "The comte had an overbite, syphilis and spots. And he didn't pursue me because I'm penniless."

Unperturbed by this indisputable truth, Maeve brushed turnip chunks into an iron kettle. "It sounds to me like that Rinalda is too old to be a decent house-keeper."

"Oh, *non*," Fiona protested, purposefully keeping her eyes lowered. "She's a very hard worker and is most kind." She nestled Lazarus in an abandoned basket that had been gnawed by several generations of rats. "But one can't help wonder about the standards of Madam Maclean. One would think she would take better care of her husband."

Maeve fixed her with a quizzical glare. "What are ye talkin' aboot, missy? There is no Madam Maclean."

Fiona's pulse gave a wild lurch. "But . . . but you said you had attended their wedding."

"Aye, and I did. But Lachlan Maclean's wife has been dead since Culloden." Maeve set down her knife, pressed her hands on her ample thighs and leaned forward. "I heard tell of it when Hector and I were in hiding with the prince, before we got away to France." Her voice lowered and grew conspiratorial. " 'Twas a terrible scandal. Terrible."

A chill trailed down Fiona's spine, as if someone had walked over her grave. She remembered little of Culloden—just sleet-choked twilight, snow blowing across a field, and twisted mounds covered in ragged tartan, which she now knew had been the bodies of slain Highlanders, but which at the time had seemed like a strange part of the gruesome landscape. And there had been a man, very tall and dark. She couldn't see him at all; she just remembered, deep in her bones, that he had been kind and needed her help.

What had happened to him? Had he died? She had touched him, but. . . . She knotted her hands in her apron and breathed a prayer to St. Sebastian, patron saint of soldiers. Then she raised her chin and scanned Maeve's dour expression. "What caused this scandal?"

"Och, I dinna ken, no' for sure. We heard several tales, Hector and I. A few stories were worse than others, just like the folk who told them. Some said Catriona Maclean died in childbed. Others swore she killed herself and her unborn bairn—overcome with remorse that the Jacobite cause was lost." Maeve snorted and shook her head. "Though why a schemin', half-Campbell loyalist like Catriona should grieve over a cause she despised is beyond me ken."

Maeve turned and gazed into the smoky peat fire. The writhing flames cast eerie shadows on her strong nose and stubborn chin, and for an instant, Fiona thought she saw a flicker of sorrow in her mother-in-law's guarded eyes. As if sensing Fiona's scrutiny, Maeve looked up and said, "But most whispered that her arrogant, black-hearted husband drove her to suicide. Or that he murdered her."

Fiona gasped and dropped onto the bench, appalled by Maeve's matter-of-fact tone. "But how can you say that? I don't believe it." She caught Maeve's rough hand, leaned forward and peered into her eyes. "Is there any evidence? *Mon Dieu!* Why in the name of St. Winifred would he kill his own wife?"

"Dinna looked so shocked. I warned ye aboot that devil Lachlan Maclean, and I'm just tellin' ye what I heard, no' makin' it happen." She stood. "Will ye hear this or no'?"

Fiona slid onto the floor, then swallowed and sat cross-legged beside Lazarus's basket. She nodded mutely and stroked the sleeping pup. Her fingers felt numb.

Maeve bent, grasped the kettle of turnips, and hung it on the iron rod suspended over the fire. "Rumor was he was wildly, violently jealous. Catriona was uncommon beautiful, and the lads would moon after her. But

I canna see a proud man like Lachlan spillin' blood 'cause he'd been made a cuckhold—unless his wife's lover was someone so close the shock turned his mind."

She snatched up the smooth, peeled branch that served as their cooking spoon and gave the turnips a poke. There was a long, strained pause, and Fiona ordered herself to remain tranquil, to focus her swirling thoughts on the flames and the puppy's soft snores. Lachlan Maclean could *not* be a murderer. 'Twas utterly ridiculous. Why, he had given her Lazarus; he had given her a job.

Suddenly a rough Scottish voice blustered through her head. *Nigs and ballocks! Is this the logical lass I married to that worthless son o' mine? Och, use what piddlin' wee brains ye have left, lassie, and face the truth—and dinna fancy there's love anywhere aboot that dreary castle. Why, ye're bonnie enough to turn a dead mon's head, and that rogue Maclean hired ye 'cause he wants to bed ye.* Hearty, jaded laughter echoed in her brain. *Ha! Ye should see your face. Now what do ye aim to do aboot it?*

Six

Fog rose from the dark fields like a strange, mystical enchantment. There was no sea wind so late at night, but as Fiona watched, phantasms of mist lifted into the air, then floated, swirled, undulated and vanished as if they had never been, leaving her to blink and clutch her cloak tight about her throat. With silent steps, she glided forward. Transparent fingers of gray trailed away from the edge of her vision until she felt as if unseen ghosts were plucking at the edge of her mind and trying to tell her—

Tell her what?

She could sense the sea through the blackness before her. It made a soft susurrus, like a sleeper's measured breathing. She heard the random slap of a wave on a boulder and the rhythmic roll of pebbles on the beach. Oh, the ocean was alive, all right. She threw back her head and dragged in a cold, damp draught of air. It smelled of salt and granite and ever so slightly of decayed life flung up by the sea. She recognized the smell of rockweed, but what else might that vast, unseen stretch of water disgorge? Dead fish? Dead sailors?

She turned her steps away from the steep embankment, which sloped down from their cottage to the tiny unseen crescent of beach below. The incline was rough and choked with heather, stunted furze and dead grass. All she needed was to stumble and pitch headlong into water so cold she would die before she could break the surface and draw breath.

She straightened her shoulders and raised her chin. 'Twould be a far better thing to stop her foolish daydreaming and walk to the castle. Rinalda had given her a key so she could let herself in before daybreak to prepare breakfast for the master and the servants, and although dawn wouldn't stretch herself awake for hours yet, Fiona could light a single candle in the silent kitchen and get a jump on the day. Something must be done about the sour ale, and 'twas high time she introduced Lachlan to the joys of café au lait and flaky, buttery croissant.

The path to the castle was narrow, and here and there nettles dragged at her skirts. Or were those goblin fingers? She smiled, and for one wild moment allowed herself to revel in the cold and the night and the mist and the potent, brazen, *alive* Scottish air. *Mon Dieu,* she never would have guessed it, but she loved the Isles. This was what she had sprung from—this secret, primitive, magical side of nature. Nothing could be more foreign to the cloistered gardens, tamed topiaries and smooth gravel promenades of Paris; and nothing could be more threatening to her carefully crafted veneer of propriety.

She frowned, remembering the one time she had defied her mother's admonitions to keep quiet, hide her gifts and blend in. She had been thirteen and a pupil at the Ursuline convent of St. Angela. The students had been learning about Louis XIV, the magnificent Sun King, and had been titillated into near obsession by Sister Marie-Josephe's lurid stories of the witchcraft and poisonings rampant at Louis' court. Of particular fascination was the infamous fortune-teller, La Voisin. Sister Marie-Josephe had intended that La Voisin— who had been burned at the stake for witchcraft—be an object lesson on the wages of sin. Instead, she un- wittingly had enticed Fiona into reading her fellow stu- dents' palms.

Fiona's predictions had caused nothing but shivers of adolescent excitement, and her fellow students hid her burgeoning practice from the sisters—until she foretold that grave misfortune would befall the family of Louise de Vernet. When Louise's father, over- whelmed by insurmountable debt, threw himself into the Seine, a heartbroken and vengeful Louise had ac- cused Fiona of witchcraft.

With the implacable inevitability of falling domi- noes, Fiona's world had collapsed. She had been sum- moned before the Mother Superior and two priests, fiercely interrogated, then expelled from the convent. The de Vernet family had sworn out a legal action of slander against the Frasers, and Ian Fraser had been dismissed from Prince Charles's service and barred from the French court. Gambling had been Ian's only source of income, and without the gold-lined pockets of witless courtiers to pick, the Frasers had sunk into poverty and obscurity.

Silently, the clouds rolled away from the face of the moon. Fiona glanced up, then smiled. Sir Hector Maclean—who had met her in a bookshop when she was sixteen, and who instantly had been taken with her wits and much-whispered reputation—at last had res- cued the Frasers. The irascible Scottish chieftain al- ways had been an iconoclast, and it had delighted him to add Fiona to his collection of scandals and lost causes—rather as if she were a rare coin.

She reached out her hands toward the glowing white

moon, so serene and mysterious, floating on its ocean of black clouds. Oh, she loved it here; she loved Mull and these people and this wondrous, strange beauty. It seeped into her pores and shot through her blood and made her yearn to dance and twirl and fling herself down onto the frost-rimed black grass. It made her long to couple with a man who was tall, brazen, faceless, and who knew her deepest longings.

A hot blush flowed down her neck and rippled like tiny waves against her nipples. She halted and clenched her eyes shut in a trance of pure desire. All at once her dark lover was no longer a remote pagan god; he was Lachlan Maclean.

That thought drove the breath from her lungs as if she had been doused with a bucket of ice water. *Mon Dieu,* she truly must be a witch, for only an unnatural being would ache for the touch of a suspected murderer. But Lachlan was only suspected; she had to remember that. And she was a demure widow in her mid-twenties whose virtue and modesty were beyond reproach. She *must* remember that.

She dug her fingers into her gloved palms and hurried forward, head bent. Earlier in the evening, when Maeve had finished her appalling tale of betrayal and murder, Fiona had wobbled to her feet and ventured that Lachlan Maclean would feature well as the villain in Sir Hector's scurrilous underground pamphlets. Maeve had not been amused with her daughter-in-law's quick tongue and had promptly accused Fiona of falling in love with a vile traitor who had enriched himself at the expense of his clan.

Fiona slowed her steps as the breathtaking black shadow of the castle rock loomed ahead of her. Had murder been committed there?

Castle Taigh sat at the pinnacle of a high rock promontory surrounded on three sides by the sea. Jagged, forbidding cliffs fell away all around it and offered perfect natural protection from invasion, a feature that doubtless had warmed the blood-thirsty hearts of Lachlan's warrior ancestors. There was only one approach to the castle from land: a dirt track that wound through the fields of Taigh Samhraidh, then ascended up a narrow ridge to the top of the cliffs.

Rinalda had told her that small boats could moor at the base of the cliffs, and that a Maclean ancestor had hewn a rough staircase from the dock up to the castle. Fiona had yet to see this marvel, and rather questioned the steps' practicality. What was the use of building a fortified dwelling atop a one-hundred-fifty-foot cliff, then rolling out a welcome mat? Clearly, that particular Maclean had been more concerned with convenience than with war.

The castle itself was a massive pile of stone, four imposing stories high—not counting dungeons, Fiona supposed. Moonlight silvered the towering, crenellated stone keep, and the black holes of the exterior windows gaped like blind, empty eyes. The sea washed on the narrow stretch of rocky beach on the southern side of the cliffs and made low, sucking, slapping sounds against the steep rock to the north and east. A brilliant, silver-white moon path stretched across the shimmering water, so wide and bright Fiona fancied she could stroll across it, dry and unharmed, to the mist-shrouded mainland beyond.

She took a deep breath and hurried up the steep gravel road to the tunnel-like passageway guarding the entrance to the castle. The stone gateway closed in around her, blocking out the moonlight and leaving her in frigid, moldering darkness. The hair rose on the back of her neck, and she thrust out a hand, anxiously feeling her way along the slimy stones.

She stubbed her toe and bit back an oath. She muttered, "Why didn't I bring a lantern?"

Suddenly she froze. Had she heard a sound? Every nerve in her body tensed, and her breath died in her throat.

At the end of the passageway she could see a rectangle of light—the moon, no doubt, reflecting off the frost-covered grounds surrounding the castle. With horrified fascination, she watched as the rectangle faded to a thick, dull gray, then slowly transformed into the shape of a man.

She stumbled backward, tripped over a loose stone and fell. She landed hard, then drew breath and screamed.

"Och, lassie, haud yer wheest. Ballocks an' oatcakes, ye could deafen a corpse. And why so shocked to see me? Havena I been tryin' to reach ye since the night I died?"

Fiona skittered backward, and her head hit the wall's cold, wet stones. She managed a gasp, then blinked. The swirling gray shadow looked uncomfortably familiar, and there was no mistaking that gruff, contentious Scottish accent.

"St. Joan," she whispered, crossing herself. " 'Tis The Maclean, back from the grave."

The shadow dissipated, and she was alone in the fetid blackness. Shivering with cold and terror, she clambered to her feet, turned and clapped a hand over her mouth. There, not ten feet away, stood Sir Hector Maclean, grinning like a naughty boy who had just played a successful prank. Her heart thundered into her throat.

" 'Ods fish, what a fankle ye're makin'," Sir Hector

said in disgust. "I took ye for a cooler head than this, lass."

Fiona's eyes fluttered shut. *Mon Dieu,* it wasn't seeing her father-in-law in spectral form that upset her; after all, he *had* taken rather theatrical control of her dreams, and she had caught herself speaking to him at odd moments. Nay, the shock came from his appearance, for all that hovered before her was The Maclean's head—a grinning, ruddy-cheeked, auburn-haired head.

She dropped her hand, then took a steadying breath and studied the apparition. Sir Hector had been shriveled, ashen and gaunt the day he had died, rather like a peeled apple left too long in the sun. *This* being was the very image of the hale and hearty Sir Hector who had met and argued about Voltaire with her in a Paris bookseller's shop nearly ten years before. She leaned forward and squinted into the darkness.

"Is that a wig or your real hair?" she asked. The specter chuckled, and Fiona saw that luxuriant auburn hair wasn't the only improvement death had wrought. This Sir Hector boasted all his teeth.

"That's me cool-eyed skeptic," the ghost replied. *"Jesu,* lassie, I was beginnin' to think ye'd gone soft on me." His long ringlets bounced as if being patted by a smug and self-congratulatory hand—an unseen smug and self-congratulatory hand.

Fiona frowned, then critically appraised her new father-in-law. His beefy cheeks glowed in the blackness of the passage with the health and vitality of a man of forty, and she almost could see life pulsing beneath his square jaw. Only his close-set, mischievous brown eyes hadn't changed.

She gathered her courage and met the specter's gaze. *"Pardon, mon père,* but should you be taking our

Lord's name in vain? I assume you have gone to heaven, and surely He doesn't like—"

"Oh-ho! Is that what ye're thinkin'? Weel, ye're wrong, lassie. Dead wrong." Sir Hector flushed at this poor choice of words, then swirled before her eyes like nuts in a cake batter. "I'm in limbo, or Purgatory, or whatever 'tis called. Nigs! What a miserable state. Cold and borin' as last week's porridge, and no lassies. Say!" He re-formed and floated nearer. "Where are all me funeral candles? Dinna they teach ye to light candles for the souls o' the dead in that fancy convent school o' yours? If ye'd lit me a few, perhaps I wouldna be in this fankle. . . ." Suddenly his voice faded, and his image grew gray and cloudy as morning fog. Then he vanished.

Fiona spun and stared about her. *Mon père?* Where are you? Don't . . . don't go." An exhausting feeling of loneliness swept over her, and her throat ached with tears. Then she sniffed and straightened her shoulders. *Mon Dieu,* what was wrong with her? Was she going mad? First to see a ghost, then to feel bereft when it left. Surely such foolishness called for a steadying glass of French cognac.

A thin, mischievous chuckle sounded a hairbreadth from her ear. She jumped and clapped a hand to her racing heart. " 'Ods bodkins, lass," Sir Hector whispered. "I had to come back, for your pure heart was grievin' me—"

"Stop that! You scared me half to death." She stared through the chill darkness, eyes straining to catch a hint of light or movement. She seemed entirely alone.

"Och, who stole your scone? No need to get snippy. Now give us a smile and admit it. Ye miss me."

"Do not."

"Do, too."

All at once, the ridiculousness of the situation hit her, and she started to laugh. In an instant she was bent over, clutching her belly and giggling helplessly. "Oh . . . really," she managed to choke, "this is too odd, even for me." She wiped tears from her cheeks, then raised her chin and strode toward the end of the passage, back the way she had come. "I don't mind talking to saints or to God, but I draw the line at ghosts."

She had almost reached the moonlit gravel path when Sir Hector's head popped up in front of her. This time she could see straight through him. She halted, then planted her hands on her hips.

"You're being ridiculous," she declared, gazing coolly into the ghost's transparent eyes. "And would you please do the kindness of leaving me alone? I don't want the people here to think I'm 'awa' wi' the faeries,' as they say. Frankly, you don't seem much of a spirit, and I certainly don't think you're worth getting in trouble over."

Sir Hector slanted her a sly glance. "Hard lass. No heart and no family feelin'. But ye're right, me fellow Scots are uncommon fond o' burnin' witches, and I dinna want ye to scorch. So I'll cut ye a deal."

"Are ghosts in a position to negotiate? I mean, I can see a clump of grass right through your nose—"

"That's 'cause I'm burnin' up me energy sparrin' wi' ye. We spirits have only so much matter, ye ken." Sir Hector looked affronted, then thrust out his pugnacious jaw. "Och, and if ye had listened to your dreams, I wouldna have to materialize."

"What dreams?" Fiona feinted forward, but the slowly fading head didn't move.

"About the treasure, lass. I told ye, 'tis enough to

make ye and Maeve rich beyond your wildest dreams. And I ken your dreams are pretty wild."

"But you never could remember where you had it hidden. You'd start nattering about the Butcher Prostitute of Provence—"

"I've remembered now!" Sir Hector crowed. His head gave an excited shimmer. "There's a map in the castle that shows the verra spot. All ye have to do is find that map—"

Fiona folded her arms across her chest and pinned the flickering specter with a level gaze. "Where in the castle?"

The ghost dimmed dolefully. "I canna rightly recollect—"

"Then how am I supposed to find it? It could take months. I have to work for a living, you know—in case you've forgotten things like food and a bed out there in limbo."

"But ye work in the castle," Sir Hector protested.

"I work in the kitchen, and Rinalda won't countenance the cook wandering about the castle on some wild-goose chase."

"Och, lassie—but the lord and master will." Sir Hector's voice took on a singularly suggestive tone. "He fancies ye, lass . . . fancies ye in his bed—"

"Stop! I'm a decent, respectable widow, and I'll not hear this." Fiona clamped her hands to her ears and started to whistle.

Sir Hector emitted a meager spurt of light. Fiona dropped her hands and felt a bit sorry for him. He *was* dead, after all. Perhaps she should be a bit more polite.

"Think on it, lassie," he wheedled. "I ken ye've feelin's for Lachlan—feelin's ye never had for that rogue Harry. And Lachlan hungers for ye wi' all the dark passion in his soul. I've watched him since the day ye came, and I ken." He floated closer, and Fiona felt a cool draft on her cheek, as if someone had opened a door to the evening breeze. "Become his mistress, lass. I ken ye want to—"

"I do not." Fiona stamped her foot, then strode forward. The ghost followed at her shoulder.

"Aye, ye do. And once ye're his, ye'll have the run o' the castle. I'll help ye find the map—"

Fiona whirled. "Are you asking me to be a whore?"

Sir Hector bobbed out of her way. "Nay, lass. I'm askin' ye to follow your heart, and to find the truth. Remember, ye promised. . . ." The specter's voice trailed away, and its image faded alarmingly.

"Wait," Fiona called. "What truth? Is it something about Lachlan? Maeve says he's a murderer and a traitor and that he's not fit to be chieftain." She knotted her hands in her cloak, then paced back and forth on the gravel road. The ghost attempted to keep up, growing paler with each passing moment. "But he seems kind," Fiona muttered. "Kind and honest. His eyes, you know. They're very . . ."

"Honest?" the ghost piped.

Fiona stopped. Sir Hector vanished. "Come back," she called. "You haven't told me what truth I'm supposed to learn."

She stood under the moonlit sky, shivering and waiting for an answer. Castle Taigh was a craggy black mass limned with silver, a breeze whistled through the heather, and ground fog drifted eerily across the fields. Then, low and far away, like the murmuring voice of the sea, she heard Sir Hector's parting words.

"Follow your heart, lass, and ye'll find the truth."

Seven

Lachlan reined his horse to a halt a quarter of the way up Ben More, then stared down over the silent, mist-shrouded fields. Sleep came hard to him most nights, but on nights like this, with a full moon, it was well nigh impossible. For years, Rinalda had tried to lull him to sleep with her various herbs and potions, all to no avail. Sorcha attributed his insomnia to loneliness, and hinted broadly that he would find relief in their marriage bed.

Lachlan gave a jaded bark of laughter, and the horse's ears swiveled backward at the sound. Marriage a solace. Ha! Marriage had proved to be the worst nightmare he had ever encountered, and he doubted not at all that wedding Sorcha would confirm this bitter truth.

The chill night breeze lifted his unbound hair from his shoulders, and he shivered. Och, what manner of fool was he, to be out here in the frost and the fog when he could be snuggled beneath wool blankets, with Sorcha's skilled lips and intoxicating curves to fire his blood?

The horse restively pawed at the frozen turf; Lachlan tightened the reins and frowned. Sure and there must be something wrong with him lately, for despite Sorcha's persistent advances, he had no more interest in her than in being bled by the surgeon. His lips twitched into a wry smile. Och, and since when had he come to think of Sorcha as a leech? Once upon a time, her dramatic beauty and flawless body had seemed the perfect anodyne for his anger and regret. Her wild Gypsy spirit had encouraged his drinking, fanned his brazen sexual appetite and applauded his hatred of Duncan Campbell. Och, indeed, once he had been besotted with his enticing mistress. Now he realized she had been nothing but a desperate distraction from the emptiness in his heart.

He shifted his weight in the saddle, and his scowl deepened. St. Ninian, this wasn't like him. He might be a womanizer who took up and discarded lasses as easily as a clean shirt, but he never had regretted his actions. His mistresses had remained his friends, to be flirted with and occasionally taken back into his bed for a night or two, for old time's sake. Certainly he never had been disgusted with himself for bedding any of them.

Until now.

Of course, there was a reason for his sudden pang of conscience. He knew it as surely as he knew every crag and cove on the Isle. He just refused to admit it. Irritably, he pressed two fingers against the bump where his nose had been broken. St. Ninian, what was the use of lusting after Fiona Fraser? She was his employee, dependent on him for sustenance and protection. He couldn't breach that trust. Besides, she had made it clear she didn't want him. Doubtless she had heard the twisted rumors about him by now and had cast her lot with his rancorous Jacobite tenants who saw only what they wished to see.

He glanced down at his mangled hand, then tucked it beneath his coat. Och, and what sensitive lass could bear the sight of such deformity? Fiona had been raised amid the exquisite beauty and artistic taste of the French court, and doubtless her dead husband had been a dashing Jacobite Cavalier who had been whole, not a cripple. He shuddered, imagining the look of disgust in her eyes should he ever touch her perfect white cheek with his deformed paw.

His horse shook its bridle and gave a low snort. Lachlan chuckled and relaxed the reins. "Ye're right, Duneen," he murmured. "Madam Fraser isna like that." Oddly, try as he might, he couldn't imagine his fey, beguiling cook wearing such a heartless expression.

He affectionately slapped Duneen's neck and allowed his thoughts to dwell on Fiona's violet gaze. Och, what was it about her? He had been puzzled and fascinated by her unconventional behavior since the moment he had found her cooing to his dogs. Those faithless little tricksters had all but abandoned him since the delectable Madam Fraser had set up shop in his kitchen. He practically had to tie a leg of mutton around his neck to get them to come when he called.

His mouth quirked into a rueful smile. Now, what could he do to get his luscious, Titian-haired cook to come when he called? Clearly, Fiona was a virtuous woman, and she came from a good family. She wouldn't countenance a meaningless tumble in his bed just for the sport and pleasure of it.

Or would she?

Lachlan closed his eyes and listened to the mournful murmur of the sea on the rocks far below. 'Twas a soothing sound, as soft and tranquil as Fiona's husky voice. But something besides serenity lay below her delightfully accented tones: there was a direct honesty and a promise of desire that, once roused, would make her more than his match in exploring the dark and forbidden passions of the flesh.

The shrill cry of a night bird scattered his thoughts, and he leaned back in the saddle, then glanced up. Despite the frigid temperatures, the weather was perfect and was likely to remain so—curse it all. The clouds had vanished from the black-velvet sky, and if it weren't for the moon's brilliant glow, he could gaze up on an eternity of stars.

He urged his horse forward, then glowered down at the shimmering sea. Nay, there was little hope of a storm to keep Duncan from crossing the Sound of Mull. Lachlan's jaw tightened ominously. His grasping brother-in-law had sent another urgent message, received today, stating that his creditors had grown importunate and the situation was grave. Therefore, he felt it best to travel to Castle Taigh to collect the necessary two hundred pounds in person.

Rage scorched through Lachlan's veins. Och, this was intolerable! He needed that money for the repairs to the tenants' cottages. Maire Rankin was dying of consumption, several families were down with ague brought on by icy drafts and muddy floors—and winter had barely begun. 'Twas his honor-bound duty to help them, not Duncan Campbell. The tenants were his kin through blood and clan ties, and laird or no, he had been raised to care for them in all things.

He clutched the reins so tightly his crippled hand began to ache. Perhaps 'twas God's judgment on his sins that Taigh Samhraidh should fall into Duncan's reptilian clutches, for all that ran in Duncan's cold veins was greed and a repulsive determination to wrest from life, preferably at the expense of others, all that he felt was due him. Catriona had insisted that Duncan's abnormal ambition stemmed from a childhood injury that had left his leg twisted and too short. The deformity had embittered him, Catriona had declared, and it behooved Lachlan to make things easy and pleasant for her brother, as compensation for his loss.

In the early days of his marriage he had scoffed at Catriona's blind spot concerning Duncan; now he conceded her point. A malformation of the body could lead to bitterness of the soul. He flexed his scarred hand and shook his head sardonically. But while Duncan demanded that others make up for his loss, Lachlan never expected folk to be anything but cruel. Certainly most of his tenants had been less than affable in their attitude toward him, but they had provocation. Why should they smile upon a traitor who had killed his wife and unborn child?

Suddenly, his hunter's eyes caught a movement on the moonlit field below. As he watched, a magnificent stag stepped from the shadows of a rowan tree, then cautiously picked its way toward the edge of the sea. The animal's head was raised, and it sniffed the air for any sign of a predator. Lachlan tightened the reins and turned to get a better view. As he did so, moonlight glinted off the stag's shaggy coat, and Lachlan discerned the distinct white scar where one of his musket bullets had torn harmlessly along the creature's hide. Four times he had had a clear shot at this wary beast, and four times it had evaded him.

Silently, Lachlan cursed himself for not bringing his musket. Brighid Maclean's three fatherless children could use the nourishing meat; and the hide, properly tanned, would clothe them through the freezing winter.

The stag paused in the middle of the field, then lowered its nose and gave its coat a sensuous shake, just as Duneen did after a bucket of oats and a day's rest in the stable. Lachlan watched, transfixed, as the animal bobbed its enormous rack of antlers, then pranced sideways, its hide as luminous as silver-shot silk under the cold white moon. A thrill rippled down his spine. It seemed as if his old adversary had come out to celebrate the wild beauty of the night, just as he had.

Something else moved at the edge of his vision. The stag froze; then a figure of a woman, bundled from head to toe in a silvery blue cloak, stepped from the pale ribbon of path at the far corner of the field and glided across the frosty grass. Although the woman approached silently from behind, the stag's keen senses detected her. Slowly, as if it were a pewter statue come to life, the animal turned. At the same moment, the woman flipped back the hood of her cloak. Lachlan's breath caught. It was Fiona Fraser.

The stag lowered its head, and Lachlan tensed, ready to dig his booted heels into Duneen's ribs. If the stag charged, Fiona would be crushed, then gored on those wickedly sharp antlers.

Fiona halted, then held out her hand. The wind and the murmur of the sea muffled her words, but there was no mistaking her meaning: she was calling the stag to her.

To Lachlan's utter astonishment, the animal snorted once, skittered sideways, then loped slowly and obediently toward Fiona, antlers joggling with each step. It halted six feet from her, then began nibbling on a low patch of heather.

Lachlan's body went limp with relief; then he urged Duneen down the rocky, grass-covered hill. He almost had reached the field when the horse's hoof dislodged a stone, which tumbled and rattled down before them. The stag's head shot up; Fiona whirled. Catching sight of Lachlan, the stag leaped forward and shot off with blinding speed, then was lost in the inky fringe of trees.

Duneen clattered to a halt a few feet from Fiona, and Lachlan swung down from the saddle.

Fiona straightened her shoulders and gazed at him accusingly. "You scared him away."

Lachlan halted, utterly enchanted. Fiona's hair had been loosed from its demure, black-velvet ribbon, and it flowed down her back in a shining river of moonlit waves. Her wide-set eyes sparkled like amethysts set in silver, and her lips parted with the agitation of her breathing, enticing him to lower his mouth to hers and savor her honeyed sweetness. It took all his willpower not to sweep her into his arms.

He bowed. "Ye have a firm grip o' the obvious, madam."

"I suppose you came galloping down here so you could shoot that poor creature and hang him in that hideous gallery of yours."

"Actually, I came gallopin' down here wi' some mad thought o' savin' ye from harm. But obviously ye dinna need help." For some unaccountable reason, he felt a stab of anger at her less-than-appreciative reception. But that was ridiculous. He was her master; he had the upper hand. He clamped control over his staccato pulse and arched a sardonic brow. "Now tell me, lass. Every time I see ye, animals are breakin' their necks fallin' all over ye. What's your secret?" He brushed a curl from her cheek. "Faery dust? Magic spells?"

Fiona scowled—an expression that didn't dim her unsettling beauty one whit. Och, she could have been the Snow Queen, sprung from the shimmering frost to lure unsuspecting men to their doom with ethereal charm. When she didn't reply, he folded his arms over his chest and asked, "How's the wee pup?"

"Oh, what a *bonne amie!*" she exclaimed, breaking into an incandescent smile. "Thank you so much for her. I've never had a gift more delightful—or destructive. Already, she has chewed up Maeve's second-best stockings." She stepped close, then reached out and stroked Duneen's velvety nose. Lachlan closed his eyes and inhaled the haunting fragrance of her hair. As if drawn by an irresistible force, he swayed toward her.

"What a lovely horse," she said, her casual tone making it clear that she was oblivious to her effect on him.

He opened his eyes, then tightened the perfectly cinched strap holding his saddle to Duneen's glossy back.

"I've always wanted a horse," she continued, "but we were too poor. And where would we have kept him? In our third-floor garret?" She slanted him a charming smile.

Lachlan stopped fiddling with the saddle. "Your husband—was he a good horseman?"

Fiona chuckled. "Harry? *Mon Dieu, non.* Harry's talents ran more to ombre and baccarat—and the wives of other men. He was a prodigious womanizer, was Harry."

"Surely ye deserved better than that."

"Oui, perhaps I did. But Harry put up with his share of . . . shall we say peccadillos? . . . from me." She caught his gaze and dimpled.

Och, St. Ninian, how he wanted this lass. Her piquant accent enthralled him; her fey beauty drove him mad. And it infuriated him that she had thrown herself away on a womanizer. Lachlan scowled. It suddenly occurred to him that *he* was a womanizer.

"Do ye miss France?" he blurted.

Fiona gazed out over the moonlit field, and her eyes grew as hazy as the mist swirling around them. *"Oui,* very much." She smiled and shivered dramatically.

"The cold here, I cannot get used to it. It seeps into my bones and makes it hard to sleep. But you know? The cold is what I remember best about Scotland. The cold and the snow. And there was someone . . . someone I cannot remember. . . ." Her voice trailed off, and her brows knit in a delicious little frown. Then she took a deep breath and laughed. *"Oui,* I miss France. I miss the Seine on soft April evenings; I miss the cathedral bells and the flocks of pigeons, the smell of roses and lilies and bergamot at the *perfumerie.* But most of all I miss *la patisserie*—and Jacques."

"Who's Jacques?" Lachlan snapped.

Fiona looked mildly surprised. "He's the chef who trained me. A great bear of a man, all bald and covered in flour."

Lachlan relaxed. "And I suppose he taught ye to like pâté?"

"Oui. And when will you let me teach you, monsieur?"

Lachlan reflected that it wasn't appreciation of French cuisine he wanted her to teach him. The bulge in his breeks gave an impertinent throb, and he cast around for something to distract his lusty thoughts. "Did ye love your husband?"

Fiona's brows arched. "Monsieur—is it the custom in Scotland to ask such personal questions? Would you like me to ask such things of you?"

"My personal affairs are none o' your concern." He glowered off into the darkness. "Forget I asked. It was rude, and ye were right to correct me. But ye must know my interest in ye extends beyond that o' a master for his servants"

Fiona eyed him warily, then said in a small voice, "I didn't love Harry."

"What?"

"That's what you asked me, isn't it? I didn't love Harry when I married him, although I grew fond of him. He was charming and useless—rather like beauty patches for the face. And he was kind in his way."

Lachlan made a *tcha* of aggravation. "Ye're a verra bonnie lass, Fiona. Why would ye marry a man ye didna love?"

"Mon Dieu, we are getting personal, *non?"* She pinned him with a level gaze for several long moments, as if she was contemplating her next response. Then she shrugged and said evenly, "If you insist on knowing, it was because I had to. I was too poor to get a better husband, and Harry's father had been very kind to my family. I . . . I had to do what my parents requested. It was for the best, safer. I would fit in—" She halted, then dropped her gaze.

"And ye'd have a husband to keep ye from bringin' creatures back from the dead?"

The question sank into the silence between them like a stone dropped in a pond. A hunted look flashed through Fiona's violet eyes; then she whirled and started to stride away. Without thinking, Lachlan grabbed her wrist, arresting her flight and spinning her to face him. She jerked back, and the relentless cold moonlight flashed on his hand—his right hand. The scars on his twisted fingers shone like gouged ivory.

He started to release her, but fast as thought, she clasped her warm palm over his disfigured flesh. He flinched, then thrust out his jaw and stared arrogantly into her wide, questioning eyes. Let her so much as dare to pity him!

Fiona slowly lifted his crippled hand and turned it so the moonlight fell full upon it. For several long moments, she studied the deep, discolored striations, then gently trailed her fingertips over the taut tendons. Her frown deepened until he doubted her brows would ever come unknit.

"Did you get this during the Rising?" she murmured.

His heart thudded into his throat. "At Culloden."

A distant look drifted into her beautiful eyes, as if she was seeing deep into the past. "Ah, I remember Culloden. 'Twas horrible."

"Ye were there?" he snapped, incredulous.

"*Oui.* Mama and I were looking for papa. He was among the wounded, and—"

"Holy Christ!" Lachlan caught her shoulders, dragged her against his chest, then hungrily scanned her face. "Was that *ye?*"

"Was what me?"

He raked a hand through his hair. "I . . . I scarce can remember anythin' aboot that day. 'Tis all a vile jumble of blood and mud and cold. And the pain, och . . ." He trailed off, clenched his eyes shut and swallowed convulsively. "But I remember one thing. Hell, 'til now I thought it was a dream—the maunderin's o' a fevered brain." He reached out and stroked her hair. It felt like living silk beneath his twisted fingers. The salt breeze lifted a few errant tendrils, and the moonlight gleamed around her like a halo.

"Aye, I remember this hair. It glowed like hearth fire through the sleet. 'Twas magic. And I remember that frown." He chuckled softly, affectionately. Then, without thinking, he leaned forward and brushed his lips over the tiny vertical groove between Fiona's delicate brows. She gasped and started beneath his touch like an unbroken foal.

He pressed his icy cheekbone against the silken warmth of her hair. "I thought I'd never seen such a frown on a bairn. And your nose was runnin'."

"Please, monsieur . . ." She struggled from his grasp, then stood her ground, shoulders heaving. "Please don't touch me this way. I don't know what you're talking about."

"Aye, ye do. Ye talked to me about your *athair*. Ye told me your name was Fiona; then ye gave me the sweetest smile and held me mangled hand between your own. I felt this surge o' warmth. . . ." He stopped, scowled down at the frozen turf and rubbed two fingers over the healed break in his nose. "Then I canna remember what happened. But ye saved me hand. I ken it. The surgeon said the tendons had been sliced clean through and that by rights I should have no feelin' at all. But ye healed me." A feeling of weary contentment washed over him, as if he had come home at last after a long and bitter journey. He sighed, then smiled down into her eyes. "I thought ye were an angel."

She blinked up at him, jaw sagging, a look of pure astonishment illuminating the perfect oval of her face. "I . . . I remember!" she gasped.

He chuckled and gently tapped her jaw shut. "Best close your mouth, *mo druidh*. Ye dinna want flies gettin' in."

"I thought it was a dream, too. I . . . I said you had a kind heart." She gripped her hands in the folds of her cloak, then shook her head wonderingly. "Truly, monsieur—"

"Under the circumstances, *mo druidh*, ye best call me Lachlan."

"I cannot believe it was you! *Mon Dieu*, for years I've dreamed about that night. Mama refused to speak of it, ever. Only once, when I was expelled from the convent of the Ursulines—"

"Ye were expelled from a convent?" Lachlan chuckled and arched a brow. Och, he was mad for this woman. If only she would stop chattering and let him kiss her.

"—did she bring it up. She said she knew then I would come to a bad end, because she had found me helping a traitor to the clan. . . ." She stumbled to a halt, then hastily glanced up. "I beg your pardon, monsieur. I . . . I didn't mean—"

Lachlan clenched his jaw until he could feel the muscle in his cheek jerk with the strain. He closed his eyes and inhaled a slow, deep breath. Och, here it was again, the wretched millstone of the past that never would lift its crushing weight from his heart. St. Ninian, *why* must this lovely, magical lass be a Jacobite? Why couldn't she truly be French and never have heard of Culloden or Bonnie Prince Charlie or that black-hearted traitor Lachlan Maclean?

And why couldn't he tell her what he had done?

Och, but that he could never do. Women couldn't be trusted; he had learned that the hardest way possible. He cleared his throat, then turned and mounted Duneen. Nay, if canny Fiona Fraser ever discovered the truth, he would lose everything, and his people would suffer in a way they never had since the Highland clans had been butchered and driven from their homes.

For a moment, he stared up at the star-spangled vault of heaven. Och, how he longed to start afresh— but he could not. He could not, and so he longed to curse God.

But he could not curse the Almighty for his own wretched mistakes.

With a sigh that reached into the very marrow of his bones, he grasped the reins, then held out his hand. "Here, lass. 'Tis dark and cold, and ye shouldna be wanderin' over the moors alone. The little people might get ye, aye?" He attempted a smile, but his lips dragged down at the corners.

Fiona gazed up at him, violet eyes filled with apprehension. Then she grasped his hand and, with a jump and a most unladylike squirm, clambered up behind him.

For several minutes, only the thud of Duneen's hooves broke the eerie silence. Then Fiona sighed softly and rested her warm cheek in the hollow between his shoulder blades. She tightened her arm around his waist, then rested her small, perfect hand over his deformed one. For an instant, his mangled fingers jerked and trembled; then a golden shimmer of warmth surged up his arm into the icy, barren reaches of his heart. Instantly, he calmed under her touch.

Later, when they almost had reached her tumbledown cottage at the edge of the sea, she sleepily murmured, "Lachlan . . . what does *mo druidh* mean?"

His hand closed over hers. *"Mo druidh?* It means 'my magic one.' "

Eight

"Come now, lassie. Ye need no' keep secrets from me. Did ye no' learn to tell fortunes over in France? Or read the oracle glass, mayhap? Or ken which stones protect from illness?" Rinalda whisked shortbread crumbs from the wide kitchen worktable and pinned Fiona with the sly gaze of a canny old parrot.

Fiona took a weary breath and cracked eggs into a massive earthenware bowl. *Mon Dieu,* but when would this week be over? Rinalda hadn't given her a moment's peace since the day she had jumped from Two-Pack's cart and stepped across the castle threshold, and the strain was beginning to fray what little nerve she had left.

She snatched up a precious white cone of sugar, then snipped off enough chunks to fill a pewter cup. "You're right," she said, keeping her eyes lowered. "Fortune-telling was all the rage at court. 'Twas from just such a reading that Madame du Barry learned she would replace Madame de Pompadour as *maitresse en titre.*" She tossed Rinalda an engaging, *entre-nous* smile. "But my father-in-law didn't approve of such rot."

Well, that much was true: Sir Hector had been a staunch devotee of reason with no patience for the occult, despite his taste for reading about sacrifices and the Black Mass in underground pamphlets. Her lips twitched. How very odd that a man of science should wind up as a ghost! If indeed he *was* a ghost. Perhaps it was all in her overactive imagination.

Rinalda appraised Fiona's guileless expression with a skeptical eye, then fiddled with the lock on the polished oaken sugar chest. "I hear tell that many ladies o' the court can cast horoscopes. Have ye had yours done, lass?"

"I . . . I don't know the exact time of my birth, so it is impossible to do a complete chart."

Her smile faded, and it seemed as if the cozy kitchen grew shadowed and cold. *Mon Dieu,* would she ever learn the truth about her origins? She foolishly had hoped, against all logic and reason, that returning to Scotland would spark her memory, or that a passing crofter might recognize her as the image of some local girl who had died in childbed and whose babe had been abandoned in care of the kirk. She frowned and dumped the sugar into the eggs. Good St. Benedict, she ought to be ashamed of such ridiculous fantasies!

Rinalda gave a loud *humph* and planted her fists on her narrow hips. "When will ye cease guardin' the truth from me, lass? I have the second sight meself. I ken your talent, and 'tis far greater than mine. Ye're fey, lass—mayhap e'en a changelin'. 'Tis as plain to me as the gold light glowin' all around ye—"

"Don't say such things! 'Tis dangerous—"

Rinalda cut her off with the shake of a gnarled finger. "Try all ye want, lass, but ye canna hide who ye truly are. No' from those who see wi' the heart." Before Fiona could protest, Rinalda turned and hobbled through the low-beamed doorway to the cellar.

Fiona's joints went loose, and she swallowed, hard. Would Rinalda scuttle to Lachlan with her suspicions?

St. Genevieve, what should she do? She had tried to be discreet since coming to work in the castle, but to her dismay, Rinalda had peppered her with questions since their first moment together. Where had Fiona been born? Who were her people? Did anyone in her family possess second sight? It had taken Fiona only a few hours in the housekeeper's presence to realize that the cunning old crone was some type of wise woman, though whether a simple herbalist or a practitioner of far more mysterious arts, Fiona hesitated to venture.

She wiped a hand across her damp forehead, then irritably whipped a wooden spoon through the genoise batter. *Mon Dieu,* she and Maeve would never find the treasure or learn the truth about Lachlan if she were run off the Isle under suspicion of witchcraft. She stifled a sickening memory of billowing smoke and cooking flesh, and shuddered. Did the Scots still burn witches? *Non,* surely not.

"St. Joan, help me," she whispered, wiping her hands on her apron. *Mon Dieu,* she felt as if she were attempting to keep a brace of fine china plates spinning in the air without letting a single one crash and shatter.

The first plate had come in the form of her stubborn and opinionated mother-in-law, who had grown restive during the crisp, clear days of early winter. To Fiona's alarm, Maeve complained ceaselessly about being cooped up in their "drafty, rat-infested hovel," and had grown increasingly daring about appearing out-of-doors without her disguising shawl.

Fiona sighed, then bent and stretched her spine. Golden, late-afternoon light slanted in through the windows, the fire popped on the cavernous stone hearth, a meaty Scotch broth bubbled in a black iron kettle, and all six dogs huddled expectantly around her feet, waiting for a scrap of oatcake or a bit of mutton. All appeared calm, but looks, like one's heart, could be deceiving.

She glared down at Fergus. *"Mon Dieu,* but Maeve has no practicality at all. How does she expect us to learn the truth about your master if he recognizes her and learns the truth about us first?" The enormous gray wolfhound cocked his ears and sat up; Fiona whipped the eggs into a lemony froth. "Am I foolish to worry about *ma mère's* behavior? *Non? Bon.* I thought you'd agree with me. You, at least, have practicality." Fergus thumped his tail and licked a splatter of egg from the floor.

Fiona poured clarified butter into the earthenware bowl. A good night's rest would set her gloomy thoughts to right. Ah, but then there was Sir Hector, the second plate spinning gleefully above her anxious head. To her intense gratification, the old curmudgeon hadn't appeared again in spectral form. Oh, no, he had much more fun haunting her dreams. Night after night, he cursed and grumbled and cajoled his way through her fitful sleep, trumpeting that the treasure map was hidden somewhere in the castle; she just had to use her brains and find it. He also urged her, with many a wink and a leer, to bed Lachlan Maclean.

She frowned, then deftly folded flour into the genoise. The choleric old ghost still wouldn't say what the treasure was, if indeed there *was* a treasure. She snorted skeptically and fixed the dogs with a stern eye. "I tell you, I need something more solid than the word of a ghost if I'm to seduce that arrogant master of yours."

Fergus whined and hung his head.

Suddenly, the sound of boots on stone echoed from the back passageway; then the arrogant master himself stormed into the kitchen. He clutched a fragrant, flaky croissant in his good hand, his long chestnut hair streamed unbraided over his massive shoulders, and his white linen shirt lay open at the throat, revealing a bone-melting expanse of tanned skin and a sprinkling of crisp, dark curls. Instantly, his raw male presence dominated the kitchen. The dogs skittered in all directions.

He halted a foot from her. "Good St. Ninian, are ye witless, or are ye drivin' me mad on purpose?" Irritability crackled from his steel-gray eyes, and he waved the offending croissant under her nose. "Three days now I've sent word down to ye that I dinna fancy these buns. They're all air and no substance. What's a mon got to do to get a bannock or an honest bowl o' porritch, and no more o' these fancy frog pastries?"

With a dramatic flourish, he dropped his hand to his side. In a flash, Rinalda's terrier leaped up and snapped at the croissant.

"Away and raffle yourself, ye wee imp!" Lachlan bellowed.

Fiona smothered a chuckle, then peeped up through lowered lashes. Instantly, she wished she hadn't. *Mon Dieu,* in all her life had she ever seen such a handsome man? Lachlan's tousled hair gleamed like burnished mahogany in the slanting sunset, and his powerful, aristocratic profile was limned in gold. As Fiona drank in his blatant virility, the red-gold light caught the tips of his long lashes and played across the web of laugh lines around his wide-set eyes.

Over the past week, except for the moonlit night on the moor, her enigmatic employer had avoided her with the ease of a guarded and cunning forest creature. When she passed him in the courtyard or brought him his breakfast tray, he greeted her with nothing more than a cold nod and a few polite words. When she saw him galloping over the fields on his way to oversee the slaughter of a pig—she shuddered at the poor animal's fate—he didn't so much as wave. He hadn't even bothered to inquire about Lazarus. In truth, he had behaved with the austere aloofness of King Louis himself—not with the seductive passion of a man burning to sweep her into his bed, as Sir Hector had so lewdly proclaimed.

Fiona folded her arms across her bosom. Only yesterday, with an air of maliciousness that hung about him like miasma, Angus Beattie, the crofter whose cottage was closest to Fiona's, had hinted that Lachlan had killed his wife, then betrayed his brothers in exchange for a life of ease and pleasure. When she had calmly inquired why an alleged murderer hadn't been brought to justice, Angus had shaken his toothless head and hissed, "No proof, lassie. No proof. That black devil's too canny for the likes o' us. But he'll get his, mark me words. Them who deal wi' Satan get a dear penny's worth."

She glanced up and found Lachlan contemplating her with a gloomy expression. Then he smiled, and it was as if the door of a dark cage had swung open, revealing the dazzling brilliance of the sun. All she had to do was fly through and she would be free. Startled, she stepped back. The tiny web of laugh lines deepened around Lachlan's warm, pewter-colored eyes, and she caught her breath.

Mon Dieu, those were *not* the eyes of a murderer.

Clearly amused by her sudden discomfiture, Lachlan eased closer, then leaned his muscular shoulder against the kitchen wall, blocking her escape. His height and strength overwhelmed her, and she swayed giddily. Ohh, what was it he smelled of? Rich, tanned leather, of course, considering that he spent most of his day in the saddle. There was an intoxicating aroma of Scots whisky, too, since that was all he would drink after the sun began its gold-and-red transmutation into night. And then there was the brisk tang of cold evergreens and the savor of salt sea air. She shivered, and her knees turned as weightless as meringue. But there was something more, some scent uniquely his—a warm, sensual musk that fired her blood and addled her wits.

"So, now," Lachlan murmured, voice intimate and dangerously seductive. "What's a mon to do to get what he wants around here?" He leaned closer, and his long hair swung forward over his granite cheek. "For surely, lass, ye ken by now that 'tis ye I want."

A mortified blush scalded her cheeks. "I know no such thing, monsieur. Besides, you . . . you've been avoiding me."

With one tantalizing finger, Lachlan brushed a curl from her cheek. "Blame it on me devilish conscience, lass. It's been grousin' that 'tis unfair to trifle wi' a virtuous widow like ye." He chuckled, and for an instant she thought she saw a faint flush of red on his high cheekbones. Then he caught her chin in his hand and lowered his mouth to hers. "But what I feel for ye is no trifle, lass."

A shiver shot across her skin, her nipples hardened beneath her black-wool bodice, and her heartbeat pounded so loudly she was surprised he couldn't hear it. She tried to skitter back. St. Valentine, this was madness. She never had cared for Harry's connubial caresses; they were rough, fumbling things that had left her agitated, empty and sad. Why, then, did she yearn for Lachlan's kiss, for the drugging heat of his embrace, for the stroke and press of his masterful hands over her aching breasts?

She dragged in a breath and longed for the forbidden sweetness of his lips on hers. "Please, I . . . I—"

The forgotten croissant slipped from Lachlan's fingers. In a heartbeat, all six dogs fell on it. Claws clattered, hackles rose, lips curled, and a chorus of barks, snarls and squeals interrupted what promised to be a dalliance worthy of the most hardened libertine in King Louis' promiscuous French court.

Lachlan's eyes clenched shut in frustrated disbelief. Then he spat an oath, spun on one booted heel and bellowed, "Haud yer wheest!" The dogs froze, then slunk to the shadowed corners of the room—except for Rinalda's terrier, who triumphantly snatched up the croissant and shot under the settle by the hearth.

Shaking his head, Lachlan sauntered to the high-backed wooden bench, then flung himself down and stretched his long legs out in front of him. Fiona noted with a blush that a large bulge threatened the confines of his wickedly tight breeks. Catching the direction of her gaze, Lachlan winked and slanted her a rakish grin, white teeth flashing against his swarthy skin. Fiona reflected with a delicious shiver that he resembled nothing so much as a handsome, taunting, alarmingly virile pirate.

He held out his good hand. "Come, Fiona. We've teased each other long enough." She shook her head. His brows slammed together. "Dinna tell me ye dinna want it, lass, for I can see it in your bonnie violet eyes."

Fiona straightened her apron and smoothed her expression into dissembling serenity. *Mon Dieu,* she had a mission to fulfill; she couldn't let tingling nipples and melting knees drag her into sinful passions of the flesh. "Sister Bernadine warned us about the danger to one's immortal soul if one fell into physical sin with a man," she declared calmly. Calm—ha! She felt as if she were about to slither into a steaming puddle on the floor.

Lachlan's black brows shot up; then he tipped his head back and laughed. "Och, lass, ye do me heart good. What else did Sister Bernadine say?"

"Marriage removes the penalty for sin," she said pertly. "Although St. Paul declared 'tis better to remain chaste in the service of God, still, 'tis better to marry than to burn."

Lachlan's teasing expression hardened into a grim mask. "Marriage, *huh*." He made a sound of disgust, then shot up from the settle. "Aye, 'tis better to marry than to burn, though in my experience, burnin's more attractive altogether." He paced across the brick floor to the cask of ale, then drew himself a cup. "How long were ye married?"

"Three years, monsieur."

"An eternity, aye? Be grateful your spouse isna alive. Sure and I am." He tossed back the ale, swallowed hard, then lowered the cup and wiped the back of his hand across his mouth. His eyes glittered like a rapier blade, and a chill shot down Fiona's spine. *Mon Dieu,* perhaps Maeve's horrible story was true, for surely only a heartless roué would speak so contemptuously of the dead.

Lachlan grimaced, then scowled at her stricken gaze. "This ale is sour as a spinster's heart. Did I no' make it clear that I want ye to assume the runnin' o' Castle Taigh? Sour ale wilna sweeten itself, ye ken."

Fiona took a sharp little breath, then strode to the worktable and snatched up the abandoned bowl of genoise. *"Oui,* monsieur. But Rinalda is an old lady. I don't want to usurp her position—"

"Can ye no' be subtle aboot it, so her feelin's wilna be hurt? Use your wits, lass."

She banged the bowl onto the table. "Monsieur, since when does subtlety, or wits, play a role in this barbaric castle? You bellow like an enraged ape at *ma belle cuisine Française;* you demand coarse dishes I do not know how to make." She stabbed a finger at a bowl of ripe chopped meat. "Like haggis! I ask you, monsieur—what, exactly, is a haggis?" Blood thundered in her ears, and before she could stop herself, she plunged a hand into the meat, then flung it on the floor. The dogs bolted from their corners and fell on it like ravening wolves. "Ugh—dead sheep and oatmeal, boiled in a stomach. A stomach! Monsieur, I do not cook things that are boiled in a stomach."

Hard, masculine dimples scored Lachlan's lean cheeks. "Och, *mo druidh,* haggis isna so bad. The French eat sweetbreads, aye? That's a fair sight worse than haggis."

She planted her hands on her hips, then noted with dismay that she had gotten bits of rancid meat on her black-wool gown. "Tease away, monsieur," she said airily. "It matters not to me. And I have made some improvements around here. The scullions actually are washing the dishes, instead of just scraping off the food—and look outside. You'll find no more rotting vegetable peelings piled up in the courtyard, calling rats. But perhaps you liked the rats. The Scots eat them as well, *non?* "

Lachlan dragged a hand down over his face, then made an effort to look serious. "Aye, ye've done right weel, Fiona—*aside* from that damned pâté o' yours, o' course." He tossed a mock-stern glare down his elegant nose. "If I could, I'd make ye housekeeper out-right. But Rinalda, weel . . ." His voice softened. "She was me nanny, ye ken. I canna put her out to pasture like some spavined old nag." He glanced awkwardly at the snuffling dogs, and Fiona's heart contracted. His cold, arrogant eyes had gone as soft as an April morn-ing in Paris.

Mon Dieu, how could she be his adversary when he disarmed her at every turn?

She turned away, then swabbed grease into a cake pan with sharp, angry little movements. Good St. Mi-chael, she had had enough of this rumor and mystery and waiting anxiously about for some sign from God that Lachlan Maclean was or was not an honest man worthy to be clan chieftain. What did she expect—for him to march up and tell her the truth? Ha! She doubted there was a man alive capable of telling the truth from a hole in the ground. And certainly Lachlan, with his bold hunter's tricks, was adept at fooling even the most worthy of adversaries.

But did hunters have adversaries—or prey?

She took a deep breath. *Non,* she had not been schooled in Voltaire, Rousseau and Descartes to trust to the whims of passion and emotion. She would use logic to extract the information she needed. But how did one find rational answers to emotional questions?

She sifted a light dusting of flour into the cake pan. "Your devotion to Rinalda is admirable, my lord," she said evenly. "I will do as you wish, and find a way to smooth the running of the household. Rinalda will not be offended, I promise." She gathered her courage and slanted him a smile. "Rinalda has been with you since you were a baby?"

"Aye. She even changed me nappies."

"She told me she used to bring you into the great

hall to greet the chieftain of your clan when he visited your papa." She paused, searching for the right off-hand tone. "My own father mentioned Sir Hector Maclean once. He said Sir Hector was one of the prince's staunchest supporters. What happened to him after Culloden?"

Lachlan's jaw hardened ominously. "As far as I ken, Sir Hector Maclean is livin' in comfort in Rome. And he can rot there, for all I care. He turned tail and skulked off to the Continent with Prince Charlie when he should have stayed and helped his people."

"But weren't several Jacobite chiefs imprisoned or beheaded when they remained behind?"

Lachlan snorted. "Hector Maclean led his clan to death and destruction, all because o' some mad Stuart dream of *Dieu et Mon Droit*. Och, if it weren't for him, me brothers wouldna—" He halted, then paced to the window and stared out over the frozen garden. Tension crackled like wildfire along the taut line of his shoulders, and he reflexively clenched his disfigured hand.

Fiona cleared her throat. "I . . . I heard you have two younger brothers. What happened—"

"Dinna ask!" Lachlan whirled and glared at her with the ferocity of a cornered wolf. Fiona flinched. Her cheeks must have paled or her eyes widened, for after a long, strained moment, he glanced away. " 'Tis personal," he muttered in a softer tone.

Fiona's hands twisted in her apron. Every caring fiber of her being cried out that Lachlan clearly was in emotional pain; it would be cruel to torture him with questions sure to rip open old wounds. Then the cool, rational part of her mind—that part artfully molded by Sir Hector and meticulously glazed with the principles of logic—declared that now was the moment to strike. Silently, she cursed herself for stifling her heart;

then she stepped forward and fixed her stormy employer with a level gaze. *"Je mendie votre pardon, monsieur.* As I recall, you don't shy away from personal questions, so why should I?"

Lachlan stared as if he had been addressed by a mouse; then he arched a sardonic brow and bowed. "Touché, madame." His thunderous expression relaxed, and after a moment he managed a roguish smile. "Does this mean your interest in me extends beyond what I like to eat?"

"Perhaps, if you're honest with me." He pulled an aggrieved face and she dimpled. " 'Tis difficult for a man, I know, but do try." She strolled to the settle, then perched on the hard wooden seat—looking, she was sure, like an escaped canary being appraised by a hungry cat. "You asked me once if I loved my late spouse. I would ask the same of you."

Lachlan sauntered across the kitchen, then nonchalantly placed one booted foot on the settle and leaned forward. His warm, whisky-scented breath caressed her cheek, and she felt herself swirling into a vortex of bewildering sensations. Every time this arrogant Highlander drew near her, wildness surged in her heart, wildness so potent it threatened her very reason. She should stop this treacherous game; stop it now, before it was too late. But to her astonishment, she found she did not want to stop.

Lachlan rested his strong chin on his hand, then placed his elbow on his bent knee, bringing his dangerously handsome face inches from hers. The glowing fire backlit his aristocratic profile, and his lips curled into a predatory smile. "Och, lassie, indeed ye are an innocent in the ways o' the world. Since when did love have anythin' to do wi' marriage?"

Fiona raised her chin and met the challenge blazing

from his silvery eyes. "Monsieur, in my estimation, love is like smallpox. The condition may be long vanished, but the scars are still evident."

Lachlan chuckled, wolfish teeth flashing in the firelight. "Och, too true, lassie. Too true." His hand shot out and caught Fiona's long auburn braid; then he trailed the end across his lower lip. She froze. "I have few rules at Castle Taigh," he hissed, "but one is inviolable. I dinna speak o' me dead wife. Ever." He straightened, spun on one booted heel and strode out of the kitchen, slamming the courtyard door so hard the wall shuddered.

Before Fiona could gather her wits, mocking laughter erupted behind her.

Nine

Fiona whirled and saw a tall, striking woman with long black hair and cruel dark eyes standing in the doorway to the back passage.

"Och, ye should see your face," the woman scoffed in a husky voice thick with Highland burr. "Jaw hangin' and eyes wide as an owl's. I bet no mon's ever treated ye like that afore. But ye'll find there are no men like Lachlan Maclean." Then the woman threw back her shoulders and sailed into the kitchen with the arrogant air of a Gypsy queen.

Fiona's jaw snapped closed with a little click, and she wondered if this beautiful stranger *was* a Gypsy, for she possessed the smooth olive skin, strong nose and dramatic cheekbones of that exotic heritage. But her clothes were like those of the local peasant women, although much too low cut in the bodice. Fiona blushed and avoided the stranger's mocking eyes. *Mon Dieu,* what type of woman was she? Even the courtesans in King Louis' court didn't reveal their breasts to this extent!

"Who are you?" Fiona managed to keep her voice tranquil and polite.

The woman's dramatic brows shot up. "Ye havena heard o' me? I'm Sorcha, the daughter of Angus Beattie. And I'm Lachlan's mistress."

Fiona's stomach lurched into her throat, and a hot, sickening surge of jealousy scorched through her veins. Only years of self-control prevented her from clenching a hand to her racing heart, and she breathed a prayer of thanks to St. Winifred that she already was sitting, for her legs suddenly felt too weak to support her. Sensing her distress, Lazarus and Fergus rose from their warm spot at the edge of the hearth and sidled up. The fluffy golden puppy whined and pawed at her skirt, and Fergus rested his great grizzled head in her lap.

Fiona stroked the hard ridge of bone beneath the wolfhound's fur and ordered herself to remain calm. What did it matter if Lachlan had a mistress? *Mon Dieu,* surely a man so bold and virile needed an outlet for his masculine desires. That was the way of men, Harry laughingly had boasted a thousand times. "Lud, Fee," he would drawl after slinking home from another woman's bed, reeking of cheap perfume. "If you never remember anything else I tell you, remember this. *Men are dogs.*"

Fergus glanced mournfully up at her, and Fiona's fingers curled around his leather collar. *Non,* she told the wolfhound silently. *Dogs are far superior.*

With a cool smile, she rose and inclined her head ever so slightly. "How do you do, madam. I am—"

"I ken who ye are," Sorcha blurted. "I've heard the rumors aboot ye and your mother-in-law." Fiona's heart gave another dizzying leap. Good St. Thomas, could Sorcha know the truth? "They say she has the leprosy," Sorcha hissed. She drew her skirts away from Fiona and scanned her from head to toe. " 'Tis a scandal that Lachlan lets ye cook for the household. What if ye spread the sickness?"

Fiona felt giddy with relief; then her lips thinned

into a sardonic line. "I wouldn't trouble myself if I
were you, or pay attention to rumors. Those who gossip tend to hear the most alarming things about themselves."

If Sorcha had been a cat, she would have arched her
back and bristled. Instead, she tossed her hair and
sniffed. Fiona smothered a smile. Clearly, Sorcha
wasn't a wit, even if she was a beauty. Squaring her
shoulders, Fiona glided past her to the worktable, then
reached for the cake pan full of genoise. Alas, at this
particular moment she would be only too happy to exchange her fine education for a mere portion of her
rival's striking looks. She halted. And just what made
Sorcha her rival? That would mean that Fiona cared
enough for Lachlan to try to win him away from his
mistress. And that she could not do.

No matter how much she loved him.

With a silent inner cry, Fiona dropped the cake pan,
then caught hold of the table to keep from crumpling
to the floor. Oh, *Mon Dieu,* this couldn't be happening.
She couldn't have fallen in love! Not after all these
years of stifling her emotions; not after all her devotion
to her role of modest Catholic widow who wanted only
to help her dear in-laws; not after so coolly and deter-
minedly hiding her true nature behind a mask of propriety and reason.

Good St. Joan, she had tried so hard to stamp out her
wondrous, strange gifts. She had denied even to herself
that she caught flashes of the future, saw ghosts, talked
to animals, healed with touch alone. She had struggled
to be like everyone else, to have a calm, normal life.
And now she had fallen wildly and passionately in love
with a stormy, inscrutable Highland warrior who had
betrayed his clan and was suspected of murder. *Mon*

Dieu, what would be next? Seeing God? Raising the dead?

Sorcha leaned her shapely bottom against the table and folded her arms below her lush breasts. "Are ye all right, Madam Fraser?" she inquired, husky voice dripping with mockery. "Ye look quite faint. It wouldna be because o' me and Lachlan, now would it?"

Fiona gritted her teeth and ordered her hands to remain still. Oh, how she longed to rake her nails down this smug creature's smooth cheeks! From the corner of her eye, she saw Fergus bare his teeth and stalk stealthily toward Sorcha.

"Let me tell ye a few things aboot Lachlan," Sorcha continued. She studied her nails nonchalantly, clearly communicating that Fiona wasn't worthy of her full attention. "Lachlan's a skirt chaser. He's brazen in his appetites. He's a bold hunter and a heartless warrior, and he takes what he wants. And what he wants forever is me." Sorcha tossed Fiona a smile of malicious triumph. "Ye're nothin' but a passin' challenge to him—a bit o' prey he must chase, like a hound after a hare."

Suddenly she turned. Like a striking snake, her hand shot out; she grabbed Fiona's forearm, then belligerently thrust her face inches from hers. "He was in me bed makin' love to me this mornin', and he'll be back there tonight. We're to be wed. Do ye hear me?"

Gray, shimmering fog descended over Fiona's stricken mind; she swayed forward and reached to break her fall. Oh, *comment très ridicule.* Who would have thought a calm head like hers would faint over falling in love with a man she could never have?

Sorcha's nails dug into her arm and jerked her closer. Lazarus whined; Fergus bared his teeth. "Stay away from Lachlan," Sorcha snapped. "He's mine, and if I catch ye moonin' around him again, I'll—"

A ferocious snarl rent the air; then Fergus sprang at Sorcha. In a flash, the dog's enormous ivory fangs closed over her arm. Sorcha shrieked and jerked back, eyes wide with panic and horror. Fergus growled low in his throat and hung on with single-minded tenacity.

"Fergus, no!" Fiona shouted. "Down. Let her go this instant." Fergus rolled his great brown eyes to look at her, then reluctantly released his hold on Sorcha's arm and backed off, still growling.

Sorcha stumbled back three paces, raven hair falling over her face, her hand clutched over the bite. "He's mad! Get him away from me. He should be shot!"

Fiona glared at Fergus and pointed to the farthest corner of the room. Fergus looked deeply disappointed, then slunk away, back stiff with wounded pride. Fiona turned to Sorcha. "Let me see the bite."

"Get away from me, ye rotten bitch."

Fiona closed the distance between them, then gently took Sorcha's arm. Her red woolen sleeve was torn, and blood oozed from two deep punctures in her olive skin. "Please let me clean it," Fiona said. "It will fester if I don't—"

Sorcha snatched her arm away, then drew it back and slapped Fiona's face with all her strength. Tears flooded Fiona's eyes; her head snapped back, and burning pain seared across her cheek.

"That dog's mad!" Sorcha shrieked. "And ye egged him on. But I'll pay ye back. I'll tell me *athair*—and I'll get me revenge if 'tis the last thing I do." She whirled and raced through the door to the back passageway—back into the castle and back into Lachlan's sheltering arms.

Fiona sank down on the cool bricks, her back against one sturdy oak leg of the worktable. Stiffly, she drew her knees up to her chin, then leaned forward and buried her face in her arms. Whining softly, Lazarus waggled up and shoved her cold, wet nose against Fiona's burning cheek. The pup gave a comic snuffle; then her little pink tongue slithered out and licked Fiona's salty tears.

Fiona gave a hoarse little chuckle and gently pushed the pup away. "All right, all right. I'll live, *mon petit bébé*." She straightened and scooped the pup's warm, wriggling body into her arms, then pressed her cheek against her soft golden fur. "Good St. Francis, what a mess." Fergus crept up, stretched out on his belly beside her, then gave a low, pitiful sigh. Fiona patted his head. "I agree, *mon ami*. And thank you for defending me. You are a creature of great honor." She leaned her head back and sighed. "Too bad your master is not."

Her lids fluttered shut, and before she could stop it, her traitorous heart called up Lachlan's virile image. His chestnut hair waved over his massive shoulders, his lashes cast crescent-shaped shadows on his high cheekbones, and an enthralling web of laugh lines radiated from the corners of his wide-set eyes. Beguiling masculine dimples scored his lean cheeks, his mouth curled naughtily at the corners, and just-out-of-bed stubble swathed his granite jaw.

Fiona shivered deliciously and hugged the puppy tighter. Every chiseled feature of Lachlan's brazenly handsome face had grown painfully dear to her, but it was his nose she loved most of all. How she adored his silver-eyed glares down that long, elegant, blade-straight nose! She dug her nails into her palms and longed to kiss the crooked bump where his nose had been broken, for it kept him just this flawed, fascinating side of absolute perfection.

Lazarus whimpered. The moment she relaxed her grip, the puppy bounded to freedom, then tackled Rinalda's crotchety old terrier. The pair rolled over in a squirming ball of nips and mock growls. *Mon Dieu,* what must it be like to be so happy and uninhibited! Would she ever feel that way?

She stood and mechanically smoothed her hair as Sorcha's bitter words burned across her mind. Lachlan was betrothed. He belonged to his mistress. Fiona was nothing but a fleeting fancy who would be cast aside like dozens, perhaps hundreds, of women before her. Tears pricked her eyes, and a thick, aching lump choked her throat.

Suddenly she heard the scrape and thump of Rinalda and her cane climbing the rickety cellar stairs. Fiona swallowed, then dug her nails into her palms. She couldn't face another of the cunning old crone's interrogations. *Non,* Rinalda's piercing eyes saw too much, and Fiona could never let anyone see the truth hidden in her heart.

She fled to the courtyard door, snatched her cloak from its hook, then dashed outside.

Ten

Far in the icy black reaches of the great hall, a grandfather clock wheezed to life and bonged the hour. Fiona froze; then her lips curved in a mirthless smile. Eleven o' the clock and all was *not* well. This winter's day had drifted into absurdity until she half-expected the iron firedogs on the massive stone hearth to sit up and bark like Fergus and Lazarus. Her smile deepened. Thank St. Francis that Lachlan's unruly pack of canines adored her. When she had slipped into the dark, silent kitchen, they merely had thumped their tails, then resumed their fitful snoring.

She shuffled forward, groping her way along the damp, labyrinthine stone passageway that led to Lachlan's library. *Mon Dieu,* when would she learn to be careful what she wished for? Back in France, she had been so afraid of living alone that she had begged Maeve to take her to Scotland. Now here she was, skulking around some haughty Highland warrior's drafty keep, searching for *le bon Dieu* knew what. Treasure—ha! Knowing Sir Hector, his deathbed revelation of untold riches was all an elaborate practical joke.

"If wishes were horses, we would be up to our necks in manure," Maeve had snapped earlier in the evening,

when Fiona had wished aloud that she had never gone
to work for Lachlan Maclean.

"I've never met such an arrogant man in all my
life," Fiona had declared as she poured tea into
Maeve's chipped cup. "Just because he looks like a
Greek god, he expects women to fall into his hand like
so many ripe apples—and I'm no apple."

"Aye, ye seem more like a prickly thistle to me."
Maeve hitched closer to the smoldering peat fire, then
rubbed her hands together. No matter how Fiona tried,
she couldn't warm their drafty stone croft, and Maeve
had taken to complaining loudly about her chilblains.
"I'm glad ye're seein' Lachlan's true colors at last.
He's no' but trouble, I promise ye."

When Fiona remained silent, Maeve gathered her
shawl around her loose, grizzled hair and stubbornly
thrust out her chin. "I want ye to go back to the castle
tonight. Search any place ye think Hector may have
hidden money or jewels or such. The sooner ye find
the treasure, the sooner we can leave this place and get
on wi' the comfortable life we deserve." She kicked at
the packed-dirt floor. "I'm sick o' this place. Believe
it or no', I want to return to France. The past is over
and done wi' and the Scotland I kent is gone forever.
'Tis high time we got some enjoyment out o' life."

"But what about Lachlan?" Fiona ventured, keeping
her eyes fixed on her teacup.

"Och, forget this fool promise to learn the truth
aboot him. Ye ken the truth. He's a black-tempered,
selfish, arrogant rogue who must have his own way, no
matter the cost to others."

As she recalled Maeve's blunt words, Fiona's shoulders sagged. Could her mother-in-law be right? Were
the kindness in Lachlan's touch and the honesty in his
eyes nothing more than a seductive ruse? Was she mad

to hope that her enigmatic employer was different from other men?

Oui, c'est vrai. She was mad, fey, odd, a changeling. She took a deep breath and tried to smooth the sharp little line between her brows. *Eh bien,* whether changeling or not, she certainly couldn't alter who and what she was. She could, however, hide it. If one wished to be loved, one had to compromise, to make concessions—*Mon Dieu,* one had to do what one did not wish to do. So here she was, prowling Castle Taigh like a starveling rat.

Suddenly the paneled oak door to the library loomed out of the darkness and blocked her way. Silent as thought, she slipped into the darkened chamber, then crossed to the hearth. Comforting warmth caressed her cheeks as she bent and thrust a splinter of fat pine into the winking embers, then lit a single candle. She held the guttering light aloft, then turned and allowed herself to admire Lachlan's taste.

Tucked off the great hall, behind a twisting stone staircase that led to the upper chambers, the library was one of the smallest rooms in the castle. It was paneled in rich, glowing oak that had mellowed to the shade of cognac, and an intricate stained-glass window rose from floor to ceiling, its six diamond-paned panels of greenish glass surmounted by tableaux of Saints Matthew, Mark, Luke and John. Cases full of leather-bound books filled two walls, and a carved and paneled oak surround arched above the cavernous fireplace. In the fitful candlelight, Fiona could just make out a tall, gilt-framed portrait centered on the surround. The subject was a beautiful young lady in a pink ball gown. Her silvery blond hair lay in neat curls behind her ears, and her long, slender hands clasped a massive jeweled brooch.

Holding the candle higher, Fiona squinted at the brooch. It was similar to the clan badges she had seen pinned to the shoulders of the Jacobite exiles who hung about King Louis' court, jockeying to gain the monarch's favor. But those badges had been more or less the same—circular, made of plain silver, the size of a woman's fist, and engraved with the clan motto.

Compared to them, the badge in the portrait appeared to be a magnificent peacock strutting among drab sparrows. It was the size of a dinner plate and made of richly gleaming gold encrusted with diamonds, rubies and emeralds. The classic badge design—a gold circle engraved with the motto of the clan—appeared in the center of the brooch, and two rampant lions with emerald eyes and roaring ruby mouths curved around the edge as if fearlessly stalking their prey.

"Virtue Mine Honor," Fiona whispered, reading the Maclean motto. Her lips curled into a smile. Lachlan must love this stunning work of art, for the stalking lions perfectly depicted his proud hunter's soul.

She lowered the candle, then bit her lower lip. Something was odd here. Lachlan's dead father had been a cousin of Sir Hector's, and although Fiona didn't completely understand the mind-boggling intricacies of Scottish blood and clan ties, she did recall that Lachlan was Sir Hector's third cousin. As such, Lachlan's family never would have rivaled the chieftain's in wealth and power. Sir Hector—indeed, the entire clan—wouldn't have allowed it. The chieftain was a nobleman and a Scottish clan's supreme authority, and as such, he must by right possess the greatest fortune.

Why, then, did Lachlan's relatively obscure family

possess such a priceless treasure, when Sir Hector himself had sported only a plain silver badge?

Fiona's breathing grew shallow; then the skin tightened at the back of her neck. Slowly, she raised the guttering candle and stared at the lady in the portrait. The woman smiled down at her coldly, triumphantly, *greedily,* as if she had pulled off a palace coup and was flaunting the spoils of war.

The spoils of war.

Fiona scrambled up on the tapestry seat of the hearthside wing chair, then thrust the candle inches from the portrait. The flame shone brilliantly on the glittering, bejeweled badge and highlighted the avariciousness in the woman's ice-blue eyes. Fiona's mouth went dry. This had to be, *must* be Catriona Campbell Maclean.

And the badge in her hand must be Sir Hector's hidden treasure.

"Verra good, lassie. I'm gratified to see your wits havena left ye entirely."

Fiona gasped and whirled. A draft doused the candle's flame; she tottered, then fell onto the thick Turkey carpet. Her ankle twisted beneath her, and pain shot like arrows up her leg.

"Qu'il aille en enfer," she spat.

A boisterous laugh echoed through the darkness. "Oh-ho, lass! 'Tis rare to hear such language out o' ye. The sea air must be doin' ye good—or is it the attentions o' that virile buck Maclean settin' ye on fire?"

Fiona crumpled into the wing chair and angrily rubbed her throbbing ankle. There was no mistaking that curmudgeonly Highland accent, or the heavy-handed innuendo behind the taunt. "Sir Hector, if that's you, so help me—"

"Arrrgh, that's it, lassie! Threaten away. Ye restore

me faith wi' every squawk. I was beginnin' to fear that *love* had addled your fine brain."

"Don't say *love* like that. You make it sound like the plague."

" 'Tis worse. Love is the affection o' a mind that has nothin' better to engage it."

Fiona glared around the inky darkness, searching for the source of her dead father-in-law's voice. "I've heard that before. Who said it? I know it wasn't you."

"Tsk, tsk. Such cynicism, and such poor memory. 'Twas Theophrastus, dear child." Fiona felt an icy draft across her cheek, then Sir Hector's voice hissed in her ear, "Listen to me, lass. Love is a mutual mistake, an hourglass that fills as the brain empties, an attempt to make a dream a reality."

Fiona snorted and waved her hand at the draft. "Now who's the cynic?"

Sir Hector chuckled. "I'm no' a cynic, lass. I tell what I see, and I say love is no more than an excuse to bed someone."

"Sir Hector! Indeed, where are your manners?" Fiona yanked her skirt down over her ankle, then groped on the floor for the candle. "Just because you're dead doesn't mean you have carte blanche to speak like a roué." Her hand closed around the candle, and she sat up. "And what's all this nattering about being in love? I assure you, sir, I am not—"

"Ha! Dinna brazen it out wi' me. I ken your mind better than ye, lass, and I say ye've fallin' for that swaggerin' haunch o' beef—"

"I have not."

"Aye, ye have." Sir Hector's tone grew cajoling. "I'm beggin' ye, snap out o' it, lass. I need your cool wits to find me treasure—and ye canna be in love and be wise."

Fiona narrowed her eyes. A filmy, swirling shadow seemed to be drifting between her and the winking embers on the hearth. "It's the clan badge in that portrait, isn't it?" she demanded. "The treasure, I mean. Please tell me you've finally remembered where it's hidden."

The haze before the fire shimmered restively. "Och, lass, ye've the tone o' a fishwife. Dinna harangue me aboot whys and wherefores. 'Tis no' your place."

"May I take it you don't remember, then?"

"*Tcha*—saucy minx. Ye try bein' a spirit and see how spry your mind is. Me memory's as faulty as Farmer George's reason. A window opens, a window shuts—"

"What's wrong with King George's reason?"

The shadow condensed and darkened angrily. "Cod's ballocks, do ye no' hear the gossip? Folk say that Farmer George is half mad. Serves him right, I say."

Fiona crossed her arms over her bosom. "Forget about the king—what about the treasure?"

The shadow swirled, and the embers blazed up. "There's a map. I canna remember precisely where I put it, but that bold cocksman ye're so enamored wi' may have run across it. If ye put your charms to good use, he may weel reveal all!" Sir Hector's raffish tone was so heavily laced with innuendo that Fiona half-expected to see him materialize, waggling his bushy brows and winking lecherously.

She sat up straight. *Mon Dieu,* she had had enough of Sir Hector's lewd remarks, and she *certainly* had had enough of his haunting. "Are you telling me to forget about love—to take what I can get out of a man instead? Are you saying there's nothing good in love but the physical part? That it's like *ghosts*"—she lunged forward and swept her hand through the shadow—"which everyone talks about but no one ever really sees?"

A clammy chill enveloped her arm; Sir Hector shrieked.

All at once, candlelight bathed the library; then Lachlan Maclean strode through the doorway, a silver candelabrum held high in his sinewy brown hand. "Just what's goin' on in here?"

Fiona clutched her icy hand to her chest and collapsed back in the wing chair. Had Lachlan seen Sir Hector's shadow? Worse, had he heard her converse with the specter of a dead man? *Mon Dieu,* he would think her mad! She bolted up and gazed wildly around. All appeared normal: no shadows, no ghosts, no grinning, floating heads. She breathed a silent prayer of thanks, then smiled demurely. "Why, there's nothing going on, monsieur."

Lachlan closed the distance between them in one long stride. "Dinna tell me that. I heard ye talkin' to someone. I heard a cry."

Fiona arched her brows. "You did? Oh, that must have been one of the dogs. You know I like to talk to them, and I think Rinalda's terrier was in here. . . ." She caught up her skirts and looked under the chair, then peered earnestly into the shadowy corners of the room. At the edge of her vision, she caught a gauzy flash of white; then she heard Sir Hector's devilish chuckle.

She froze. Did Lachlan see or hear it? Good St. Joan, was there a ghost, or was she mad?

She peeped up through lowered lashes and found Lachlan scanning her face, shrewd eyes glittering like tempered steel. "Ye're pale," he snapped, "and ye're actin' odd. Are ye sure ye're no' drunk?" He slammed the candelabrum on a side table, then clasped her arm in a firm grip and lowered his face to hers. Her heart vaulted into her throat, and for one giddy moment she thought he was going to kiss her. But he merely inhaled, then released her and stepped back.

"Now, madam, would ye care to tell me what ye're doin' in me library in the middle o' the night?"

Eleven

Lachlan's voice was velvet smooth, underpinned with a flash of steely challenge. To Fiona's enormous relief, he didn't seem to notice the hammer of her heart or the surge of her blood—or the haze of Sir Hector Maclean's troublesome spirit swirling about by the bookcase. Fiona wanted to stamp her foot and demand that Sir Hector go straight to Purgatory, then tell her lazily smiling employer to do the same. Instead, she dropped her gaze and blushed.

Two elfin dimples appeared at the corners of Lachlan's firmly molded lips. "What, no pert reply? Ye disappoint me, Fiona. I've come to expect all sorts o' peculiarities from ye—such as talkin' to thin air."

A shiver rippled down Fiona's spine. There was no mistaking the predatory tone in Lachlan's husky voice. She glanced up, determined to be calm, cool, reasonable, to brace herself against the mastery of his seduction. Immediately, she cursed herself for a fool. *Mon Dieu*, never had she seen such a desirable man.

With the firelight burnishing the slant of his sharp cheekbones and with his long chestnut hair streaming down over his shoulders, Lachlan looked like a savage who had slipped from the wilderness into the sensual comfort of a black-silk dressing gown. This incongruous garment lay open to his waist, revealing a truly dizzying expanse of tanned and sculpted flesh. Fiona swallowed. Delicious dark curls dusted the chiseled muscles of his chest, trailed down over his taut belly and disappeared into the waistband of his breeks. Wickedly tight and of softest doeskin, that particular garment revealed every tantalizing plane of Lachlan's long, muscular thighs—and the virile bulge of his erect manhood. Her jaw dropped; she gaped, then prayed he hadn't noticed. Unfortunately, he had.

He gave a low chuckle and tapped her chin with one warm finger. "Best close your mouth, *mo cridhe.* Ye dinna want flies gettin' in."

Fiona blushed to the tips of her ears. "There's no need to tease, monsieur," she said sourly. "If I was staring, 'twas only to verify that you've not taken to smuggling contraband whisky."

Lachlan threw back his head and laughed, all wolfish white teeth and crinkling eyes. Instantly, she regretted her retort. *Mon Dieu,* why was she compelled to cross wits with this maddening Highlander, when all she wanted him to do is sweep her into his arms, cup his hands over her breasts and thrust his tongue into her mouth?

"Och, *mo cridhe,* ye lift the gloom o' a chill winter's night. I never ken what to expect from ye. First 'tis talkin' to me dogs, then savin' me pup's life"—he caught her arm and drew her against his chest, silver eyes warm, yet puzzled—"then I catch ye in me study talkin' to ghosts—"

"What?" she blurted.

His expressive brows drew together in teasing consternation. "Och, hasna Rinalda told ye aboot the ghosts o' Castle Taigh?" He slid his strong hand around the small of her back and began a slow caress, urging her closer and closer to his body's startling warmth. Fiona's nipples tingled with anticipation; then she bit back a gasp as he settled her hips against the hard muscles of his thighs. His free hand caught her chin, then tenderly tilted her head to the perfect angle for kissing.

"First, there's the sobbin' bride jilted on her weddin' day." He lowered his mouth to hers, then captured her lips with a soul-searing kiss that swept away all resistance. His deft tongue teased her teeth apart, then plunged into the yearning recesses of her mouth, swirling, twining, gliding, then thrusting into her in a maddening imitation of the act of love. She melted against his naked chest; her head lolled back, her nipples hardened, her knees weakened. She would have fallen if not for the protective circle of his arms.

He bent her back, then stripped away the soft black shawl covering her tightly laced bodice. "And there's the wee lad who drowned in the sea loch." He flicked his tongue around the sensitive whorls of her ear, then languidly kissed and nibbled his way down the curve of her throat. She sighed, and gooseflesh shot across her shivering skin. Lachlan gave a predatory growl of approval, then cupped his hand around her breast and expertly kneaded her flesh. Her blood surged, and she molded her body to his.

He pulled her against his iron-hard length, then pressed his stubbly cheek to hers. He smelled of whisky, peat smoke and rich, musky leather; when he smiled, she could feel his skin crinkle into lean, masculine dimples.

With a hoarse sigh, she clenched her eyes shut and allowed the wildness in her soul to crash its way to freedom. Ah, this was it; this was life. This surge and fire and shimmer, this need and ache and rhythm.

Lachlan chuckled, pleased with her response, and

his skilled thumb and forefinger swirled around her
diamond-hard nipple until she thought she would faint.
He cupped a hand around her bottom, then impishly
whispered, "And I must no' forget the kilted piper who
plays on the cliffs whenever a Maclean chieftain
dies—"

"Arrrgh! That's no' true!" Sir Hector Maclean's outraged voice bellowed through Fiona's mind. "Get your
boobies back in your bodice, lass. The mon's playin' ye
for a fool!"

Panic jolted through Fiona's veins; she jumped like
a scalded cat, then lurched from Lachlan's arms.
Clutching a hand to her quivering belly, she bent and
gasped for breath.

"That bloody piper's no' a proper ghost! He told me
himself he canna make his bletherin' bagpipes heard—
thank God for wee mercies—and he hasna appeared in
eighty years, on the cliff or no'." Sir Hector's voice
blustered on, as real to her as if he stood at Lachlan's
elbow. She squinted and peered into the shadows. Actually, it looked as though Sir Hector *was* standing
beside Lachlan, for a hazy mass seemed to hover like
a rain cloud over the towering Highlander's shoulder.

"Fiona, what's wrong?" Lachlan's wide brow furrowed almost comically. "Ye look like ye've seen a
ghost—"

Fiona broke into hysterical laughter, then collapsed
into the wing chair. Sir Hector swirled in a smoky huff
between her and the fireplace, then disappeared, trail-
ing a long string of oaths behind him.

Scowling, Lachlan strode over and scooped her into
his arms, then sat in the wing chair and settled her on
his lap. When her laughter had subsided into sporadic
giggles, he slanted a fierce gray-eyed glare down his
blade-straight nose and said in a mock-aggrieved tone,

"Och, that's the first time a lass has burst into hysterics when I tried to seduce her."

Even though his tone was teasing, there was no mistaking the passion in his deepening voice. He wanted her. Now. Fiona's limbs grew as watery as her eyes, but she braced her hand against the warm span of his chest and prepared to flee.

How could she resist him, resist her own devastating desire? Sorcha, Maeve, even the overheard gossip of the tittering scullions had made it plain that this bold and subtle warrior was an inveterate womanizer. Fiona frowned sardonically. *Mon Dieu,* what a constitution he must have! Doubtless he had bedded Sorcha earlier in the day—perhaps even earlier this night—yet here he was, sliding his muscular hand under her hair, gently rubbing the back of her neck, firmly settling her bottom against the rock-hard curve of his erection. St. Valentine, he was worse than Harry!

All at once, a terrible realization barreled through her mind. *Non,* Lachlan was far more dangerous, for she never had loved Harry.

She averted her face and pushed away with all her strength. Lachlan went as still as a crouching wildcat; then his warm silver eyes turned to frozen pewter. "Tell me," he said, voice cool and dangerously even. "Why must ye fight me?"

Fiona lurched to her feet. Her hearing had become painfully sensitive, she felt flushed and prickly all over, and the room had grown as hot as a furnace. She prayed she wouldn't faint, then desperately searched for the light, bantering tone of the accomplished Parisian wit. "You mistake me, monsieur—and you remind me, most regrettably, of my late papa. He believed, as did my late husband, that all French women were lightskirts, and behaved accordingly." All at once her brittle insouciance gave way, and she planted her hands on her hips. "Just because I was raised in France does not make me a whore."

Lachlan's jaw hardened to granite. "I ken ye married a philanderer, lass, and I'm sorry to hear your *athair* was one as weel." He rose and prowled toward her on lithe tiger feet. "But ye have me word as a Maclean that I'm no' o' that ilk."

"No, you're worse—" Fiona halted, appalled that her voice had grown as shrill as a fishwife's. She dug her nails into her palms and edged backward until the sharp corner of the bookcase bit into her spine. Oh, St. Benedict, she wanted to say more. She wanted to shout out her real identity, to reveal the true reason she had returned to Scotland, to confess her paralyzing fear that Lachlan was a liar and a traitor and far, far worse. Most of all she wanted to sob out the devastating waves of love and fear that crashed over her, sweeping away all logic and reason.

Lachlan reached for her, and she thrust up both hands. Her throat constricted; she swallowed. "I met Sorcha—your mistress. Your *official* mistress." She bit sarcasm into the word, desperate to hurt him, to ward him off. She couldn't abide the swift flash of kindness and understanding in his eyes. "She told me I was nothing but a passing challenge to you, like a hare to a hound. She also told me you were to be wed. I don't know what type of women you usually consort with, monsieur, but I do not bed men who are betrothed."

Lachlan's sensual mouth curved at the corners. "Is that what's fashin' ye, *mo cridhe?* I assure ye, what Sorcha told ye was a lie." She opened her mouth to squawk, and he held up his good hand. "Aye, she was me mistress for a time. What can I say aboot that?" He grinned rakishly, shrugged his massive shoulders, and

turned his hands palms up in a gesture that was discon-
certingly French. "A mon has needs, aye?"

Suddenly, all humor vanished from his chiseled features; he reached out and stroked Fiona's unpinned
hair. The strong, tanned fingers of his good hand
twined gently around an errant curl; then he lifted the
gleaming auburn cascade from her nape and smoothed
it down over her left shoulder. A shudder of longing
swept through her, and she steeled herself against the
urge to melt into his arms. *Mon Dieu,* surely he could
sense her need and would ruthlessly press his advantage—now, when she teetered at the brink of complete
surrender.

But he didn't. Instead, he eased his warm hand back
to the sensitive skin of her neck, then deftly rubbed his
thumb in a circular pattern. Hot, aching desire pooled
low in her belly; she expected at any moment to slither
into a puddle at his feet.

"I havena lain wi' Sorcha since the day I met ye, *mo
cridhe.*" Lachlan stroked his hand around to her cheek,
then gently traced his callused thumb across her trembling lower lip. His accent thickened, and his eyes
grew heavy-lidded with desire. "Och, lass, ye're so
beautiful, wi' your hair long and glowin' like banked
embers in the firelight."

He lowered his head, and for one wild moment she
prayed he would kiss her. Her lips parted, quivering in
anticipation for the heat and thrust and wetness of his
maddeningly skilled, whisky-flavored tongue.

He paused, his slightly swollen lips hovering at the
corner of her mouth. "I canna even look at another lass
since ye bewitched me, *mo cridhe.*" There was no mistaking the raw, agonized emotion behind the beguiling
words.

He lifted his head and gazed down at her, steel-gray

eyes soft as mist, sure as bedrock. His lips quirked in surprise, and he shook his head ruefully. "I'll no' play games, lass. To me verra great astonishment, I find meself longin' for ye every minute o' the day. I want ye in me bed and at me table, but I'll no' force ye. If ye come to me, ye'll come willingly." He lowered his mouth once more. With a tiny sigh, she swayed against the warmth and strength of his bare chest. He chuckled, then murmured, "Your body's ready for me, lass, even if your mind isna. And I'll wait, but no' for long."

He brushed a feather-light kiss across the bridge of her nose, then spun away, his black-silk dressing gown swirling with the lethal grace of a highwayman's cape. He caught up the candelabrum, strode to the library door, then paused, silver eyes glittering. "Ye best ready yourself for a siege, *mo cridhe*. This is one battle I wilna lose."

Twelve

Rain had been falling for twelve hours straight; implacable, icy rain that stung Lachlan's cheekbones and turned the castle's dead lawn into a sodden, grayish brown swamp. The sky was a leaden expanse of cloud, the towering sea cliffs glistened like black mirrors, and the mist rising from the wind-bent gorse looked like sullen puffs of smoke from the unseen dwellings of the *daoine stith*,

This strange thought caught him off guard, and he smiled. 'Twas not like him to entertain such fancies, despite countless generations of superstitious Celtic blood and Rinalda's sporadic dabbling in the old ways. But then again, a fey beauty with odd healing powers and a tendency to talk to thin air never had bewitched him before.

He turned and looked down at Fiona. She was bundled against the rain and bitter cold, with a heavy gray shawl wound peasant-style over her head and the hood of her Madonna-blue cloak pulled as far forward over her face as possible. Her small, graceful hands were swaddled in thick woolen mitts, and hem of her black-wool skirt was caked with mud. She was staring down at the heaving, pewter-colored sea, intent on the efforts of a shallop to come alongside the boat ramp that jutted out from the base of the jagged cliff. He reached to take her hand, then stopped. He couldn't rush her. She was like a wary, skittish doe who would bound away into the mist if he made even the slightest false move. But he was a cool and expert hunter; he knew the value of patience.

"I shouldna have asked ye to come out in this weather," he said in a light, conversational tone. " 'Tis no place for a lassie." She glanced up at him, her wide violet eyes gleaming like amethysts in the gathering gloom. Her level gaze was composed, and he gave in to the temptation to tease her. "But perhaps ye like it, aye? 'Tis said the *daoine stith* favor mists and fogs."

"What are the *daoine stith?*" Her charming, half-French accent stumbled slightly over the unfamiliar words.

"The little people, the fair folk. The faeries, if ye will." The air was so wet that diamonds of mist clung to her long, dark lashes. He caught his breath, distracted for one delicious moment from the damnable reason they were waiting here at the top of the steep sea stairs. She was so lovely—as slender and supple as a reed, even swathed in bulky black wool. Och, and how he would love to sweep her into the castle, lay her on the carpet before his bedchamber fire, then strip away her damp garments until she stretched naked and glorious before him, pale and pure as alabaster in the glowing firelight.

"The faeries? Isn't that all superstitious nonsense?" Her exquisitely cut lips curved into an elfin smile.

A fierce gust of wind buffeted the cliff top, flinging glistening water droplets from the branches of a rowan onto her velvet cheeks. Before she could protest, he pulled off his glove and smoothed the drops away. Her skin was surprisingly warm to his touch. "Aye, perhaps, *mo druidh*. But it seems to me I've found me verra own changeling."

She pinned him with mock-stern gaze. "Haud yer wheest, Lachlan Maclean. Just because ye're laird doesna gi' ye the right to tease your new housekeeper."

Lachlan threw back his head and laughed, delighted with her perfect imitation of his Highland accent. "Touché, madame," he retorted in rusty French. He flourished his arm and made a leg in a courtly bow. "Please accept my most humble apology."

She frowned. "Forgive a rogue like you? *Quand les poules auront des dents.*"

Despite the frigid temperatures and gusting rain, a tide of warmth washed over him. Och, but what was he doing? In less than five minutes he would be facing his bitterest enemy, yet here he was, flirting with a woman he knew nothing about—and who knew nothing about him. "St. Ninian," he muttered, "I'm bewitched, indeed."

"Pardon?"

"Nothin', *mo cridhe*." Gently, he put his arms around her and drew her against his chest. She didn't try to jerk away, and his heart thundered to life. "I just wish I'd brought me plaid. Then I could warm ye properly while we wait for the bastard."

Fiona smiled uneasily. "Isn't it a bit rude to call your brother-in-law a bastard?" When he didn't reply, she shivered and clutched her cloak tight about her throat. "Lachlan? Why have I never seen you, or anyone else for that matter, wearing the kilt and plaid in Scotland? I'd rather looked forward to seeing that, since I've always heard 'tis a proud and thrilling experience."

Lachlan's crippled hand spasmed into a fist behind Fiona's slender back. "Do ye no' ken 'tis outlawed?" he snapped. "By the king's order, no Scot may wear the kilt, the plaid, the clan badge or crest, or any type o' tartan. The idiot Sassenachs think a mere scrap o' cloth will incite further rebellion—the miserable dogs. Wearin' the kilt is a hangin' offense."

"What?"

"Aye. A few years after Culloden, some Highlanders tried to bring back the kilt. Three men were hanged, and many more were banished to the Colonies."

At his foolish, careless mention of the Colonies, a lance of pure agony stabbed through his heart. Dear God in heaven, why could he not control his thoughts? Good St. Ninian, would he ever see them again—his proud, arrogant brothers? He clenched his eyes shut and swallowed, hard. He missed them, och, how he missed them. Brilliant Diarmid, with his scholar's mind and warrior's fire, and light-hearted Jamie, with the charm of the devil and hair the color of Fiona's—

He must have made some sound of pain, for Fiona scanned his face, violet eyes dark with concern. "Lachlan? Are you all right? I didn't mean to bring up unhappy memories."

Lachlan smiled mirthlessly at her naive choice of words. Och, the fortunate lass had been raised far from the endless horrors of war's aftermath, which had rippled out from Culloden as if the battle were a stone thrown into the bitter water of Highland life. She hadn't seen a kirk full of Jacobite men, women and children burned alive. She hadn't seen homes razed, cattle slaughtered, crops destroyed, women raped and children wandering the barren hills—gaunt, starving, riddled with disease.

Wearily, he folded her into his arms, then rested his chin on top of her head. "Och, *mo cridhe,*" he sighed. Whether it was wise or not, she was part of his life now, and he would protect her. If she pressed him, he

would tell her about the appalling destruction of the
Highlands, but he could never, *never* tell her of his own
sins, his own demons.

To his joy and astonishment, Fiona gripped the la-
pels of his greatcoat, then turned and pressed her
cheek against his chest. They stood silently, wrapped
in a strained and fragile communion, while the rain fell
and the mists swirled and the twilight lowered its
mournful wings.

Lachlan heard the clump and scrape of boots on the
hewn black rock of the sea stairs; he released Fiona
and turned just as Duncan Campbell's head appeared
above the cliff. With the awkward hop and shuffle of
the lame, Duncan gained the top step, then stumped
across the muddy grass, leaning heavily on a carved
mahogany crutch.

Lachlan stepped forward and attempted to appraise
his loathsome brother-in-law with Fiona's calm eyes. It
pained him to admit it, but a lass might consider Duncan handsome, in a weak sort of way—although he
barely reached Lachlan's shoulder and he was humpbacked from leaning on his crutch. His right leg looked
shriveled and useless, even under his expertly tailored
and padded green broadcloth breeks, and he was as
thin as a whippet.

Catching sight of Fiona, Duncan darted forward
with the nervous energy of a rat. Lachlan bowed stiffly
and struggled to form a civil introduction, all the while
deciding that the rodent image fit his brother-in-law
perfectly. Because of the foul weather, Duncan had
eschewed his usual curled and powdered wig, and his
mouse brown hair fell over his forehead, giving him
the impression of boyishness. Lachlan glowered,

knowing all too well how Duncan used his innocent appearance to throw people off his true nature.

"Well, Maclean, I see this bloody Highland weather is as foul as ever." Duncan stumped to a halt before Fiona, and his pale-blue eyes appraised her figure.

Lachlan nodded coolly. "As are your spirits, it appears." Och, so much for a civil introduction.

Duncan jutted his weak chin at Fiona. "And who is this lovely lass?"

Lachlan itched to grind his fist into Duncan's sharp nose. "Allow me to introduce Taigh Samhraidh's new housekeeper, Madam Fiona Fraser. She came to us from France, with excellent references."

Fiona curtseyed demurely.

Duncan's oily smile fell a notch upon hearing that Fiona was a mere servant. Then, as if realizing the lovely creature before him was his to command, he grinned, revealing yellowed and rotting teeth. "Hmm, and what, ah . . . *skills* did you learn in France, my dear?"

Even in the twilight, Lachlan could see Fiona blush. Before she could reply, he nodded at her and said offhandedly, "Ye best head back to the castle and see to dinner. Oh, and be sure the brandy's laid out in the library."

Fiona tossed him a grateful glance, bobbed a silent curtsey, then fled around the high stone wall that separated the cliff top from the castle lawn.

Duncan glared at Lachlan, and the livid, purplish scar on his cheek seemed to pulse with annoyance. "I see you're still playing lord of the manor, Maclean. I'll thank you to remember that *I'm* master here. Taigh Samhraidh is mine, thanks to my unswerving devotion to our noble British crown, and *I'll* give the orders to the delectable Madam Fraser."

Lachlan thought he heard the skitter of pebbles on the other side of the wall, but Duncan's affected English accent drowned out any further sound. "Now get me out of this dreadful rain. Lud, what a curse, traveling to the West Highland isles in December. My leg is paining me quite cruelly. Perhaps the fair Madam Fraser will rub my special liniment on it. 'Tis the Prince of Wales's own remedy, and of course it costs the earth." He slanted Lachlan a sly gaze. "And how is *your* deformity, Maclean? That claw of yours still shriveled like a dried toad? Still weak and useless? Oh, I forgot. No Highland warrior ever admits a weakness."

Duncan turned and waved on the liveried lackey who was struggling up the last step with his master's brass-studded trunk. "Hurry up, you useless sod. I'm soaked through and would change into something warm and dry—*if* you've managed to keep that box out of the mud."

The rain had stopped, and the sea wind had risen to a knife's edge, but Lachlan hardly felt it. Sweat beaded on his brow, and he stood as though carved from granite, loath to move or speak in case his iron control should snap, sending him lunging toward Duncan's throat, ready to throttle the scrawny pipsqueak with one bare hand. His lips thinned in a wolfish smile. His *crippled* hand.

Och, how he hated this cunning spawn of the Sassenach-loving Campbells! He instinctively had disliked Duncan long before he had married the beautiful Catriona—who was this vile rat's twin—but love had made him overlook the strength of blood ties and the perverse, selfish temperament the siblings shared. He stifled a bitter surge of rage. Perversion was the perfect description for the unholy bond between the two.

Duncan turned from berating his lackey and caught the fierce expression on Lachlan's wintry face. "Lud, Maclean, what are you standing there for? Help Peter with my trunk."

Lachlan ground his teeth until he actually could hear them scrape together. "I'm your steward, Campbell, no' your slave."

"My, my. I had forgotten that fierce Celtic temperament of yours. My sister may have found it appealing, for perhaps a minute, but *I* certainly do not." He disdainfully shook water off his fur-lined cloak, then thrust his suede-gloved hands in his pockets. "Oh, I almost forgot. I was asked to give you this. Your London solicitor said you were expecting it. A love letter, perhaps?" With a supercilious smirk, he tossed a folded, sealed paper in Lachlan's direction. It fluttered in the wind, and Lachlan caught it with one deft hand. "Don't expect me to make any more deliveries."

Lachlan ignored his brother-in-law and stared down at the smudged, dog-eared parchment. His pulse began to pound, and the elegant, sloping handwriting that sprawled across the letter seemed to lunge up at him, then undulate before his stricken eyes.

"Are you listening, Maclean?" Duncan's petulant voice sliced through Lachlan's paralysis. "As long as you're in my employ, you *will* do as I say. Remember, I can turn you out in an instant, without so much as a brass farthing. You'd never see your precious Taigh Samhraidh again. And what would happen to those oafish clansmen of yours? Those few who survived their ill-advised loyalty to the Young Pretender, that is." He hobbled forward, thrust his rodent's face as close as possible to Lachlan's, and giggled with perverse triumph. "I know you love them, but they're nothing to me, Maclean. Mere beasts of burden whose lot it is to grind themselves down under my yoke. They work, they pay rent, and I live off their sweat. What could possibly be more just?"

Duncan's fetid breath smelled of rotten cheese and soured ale, and Lachlan nearly staggered back. Instead, he thrust the letter in his pocket, nonchalantly flicked a few raindrops from his sleeve, then fixed his brother-in-law with a cool, unruffled gaze—a little trick he had learned from Fiona, and one that he knew could be astoundingly infuriating. He appraised Duncan's pale face—taking special note of the livid spots of red floating high on his cheekbones—then tossed him a shrewd smile. Duncan might be laird now, but he still harbored the gnawing insecurity that had led him to destroy Lachlan's family.

Duncan flushed under Lachlan's knowing gaze. "Don't worry, Maclean. I'll be returning to London tomorrow. When me debts are settled and I've gained me title, I'll need your precious crofters more than ever. A peerage is expensive, ye ken, and as long as I get me rent money, I'll leave ye Highland dogs to lick your wounds in peace."

Lachlan noted that Duncan's aristocratic accent had given way to a rough Scots burr. He arched a sardonic brow and drawled in sterling British tones, "Do keep watch on your accent, Duncan. I'm certain you don't want the Prince of Wales to discover that you were born in a sod-roofed croft and grew up eating cow's blood in your bannocks."

The hulking lackey named Peter stifled a guffaw, and Duncan's eyes nearly bulged from their sockets. "Don't trifle with me!" he snarled. "I know your scheming tactics, and you're stalling about something." He stopped short, his appalled gaze riveted to

Lachlan's face. "You've done something with the re-served rent money." It was a statement, not a question.

"Three o' your tenants have died since Michaelmas. There's consumption and ague gallopin' through this estate because ye wouldna allow me the money to make proper repairs to the roofs and fix those damned, disease-ridden drains—"

"What do I care about the drains! That money is mine! How *dare* you steal it for your own crazy schemes—"

"They're no' crazy schemes!" Lachlan roared. " 'Tis people's *lives* we're talkin' aboot here. I wilna let me kinsmen die so ye can mince around in satin and kiss the king's arse." He caught Duncan's shoulder in a steely grip, then glared down his nose at the selfish, puerile little worm he was doomed to serve. He despised Dun-can Campbell with every fiber of his being, but he never could leave his service. To do so would consign the Maclean tenants and clansmen to the bitter fate of tens of thousands of Highlanders—a fate of hunger, disease, brutality and despair.

Duncan paled, then jerked free and hustled back sev-eral paces. Furiously, he gestured Peter forward, as if desperate for physical protection. The strapping young lad stepped between Lachlan and his employer; Dun-can clutched his cloak to his throat and hissed, "You'll pay for those words, Maclean. Mark me here and now. In the meantime, I care not one pot of piss for your forelock-tugging kin." He dragged in several harsh breaths, straightened up as much as his crutch would allow, then thrust out his chin. "You said my money has gone for cottage repairs."

"Aye."

"Then you will stop those goddam repairs this in-stant! And I'd better have my money in twenty-four hours, or God help me, I'll have you arrested like the common criminal you are."

Fiona slammed the courtyard door and strode into the castle kitchen, mud-soaked skirts slapping about her ankles. Warmth from the dancing hearth fire washed over her like a blessing, and the dogs leaped up to greet her, all whipping tails and delighted whines. Fergus thrust his massive, grizzled head into her gloved hand, and Lazarus rolled onto her back on the red brick floor, then writhed about like a landed fish, begging Fiona to scratch her belly.

"*Chien de singe.* Monkey dog," Fiona said, chuckling despite the clammy tendrils of dismay curling down her spine. "I've only been gone an hour. You act as though you haven't seen me in days."

She rubbed Lazarus's soft, pink-and-white belly with the muddy toe of her boot, then stiffly unclasped her sodden wool cloak. Sir Hector often had told her that eavesdroppers could learn the most interesting and instructive things, to which she always replied, "Interesting and instructive, perhaps, but never beneficial." Well, both she and Sir Hector had been proved right.

Moving as if in a daze, she pushed her way through the milling pack of dogs and hung the cloak on a peg by the hearth, where it began to steam in the fire's heat. Of course, she hadn't really meant to eavesdrop. She just had been curious about Duncan Campbell, or more specifically, about Lachlan's obvious aversion to him. She had paused behind the stone wall just for a moment, then had been so shocked by what she heard that she found herself rooted to the spot.

Holy St. Isidore, she still couldn't believe it. Lachlan did not own Taigh Samhraidh.

She waved her frozen hands in an attempt to regain some feeling, then wondered exactly how she was going to break the news to her formidable mother-in-law. Just this morning Maeve had been plotting a battle plan about telling Lachlan flat out that he was the new chieftain of Clan Maclean.

"To the devil wi' whether or no' Lachlan's virtuous enough for the job," Maeve had snapped. "We know damn weel that he isna, and I'm sick o' hangin' aboot in this icy, rat-infested hovel. As chieftain, Lachlan will be honor-bound to look after both o' us, and in my case that means a tidy annual sum to keep me in comfort in Paris." Maeve had scoffed at Fiona's description of the jeweled gold badge in the portrait; then she had flourished her stout arm toward the shuttered cottage window and the unseen fields beyond. "Look, missy, even if there is a treasure, Lachlan surely has found it and spent it by now. 'Tis equally sure that he makes a fine livin' from this estate. I say we tell him the news, claim the financial support that is our due, then sail back to France—because I'm tellin' ye, lass, I canna stand another day o' this cold."

Fergus made a low sound that in a less dignified dog would have been a whine, and Fiona reached down to scratch behind his ears. *Mon Dieu,* if Lachlan wasn't laird of Taigh Samhraidh, then he had nothing with which to support his kin. She shut her eyes. She cared little what happened to her; she could always find a job as a cook or housekeeper. But if there was no treasure and Lachlan had no money, what would become of Maeve? Fiona would never let her starve, but she barely earned enough money to support herself here in Scotland. She never would be able to support Maeve back in Paris.

Fergus nudged her hand with a cold, wet nose. "I

can't believe it," Fiona murmured. She caught the dog's head between her hands and stared into his soulful brown eyes. "Why didn't you tell me?"

"Tell ye what?"

Fiona jumped and turned to see Rinalda hobbling in from the back passage. An icy draft accompanied her, and she awkwardly closed the heavy oak door behind her. Fiona gaped, then struggled to regain her composure.

Instead of her usual shapeless homespun skirt, faded linen shift and stained leather bodice, Rinalda wore a stylish gown of shiny black bombazine with long, tight sleeves, a full skirt and a high, white-lace collar. A pert white cap covered her thinning hair, and a snowy, starched muslin apron was tied with a perfect bow around her gaunt waist.

"Why, you look lovely!" Fiona said.

"Dinna sound so shocked."

Fiona grinned. The wise woman's new finery never could camouflage her sharp tongue or piercing eyes—or her canny knack for seeing straight to the heart of things.

Rinalda bobbed across to the fireplace, leaning heavily on a shiny mahogany walking stick.

"Why, that's lovely." Fiona nodded at the cane. "Wherever did you get it?"

"Och, dinna the French ken any other words but loovly?" Rinalda gave a dismissive *humph,* but Fiona caught the look of pride in the sunken eyes. " 'Twas Lachlan gi' me this stick. I got no use for it most days, and most times I like to devil him by no' carryin' it." She winked and grinned, revealing wooden false teeth. "I'm beginnin' to think ye're learnin' what a lark it is to tease the strappin', hot-tempered laird o' Castle Taigh, aye?"

Fiona turned away and unwound the damp shawl from her head. "Since you asked me a moment ago, *that's* what I wish someone had told me. Why are you calling Lachlan the laird, when he clearly is not?"

"Who have ye been talkin' to?"

"No one. I, ah . . . overheard Duncan Campbell say that he owned Taigh Samhraidh. He said Lachlan was his steward."

Rinalda flourished her cane and shooed Lazarus out of her way. "Aye, lassie. That's true enough, and sure and we never tried to hide such from ye. 'Tis no secret. The bloody Sassenachs gave Duncan the estate for lickin' their arse and fightin' the Jacobites at Culloden."

"But why did he keep Lachlan on—"

A sudden, horrible thought assailed Fiona; she clapped a hand over her mouth. St. Francis, this had to be it. This was what had led to the rumors and whispers that Lachlan had betrayed his clan. She sank down onto the wooden settle and stared into the fire. A wave of nausea churned through her stomach, and she suddenly felt like sobbing. Instantly, Fergus and Lazarus huddled about her, panting anxiously.

Mon Dieu, how could she have been so wrong? She had been *sure* that Lachlan was falsely accused, that petty clan jealousy had spawned the rumors of his betrayal. Now she saw it as clearly as she saw the writhing orange flames: Lachlan had been allowed to stay on as estate steward because he had fought with the English against his own people. He had been a cunning, selfish traitor who had sacrificed his own brothers for his own ease and protection.

And if he had done that, couldn't he also have killed his wife and child?

"Here now, move your arse." Rinalda smacked Fer-

gus's tall, bony haunch, then eased her lame old bones
onto the settle beside Fiona. "Och, lass, these hounds
adore ye, so they do. They see your kindness, ye ken.
And so do I." Fiona turned and stared at the wise
woman, momentarily jarred from her shock by Rinalda's urgent tone. Gone was her usual breathy, sing-
song peasant's burr. In its place was a voice of ringing
authority.

"Listen to me, Fiona Fraser. I ken who ye are, and I
ken ye come here for a reason. There's much I canna
tell ye, for Lachlan will no' let me. Och, he's a proud,
hard, stubborn mon, as are all the Macleans. Down-
right bull-headed, he is, but he has his reasons. And
like ye, he shies from the truth."

Suddenly a tarnished silver bell on the servants' call
board jangled to life. Rinalda glared at it, then struggled to her feet. "Och, 'tis that puny whelp Duncan,
ringin' for his tea. Nay, lass"—she held up a wrinkled
hand—"sit ye there and dry the cold out o' your bones.
I'll see to that Campbell scum." She paused and half
turned, then made her usual *humph*ing sound. "And
notice I dinna call him laird. He may own this land, but
Lachlan was born laird, and he'll die the same."

Fiona averted her face and gazed into the fire as
Rinalda stumped about the kitchen, preparing Duncan's tea tray. She desperately wanted to cry, but she
didn't want to upset the dogs more than they already
were, for Fergus had subsided into a mournful bundle
of misery on the hearth, and Lazarus was whining and
nosing her hand in extreme agitation. Fiona made a
choked little sound and dragged the gawky, squirming
puppy onto her lap.

"Hush, *bébé*," she crooned, stroking Lazarus's velvet nose. Oh, St. Valentine, why had she been so irrational as to trust her emotions, even for one little

minute? Her foolish heart had never done her a bit of good, and truly, it had caused her more than a bit of trouble. After all, it was her heart that led her to heal, and hadn't her own mother warned her against the dangers that lay down that road? Fiona squinted her eyes shut and heard Deirdre Fraser's voice as clearly as if she stood by the fire.

'Tis a cruel, ignorant world. And if ye wish to survive, ye must hide the truth.

Fiona smothered a snort. Well, Monsieur Maclean had hidden the truth, and he seemed to have benefited.

"Lass, pay attention." Fiona's head whipped around; Rinalda stood before her. "I'll tell ye one more thing," the old crone said. "Things are no' as they seem wi' Lachlan Maclean. He's as secretive as the grave, he is. But keep ye on the path, and one day he'll let ye in. Then ye'll ken the real truth."

Thirteen

The shrilling, clamoring, clanging of a bell jangled its way into Fiona's dream. She awoke at once, but the all-too-familiar nightmare clung to her mind with cold, tenacious fingers, and her heart fluttered like a panicked bird against her rib cage. Muzzily, she dragged her head from the settle's rough wood, then glanced about the warm, shadowy kitchen. Outside, rain poured down in drumming sheets; inside, the fire popped and the dogs snored.

Mon Dieu, what *was* that clanging? She swiveled her head on a neck gone sore from sleeping on the hard bench. Ah, that was it—a bell on the servants' call board. She stumbled to her feet and peered through the flickering firelight, trying to determine from which room the summons came. Her bleared vision focused, and she blinked, startled. The call was to an unused bedchamber in an empty wing of the castle.

St. Genevieve, who could want a servant in a room no one inhabited? She smoothed her hands over her rumpled apron, unsure she could find her way through the forbidding, labyrinthine stone passages. And what if it was Sir Hector, playing one of his spectral jokes? The bell jangled again, urgently, and she started forward. Rinalda had taken up Duncan Campbell's tea tray, and the housemaids had disappeared, no doubt to hover and titter outside the expensively dressed Londoner's bedchamber. She would have to go herself.

She hurried to the covered copper kettle that sat on the hearth, yanked off the lid and splashed tepid water on her cheeks. After drying her face on a linen dish towel, she lit a tallow candle, then strode through the kitchen door into the icy passageway.

Five minutes later, after losing her way three times and barking her shins on two uneven steps, she halted outside an ancient, carved-oak door hung on rusty iron hinges. A thin ray of light shone from beneath the doorjamb, and she heard quick, light footsteps within. She rapped briskly.

"Who's there?"

Fiona's lips thinned. No mystery here, for that deep, beguiling Highland burr could only belong to Lachlan. "It's Fiona, monsieur. You rang?" She couldn't resist a certain arch tone.

The door whipped open, and she stifled a gasp.

It was clear that this remote chamber hadn't been inhabited for years, perhaps decades. What little furnishings it contained—a massive bedstead, several high-backed chairs and a small round stool—were swathed in ghostly white dust covers that had gone gray with time and filth. The bare stone floor was covered with a thick layer of dust, and skittery footprints, dried droppings and the acrid stench of rat urine bore witness to an active and sizable rodent population. The single narrow window was covered with a faded green-serge curtain, and tattered cobwebs trailed from the primitive wrought-iron chandelier hanging from the sloping ceiling.

On the bedstead, covered by Lachlan's wool greatcoat, lay a gaunt, black-haired young woman. A mewling baby wrapped in a ragged and filthy shawl was clutched to her bosom, and both mother and infant were as pale as corpses. Fiona crossed herself and hurried forward. She didn't need to touch this poor creature to recognize the muddy aura hanging over her. Indeed, death assaulted Fiona's senses far worse than the forgotten bedchamber's icy air and choking stench.

She raised her candle high overhead, then laid a hand to the woman's clammy brow. Instantly, she felt as if she were being sucked down into a swirling brownish flood that grew colder and stronger with each passing moment. She closed her eyes and gasped a prayer, then drew back.

"Who is this?" She struggled to keep her tone low and soothing.

Lachlan took the fat tallow candle from her trembling hand, then set it on the floor, where it cast grotesque, writhing shadows on the moldy stone walls. "This is Maire Rankin. She's the widow o' a crofter on the estate. He died o' the consumption these three months past, and I fear Maire and her bairn have got it as weel." Without meeting her questioning gaze, he knelt beside the bed. His long, rain-wet hair glowed like polished mahogany in the guttering candlelight, and the curve of his stern lower lip trembled slightly, as if he struggled with deep remorse. "Seventeen years ago I swore to an old friend that I'd always look after his family, and now they're all dead or dyin'."

Startled by the hoarse agony in Lachlan's voice, Fiona instinctively reached out to comfort him, then pulled back. She knew nothing of the situation here; it wouldn't be proper—or wise—to intrude on her employer's shadowed past.

Suddenly Lachlan groaned and smashed his fist into the bedstead. In an instant she was on her knees beside him, all thoughts of propriety flown. "Shh," she whis-

pered, checking his hand for injury, stroking his tousled hair. It slipped through her fingers like cool, liquid
fire. "There's nothing you could have done, *mon
cher*—"

He turned and grasped her shoulders, his handsome
face twisted with guilt and rage. "But ye can do somethin'. Ye can save her—"

"Hush." Fiona pressed two fingers to Lachlan's
warm lips. "You ask too much. I have no special
skills—"

"Dinna say that! I saw ye bring that pup back from
the dead, and when ye were but a wee lass, ye saved
me life on Drumossie Moor." He thrust out his crippled wrist, and his lips twisted in a bitter smile. "Ye
forget, *mo druidh*, I have first-hand experience wi'
those special skills ye dinna have." He swayed toward
her, and she caught the unmistakable tang of whisky on
his breath.

She averted her eyes from Lachlan's tortured face,
then wildly wondered why her wits had deserted her
with the speed of a winging arrow. Oh, St. Benedict,
what should she do? One brush with Maire Rankin's
dismal, churning aura had demonstrated that her disease was beyond Fiona's power to heal. In truth, it had
been so long since Fiona had used her ability that she
doubted she could heal so much as a bruise. Certainly,
consumption was out of her reach.

Besides, it was clear her aloof, enigmatic employer
was well on his way to being royally drunk. At the
moment, calling upon her unusual talent might seem
the right and reasonable thing to do, but what would
happen tomorrow, when he was sober?

"Why did you bring her here?" Fiona asked, stalling
for time.

" 'Cause o' that bastard Campbell!" Lachlan

snarled. "I took two hundred pounds from the estate account to fix a bunch o' crofts that are fallin' apart—Maire's among them. Now Duncan's demandin' the money back. He even went over me head and ordered the work to stop. I couldna allow Maire or any other o' the tenants to suffer through another freezin' winter, so I hustled along behind Duncan's back and told the carpenters to continue. I'll pay 'em meself, no matter how long it takes."

Lachlan dragged his fierce gaze from Maire's ashen face, then reached into the pocket of his breeks and drew out a leather flask that doubtless contained Scots whisky. Tipping his head back, he drank with great, angry gulps; despite the room's bitter cold, sweat glistened on his tanned cheeks. He wiped the back of his hand across his mouth and restoppered the flask. "I hated bringin' Maire to this rat hole of a room, but if Duncan kens she's in the castle, he'll turn her out in the snowbank."

He leaned over the bed and lifted Maire's baby with strong, gentle hands, then cradled it against the comfort of his chest. "Mayhap 'tis too late for Maire, but no' for this wee bairn." His Scottish accent thickened as he smiled down at the babe; Fiona realized with a spurt of pure tenderness that he barely held his emotions in check.

Suddenly, a base, shameful worry blasted its way through her swirling thoughts. She darted a glance at Maire, who, despite the ravages of poverty and disease, clearly had been a handsome woman. Fiona dropped her gaze and struggled to control the jealousy that swept over her like a winter storm.

"Is . . . is the baby yours?" she blurted, losing the battle for reason.

Lachlan's expressive black brows flew up; then he

chuckled, a surprisingly deep, affectionate sound. "Nay, lassie. Och, what ye must think o' me." Two hard, masculine dimples hovered at the corners of his mouth. "Should I be angry or flattered that ye take such an interest in my, *ahem* . . . amorous pursuits?"

"Well, monsieur, you do seem to have cut a rather wide swath hereabouts."

Lachlan dandled the cooing baby over his massive shoulder and slanted Fiona his severest glare. "Watch yourself, madam." Then he scowled, anger gaining ascendance over flattery. "St. Ninian, do ye really think I'd leave me own flesh-and-blood to suffer in a hovel scarce fit for a weasel?"

Fiona blushed miserably. *"Non,* monsieur. It's just that, well . . . doubtless Harry left a few fatherless babes about Paris, and—"

"Och, I've aboot had enough o' ye comparin' me to dear departed Harry." Lachlan cuddled the baby to his shoulder with one hand and unstoppered his flask with the other. "Not all men are dogs, *mo cridhe.*"

Fiona struggled to smooth her face into a mask of deceptive tranquillity. This line of talk was going nowhere, but at least she had distracted him from the notion that she could heal the dying.

Lachlan took another swig of whisky. "Now, lassie, aboot ye healin' Maire."

Mon Dieu, there was no distracting this stubborn, arrogant, headstrong Highlander. Fiona jumped to her feet, then lifted Lachlan's coat off Maire's frail body. As she did so, a smudged and dog-eared letter slithered from the pocket. The word *Virginia* arrested her attention. She reached for it. "Is this yours?"

Quick as a striking snake, Lachlan's hand flashed out, snatched the letter, and stuffed it in his breeks' pocket. "Aye."

She waited for something more. Nothing came. She fixed Lachlan's flushed face with a level gaze. "I'll do what I can, monsieur, but I make no promises. *C'est vrai,* consumption is almost always fatal, but I'm sure *le petit bébé* will be safe, now that you've rescued . . . him? Her?"

"Him." Lachlan stood and towered over her in the candle's meager light. She could feel the heat radiating from his body. "His name is Hugh. Hugh Rankin."

Maire muttered something in Gaelic, then began to cough with great, wracking gasps. Lachlan caught the dying woman's hand, and to Fiona's utter astonishment, a single tear trickled down his granite cheek. Without thinking, she raised a finger and traced the teardrop's slow path until the salty diamond disappeared. Lachlan's eyes held hers for what seemed like eternity, and she caught her reflection there, swimming in twin pools of gray and silver.

He tenderly nestled the sleeping baby in Fiona's arms. "Save them, *mo cridhe.*" He strode toward the door, and she heard him mutter, "Then save me."

Two hours passed before Maire Rankin regained consciousness. In that time Fiona ran Rinalda to ground, and they managed to light a cheery fire in the frigid bedchamber, strip the filthy dust sheets from the heavy furniture, sweep up the dirt and mouse droppings, swipe down the cobwebs and make up the bed with fresh linen and a pile of thick wool blankets.

Rinalda, somehow divining that Fiona was powerless in the face of such dread disease, brought out an ancient-looking cedar box that contained a dazzling array of dried herbs, silver instruments, green-glass vials and tiny pots of aromatic salve. As Fiona watched, the withered old crone picked up a cobalt-glass vial, then sloshed dark, pungent liquid into a cup of steaming water. "There's no point in aught but makin' her easy now," she said with a pitying cluck of the tongue. "When she wakes enough to swallow, give her this." She handed the cup to Fiona, then levered herself up with her cane.

"What is it?"

"This and that. Skullcap for pain, valerian and hops for sleep, horehound and comfrey to help the lungs—although 'tis too late for that, I fear. Did ye never learn aboot simples in France, lassie?"

"Blessed Jesu, *non!* I had enough trouble with church and law without being suspected of poisoning." Fiona sniffed the murky mixture and grimaced. "Whew! It smells awful. I wonder how one is ever poisoned if herbs smell so terrible."

Rinalda chuckled. "Och, lass, the frogs are idjits. If *I* wished to poison someone, they'd sure never ken it—'til 'twas too late."

Fiona plucked a tiny pair of silver scissors from the cedar chest. "Rinalda, why do you think Lachlan brought Maire and the baby here?"

Rinalda appraised her shrewdly. "Is that suspicion I see, lassie?"

"No, I—"

"Och, I'm gettin' too old for this." Rinalda snatched back the scissors. "Who's been fillin' your ears wi' tripe?"

"My mother-in-law has heard rumors about Lachlan's wife, and how she died—"

Rinalda banged down the lid of the chest. "Stop ye right there. I'll no' hear gossip aboot the laird—"

"But he's not the laird, not anymore."

The polished mahogany cane shot out and whacked

Fiona in the calf. "Have done. If ye want the truth, ye'll have to get it straight from the horse's mouth." She stumped righteously from the room, then slammed the door behind her.

Maire gave a weak cough, and Fiona turned. "How do you feel, *cherie?*"

"V-verra bad." The young woman gazed around the room, her ravaged face anxious. "W-where's wee Hugh?"

Fiona nodded at a warm nest of fleecy blankets in a basket by the fire. "There. He's a bonnie lad. You must be proud."

Maire managed a wan smile. "Aye. Me husband named him for his brother what was banished to the Colonies after the Risin'."

"Your brother-in-law fought against the English?"

"Aye. He was *gillie ruith*—aide and runner—to the laird's uncle Alexander. When the laird's brothers were banished for fightin' the king, Hugh was banished, too."

Fiona smoothed Maire's blankets and offered her a sip of Rinalda's potion. Maire managed a few swallows; then her eyes fluttered shut. Fiona gnawed at her lip. She knew she should let the poor lass rest, but there was a story here, perhaps some piece of the puzzling truth she sought, and she couldn't rest until she had sorted out all the nagging mysteries around her.

"By the laird, you mean Lachlan?" she asked softly.

"Aye," Maire muttered.

"And his brothers were banished?"

"Aye. Jamie's in New England. Och, he were a handsome lad. And there's Diarmid, too. He got shipped to Virginia."

Fiona's pulse quickened. "How do you know all this?"

"Lachlan's been searchin' for 'em like a mon possessed. Searchin' for years. He kept me husband posted of it, 'cause o' Hugh."

"But if Lachlan found his brothers, why aren't they here with him?"

Maire eyed her as if she was daft. "Why, they be banished for life, ma'am. Treason's a hangin' offense, ye ken." Her eyes fluttered shut; then her breathing grew light and shallow.

Thinking her patient had drifted to sleep, Fiona rose to check on the baby. Suddenly she heard a ragged gasp and turned. Maire was choking for breath, and the skin around her lips had turned an appalling shade of blue.

Fiona flew back to the bedside and clasped her patient's icy hand. "Oh, Maire, Maire. Hang on. Good St. Joseph, please don't die." Hot tears slid across her eyes. "You've little Hugh to live for—"

"N-nay," Maire croaked. " 'Tis too late. Ye care for him . . . ye and L-Lachlan." Her voice grew faint, and her hollow, blue-veined cheeks went ashen. "And . . . and if ye ever meet up wi' me bairn's uncle, tell him he's wrong. Th-they're wrong."

"Who's wrong? About what? I don't understand!"

"J-Jamie and Diarmid. Tell 'em Lachlan's been so verra kind." Maire's breathing grew fitful; then her hand unfurled from Fiona's like a dying flower. "Tell them . . . no matter what they believe he's done, no matter how black they think his heart . . . 'tis really made o' gold."

Fourteen

Lachlan twitched the thick, brown-velvet curtain from the narrow window of his bedchamber, then gazed out over the lawn toward the sea. With the coming of darkness, the afternoon's rain had turned to snow—the first snow of the Western Isles' long, bitter winter. Thick, wet flakes swirled down from the sky, blowing this way and that in the wind gusting from the Sound of Mull, and although the sullen cloud cover blocked any hint of moonlight, a strange white glow emanated from the undulating land. Lachlan always had been enchanted by this phenomenon, for how could mere specks of frozen water emit their own magical light?

The snow piled up on the castle's high stone wall like caps of fluffy wool, and the wizened old rowans, which had survived many a sea storm, seemed glittering, ethereal things, like trees spun entirely from precious white sugar. Surely they would splinter and shatter with the slightest touch.

With a sigh, he closed his eyes against the silvery fairyland and took another sip from his whisky flask. The rich, peaty aroma seduced his nose, and he inhaled, luxuriating in the smoky vapors. St. Ninian, he wished Fiona were here with him, admiring the hushed miracle of the winter's first snow.

This thought startled him so badly he almost dropped his flask; then he shook his head and smiled. Why should he be surprised to think of Fiona? She— violet-eyed enchantress that she was—had beguiled him as surely as if she were queen of the mystical world below. Och, in truth, he half expected to see her sylphlike form materialize as if from thin air, then ghost to the cliffs above the yawning black sea, leaving no trace of her passing on the snow's shimmering surface.

He pressed his forehead against the window's frosty glass and savored the cold bite against his fevered skin. Sure and the whisky was getting the better of him, if he was beginning to believe his beautiful housekeeper was one of the *daoine stith*. Och, but what did it matter if he got dead drunk? It hardly could make things worse.

Gritting his teeth, he turned from the window, then paced across to the hearth, where a crackling fire glowed through the chamber's warm gloom. Good St. Ninian, this infuriating situation was getting out of hand. What had happened to him since the day he had hired Fiona, with the thoroughly male intent of seducing her, enjoying her, then sending her back below stairs? How had he been brought to this miserable pass, mooning out frosty windows like a callow lad?

He threw himself down into the tapestry wing chair and glowered into the flames. Now it seemed that another man had designs on his housekeeper's virtue, for there had been no mistaking the predatory lust in Duncan's eyes when Fiona had smiled and curtseyed to him. Damn the lecherous weasel to hell!

Lachlan irritably wriggled his shoulders, trying to find a comfortable position on the chair's lumpy horsehair. His mouth quirked to one side, and he pinched the healed break in his nose with thumb and forefinger. Och, but why was he surprised at Duncan's interest? He should have known such an enchanting lass would stir up trouble. He took another swig of whisky. The question was, what had she stirred up in him?

Flaming desire scorched through him, and he inhaled through his teeth as fire burned in his loins. Och, good Christ, what had he gotten himself into? He could open his chamber door this very moment and bellow for a lackey to fetch Sorcha or any of the lassies he had enjoyed to the fullest over the years. He could plunge his manhood into a wanton, willing body and spend his lust without a single worry. But since the moment Fiona had caught him in her tranquil amethyst gaze, no other woman tempted him.

With a harsh laugh, he rubbed two fingers between his brows, then took another gulp of whisky. Och, this was too rich! He, the shrewd hunter who swore he never again would hazard his heart, who had learned in the cruelest possible fashion that love was a bitter trap—he, Lachlan Ailm Adair Maclean, was ensnared.

Now would come the battle of wills. He snorted and lunged to his feet, then flung his empty flask to the floor. Hadn't Catriona taught him the rules? First, the man determines to get the woman in his bed. *His bed.* Lachlan clenched his eyes tight and actually felt Fiona beneath him, all warm belly, soft thighs and succulent breasts. His manhood grew heavy and erect, and his fingers twitched with the desire to touch, to caress. He dragged a hand down over his face. Och, he had to stop this.

Then the woman realizes the power she wields and resolves to lead the man a merry chase. Only with Catriona, the chase hadn't been merry. It had been perverse and sordid and had ended with an appalling finality that cursed him still.

The breath hissed from his pinched nostrils, and he opened his eyes. On the hearth rug, half hidden beneath the wing chair, lay a chewed up old brogue that had been Lazarus's favorite toy. The pup had been banned from Lachlan's bedchamber after numerous acts of destruction, but of course that hadn't stopped the wee imp. The skin around Lachlan's eyes crinkled into a smile. Och, Fiona loved that dog almost as much as his traitorous hounds loved her.

Abstractedly, he rubbed at the knotted sinews of his crippled hand. It ached like the devil when the weather turned wet and cold, and he longed for another draught of whisky to dull the gnawing pain. He gave a regretful half smile, then forced his thoughts away from the wee, redheaded lass who had saved his sense of touch all those years ago on Drumossie Moor. Nay—he couldn't let down his emotional armor. He had learned the hard way that women moved in for the kill the moment they gained the upper hand.

He glanced back at the pup-chewed brogue, and his lips curved with warm affection. Och, but was there any possibility—any hope at—all that Fiona was different?

A sharp rap sounded on the bedchamber door. "Maclean, are you in there?"

Lachlan muttered a curse and shot to his feet. "What do ye want?"

The heavy oak door swung in with a *skreek* of hinges; then Duncan Campbell stepped into the room. He raised his candle and blinked through the fire-flickered shadows until he caught sight of Lachlan. "I've come to make a deal." He stumped across to the hearth, then leaned on his crutch and cupped his hands to the fire's smoky warmth. "I'm giving you one last chance to save your sorry hide."

Lachlan's mouth twisted with cold amusement. "Have ye no' heard that old Scots proverb? They that deal wi' the devil get a dear penny's worth."

Duncan avoided Lachlan's challenging gaze and belted his gold-and-green brocade dressing gown tight about his waist; Lachlan reflected that he looked like a gigged frog. "Lud, this castle is a mausoleum. Tell me, how do you keep your balls from freezing?" When Lachlan ignored this sally, Duncan deepened his insufferable drawl. "That housekeeper you hired—Fiona Fraser. How much do you know about her?"

"Enough."

"It seems rather odd to me that a beautiful woman would leave the delights of Paris for a frozen, godforsaken island overrun with boorish Scots."

"Madam Fraser is o' Scottish blood," Lachlan replied tersely. "And I find nothin' odd aboot her."

"Perhaps. But then it appears to me that you're thinking with your cock, hmmm?" Lachlan's brows slammed together. "Not that I blame you," Duncan blurted, his voice rising a notch. "She would turn heads at St. James court. Lud, those killing eyes—"

Lachlan gave a low growl of anger.

"Lud, Maclean, there's no need to glower so. I vow, you look quite the fierce Highland warrior. Mistress Fraser must find that appealing, after those limp-wristed Paris fops."

Lachlan folded his arms over his chest and jerked his head toward the door, but Duncan hurried on. "That's what I'm here to talk to you about. Angus Beattie took me to the Rankin cottage to order a halt to those demmed repairs of yours. Now wait"—Duncan held up a hand—"hear me out. Quite a gabby old peasant, that Angus. He told me his daughter was your mistress, or had been, until that enchanting, red-haired housekeeper came along. Now it seems you only have eyes—or should I say other body parts?—for Fiona."

"That's none o' your business—"

"Lud, Maclean, I beg to differ. You're here on my sufferance, remember? Who you bed is of no interest to me, unless it's the delectable Mistress Fraser. Then it's very much my business. Since Taigh Samhraidh is mine, isn't it proper that the housekeeper should be as well? *Droit de seigneur* and so on. But being a fair man, I'm here to make a deal."

Lachlan dug his fingers into his folded arms, keeping iron control over the urge to smash his fist into Duncan's ferret face. "I said I dinna deal wi' the devil."

"I don't flatter myself on my attractiveness to women." Duncan's narrowed eyes registered the insult, but he went on, voice as matter-of-fact as if he were horse trading at the market fair. "Wealth and power are all I've got, and for most women, that's enough. But your violet-eyed sweetheart is different. She's the knight-in-shining armor type, and she'll never lay with me as long as you're in the picture. So the deal is this."

Duncan turned. Backlit by the fire, his perverse smile became almost demonic. "Break it off with Fiona in the cruelest possible way. Better yet, let her find you in bed with Angus's daughter. If I know women, which I do, she'll despise you and run straight to my comforting arms. In return, I'll offer you what your dutiful heart wants most. You can continue with the repairs to those miserable huts.

"You'll still have to give my money back," Duncan added hurriedly, seeing the wariness in Lachlan's eyes, "but the carpenters will work on credit. Lud, with that dubious Highland charm of yours, you ought to be able to string them along for years. Wish I had the likes of you dealing with my London creditors." He tossed Lachlan an ingenuous smile. "So, what say you? Fiona Fraser in return for the health and comfort of your beloved tenants? Even crusty old Angus ought to approve such a noble sacrifice."

Lachlan ground his teeth. Duncan was a fine one to blather on about winning approval. At least *he* wasn't trying to buy a title! He stalked across the faded Turkey carpet and flung himself down in the wing chair. But, God help him, Duncan was right. Lachlan had been raised from birth to be the laird of Taigh Samhraidh. Since the age of four, his father had pounded into his head the necessity, the duty, the *command* to always place his kin, clan and tenants first. Their care, their health, their happiness—that was the highest calling for a Maclean. Every choice Lachlan had made since becoming a man had adhered to that call. Och, he had been proud to sacrifice for their sake. Until now. He never could sacrifice Fiona.

He stood and drew a harsh breath through gritted teeth. Then he loomed over Duncan and glared down his nose with frigid fury. "I've told ye twice that I dinna deal wi' the devil. Now go back to hell where ye belong."

Fiona halted before the door to Lachlan's bedchamber and raised her hand to knock, then hesitated. Light from a torch thrust in an iron sconce guttered across her fingers, and she noticed that they trembled, though whether from fear or cold she couldn't say. Good St. Joseph, how would she ever find the words to tell

Lachlan that Maire Rankin would be dead by morning?

Gathering her courage, she knocked, then whispered, "Lachlan? May I speak with you?"

She heard light, quick footsteps; then Lachlan opened the bedchamber door and stood before her, tall and powerful as a Viking god in the fire's golden glow. "Aye, madam?" His voice was slurred and suspiciously polite.

"It's about Maire," Fiona said. "She's resting now, but I . . . I'm afraid it's just a matter of time. Rinalda and I are doing what we can, but . . . but I'm afraid Maire will die. I'm so very sorry." She peered through the flickering shadows and tried to read his face. As he motioned her into the chamber, the firelight burnished his austere features and illuminated an expression of keen anguish. She knotted her hands in an attempt to still their trembling. *Mon Dieu*, what was she doing here? How could she help him?

She must have looked like a panicked deer, or perhaps he caught the worry in her eyes, for his tortured expression vanished instantly, replaced by his usual enigmatic coldness. "Thank ye for tryin'," he said tersely. "The thought o' poor Maire's passin'—" He halted, and a phantom of unfathomable despair ghosted across his taut features. She reached out her hand, desperate to comfort him, to beg him to pour out his grief and pain, but he folded his arms across his chest and stared down into the fire, jaw clenching into lines of adamantine control. "It . . . grieves me deeply," he ground out, the harshness of his voice betraying the depth of his emotion. "But dinna trouble your tender heart. 'Tis my conscience that must suffer." He abstractedly waved his hand toward the wing chair, and the firelight caught the long, concealing ruffles at his shirt cuff. "Sit ye down, lass. Ye must be tired."

She perched on the chair, and he walked to the stone mantel, caught up a clay pipe, filled it with tobacco, then bent and lit it with an ember from the fire. She tried to relax against the chair back and managed a wan smile. So that was it. The masculine scent that clung to her moody employer wasn't danger after all, only tobacco.

He cupped the pipe in his twisted hand, then made a tiny, involuntary sound of pain. Instantly, she was on her feet, standing so close she could feel the drugging heat of his powerful body. She gently stroked the scars on his wrist and willed warmth through her fingertips into his stiffened joints. *Mon Dieu,* if only she could take his pain, but her gift seemed to have withered and died along with her dreams. "Does your old wound still hurt you, monsieur?"

"Nay." He jerked away as if he had been burned. "And dinna keep callin' me monsieur."

She stepped back and coolly met his searing gaze. "And what, exactly, should I call you? *Mo cridhe,* perhaps?"

Surprise rippled across his taciturn face; then he peered down at her, silver eyes sharp and assessing. "Aye, if ye will. In truth, 'twould make me verra happy." Suddenly he smiled—quick, brilliant, all gleaming teeth and masculine dimples. Her heart stalled. 'Twas like looking into a secret, intimate heaven, that smile.

"Well. . . . *C'est bon,*" she stammered, cheeks flaming beneath his bold appraisal. "But, I'm afraid I must confess, I don't know what it means."

His seductive smile never wavered. *"Mo cridhe?* It means 'my heart'."

Fiona choked back a sudden, irrational urge to cry. Couldn't he see how she longed to tear down the walls

between them? How she ached for his love? She
wanted to comfort him, to touch and heal his tortured
soul, but *non*. He must withdraw into the safety of
practiced seduction.

She spun, then knelt before the fire, desperate to
hide the fear and desire swirling through her veins.
Good St. Augustine, she *must* get her emotions under
control, for if ever there was a time to be logical and
practical, now was it. She should sit Lachlan down and
have one true, honest conversation that would set everything straight. But how could she expect the truth
from him when she was living a lie? How could she
tell him she had given him a false name, had pretended
to be someone she was not? Would he understand why
she had done it?

Ha! In her experience, men understood nothing but
their own needs. *Non*. No matter how much she
yearned for this seductive Highlander's love, she must
follow the path of reason.

"Please stop," she murmured. "Why must you tease
me?"

"I'm no' teasin'." Lachlan gazed down at her, boldly
appraising the fullness of her breasts and the flare of
her hips. "I ken ye have your secrets, *mo cridhe*." His
warm hand clasped her chin; then he knelt and turned
her toward him. "In truth, so do I." His silver wolf's
eyes burned into hers, and his fingers soothingly
stroked her jaw. "I'll risk me stubborn pride, a terri-
fyin' thing for a Scotsman"—he slanted her an impish
wink—"and tell ye truly. I could wish for a future with
ye, *mo cridhe*. But I wilna dig up the past. 'Tis over
and done, aye?"

"Is it?" She jerked away. "Can you honestly say
your past is dead and buried? I've heard the rumors
about Catriona—"

His eyes narrowed, and his fingers tensed. Instantly, she regretted her rash words, regretted her clumsy attempt to force the truth about his wife and child. "I'm sorry. I didn't mean—"

"Hush, *mo cridhe.*" He cupped her face with both hands, then lowered his mouth to hers. Melting desire pooled in her belly, and a tiny moan escaped her lips. Lachlan paused, eyes heavy-lidded with desire. She caught her breath.

"Please, Lachlan. I've got to know the truth—"

He hooked one strong arm under her knees and one under her arms, then whisked her off her feet into a powerful embrace. "I said hush. I need your comfort tonight, *mo cridhe,* and I will have it." His lips were warm against her ear, and the sibilance of the sound vibrated a tingling path to her toes. Her nipples hardened exquisitely, puckering into sensitive nubs that ached for his touch.

"Mmm." He gazed with subtle knowing at the stiff little points. Then he grazed his tongue across the trembling curve of her lower lip and chuckled wickedly. "Are ye cold, *mo cridhe?*"

"N . . . no," she squeaked.

He sank down on the bed, then clasped her waist with commanding hands and slowly, expertly ran his palms down over her belly and thighs, urging her back against his hardness. She felt the unmistakable jut of his manhood against her buttocks, and a jolt of pure sensation shot through her. She closed her eyes and bit back a moan.

"L-Lachlan, please . . . we need to talk. We shouldn't be doing this."

His fingers found the lacing up the front of her bodice; her bones turned to water, and she dissolved against the broad strength of his chest. "We should and we are," he rasped in her ear. His voice was low and husky with need, and she felt herself sinking into a maelstrom of primitive sensation. "I've fallen under your spell, sweet witch. Now ye'll fall under mine." Deftly, he unlaced her bodice, then pulled it away and flung it to the floor.

Fiona gasped. *Mon Dieu,* she was burning alive. Her skin, her breasts, her nipples, her entire body was consumed by the startling heat and maleness of his flesh.

"Ye're blushin'." Lachlan's whisky-scented breath caressed her cheek as he untied the drawstring of her skirt, then whisked it off over her ankles, leaving her in nothing but her shift.

"Non," she sighed.

He murmured something in Gaelic; then one expert hand cupped her breast and rolled her tingling nipple between thumb and forefinger. His other hand roved down over her bare thighs, teasingly stroking her sensitive skin until she thought she would faint. A tiny part of her mind whispered that she should feel embarrassed and ashamed, but she didn't. He rucked her chemise up around her lap, then eased her thighs apart. His long, knowing fingers trailed along her inner thigh, and she shivered and cried out as he nipped at the sensitive flesh of her ear.

"Did I hurt ye, *mo cridhe?"* His fingers raked through the crisp, red-gold curls covering her womanhood, catapulting her into a near swoon of ecstasy.

"Non," she whimpered, blushing wildly. A hot, yearning wetness blossomed between her thighs, then unfurled into full-blown need.

"Aye? Weel, I'll take that as encouragement."

With a sigh of surrender, she turned sideways, wrapped an arm around the sinewy column of his neck and pressed against him, reveling in the granite hardness of his chest, longing for him to ease the ache that throbbed between her legs.

Pulling her along with him, he lay back against the soft billow of quilts, then gently eased her shift from her shoulders, exposing her breasts to the warmth of the fire and the scorch of his gaze.

"Och, ye're so beautiful, so beautiful," he sighed, cupping and kneading her flesh, dragging his callused fingertips across her quivering skin. He lowered his head, and his lips closed over her ripe nipple. Groaning deep in his throat, he suckled firmly, rhythmically, urgently, and each suck sent a maddening vibration straight to her aching womb.

His hand gripped the shivering flesh of her thigh, then trailed higher until his fingers touched the wet heat of her womanhood. She arched her back and cried out; he took advantage of her open lips and captured her mouth with a low, possessive growl.

His kiss was devastating; her blood surged, and she instinctively molded her flesh to his. His tongue thrust against hers with heart-rending skill, and his hands roamed over her nipples, her breasts, her hips, her thighs. Then—slowly, teasingly, relentlessly—his fingers slid down over the aching flesh of her womanhood. She moaned and lifted her hips to meet him, and he deftly parted her slick lips, then began a rhythmic stroking.

She gasped, "Oh, Lachlan, please don't stop."

Chuckling wolfishly, he eased one long finger inside her. Time stopped. All her senses sharpened, tightened, focused, taking her to the verge of pleasure so intense it was pain. Desperate for release, she ground herself against the hardness of his palm and cried out with quick, helpless little pleas, "Lachlan. Oh, please, yes, please. Take me."

Every fiber of her being tensed. Her breathing stopped. Then sensation exploded through her. She arched against him, froze, then arched and shuddered again and again, riding each wave of pleasure as if it were her last.

She collapsed back against the warm quilts and struggled to slow her breathing. At last, boneless and content, she smiled and stretched her sated limbs.

"Och, lassie, ye look like a wee cat," Lachlan whispered in her ear. He chuckled naughtily. "Or should I say a wee pussy?"

Suddenly too embarrassed to meet his burning eyes, her gaze drifted down his long, iron-muscled body, and landed on the formidable bulge straining for freedom under his breeks. Without a moment's thought, she reached out and cupped her hand over him, exulting in his thick, jutting maleness. She heard his sharp intake of breath, but pulled away before he could roll and mount her.

With a chuckle nearly as naughty as his own, she clambered off the bed and stood before him, hair loose and curling down to her belly. She arched a brow at his disheveled clothing. "Is this how men make love in the Highlands, monsieur? Without even so much as removing their boots?" He started to snap a retort, but she held up an admonishing finger. "Ah, ah. Remember, you're the master and I'm the servant. So, monsieur, let me serve you."

Kneeling naked before him, silky hair curtaining her face, she tugged off his tall leather boots, then stood and pulled his linen shirt off over his head. He chuckled at her determination, all elfin eyes and roguish dimples. *Mon Dieu,* she could understand why he had cut such a staggering swath among the island's women,

Introducing Ballad,
A LINE OF HISTORICAL ROMANCES

As a lover of historical romance, you'll adore Ballad Romances. Written by today's most popular romance authors, every book in the Ballad line is not only an individual story, but part of a two to six book series as well. You can look forward to 4 new titles each month – each taking place at a different time and place in history.

But don't take our word for how wonderful these stories are! Accept our introductory shipment of 4 Ballad Romance novels – a $23.96 value – ABSOLUTELY FREE – and see for yourself!

Once you've experienced your first 4 Ballad Romances, we're sure you'll want to continue receiving these wonderful historical romance novels each month – without ever having to leave your home – using our convenient and inexpensive home subscription service. Here's what you get for joining:

- *4 BRAND NEW Ballad Romances delivered to your door each month*
- *30% off the cover price with your home subscription.*
- *A FREE monthly newsletter filled with author interviews, book previews, special offers, and more!*
- *No risk or obligation...you're free to cancel whenever you wish... no questions asked.*

**Passion-
Adventure-
Excitement-
Romance-
Ballad!**

To start your membership, simply complete and return the card provided. You'll receive your Introductory Shipment of 4 FREE Ballad Romances. Then, each month, as long as your account is in good standing, you will receive the 4 newest Ballad Romances. Each shipment will be yours to examine for 10 days. If you decide to keep the books, you'll pay the preferred home subscriber's price – a savings of 30% off the cover price! (plus shipping & handling) If you want us to stop sending books, just say the word...it's that simple.

4 FREE BOOKS are waiting for you! Just mail in the certificate below!

BOOK CERTIFICATE

Get 4
Ballad
Historical
Romance
Novels
FREE!

Yes! Please send me 4 Ballad Romances ABSOLUTELY FREE! After my introductory shipment, I will receive 4 new Ballad Romances each month to preview FREE for 10 days (as long as my account is in good standing). If I decide to keep the books, I will pay the money-saving preferred publisher's price plus shipping and handling. That's 30% off the cover price. I may return the shipment within 10 days and owe nothing, and I may cancel my subscription at any time. The 4 FREE books will be mine to keep in any case.

Name_____

Address_____ Apt._____

City_____ State_____ Zip_____

Telephone (_____) _____

Signature_____

(If under 18, parent or guardian must sign)

All orders subject to approval by Zebra Home Subscription Service.
Terms and prices subject to change. Offer valid only in the U.S.

DN101A

If the certificate is
missing below, write to:

**Ballad Romances,
c/o Zebra Home
Subscription Service Inc.**

P.O. Box 5214,
Clifton, New Jersey
07015-5214

OR call TOLL FREE
1-888-345-BOOK (2665)

Passion...
Adventure...
Excitement...
Romance...

Get 4
Ballad
Historical
Romance
Novels
FREE!

BALLAD ROMANCES
Zebra Home Subscription Service, Inc.
P.O. Box 5214
Clifton NJ 07015-5214

and doubtless across the whole Scottish Highlands as well. He was utterly, impossibly irresistible.

The firelight danced across his sculpted muscles, and a dizzying rush of love and desire nearly sent her to her knees. He was so beautiful, so perfectly male. Long, tousled waves of midnight-dark hair rippled over his chiseled shoulders. And oh, St. Genevieve, how she longed to run her fingers through the curls on his chest, then kiss her way across his taut stomach and down the tantalizing trail of hair that disappeared into his wickedly tight breeks.

With the air of a brazen and lusty demon, he beckoned her forward, then pressed her hand to the brass buckle of his belt. "Dinna stand there gawpin', lass. There's work to be done." Her fingers fumbled with the snug clasp, and his strong hand guided her until the buckle sprang open. Then he stood and swiftly skinned off his pants. She stared in frank appreciation at his hard, round buttocks and the long, knotted muscles of his thighs. His manhood jutted up from a thatch of dark pubic hair as if it were a sculpted bar of ivory—thick, proud and erect against his hard belly.

Her heart leaped into her throat. "Good St. Valentine," she blurted, "you're as big as a bull!" Appalled, she clapped a hand over her mouth and blushed furiously.

Lachlan tilted his head back and laughed, the sound bold and roughly male. "Och, *mo cridhe,* ye'll be the death o' me. The French are nothin' if no' direct, aye?" He brushed tears of amusement from his glittering eyes, then clasped her hand around his straining member and showed her the rhythm he liked. Her fingers teased their way across the deliciously smooth head, instantly hardening him to marble.

"St. Ninian," he moaned, "what are ye doin' to me?"

With a hungry growl, he pulled her down on the bed and took possession of her mouth. His tongue thrust deep into her, preparing her for his entrance. With a low, husky cry of need, she writhed against him, and his elegant nostrils flared as he inhaled the rich, musky scent of her desire. She reached down and gripped his manhood with firm, feverish fingers. His breathing stalled.

"Good Christ, dinna stop," he panted, head thrown back, neck corded. He shuddered under her touch like an unbroken stallion, and she reveled in her power over him. Suddenly she longed to mount him, to clasp her thighs around his narrow hips, to make him beg and moan beneath her, to ride him until his essence erupted into her with a primal burst of ecstasy.

She knotted her fingers in his long hair, then raked her nails down his sweat-slick back. "Lachlan, *please*. I want you. Now."

The slight pain spurred his passion, and his control vanished. Rearing up, he straddled her slender thighs, then ran his hands over the quivering softness of her belly. Her lush breasts heaved under his touch; then the muscles of his arms bulged as he lowered himself and kissed her. She whimpered and suckled his lower lip, taunting him with tiny nips. Her nails raked down his back, and she grasped his buttocks, urging him closer, urging him to penetrate her, urging him into frantic, mindless lust.

He parted her thighs with one fluid motion. Then, gritting his teeth to keep control, he eased the crown of his manhood into her molten heat. Och, St. Ninian, he loved this, loved the tight, slick clasp, the delicious resistance as his burning flesh pressed forward. He inhaled and plunged home. She cried out beneath him, not with pain but with passion, with welcome, as if he had been born in her, grown in her and had returned to her at last.

He forced himself to hold still, giving her flesh a moment to adjust to his invasion. When she gave an urgent little wiggle of encouragement, he clenched his buttocks and thrust into her—slowly, firmly, relentlessly. He captured her lips, his tongue swirling and plunging, matching his body's rhythm, then served her with intense concentration, his movements measured thrusts of barely restrained power. Her inner muscles gripped his manhood, and she bucked her hips, frantically riding the hardness of his shaft.

"Lachlan, don't tease. More . . . please. *Do* it."

"Hush now," he murmured. "Patience." Leisurely, tantalizingly, he rotated his hips. She whimpered and squirmed against him; tears glistened in her eyes. Nearly frantic with need, she wrapped her legs around his buttocks and pulled him deeper. With a gasp of surrender, he lowered his head and drove home.

Her body convulsed beneath him. She bucked, writhed, cried out. Then she dug her nails into his buttocks and bit his shoulder. Instantly, his climax thundered over him like a raging tide, its raw, primitive intensity taking him utterly by surprise, leaving him helpless, dashed open, washed clean.

And for the first time in his life, amazingly, perfectly alive.

Fifteen

Fiona let her eyes drift shut, then stretched and snuggled back into the warm cocoon of quilts. Contented happiness rippled through her like honeyed wine, followed instantly by a surge of wild, giddy excitement. *Mon Dieu,* sleep was impossible. Her eyes shot open, and she gazed around Lachlan's bedchamber, smiling like an idiot. The cool, filtered light of dawn was seeping through the diamond-paned windows, and Lachlan thoughtfully had built up the fire so the room would warm before she arose.

Her smile broadened into a grin, and she curled her toes against the soft linens. Who would have thought the brazen lover who had plumbed every carnal secret of her body could be so considerate? She had expected to wake to wintry aloofness. Instead, Lachlan had kissed the top of her tousled head and whispered, "Stay ye asleep, *mo cridhe.* I'll fetch ye ale and water to wash before the rest o' the castle wakes."

"Porridge, too," she mumbled, burrowing into the warm, musky spot he had just vacated. He chuckled, and she cracked open an eye to devour the masculine power and beauty of his naked body.

He winked and threw on a dressing gown. "Och, ye dinna want to eat me cookin', lass."

"*Non* . . . but I'm happy to eat anything else of yours."

Laughing softly, he thrust his big feet into scuffed brogues, then slipped into the icy hall, gently closing the door behind him.

Fiona rolled over and debated pinching herself. *Mon Dieu,* this had to be a dream, for never in her life had she been so happy. She hugged herself, then stared up at the brown-velvet bed hangings. "I love you, Lachlan Maclean," she whispered.

Oh, how she longed to murmur that in his ear as she pressed wet, teasing kisses against his salty flesh! But she would wait. It didn't take French practicality or second sight to know that men could be skittish about such things.

She flung back the covers, then gasped as the icy air hit her naked skin. She dragged a quilt from the bed and wrapped it around shoulders, then dashed to the hearthside wing chair, where she sat, drew her knees up to her chin and surveyed the wreckage of the long, passionate night she and Lachlan had shared.

Her shoes, stockings and chemise lay in a heap on the floor by the bed, her skirt hung from the bedpost, and her bodice had narrowly missed being flung into the fire. She curled her toes once more, then glanced about, looking for Lachlan's clothes. Good St. Valentine, had she—the modest and repressed widow—really torn off his shirt and boots, then hurled them into the far corner by the wardrobe? And where were his breeks?

"Oh, there you are," she said, spying the crumpled suede garment lying halfway under the bed. Suddenly her smile faded. Protruding from Lachlan's breeks, more than three-quarters of the way out of the pocket, was the mysterious letter from Virginia.

A slow, relentless curiosity gnawed like a hungry rat at the corners of her mind. Doubtless Lachlan knew a tobacco planter in Virginia, since he seemed to cherish a clandestine smoking habit. But what gentleman would snatch up a letter from a merchant as if it were a flaming brand? Could it perhaps be a letter from the brother who had been banished to that colony?

She bit her lip and debated the ethics of the situation. Of course, every person knew that only the lowest of the low snooped into another person's correspondence. In the convent of the Ursulines, even the nuns had respected the girls' letters from relatives. Letters from friends had been a different matter, of course, but still. . . .

"Well, Sir Hector"—she darted a baleful glance into the shadowy corners of the room—"where are you when I need you?" Her spectral father-in-law had been noticeably absent of late, and she certainly didn't miss him. But in this situation, a canny ghost well versed in philosophy and ethics would come in handy. The cold dawn light grew stronger, and Fiona glanced toward the door. Lachlan would be back at any moment. Oh, St. Benedict, what should she do?

Then, as if the curmudgeonly specter had heard her call, Sir Hector's voice rang through her mind. *Ye must find out the truth. Promise me. Promise me ye'll find it—*

She jumped up, then winced as her bare feet hit the icy floor. She had pledged to find the truth, but somehow in all the confusion of recent days she had lost sight of that deathbed promise. She had tried asking Lachlan straight out, but he had kept his dark secrets and evaded her with expert kisses and caresses that would make even an Ursuline drop her skirt in the rue de Palais. *Non*, logic dictated that she must find the truth herself. And if that meant reading a letter not addressed to her. . . .

Her fingers closed over the smooth parchment; she snatched it up. A glance at the address confirmed that the letter was indeed for Lachlan, that it had come from Virginia, and that the writer obviously was finely educated, or she was no judge of Spencerian script. She lifted the broken wax seal.

The brief note inside had been torn nearly in half, as if Lachlan had taken out his fury at the messenger on the missive itself. Fiona muttered a prayer for forgiveness, then began to read.

Williamsburg, Royal Colony of Virginia
August 3, 1763

My Dear Sir,

It is with Mix'd Feelings that I take up my Pen and compose this epistle to you, as your London Solicitor, David Morrow, Esq., requested. I Beg that you will Forgive any Distress I might cause in conveying this News, which I fear must bring you Pain.

Firstly, it is my Honor to report that my Esteem'd Acquaintance, Diarmid Niall Altan Maclean, Esq., of Stanton's Grove Plantation, is indeed your younger Brother. I rejoice at the Happiness this must provoke in your breast after your long and arduous Search for this Relative, whom you believed Lost to you Forever.

However, it now becomes my unhappy Duty to convey to you Mr. Maclean's wishes in this Matter. He has direct'd me to inform you that he has no Desire to communicate with you, and he refuses utterly your generous Offer of Money. Sir, he is most Adamant in this, and will not Sway, despite my earnest Pleas on your behalf. It Grieves me to commit such Words to paper, but your Brother bids me tell you that he considers you Dead. He cannot forgive the Wounds of the Past, and begs that you never again attempt to contact him.

However, my dear Sir, there is one last Bright Note in this unfortunate Matter, which must surely be a Sore Trial to you. It brings me great Joy to report that your youngest Brother, James Iain Alasdair Maclean, is Alive and Well, and lives in the Province of Maine, which is, as I am sure you know, a part of Massachusetts Colony. However, Mr. Diarmid Maclean has instruct'd me to say that Mr. James Maclean joins him in wishing to be left Alone, and that he, too, considers you Dead.

Sir, I know not what Sins have driven you from your Brothers' Esteem. Nor do I know if you are a Religious Man. However, the Bible tells us "To every Thing there is a Season." Therefore, my dear Sir, I beg you to possess your Soul in Patience, and perhaps your Brothers will some day see Fit to Forgive you.

Until that time, I once again Crave your Pardon, and I remain

Your most Faithful Servant,
Josiah Carter Cummings, Esq.

"Madam, may I inquire what you are doing?"

At the sound of those frigid British tones, utterly devoid of beguiling Highland burr, Fiona spun, and her heart leaped into her throat. Lachlan stood in the doorway, holding a tankard of ale and a jug of steaming water and glowering at her with the coldest expression she had ever seen on the granite planes of his face. She tried to reply, but no sound issued forth.

He slammed the jug and tankard on the table; ale and water sloshed onto the age-blackened wood. "I wouldna have expected ye to be the type who reads other folk's letters, but mayhap things are different in France. Tell me, did ye learn anythin' interestin'?" His tone was icily polite; but now his Highland burr had returned, and his *r*'s rolled like winter wind.

"Lachlan, please. I—"

He snatched up her skirt and bodice. "I think ye best be leavin'."

"Wait. Please listen. I was just trying to find out more about you. I tried to talk to you last night, but . . . well, you distracted me." His lips thinned into a mirthless smile, and she hurried on, heart hammering against her ribs. "Ever since I've been here I've heard rumors about you—"

"What rumors?"

"That . . . that you betrayed your clan by fighting for the English. That Duncan Campbell keeps you on as steward because you spied for the king." A pained expression shot through Lachlan's ice-gray eyes, and his handsome face grew strained. Fiona cursed herself for a fool, but blundered on. "Last night Maire told me about your brothers. She mentioned that one of them lived in Virginia, so when I saw the letter—"

Lachlan closed the space between them with one lightning-quick stride. "What other rumors have ye heard?" His hand gripped her forearm, and he dragged her roughly against his bare chest. "There's more. I can see it in your eyes."

She tried to jerk away, but he held her in an iron grasp. The searing heat of his body seeped through the thin quilt straight into her blood, and her traitorous flesh went weak with longing. *Mon Dieu,* she loved this man; loved him deep in her very being, as if she were a fragile tree and he the granite bedrock that enabled her to withstand the gales of winter. With every thoughtless word she risked losing him forever, but she had to find the truth.

He shook her. "Tell me!" Her teeth clacked together, and panic roared through her veins. He caught her jaw in a painful clasp, eyes glittering like steel blades in the cold dawn light. "Say it," he hissed.

"I heard you killed your wife!" she shrieked. "That you killed your child. *That's* what I've been trying to find out!"

He released her so quickly she staggered back. Her elbow struck the bedpost, and tears of pain and hopeless frustration sprang to her eyes. Lachlan spun away and stood with his back to her, massive shoulders as tense as a crouching wildcat's. She reached out a trembling hand and tried to speak his name, but a choking ache clogged her throat.

"Do ye believe that?" Lachlan's voice was so choked she scarce could hear him.

She dragged a despairing hand over her eyes, then collapsed on the bed. "Oh, Lachlan, how can you ask me that? Of course I don't—"

"Why in hell are ye readin' me private correspondence?" He whirled and glared down his blade-straight nose, eyes blazing with rage.

"Why in hell won't you tell me the truth?" she wailed. "Why in hell won't you trust me?"

His wickedly peaked brows lifted a fraction; then one corner of his hard mouth quirked into a rueful smile. Slow as a winter's dream, he walked forward. Then he stood before her and smoothed his stiff hand

over her disheveled curls. "Trust ye? Och, *mo druidh,*
I'd as soon trust the devil." His voice was hoarse and
heartbreakingly bitter.

A great, shimmering warmth rippled through her.
She caught his wrist, then pressed a kiss against the
scarred brown skin on his palm. "Oh, Lachlan, please
forget everything I've said. I love you—"

He stiffened. "Hush. Dinna say such things. Ye
wouldna feel that way if ye kent the awful things I've
done. Now get dressed. 'Tis better if we forget that last
night ever happened."

"You . . . you don't care for me?"

He drew a harsh breath, and his wintry eyes grew
veiled. "Nay. No' in that way."

She blinked. "I don't understand. We made love—"

"Please. I never should have bedded ye. But ye're so
beautiful, so magical. I . . . I couldna help meself. I'm
only flesh-and-blood, aye?" He attempted a rakish
smile, but failed miserably. He grasped her elbow and
lifted her to her feet, his fingers cold and frighteningly
impersonal. "Come now, ye best be off. The household
will be awake soon, and we dinna want them findin' ye
in me room."

Fiona pinned him with a cool, level gaze. Relative
to Lachlan's vast experience, she might be an innocent,
but she *had* been raised in France. Indeed, she had
been married to Harry—Don Juan *extraordinaire.* She
knew the demeanor of a man who bedded women for
sport, then hastened to be rid of them when the sun
rose. And Lachlan's tortured expression and haunted
eyes did not belong to such a man.

"Lachlan, I'm sorry. Please don't shut me out like
this."

He turned away. In the cold dawn light, his austere

features resembled the profile of a remote, pagan god. "Och, lass, there's so much I canna tell ye."

"Like what?"

For a split second, his steel-gray eyes blazed with bitter regret; then his stark face froze into an in icy mask. On the swift, silent feet of a hunter, he strode from the room.

Fiona opened her mouth, then closed it with a click. She had destroyed all hope of trust between them. What more was there to say?

Sixteen

The lowering December sun disappeared behind the bulk of Ben More, limning the mountain with a blurred band of gold and backlighting the bare trees' wizened branches. Tiny diamond stars littered the blue-velvet sky, and lavender evening shadows stretched long across the snow. Here and there, the last scarlet rays of sunset pierced through the dark evergreens, staining the undulating crystal blanket, as if heart's blood had been spilled, then frozen forever into haunting beauty.

Lachlan paused, then listened. The air was keen with the stillness of snow-shrouded woodlands at dusk, and he could hear neither the click of the ice-sheathed branches nor the sigh of the wind through boughs of pine. He relaxed his shoulders, then lowered his musket, muzzle down, toward the ground. Even though the stag's tracks were clear as ink blots in the blue-shadowed snow, he no longer felt the urge to hunt the poor beggar down. His half-frozen lips twitched into a wry smile. Och, Fiona wouldna approve.

He swallowed the swift, sharp ache that rose in his throat. Good St. Ninian, but he was a fool. He had thought Fiona different, but she was like all the others—far too willing to believe vicious rumors and snoop about for evidence damning him as a traitor, and worse. Och, if his violet-eyed housekeeper truly had second sight, why couldn't she see what was right under her delicate nose?

He raised one icy foot and irritably knocked clinging snow from his black-leather boot. She thought him a liar. Aye, and so he was. Over the years he had learned the value—and the high price—of the half-truth, even of the outright falsehood. And now he had told the biggest lie of all.

He had told Fiona he didn't care for her.

What price would he pay for his dishonesty? Good St. Ninian, he already was paying, for after only half a day he missed Fiona so badly he thought he would go mad. He missed her beguiling, half-French accent and the way she was forever trying to keep her irrepressible curls demurely pinned beneath a plain black ribbon. He missed her level, infuriatingly logical gaze and the violet tranquillity of her eyes. Most of all, he missed her in his bed. His flesh burned at the mere memory of her rose-tipped breasts, succulent and quivering beneath his tongue—

"Lachlan!"

Lachlan spun and swiftly raised the musket to his shoulder. His pulse thundered to life; then he spat a Gaelic curse and dropped the gun to his side. Even after all these years he retained the survival instincts of a jaded, battle-scarred warrior. And 'twas likely a battle he was facing.

A cloaked feminine figure hurried toward him through the snow, boots squeaking in the powdery crystals. "St. Ninian!" he bellowed, "how many times have I told ye no' to startle a man wi' a gun?"

Sorcha halted before him, puffing little whorls of steam into the frigid air. "Dinna snap," she retorted. She planted her hands on her hips, then bent forward, gasping for breath. "I shouted your name. Could ye no' tell 'twas me and no' a wild boar?"

Lachlan bit back a terse rejoinder. "What are ye doin' out here in the woods?"

Sorcha straightened, brushed a strand of coarse black hair from her cheek, then smiled suggestively. "Perhaps I was lookin' for a romp in the snow. What say ye, sweeting? Care for a saucy tumble?" When Lachlan refused to rise to the bait, she dragged a woolen mitt across her dripping red nose and shot him a belligerent glare. "Aye, then. I been lookin' for ye all day—ever since the 'tween maid told me she saw that odd little French bitch comin' out o' your room at dawn."

Lachlan felt his face stiffen into a taciturn mask. He grasped Sorcha's arm, then began to march her through the ankle-deep snow. "I'm no' havin' this discussion. Now let's be gettin' ye home."

Sorcha dug in her heels and pulled free. "Aye, ye are. Ye'll listen to what I have to say, then ye'll do somethin' aboot it, or by God, me *athair* will ken the reason why."

Lachlan glowered at the trees. "Talk fast, then. Me balls are freezin' out here."

"Weel, that's more than ye can say for 'em two months ago. I vow they were hot enough then—and workin' better than ever."

Something in her tone sent a sliver of ice down his spine. His brows slammed together. "What do ye mean?"

She thrust up her chin and smiled triumphantly. "I mean I'm carryin' your bairn, Lachlan Maclean. I've caught your seed in me belly. Ye'll marry me now—"

"What kind o' trick do ye think ye're playin'?" He caught her arm and jerked her toward him.

" 'Tis no trick, sweeting. Rinalda's seen to me. She'll tell ye I'm wi' child. Ye said ye'd do right by me if I caught your bairn in me belly, and so ye will, for ye're a gentleman." Sorcha stroked her rough, soggy mitten down his cheek, then pressed her ample bosom against his arm. "Oh, Lachlan, 'twill be prime fun—a weddin' and a new baby."

The blood drained from his face, and his crippled hand twitched against the musket. Struggling for control, he dragged in an icy breath of air. Och, St. Ninian, this couldn't be happening. 'Twas a nightmare. Nay— 'twas a fitting consequence of his weakness, his folly. He stared down at Sorcha. *She* was but one of the many wretched reasons he had lied to Fiona. He couldn't bear Fiona's pure amethyst gaze to rest on his wicked past, to be averted in disgust from his penchant for drowning his sorrows in whisky and wanton female flesh.

"Come, sweeting," Sorcha cooed, "will ye tell me da we're to wed, or should I?"

Lachlan's mind reeled. Good St. Ninian, what had he done? He couldn't marry Sorcha, for he was deeply, wildly, passionately in love with Fiona. He loved her as if she were his very heart, as if they were one indivisible soul. Och, why in God's name had he ever told her he didn't care? And who would have thought he would pay for his lie this quickly? He ground out a Gaelic curse, then gave a harsh bark of laughter.

Sorcha's olive skin flushed an unbecoming red. "That doesna sound like happiness over marryin' me, Lachlan Maclean."

He shook his head sadly, then gently set her away from him. "I never promised to marry ye. I'll take fine care o' the bairn—"

"What!" Sorcha's shriek tore through the twilight

woods. "I canna believe it! That French whore ye're beddin' has bewitched ye! Me da warned me. He said she brought your wee pup back from the dead, but I wouldna believe—"

"That's enough!" Lachlan slammed his musket into the snow. "Madam Fraser has nothin' to do wi' this, and she's none o' your concern."

Sorcha snorted and rolled her eyes. The gesture had always annoyed Lachlan; now annoyance turned to livid disgust. "That's what ye think, ye black-hearted, skirt-chasin' cocksman," Sorcha hissed. "She's my concern when she's keepin' me from bein' your wife! And if ye kent who she *really* is, the whey-faced little bitch would slip from your graces mighty damn quick."

He whirled and stalked toward the castle. Despite the frigid air, sweat broke out on his brow and crawled like icy insects down his ribs. St. Ninian, he wouldn't listen to any more of Sorcha's lies. He knew who Fiona was; she was a Scottish widow raised in Paris and come back—

His stomach clenched. Why had Fiona come back? She never had given a satisfactory explanation, beyond the unlikely excuse of wanting to see the land of her birth. He had been so dazzled by her beauty and his own overwhelming desire to bed her that he hadn't bothered to pursue it. In truth, he hadn't wanted to know. He preferred that the past remain buried—for both of them.

Halfway through the woods, Sorcha caught up with him. She grabbed his arm and dragged him to a stop. "Listen to me, Lachlan. Fiona Fraser isna who ye think."

"I dinna want to hear another word."

Sorcha raised a hand to her throat, then scanned his

face with astonished black eyes. "My God, she truly has bewitched ye."

Lachlan wiped the sweat from his brow. "Och, stop your bletherin'. Me only concern with Madam Fraser is that she no' be the victim o' vicious rumors. We've had enough o' those already, aye?" He spun on his heel and strode forward.

"Lachlan, dinna do this." Sorcha stumbled through the snow beside him. "Ye canna truly love that schemin' adventuress."

The harsh set of his mouth eased into a smile. "If Madam Fraser's a schemin' adventuress, then I'm the Prince o' Wales."

Sorcha lunged close and tried to tug him to a halt. "She's no' Madam Fraser, ye bloody fool. She's Madam Maclean! She was married to Sir Malcolm Henry Maclean—better kent to ye as Harry, son and heir to Sir Hector Maclean. Lachlan, listen to me. She's the daughter-in-law o' the chief o' Clan Maclean."

Lachlan's heart went deathly still, like a ship becalmed in the eye of a tempest. For a long, agonizing moment the only sound through the twilight woods was the whistle of the rising wind and Sorcha's labored breathing. For what seemed like an eternity, his gaze riveted on the black, snow-heavy boughs of a towering fir; then he slowly turned his head and looked down at Sorcha. She smiled up at him, smug triumph leaping from every line of her face. His lips parted, but no sound came out.

"Me da heard 'em talkin'—" Sorcha began.

"Who?"

"The French whore and her mother-in-law."

Lachlan's eyes fluttered shut. "Ye wouldna be speakin' o' Madam Maeve Maclean, now would ye?"

"Aye. The old bitch kent ye'd recognize her. That's

why they put out the story that she'd been burnt and
wanted to stay in hidin', 'cause o' her scars." Sorcha
stamped her feet and wrapped her arms about her ribs.
"Brrrr. Canna we finish this inside?"

"Tell it. Now."

She pulled a face. "Me da's been spyin' on 'em,
'cause I kent there was some feelin' between ye and
that French whore, and I thought it best to keep an eye
on things. It seems old Sir Hector died penniless—and
guess what? Ye're the next chieftain o' Clan Maclean!"
She gave a snort of laughter. "Isna that a hoot?"

Lachlan clenched his jaw and prayed for the strength
not to throttle her before he got the whole story. "I am
the man's third cousin. 'Tis no' so great a stretch."
Och, but it was. It was a bloody, goddam miracle. He
blinked, then swallowed, torn between shock, rage and
jubilation.

"Weel, dinna be celebratin' yet," Sorcha retorted.
"Sir Hector was stone broke. And that's why that
French bitch has been suckin' up to ye like a barnacle.
She and the old bawd are penniless. They'd planned to
come here, swindle some sort o' treasure out o' ye, get
their claws into the estate, then sail back to France,
leavin' ye wi' nothin' but a stupid Jacobite title likely
to run ye afoul o' the king."

A fierce pulse began to throb at the base of Lachlan's throat, and he curled his hands into fists. Now it
all made sense. Och, what a fool he had been to believe
that Fiona loved him—the lying, scheming, duplicitous
little bitch! She had been scheming to sink her claws
into a fortune he no longer possessed. And to think he
had been ashamed of *his* past! At least he had given her
his real name.

A terrible, livid heat spread across his icy cheeks.
Sorcha smiled and nestled against his chest, smug and

complacent now that she had aroused his fury against her rival. "So now, sweeting, when should we set the date?"

Lachlan ground his teeth until he actually could hear their rasp through the quiet woods. Drawing in a harsh breath, he grasped Sorcha's shoulders, then lifted her and set her out of his way. "I'm sorry, lass, but I wilna marry ye. The bairn will have me name and protection as long as I live—"

Fast as a striking snake, Sorcha's mittened hand shot up and cracked across his cheek. He rocked back with a soft gasp of surprise. "Ye listen to me!" Sorcha shrieked. "Ye'll marry me or so help me, I'll slip this bairn. Rinalda wilna do it, but there's others who ken how to tear a babe from the womb—"

Fury ripped through him like chain lightning; his pulse accelerated until it roared in his ears. He snatched her elbow in an iron grip and jerked her face inches from his. "Never say that again! I'll never have another bairn o' mine killed by a selfish, heartless—"

He shoved her away from him and stormed forward, drowning in seventeen-year-old grief and an awful, eternal rage. Then he turned and bellowed an oath, his Scots accent as rough and wild as any ancient Gael's. "I wilna tolerate blackmail, Sorcha Beattie. Ye tell your father that. But neither will I let ye kill me babe—" His voice cracked, and he bit his lip until blood spurted in his mouth. "I canna discuss this now. Come to me tomorrow."

He turned and strode through the icy blue twilight, dodging snow-covered tree limbs, jumping black clumps of heather, skirting ghostly granite outcrops. He ran away from the castle, out onto the windswept cliffs, out to where it had all started that wretched April night of 1746.

He skidded to a halt, boots barely gripping the icy rock. Below him the sea stretched away to the west like one long, blue-black plane of liquid night, indistinguishable from the leaden sky above. His shoulders heaved as he drew frigid gasps of air into his lungs, then exhaled white clouds of vapor. Hot tears blurred his vision, then spilled over and froze against his cheeks like scalding, salty diamonds. He shuddered and listened to the crash of the white-capped waves on the jagged rocks sixty feet below. This was where Catriona had played her final card; this was where his life had gone hideously wrong.

He clenched his fists and bellowed to the silent heavens, "Och, good Christ, help me!"

Seventeen

Fiona perched on the edge of Maire's bed, then reached for the green-glass vial that contained Rinalda's sleeping potion. As she did so, her gaze caught the peculiar, luminous lavender of the evening sky outside the diamond-paned window. Her breath caught. She had never seen such crystal-clear winter twilights back in France. She had never known such serene, secret beauty could exist, to be revealed only in moments of solitude, when one's mind was open and one's heart was engaged. It was almost as if God was revealing an overwhelming truth, if only she had the desire and the wisdom to comprehend its scope.

She eased a silver spoonful of medicine between Maire's bluish lips, ascertained that her patient had swallowed, then sat back and wrapped her cold hands in her apron. Through the silent, interminable day, Maire's condition had grown worse. Rinalda's best herbal remedies had kept Maire's cough—and the blood from her damaged lungs—at bay, but the poor lass was slipping into a stupor that would lead to her death.

Fiona closed her eyes and whispered a prayer, first to God, then to the Holy Mother, then to St. Joseph, patron saint of the dying. Slowly, Maire succumbed to the sedative effects of the skullcap and valerian, and her labored breathing eased into light, even snores. Fiona shivered and glanced out the window. Was Lachlan out there?

Suddenly, a surreptitious skittering sound filtered through the drafty bedchamber, and a gray field mouse peeked out from beneath the bedside table.

"Bonjour, petite souris," Fiona said softly. "I'm glad to see I'm not alone tonight." The mouse cocked its velvety head and busily sniffed the air. *"C'est vrai,* I would have been happy to leave this dreary place after what happened with that arrogant Highland seducer this morning, but poor Maire needs nursing, and Rinalda is too old to do it all by herself."

The mouse sat up on its haunches, clasped its tiny pink paws and fixed Fiona with a shrewd, if slightly anxious, expression. Fiona chuckled. "You're right, *ma petite.* I'm fooling no one, pretending to outraged virtue after I all but threw myself at that arrogant black lord last night. I'm too practical, like the French, eh?"

Tears rose in her eyes, and she blinked. Too practical, and too much in love. Lachlan's cold declaration that he didn't love her had hurt her to the quick—much more than she thought her calm, rational heart could be hurt. But she was too sensitive to blame his callous behavior on a lack of feelings. There had been much going on behind his glittering silver eyes. If he was uncaring, then she was—

"Then I'm a field mouse," she told her timorous visitor, with a defiant nod of her head.

Suddenly, footsteps flew down the passageway; the startled mouse darted back beneath the table. The heavy oak door swung open, and Sorcha strode into the chamber. Her slanted black Gypsy's eyes locked onto Fiona's, and a feverish, nauseating wave of jealousy surged through Fiona's veins.

"Rinalda told me I'd find ye here," Sorcha snapped.

Fiona ordered herself to remain calm, then fixed Lachlan's former mistress with an unruffled gaze. "What do you want?"

Sorcha sailed across the room, elbowed Fiona out of the way, and raked Maire's sleeping form with a cruel, derisive gaze. "She'll die," she declared. "Where's her babe?" Fiona nodded to the basket by the fire where little Hugh slept. Sorcha didn't spare the child so much as a glance, but thrust her chin toward Maire. "I suppose this useless sack o' bones has thrust the wee beggar on Lachlan." Her black eyes took on a speculative gleam; then she shrugged out of her red-wool cloak with the slow, predatory movements of a jungle cat. "Lachlan's always wanted a son, ye ken."

A sharp pain jabbed beneath Fiona's left breast. She flushed, remembering the long, passionate night in Lachlan's arms. What if his seed now grew inside her? " 'Tis a normal wish, for a man of his station," she murmured. She plucked a linen cloth from a basin of cool water, then gently placed it on Maire's fevered brow. Why on earth was Sorcha hanging about, anyway? A sudden, horrible thought struck her. *Mon Dieu,* what if Sorcha had seen Fiona coming from Lachlan's bedchamber this morning?

"Aye, weel." Sorcha sauntered to the crackling hearth fire, then shook out her waist-length hair. It shone like raven's wings in the red-gold light. "He'll no' have time for wee Hugh—no' now that I'm bearin' his child."

Sorcha's words hissed through Fiona's mind like a venomous snake. Fiona's heart thundered into her throat, and her stomach heaved until she had to press a hand to her mouth. Stunned and half blind with actual physical pain, she rose and wobbled to the window, desperate to hide her ashen face.

"Ye look pale," Sorcha taunted. "Are ye no' goin' to offer me your best wishes?"

Fiona blew her nose on one of Maire's linen wash-cloths, collapsed on the bed beside her sleeping patient, then broke into a tempest of wrenching sobs. Oh, *mon Dieu*, why couldn't she control herself? Where were logic, reason and rationality now? Where were God, the Holy Mother and the saints? Where was Sir Hector?

Eh bien, she still could be thankful for something. At least Sorcha wasn't here to witness her complete and utter destruction. With a furious, agonized wail, she pounded her fist into the musty mattress, then sobbed louder.

After several wretched minutes, she gasped for breath, then dragged a hand over her tear-fevered cheeks. *Mon Dieu*, how long had she been crying like this? Long enough so that her throat burned, her stomach heaved, and her nose had clamped shut against any attempt to breath. She rolled onto her side, then wrapped her arms around her ribs. St. Joseph, she wanted to die.

"Fool, fool, fool!" she whispered hoarsely.

How could she have been so *stupid*? Sir Hector must be spinning in his grave! She had bought it all, lock, stock and barrel. She had believed that moody, black-hearted cocksman when he said he and Sorcha were no longer lovers, that he wanted a future with Fiona. Ha! A future between her thighs, perhaps.

She flounced onto her back and conjured Lachlan's dangerously handsome face. For one bittersweet moment, she let herself admire his elegant profile, his teasing smile, his enigmatic gray eyes shimmering with enchanting silver flecks. She knew the strength and gentleness of his hands—hands that had comforted poor, dying Maire and cradled wee, innocent Hugh. She had felt the soul-stealing thrill of those masterful hands on her skin; she had known the wild, jubilant glory of his touch, surging with mystery and heat and life.

Oh, Lachlan. . . . She dug her nails into the soft eiderdown. What could she do? What did she want? She felt helpless, adrift, as if her mind and will were scattered to the winds like a thousand crushed leaves whirling in a gale. And yet. . . .

And yet she knew. No matter how foolish the desire, she wanted Lachlan. She craved the tenderness he showered on little Hugh; she yearned for the selfless devotion he gave his ungrateful, gossiping tenants; she longed for him to wrap her in the comforting strength of his arms and call her his heart. And she ached for the hot pressure of his mouth on hers, for savage, demanding kisses full of passion—and love.

With a tiny wail, she flung an arm over her eyes. Why did she torture herself with hopeless dreams? Lachlan didn't love her. Worse, he had gotten a child on his mistress, and to hear Sorcha tell it, they were halfway to the altar already.

"St. Andrew, what's wrong with me!" she cried.

"Weel, lassie, for starters ye've let your patient die."

Fiona leaped up, heart pounding. There, lurking like a naughty schoolboy in the corner beyond the window, was her father-in-law's ghost.

"Sir Hector," she gasped.

"In the spirit," the ghost jauntily replied. His blurred

gray image brightened, and he swirled about, as if pleased with the sensation he had caused.

"This better be a joke." Fiona raced around the side of the bed, then grasped Maire's icy hand and chafed it briskly. "Maire? Maire!" She leaned over and rested an ear on the young woman's gaunt chest. "Oh, this can't be happening. She can't have died—"

Desperately, she pressed her hands over the girl's heart. No light or warmth met her touch. Oh, *mon Dieu*, she couldn't let Maire die. 'Twas too sad, too unfair—and it would kill Lachlan. She clenched her eyes shut and tried to force the healing golden light down through her arms into Maire's still chest. Nothing happened. She bit her lip and clenched her eyes tight. She was a failure. What good was her gift if she couldn't use it out of love?

"It happened, missy, while ye were fashin' over that strappin' haunch o' beef ye've bedded." Sir Hector swarmed closer, then hovered disapprovingly at her elbow. The air around him was bitterly cold, even by the appalling standards of Castle Taigh.

Fiona slumped down on the bed, too shocked and despairing to retort. Maire's chest was still, her heart silent, her breathing stopped. She hadn't been able to save her. "She slipped away so fast," she whispered.

Sir Hector gave a *tcha* of aggravation. "Dinna start blubberin' again, lassie. 'Twas for the best. Ye couldna have saved her, ye ken. 'Tis beyond your power—"

"It seems everything is," Fiona blurted.

"But she wasna in pain, lass. Rest easy on that score. And she didna blame ye for howlin' over me cousin when ye should have been watchin' her to the next life."

"She wasn't? She doesn't?" Fiona gaped at her head father-in-law. "How do you know?"

Sir Hector swirled about and peered in Rinalda's medicine box, then inspected the blissfully sleeping Hugh. "Because, me dear dimwit, she told me on her way out."

"Out where?"

"To the other life, lassie. Have ye no' learned a thing, consortin' wi' a ghost the way ye do? Och, love has addled your wits."

"You mean you talked to, er . . . Maire's spirit?"

"Aye, I did," Sir Hector blustered. "And stop badgerin' me. Ye canna even find out the truth aboot that arrogant Highlander. Do ye really expect to grasp the finer points of metaphysics? Now stop gawpin' and get the poor lass laid out before that scoundrel Campbell learns she's in the castle."

Fiona swallowed the agonizing ache in her throat, then eased the eiderdown from Maire's still form. The young mother's frail limbs appeared waxen in the firelight, and her tangled black hair clung about her cheeks like wet black feathers. Fiona smoothed a tender hand over Maire's brow. In death, all signs of pain and struggle had vanished from her thin face, and she appeared to be smiling.

"She . . . she looks peaceful," Fiona murmured, woodenly catching up a cloth and the basin of water.

"Aye. No Purgatory for her, lucky lass." The ghost whiffed at an open medicine bottle, then grimaced. " 'Tis enough to make ye believe in Calvinism." He floated directly over the bed, then watched with clinical interest as Fiona gently washed Maire's body and murmured prayers for the repose of her soul. "By the by, she gave me a message for ye."

Fiona dropped the cloth and stared. "She did?"

"Aye. It seems Sorcha—who *is* Sorcha, by the way? That divine Gypsy beauty your beloved was bedding?

Lucky sod. Anyway, it seems this Sorcha lied to ye, lass. She *is* carryin', but the bairn isna Lachlan's. Accordin' to Maire, he told ye the truth aboot no' touchin' Sorcha since the day he met ye." Sir Hector rolled his eyes and sarcastically shrugged what passed for his shoulders. "Och, it must be love."

"Is that true?"

"Och, lassie, in my experience, the newly dead dinna lie. 'Twould hardly be beneficial to their, er . . . future happiness."

A flood of joy and gratitude and relief rippled through Fiona, leaving her weak and suddenly, dreadfully tired. She clenched her eyes shut, then whispered, "I knew it. I knew he wouldn't lie to me."

" 'Ods ballocks!" Sir Hector went black with disapproval. "Ye couldna tell a lie from the truth if it came up and bit ye. Here the new chieftain o' Clan Maclean all but hurls his heart at your feet, and ye go pokin' aboot, believin' rumors and stirrin' up trouble—"

"But you asked me to find the truth." Fiona jumped up and planted her hands on her hips. "You said there was something on your conscience—"

"Aye, there was. And I've learned the truth—on me own, I might add. The question is, have ye?"

Fiona opened her mouth, then closed it with a click. *Mon Dieu,* what was the truth? Suddenly, she saw a vivid image of her mother as a young woman, spitting on the frozen earth of Culloden battlefield, inches from Lachlan's face. "Can ye no' see, ye fey, addle-witted changeling?" her mother had shrieked, kicking her booted toe into Lachlan's side. "He's a bloody Campbell—a bloody traitor to the cause! Look there. 'Tis the Campbell badge. He's the enemy, and he likely killed your pure father."

But Lachlan hadn't killed her father; drink and the

French pox had. Fiona sank down on the bed. Deirdre Fraser always had gone for appearance over reality. She had kept up the illusion that her husband wasn't a philanderer, she had pretended Fiona was just like the other girls at the convent of the Ursulines, and she had schooled her daughter well in the art of repressing one's true self. Fiona shot a scathing glance at the ghost. So had Sir Hector, for that matter. He had rewarded her for projecting the image he preferred: that of a cool, logical, educated woman.

Fiona bit her lip. Her mother and Sir Hector might have been wrong in championing appearance over reality, but they had only meant to protect her. *Non*, they had protected her. She hadn't been shunned, or burned as a witch, or excommunicated from the church, and she had been able to survive the emotional abuse of a cheating husband who had loved his three-inch, red high heels more than he loved her. Her reserve and rational outlook had helped her survive.

She clenched her eyes shut, then surrendered to overwhelming exhaustion. Lachlan may not have lied about bedding Sorcha, but he still didn't love her. He hadn't chosen to peel away his mask and reveal his true self. Quite the opposite, he had refused to offer even the tiniest glimpse into his heart. She had told him she loved him; she had told him the truth. What had he done for her?

Her eyes flew open just in time to catch her father-in-law chucking baby Hugh under the chin. The infant woke and began to fuss; Fiona stood and hurried across the icy plank floor. "Sir Hector, get away from that baby," she snapped.

She scooped Hugh into her arms, then settled him over her shoulder. He was warm as fresh brioche and smelled delightfully of milk. "As for the truth, I've found it brings nothing but pain, rejection and trouble. Right now I'm much more concerned about Maeve's and my—and *ce petite bébé's*—future. So unless you can help with that, go back to Purgatory or wherever restless souls reside and leave me alone."

The ghost dissolved, literally, into raucous laughter. "Weel said, missy, weel said. Ye're a lass after me own heart."

Fiona wrapped Hugh's pink, flailing limbs in a soft wool shawl, then shot Sir Hector a critical glare. "By the way, how did Maire know that Sorcha's baby isn't Lachlan's?"

Still chuckling, the ghost swarmed close, then whispered in her ear. Icy air accompanied him, wee Hugh began to howl, then Fiona burst out laughing. "Och, *mon Dieu!* That's too rich. Wait 'til I tell Lachlan."

Sir Hector waggled his filmy brows, then leered. "Does that mean ye're givin' that brazen cocksman another chance?"

"I don't think that's up to me. Lachlan's the one who said . . . who said he didn't care for me."

"Och, lass, and ye believed him?" The ghost swooped about beneath the stone ceiling, making exaggerated faces, attempting to get Hugh to stop wailing. " 'Ods ballocks, love has addled your fine wits, lassie. Dinna ye ken that men *always* say that? 'Tis the male code!" He winked both eyes owlishly, and Hugh gurgled down to amused cooing. "A jackass always digs in his stubborn heels, ye ken—right before he takes that final plunge."

Fiona snorted, then tried to quell a tiny spurt of hope. *"Oui,* that sounds like Lachlan. But jackass or not, I'm afraid he's made it quite clear that he wants nothing further to do with me."

Sir Hector bounced across the room, then hovered

agitatedly before the tall window. A brilliant crescent moon had risen over the snowy cliffs, high into the blue-velvet sky. It shone straight through him. "He will, lass, when ye hand him the treasure."

Fiona froze halfway to Hugh's basket. "Don't tell me you've finally found it."

"Nay, I havena found it, ye saucy baggage. But I have remembered where I hid the map. Now 'tis up to ye to find the treasure."

Eighteen

Fiona clutched the smoking tallow candle, took a deep breath, then gazed up at the cold, echoing blackness high above her head. Could Sir Hector's elusive treasure map really have been hidden here, almost in plain sight, for all these years? An icy draft wafted through the great hall, as if a door had been opened, then silently closed. She shivered and wondered, not for the first time, why she had left the relative warmth and comfort of her Paris garret for this dank and musty castle.

A guttering beam of candlelight caught the glassy-eyed gaze of the animal heads on the paneling above her. Her shiver turned to a shudder. "How awful," she murmured, gazing pityingly at the stuffed boar. "How awful to die for a selfish whim."

"Your soft heart adds to your attraction, Mistress Fraser. But, alas, many innocent creatures have died because of selfish whims."

Fiona whirled, then peered into the blackness, searching for the source of the low, sibilant whisper. "Who's there?" she demanded, desperately trying to slow her galloping heart.

"Your laird and master, my dear." The whisper rose into a high-pitched, predatory giggle. Tendrils of fear curled down her spine.

She stepped back, then gasped as the corner of the refectory table bit into her buttocks. The frigid, black-shadowed hall had grown silent and oppressive as a tomb, and she brandished the candle before her like a shield. She didn't recognize the whisper, had never heard such a lurid, menacing tone in her life, and certainly not here at Taigh Samhraidh, where she had met and conversed with every servant, every crofter. Could a stranger have come to the island, hidden on Duncan Campbell's boat? Her stomach roiled, and she pressed back against the table. What if the voice didn't belong to a stranger? What if a madman lived undetected on Mull?

She jerked up her chin and forced her voice into calmness. "Lachlan Maclean is laird here, and you're not him."

"Oh, I forgot." A hiss sounded from behind her. " 'Tis that swaggering, bleeding-heart Highlander you wish to bed."

"How dare you say such a—"

A blurred shape hurtled out of the shadows. From the corner of her eye, Fiona caught the impression of a hunched male form; then a hard body hit her, knocking the air from her lungs. Arms of iron gripped her shoulders and jerked her off balance; she grunted and dropped the candle. It hit the floor, rolled against a chair leg, and guttered out. The hall was plunged into blackness.

A blast of sour, whisky-drenched breath hit her cheek; then the man dragged her against him. His pawing hands seemed to be everywhere, stroking her hair, pinching her bottom, groping her breast. "I'll make you forget him, beautiful enchantress." Burning lips crawled across her temple, searching inexorably for her mouth. "God, how I want you. Since the first moment—"

The man's wind-roughened lips dragged across hers. Wild to free herself, Fiona landed a vicious kick on his shin, then lunged back and screamed.

Her attacker gave a hiss of pain. "You little bitch—"

A door slammed; then she heard the pound of swift, booted feet against the flagstones. A towering male body brushed past her, then barreled into her attacker and knocked him to the floor. There was a grunt of pain, then the dull, wet thud of a fist connecting with flesh.

Fiona staggered back, then groped her way along the edge of the table. Stumbling over chairs and barking her shin against a footstool, she managed to find the door to the passageway, where a torch always burned. She heard another cry of pain and a string of hoarse Gaelic curses, then dragged open the hall door, gritting her teeth as the hinges gave a loud *skreek*. She dashed forward, grabbed the smoking torch from its wrought-iron sconce, whirled and plunged back into the great hall.

As she stumbled forward, the torch's light gyred like writhing demons across Lachlan's broad back. He crouched atop a smaller man, his crippled hand around the man's throat, his good hand raised and curled into a fist.

"Stop!" she cried. "Lachlan, stop. You'll kill him!"

She lunged forward, grabbed Lachlan's collar and hauled with all her strength. The rough linen tore with a loud *rrrrpt!* Lachlan spat another oath, reared up and spun to face her. The torch's guttering flames caught the sharp planes and angles of his face, and for a single, mad moment, he resembled a savage Gaelic warrior risen from the mists of time.

"Get back, ye wee fool," he snarled. His shoulders heaved, sweat beaded his brow, and his teeth gleamed wolfish and white. He made a grab for the burning brand, but she sidestepped, then lowered it toward her attacker.

" 'Tis Duncan Campbell," she blurted.

Duncan rolled onto his side and clutched a hand to his bleeding nose. "Get away from me." He scrabbled sideways like a crab. "I'll kill ye for this. So help me—"

Lachlan grabbed for him.

"Lachlan, don't you dare!" Fiona blocked the Highlander's way, then shoved her shoulder against his chest, savoring the solid warmth of chiseled muscle and hard bone beneath the wool of her sleeve.

"Fiona, this scum just attacked ye—"

"He's drunk," she replied calmly. "Have you never done anything you regretted when you were drunk?" She arched a brow and fixed him with a cool gaze. His lean cheeks flushed under her scrutiny, and his eyes flashed like silver swords.

"Aye, many things," he spat, raking a hand through his long, tousled hair. He turned toward Duncan, seemed to contemplate kicking him in the ribs, then grabbed his hunched shoulder and dragged him to his feet. Duncan wrenched free, then slouched forward over the refectory table, hand still clenched to his nose.

"Touch me again, Maclean, and I'll kill—"

"That's enough," Fiona said. "You're bleeding. Let me help you." She reached toward Duncan; he turned on her like a rabid dog.

"Aye, now ye pay me some attention." Duncan's carefully cultivated English accent gave way to a rough Highland burr. "Now that your cavalier has saved your pretty little arse."

"That's enough." Lachlan's voice cracked like musket fire.

Duncan straightened as much as he could, then looked from Lachlan's glowering face to Fiona's flushed one. His eyes glittered like polished jet in the guttering torchlight. "Ah, so that's how it is. Fallen for the housekeeper, eh? I should have known that's why you wouldn't let me have her." He sniffed, then managed a vile smirk. "I must say, Maclean, it seems you've finally sunk to your proper level—"

Lachlan's hand shot out and caught Duncan by the throat. "Shut your foul mouth."

Fiona gave a squeak of protest. Duncan jerked free, then tossed her a vicious glare. "Save your pity, wench. And I'd advise you to save your tender little heart. Don't you know my esteemed brother-in-law still mourns his dead wife?" Duncan's voice dripped venom; then his reptilian face twisted with an emotion that seemed very like grief. "Oh, yes, he adored my beautiful, darling sister." His voice tore into a ragged sob. "My Catriona, my only love. He worshiped her like a man possessed—"

"Shut up, Campbell!"

"—right up 'til the day she died." Duncan braced against the black-oak table, then took a hobbling step toward Fiona. "You've never seen a man grieve so violently over a beloved's death." His voice grew light and conversational. "Which is odd, considering that he killed her."

Fiona slumped into the tapestry wing chair in the corner of the great hall, then gazed numbly out the tall windows. The wavy, greenish glass took on a leaden sheen as the night sky lightened ever so slightly into the first frozen gray of dawn. She drew her icy feet up onto the chair, then rested her chin on her knees. *Mon Dieu,* this was the second night in a row that she had gone with little or no sleep. No wonder she was seeing ghosts!

Her smile faded, and she pressed the back of her hand to the sharp vertical line between her brows. Good St. Genevieve, how she would love to tear the last few minutes from her mind, to float back in time to just an hour before. But she couldn't. She had wanted the truth, and now she had gotten it. Lachlan Maclean had killed his wife. Catriona's own brother had said so.

She clenched thumb and fingers to her temples and rubbed the dull ache that throbbed there. Only minutes earlier, Duncan had flung out his bitter revelation, then turned on Lachlan, angular face contorted with rage. "As soon as it's light, Maclean, I'm going for the sheriff. You've defied me long enough. You've countermanded my orders and stolen my money. But now, at last, I'll get the great pleasure of making you pay for your crimes." Before Lachlan could react, Duncan snatched up his abandoned crutch, then stumped from the room.

Lachlan's unfathomable gray eyes went blank, his brow wrinkled and his lips parted, but no sound came out. She stared up at him, too stunned to speak.

"Is it true?" she croaked.

Lachlan expelled his breath as if a savage blow had knocked it from him. He jerked the burning torch from her grasp, thrust it into the fireplace until the kindling flamed, then stormed across the room and thrust the brand into an empty sconce.

For tense, endless minutes he paced back and forth, pounding his fist into his thigh with each long stride.

Suddenly, a tremor shuddered down the entire rigid length of his towering frame. With a strangled cry, he shot forward and smashed his fist into the stone wall. Then he whirled and was gone.

Fiona clutched her arms about her knees; her head dropped forward against them. At any moment she expected to hear a blood-curdling scream as Lachlan's glittering dirk ended all threats to his safety.

Agonized tears welled in her eyes, and she gave herself over to her emotions. *Mon Dieu,* what use was love if it only led to such pain, to such cruel, bitter heartbreak? She had been better off within the cool, carefully constructed fortress of reason. At least there she had been safe, if only half alive.

A sob tore from her throat, drowning out the sound of quick, determined footsteps striding down the passageway. The door to the great hall creaked open; Fiona's head shot up. To her astonishment, Lachlan stepped in, tugging someone behind him. Firelight licked the sharp planes and angles of his face, bathing his high cheekbones and severe nose in flickering shadows of black and gold. His eyes locked onto hers, searing a raw challenge straight into her soul.

Fiona struggled to her feet. "Why have you come back?"

Lachlan's lips thinned into a grim line. "Ye asked for it, so I'm bringin' ye the truth." He stepped aside.

Rinalda stood behind him, clad in a billowing muslin nightshift, a frayed wool shawl and a lacy white bed cap. Her thinning, yellowish hair crawled Medusa-like over her frail shoulders, and she blinked owlishly in the fire and candle glare. "What is all this, laddie?" she demanded querulously. She rounded on Lachlan and jabbed a clawlike finger into his broad shoulder. "Draggin' me from me watch over wee Hugh—"

"Rinalda, tell Madam Maclean how me wife died."

"Madam Maclean? Her name's Fraser, lad."

Lachlan's wintry gaze raked Fiona from head to toe. "So she said. But she lied. She's the daughter-in-law o' Sir Hector Maclean."

Rinalda's mouth fell open, revealing a complete lack of teeth, real or false. Then she peered through the shadows, blue eyes sharp as a falcon's. "Is it true, lassie?"

Too shocked to speak, Fiona nodded. *Mon Dieu,* how had Lachlan learned her true identity? And now that he knew, what would he do to her? An icy wave of dread washed over her; she clenched her teeth to keep them from chattering.

Rinalda limped closer, minutely appraising Fiona's face. "I heard tell that Sir Hector's son married a Jacobite lass from the mainland, from roundabout Loch Linnhe. Adopted daughter o' Ian and Deirdre Fraser. Dinna tell me that would be ye, now."

"Oui," Fiona managed to choke out. " 'Tis true."

Lachlan arched a bitterly sardonic brow. "Ah, the truth. We canna escape it, aye?" His taut bearing relaxed a bit; then he ran a large, reassuring hand down the old wise woman's arm. " 'Tis all right, Rinalda. I dinna care who she is. Tell her the truth about Catriona's death."

Rinalda scowled crossly. "Och, ye'll be the death o' me, laddie—ye and your proud, stubborn heart. Canna ye tell her yourself? I've told ye forty times—"

"She wilna believe me." Lachlan's silvery eyes took on a mocking glint. In the flickering, black-and-gold light he resembled a cruel and tortured demon. "She thinks all men are lyin' dogs—"

"Humph. And so they are." Rinalda swayed forward and caught the arm of the wing chair, then leaned

down until her withered face hovered a few inches from Fiona's tear-streaked cheeks. "This lad o' mine's a prime rascal, lassie, and I'll no' tell ye otherwise. But if ye're in love wi' the mon, ye must ken the truth aboot him, aye?"

Fiona began to protest that she most certainly did *not* love Lachlan Maclean. Rinalda pressed a dry, leathery finger to her lips and muttered, "Hush, lass. I ken your pure heart, and I ken who ye are. Your soul's too old and wise to believe fiddle-faddle from the likes o' Duncan Campbell." She perched her scrawny haunch on the arm of the chair and gazed at Lachlan with proud, admiring eyes. "Lachlan's a fine mon, is he no'? Handsome, brazen, strong—"

"Och, haud yer wheest." To Fiona's astonishment, Lachlan actually blushed. Catching her startled gaze, he drew himself up to his full six-foot, four-inch height and glared down his knife-straight nose—the very image of the imperious Highland laird.

"All right, all right. Now listen to me, lass." Rinalda grasped Fiona's wrist with surprising strength. "I ken ye've heard a pack o' rumors and Duncan Campbell's wild tale, but the truth is this. Catriona died tryin' to slip a bairn."

Fiona's brow wrinkled. "Slip a bairn?"

"An abortion, lass. An abortion gone wrong." Rinalda shook her grizzled head; the long lappets on her nightcap slapped back and forth like hounds' ears. "She was carryin' Lachlan's child—or at least she said 'twas his." The old crone cast her employer a keen, assessing glance. "While he was near death and stark out o' his mind after Culloden, she took her chance and decided to be rid of it."

A cold, appalled horror uncoiled in Fiona's belly,

then slithered its way through her veins. She crossed herself. "It . . . it wasn't you who did—"

"Nay, lass. She went to some upstart on the other side o' the Isle. They called me in when it all went wrong. They'd used a needle, and the blood—"

Catching sight of Lachlan's tense, ashen face, Fiona said, "Please . . . that's enough. I understand what you mean."

Rinalda patted Fiona's arm, then stood and hobbled toward the door. "Good. Then I'm back to wee Hugh and bed 'til the sun's up. Now ye ken the truth, lass." She paused on the threshold, wrapped her shawl about her shoulders, then pinned Fiona with a shrewd gaze. "Or at least part of it." Then, fast as mist in the morning sun, she disappeared.

Fiona gaped at the empty doorway. Her mind swirled with a thousand conflicting emotions, yet she felt strangely numb, as if her body had sunken into cold, stiff paralysis. She swallowed hard, then glanced at Lachlan. A day's growth of stubble covered his tanned cheeks, lines of exhaustion creased the corners of his eyes, and he stared down into the crackling fire with the remote expression of a man who had withdrawn forever from the betrayals of the heart.

"Lachlan?" *Mon Dieu,* what could she say? Where should she begin? She cleared her throat. "Lachlan, I . . . I was coming to tell you. Maire died an hour ago. She went in her sleep, and there was no pain."

"I ken," he snapped. "Rinalda told me when I fetched her."

"What . . . what about Hugh?"

Lachlan made a quick, aggravated sound. "Dinna worry yourself. He'll always have me protection and as fine a home as I can give." Silence loomed between them—tense, hopeless, insurmountable. Lachlan began to turn away.

"I'm sorry about Catriona," she blurted, desperate to keep him from going.

His head whipped up, and his frigid gaze seared across her face. Then, deep within the frosty gray of his eyes, she caught a blaze of pure grief, like torch fire gleaming beneath ice.

Her heart gave a long, agonized contraction. Oh, she was a fool to have believed she could find love in the warmth and strength of Lachlan's arms, a fool to believe that she could escape the loneliness of her existence by coming to Scotland. She pressed a hand to her ribs, then bent, trying to dull the pain clawing its way through her gut. But she had found love: she loved this stormy, enigmatic Highlander. She loved him even though he still loved his dead wife.

"Save the apologies, madam." Lachlan's harsh voice cut the steely tension.

Fiona started up, then clutched at the chair as her knees threatened to buckle. Now she must face it; now she must tell him why she had come. Oh, *mon Dieu*, would he understand, or would he turn from her in disgust? She drew a quavering breath. "I . . . I am sorry, though. I never wanted to lie to you—"

"Indeed. I thought 'twas only men who lied."

"There's no need to take that snappish tone with me, monsieur." She raised her chin and attempted to smooth her face into tranquillity. Lachlan clearly apprehended her struggle, and his frosty gaze thawed just a bit.

"Dinna call me monsieur," he growled, *r*'s rolling like distant thunder. He sauntered toward her, then nonchalantly folded his arms across his chest. She watched in helpless fascination as his biceps bulged.

His soft muslin shirt lay open at the throat, and she couldn't seem to drag her gaze from the dusting of dark, tantalizing curls on his chest.

"What should I call you?" she retorted, trying to muster a tone of tart asperity.

He looked down at her, face utterly impassive. "Weel, *mo cridhe* seems to be out o' the question."

She smiled wanly, unsure if he was furious, teasing, or completely uninterested. When he didn't speak, she said, "Do you want to know why I came to Castle Taigh?"

A mask of bland politeness slipped over his features, but his eyes blazed like shooting stars. "Och, I already ken that. Ye came back to use me, to toss me an empty title like ye'd toss a dog a bone, then sink your claws into whatever money ye could before sailin' back to France."

She felt the color drain from her cheeks. How had he managed to put such a vile intent to what had been a well-meant, if not particularly forthright, endeavor? Her eyes devoured his handsome face, so wild-looking with that dark shadow of beard. How should she answer him? She pursed her lips and gathered her courage.

"That is a lie, monsieur. Sir Hector's widow and I came here to help you. Whether you wish it or not, you are now the rightful, hereditary chieftain of Clan Maclean. I had hoped to be the first to tell you such good news, but it seems someone has beaten me to it. Shall I guess who?"

He lowered his face until their lips were a finger's breadth away. She felt the manly heat of his body, heard the icy rage in his voice. "Ye've no need to guess, witch. Ye've the second sight, aye?"

Oui, she didn't need to guess. She didn't know the why, but she certainly knew the who. "It was Sorcha."

He spun on one booted heel, then stalked to the hearth, leaned both hands on the paneled surround and hung his head between them.

She held out a hand. "Lachlan, I don't understand. I thought you'd be happy to hear that you're chieftain—"

"Happy!" He whirled, cheeks livid, eyes blazing. "What good is a useless title when I dinna have the means to help me fellow clansmen? What good is bein' chief at all, when half me people have been slaughtered or sent across the sea forever?"

She stepped back, startled by the raw agony in his harsh voice. They stood in silence for several long moments, the only sound the soft popping of the fire. Outside the tall windows, the sky had lightened to a dull, pearly gray, and she shivered, suddenly cold and disgusted with her naive assumption that merely by telling Lachlan that he was clan chieftain, she could heal the scars he bore.

The chill dawn light shone on the carved-oak screen that stood behind the refectory table, and once again, she felt her gaze being drawn upward. The dead animals stared silently down at them as if in judgment. She bit her lip, desperate to hold back tears, and counted. There was the deer, stag, bear, fox, wolf, boar—

Her heart gave a startled leap; then she walked toward Lachlan, hand outstretched, eyes level and calm. At last she knew how she could help him.

Nineteen

"What's the most important thing in the world to you right now?" Fiona gazed up into Lachlan's tense face.

He slanted a scathing glance down his blade-straight nose. "Ye mean aside from tannin' your arse and sendin' ye back to France?"

"You're not at all witty, monsieur."

"Aye, weel. I'm funnier in Gaelic." The corners of his mouth twitched.

She folded her arms across her chest, leaned her chin on one finger, then gazed in mock speculation at the gallery of animal heads. "I'm a woman who prides herself on her devotion to logic over emotion, monsieur, and if I were to deduce anything, I would say that you would do just about anything to win back Taigh Samhraidh, secure the well-being of your clansmen, and win the forgiveness of your brothers in the Colonies." She arched a brow. "Would that be correct, monsieur?"

Lachlan glared as though he would happily throttle her with his bare hands. "That's none o' your business—"

"Ah, but it is. That's why I'm here. Sir Hector carried a great burden of guilt—"

"As weel he should."

"—until the day he died. On his deathbed, he alluded to some troubling mystery about you. I assume he meant whether or not you had betrayed your clan."

Lachlan ran a stiff hand over his face. "It seems ye've made up your mind on that score." He dropped both hands to his sides, then held them palms up in an eloquent shrug. "So why are we standin' here discussin' it?"

She tilted her head and studied the granite angle of his jaw. "Frankly, monsieur, that's the least of my worries right now. My first—and it should be yours as well—is that Duncan Campbell is about to have you arrested." She grasped his forearm. "Quick, what is the one thing that could stop him?"

"Money, of course. But that's the one thing I havena got."

"Ah, but you will—*if* you agree to help me. As they say in France, *Une main lave l'autre.* One hand washes the other."

He stared down at her as if she suddenly had metamorphosed into a fascinating and rather distasteful insect. "Aye?"

"Sir Hector Maclean hid a map somewhere in this castle just before the Rising. You remember that time, monsieur? He came here on one last visit to try to convince you to fight for Bonnie Prince Charlie. He also came to hide an item of great value, as surety against the future in case the Jacobites didn't prevail. He knew he would need money after all was said and done, and Mull was the safest place he could think of to hide a treasure. *C'est vrai.* You know what I'm talking about, don't you?"

Lachlan's face grew as austere as the North Sea. "And if I do?" He eyed her warily.

"Then you'll know I'm telling you the truth. The

map Sir Hector hid leads to a treasure as valuable for its symbolic meaning as for its actual worth." Lachlan's blazing eyes riveted on hers, and she flashed a smile of triumph. "Care to guess what I mean?"

Sudden, stunning knowledge rippled across his aristocratic features; he expelled his breath in a long, slow exhalation. He paced forward with the predatory grace of a jungle cat, then towered over her, blocking the pale dawn light. "How do ye ken all this? How can ye ken such a secret?"

"Never mind." Fiona lowered her gaze and edged sideways, refusing to meet his gaze. "Please just trust me."

Lachlan grasped her arm and dragged her against his chest. "Trust ye? Trust *ye,* who believe I'm a traitor and a murderer?" His voice had gone soft as velvet, but she caught the steely rage beneath his tone. Frightened by the intensity of his silver gaze, she jerked back. His closed his hands around her shoulders, then jerked her closer.

"Do ye change so quick, then, *mo cridhe?* From loving me to fearing me, just like that?" He snapped his fingers, and his whisper burned like acid, scalding her ears, her brain, her heart. "Why should I trust yet another woman who's lied to me, who's used me, who doesna care if I betrayed me own flesh, as long as it doesna stand in her way?" He inhaled sharply, then grasped her face between his hands. "Och, ye're a credit to your sex, madam. In truth, if I were half the Bluebeard ye think me, I'd lock ye in me dungeon right along with Catriona, for sure and ye're birds of a feather."

Suddenly, the tempo of his breathing changed— grew slow, ragged and unmistakable in its meaning. His feverish fingers crawled across her cheekbones, then pressed hard, harder, as if he meant to crush all lies from her skull. Fiona squirmed, heart thundering. "No ye don't," he murmured, lowering his lips to hers. "I'll let ye go when I'm damn good and ready." He kissed her, violently thrusting his tongue between her parted lips and grinding his mouth against hers until she tasted blood.

She squealed and staggered back, hand pressed to her lip. "What's wrong with you? Are you mad?"

"Aye, mad I am, *mo cridhe*. Mad enough to have believed ye could revive a dead heart."

She scowled. "Listen, it's getting lighter. We don't have time to stand here and argue, not if you plan to stay out of prison. Now do you want Sir Hector's map or not?"

He languidly scrutinized her heaving bosom. "Ye seem to be mighty eager to give me somethin' so valuable, lass." The skin around his eyes crinkled mockingly. "Why do I have the feeling there's a Part Two to this offer o' yours? The part where one hand washes the other?"

She sighed. "Of course there is, monsieur. 'Tis only logical. We cannot find the treasure without each other. Sir Hector said the map is in Gael—" She halted, then hurried on. "I need you, but you need my help as well—and Maeve's. Only I know where the map is hidden, and as Sir Hector's widow, Maeve has the power to establish you as the rightful clan chieftain. The clan will listen to her, and she's a friend to the Earl of Bute, who I believe is former prime minister of the realm. He can smooth any difficulties with the king, I'm sure. But without her official sanction, you'll remain as you are now—a brooding outcast with dreadful rumors swirling about you. So it's only fair that in return for helping you regain your fortune, your position, and the forgiveness and approbation of your kin and brothers, my mother-in-law and I should get a small stipend. Just enough to live in comfort in Paris."

His teasing expression vanished. "A small stipend? Why should I believe that? How do I ken ye wilna bleed me dry—or worse, stay on here like a pair o' leeches?"

Vicious pain stabbed at Fiona's heart, and her calm expression crumbled. She dropped her gaze from Lachlan's cruel, mocking face, then stared down at her shoes. How could he hate her so much? *C'est vrai*, she had been stupid enough to doubt him and foolish enough to show it, but surely, *surely* he knew that she loved him—and oh, *mon Dieu*, that she would love him forever.

She swallowed, then raised her chin. "We will not bleed you dry, monsieur. I've already decided that upon our return to France, *ma mère* and I will enter a convent."

Lachlan threw back his head and roared with laughter. "Och, lassie, ye'll be the death o' me. Madam Maclean in a convent I'd believe—but *ye!*" He actually bent and slapped his knee, laughing uproariously all the while.

"I'm glad to be such a source of amusement to you, monsieur."

His arm snaked out and hooked around her waist. "Och, lass. A convent is for saints and biddies, no' for a fey, passionate wee changeling like ye. Better ye warm a mon's bed than sing psalms, aye?" His eyes glittered like wicked elfin jewels.

She eyed him coolly, then smoothed back an errant curl. "Whatever you say, monsieur. Now, will you help me or not?"

His boldly seductive gaze settled on her lips. "I'd

have to have some sort o' token o' your good faith—such as it is."

"If you think I'm going to lay with you again, *monsieur,* you're very much mistaken."

He arched a sardonic brow. "Who said anythin' about beddin' ye? Och, such lascivious thoughts from a future nun. *Tsk, tsk.*" She flushed, and he stepped back, clearly pleased that he had flustered her. He nonchalantly adjusted the ripped collar of his shirt, then flicked invisible dust from his sleeve. "I had in mind somethin' more along the lines o' your word o' honor. If ye possess such a thing."

"I've had just about enough of this, monsieur. If you want a gesture of good faith, I'll be happy to give you one." She appraised him coolly. "I know how you can be rid of Sorcha's child—"

"Shut up." Lachlan's brows slammed together, and he shot forward, hand raised.

"Lachlan, I—"

"Dinna say another word." He halted awkwardly, as if an unseen fist had knocked him back. "Ye just heard how me only child died!" he bellowed. "At the foul hands o' an abortionist and me own vicious wife. Have ye no idea how much I've longed for a bairn, for an heir? Sorcha may no' be a fine lady like ye, but she'll no' have reason to kill me child!"

Bitter jealousy slammed its fist into Fiona's belly. "You . . . you cannot mean that you love her," she gasped, eyes scanning his face

"Nay. Nay, I dinna." He raked a hand through his hair, silver eyes fierce with anguish. "I've only loved—*truly* loved—one woman in me life. And she broke me heart."

Hopeless, aching tears clogged Fiona's throat. She

clenched her eyes tight, then swallowed, hard. "Catriona."

"Nay, no' Catriona."

Lachlan's hoarse voice rippled through the silent hall like a stone tossed into a pond. For one endless moment, Fiona stood, frozen to the flagstones. Then she spun, dashed across the great hall, yanked open a sideboard drawer and pulled out a long carving knife.

Lachlan paled, then strode forward, hand outstretched. "Give me the knife, lass."

She tugged one of the carved dining chairs directly under the grim row of animal heads. Lachlan lunged at her, but she dodged, then gathered her skirts and leaped onto the chair's frayed seat. She raised the knife over her head.

Lachlan spat an oath. "Fiona, no!"

She stretched as high as she could; the chair wobbled on the uneven stones. "Damn," she muttered, "I can't reach." She glanced over her shoulder. Clearly relieved that she hadn't stabbed herself, or him, Lachlan stood with muscular arms folded, glaring at her with mingled fury, exasperation and puzzlement. Stifling the last of her tears, she mustered her most beguiling smile. "Lachlan, *mon cher,* can you get it for me?"

He stepped forward, grasped her about the waist, then lifted her over his shoulder like a bag of potatoes. "Dinna '*mon cher*' me, lassie. Save your charm for the nuns in Paris." He dropped her roughly to her feet. "Now what's this—"

"*Mon Dieu,* I've been trying to tell you. I just thought it would be faster to show you." She smoothed her skirts, took a calming breath, then held out the knife, hand flat, palm up. "Take this, climb up on that chair and slit open the boar's throat."

"Are ye mad? I thought ye loved animals. Why do ye want to slit a dead boar's throat?"

Silently, she entreated St. Jerome for patience. "Because, monsieur, that's where Sir Hector hid his map."

Twenty

The golden light of dawn glittered through the crystalline air and sparkled on the new-fallen snow until the endless white expanse resembled a field of powdered diamonds. The sky overhead was pale, delicate blue, and in the distance beyond the snow-capped cliffs, a glazing of rose melted across the still, sapphire sea.

Fiona gasped for breath. The frigid air—so cold it was nearly brittle—stung her nose and brought tears to her eyes. "Lachlan, please, can't we slow down?"

She darted a gaze at her employer's stern face. A few stray snowflakes clung to his long black lashes, and the icy air and the exertion of plowing through knee-deep snow had flushed his high cheekbones a healthy red. His chestnut hair was loose and streamed down the back of his greatcoat, and gold-shot strands lifted here and there in the fitful breeze. His eyes were fixed straight ahead, and a muscle twitched at the corner of his adamantine jaw.

He shot her a brooding glance. "Nay, lass. Ye want to get there in time, aye?" His features didn't relax from their austere mold, but his gray eyes warmed and spoke to her with a quiet intimacy that was nearly deafening.

She caught her shawl tighter under her chin, then

floundered on through the drifts. Tossing her a pitying glance, Lachlan stepped in front of her to pack down the snow and break her way. They headed west in silence across the windswept fields, toward the cluster of crofts where most of the Taigh Samhraidh tenants resided. Fiona kept her gaze riveted on the small of Lachlan's back, alternately admiring his long legs and easy stride and worrying what they would find when they reached the blacksmith's cottage. What if Sir Hector's information was wrong?

Lachlan certainly hadn't been open to her assertions that he had not fathered Sorcha's bairn. *C'est vrai,* he hated to admit that his mistress might find another man desirable—and that man a blacksmith, no less! With a wry smile, she swiped a mittened hand across her streaming nose, then floundered forward. Men.

"Fier et têtu, chacun," she murmured. Proud and stubborn, every one.

"What's that, lass?"

"Nothing," she called, biting back a breathless giggle.

Lachlan stopped and turned, then pinned her with a mock-stern gaze. "I do speak French, ye ken."

Thoroughly grateful for the chance to rest, Fiona pressed a hand to her ribs and bent forward, panting. *"Oui,* monsieur. But not well."

Lachlan made a low Scottish noise that sounded suspiciously like an insult, then turned and slogged on, tall leather boots squeaking in the sun-dazzled snow. Fiona straightened. "Lachlan, please stop. I-I can't go another foot. 'Tis too c-cold. I can't c-catch my breath."

Glancing past Lachlan's wide shoulders, she saw that they had almost reached the tiny village of Taigh Samhraidh. She slowed her breathing and eyed the low, gray-stone crofts, which were barely visible above the drifts of snow except for a smudge of smoke drifting from each squat chimney. From what she could tell, the dwellings were in tolerable repair. Obviously, her employer had found the means to ensure that these tenants, at least, were warm and safe.

Lachlan stopped and turned. His wide, expressive mouth twitched up at the corners; then he adopted a disapproving scowl and strode toward her. His stern eyes blazed with devilry, and a frisson of fear shot down her spine. "Lachlan?" she said warily. "W-what are you doing—"

With the lithe swiftness of a hunter, he bent, clasped her beneath shoulders and knees, then swept her up into his arms. She flailed wildly, clutched the iron-hard curve of his neck, then squealed in his ear. Lachlan grimaced and jerked his head to the side.

"Wheest, lass," he growled. "Ye'll be wakin' the dead wi' such screamin'—and then what will happen to our big surprise?"

"Put me down! I can walk."

He snorted and strode forward, his long, powerful legs making quick work of the drifting snow. "That's no' what ye said a moment ago. And I've aboot had enough o' your fashin'." He slanted her a stern glance; she noticed that snowflakes had melted on his long lashes and clung there like tiny, glistening moonstones.

She went limp against him, suddenly feeling light and helpless and giddily feminine. Good St. Genevieve, what a man! No matter what she threw at him, he tossed it right back. He was fearless and strong, seductive and sensuous, wise and proud.

He caught her bedazzled gaze, and his eyes warmed, then crinkled at the corners. "Shut ye up for once, didn't I?"

Her heart melted; her bones melted; her reason
melted, like a crystal of snow beneath the sun's blazing
glory. She managed a tremulous smile, then nestled
against his broad, warm chest. His wind-tossed hair
brushed her cheek, and she inhaled, then curled her
frozen toes. He smelled delicious, this kind, stubborn,
exasperating and honest man; all musk and leather and
tobacco, and that spicy, indefinable male scent that
was all his own.

"I'm sorry I ever doubted you," she murmured.
"Can't we work together to make things right?"

"Aye, weel. We'll see aboot that. I'm makin' ye no
promises."

They reached a sturdy dwelling in the midst of the
sparse village. Lachlan assessed it, then nonchalantly
set her down in the snow. No footprints led to or away
from the rough oak door; clearly, whoever slept within
had been there all night. He grasped the wooden door
handle, then set his shoulder to the door.

"Wait," Fiona protested. "Aren't you going to
knock?"

Lachlan shot her a quelling glance, then heaved
against the sturdy oak portal. It flung inward, then
banged against the inside wall. An elderly, pinch-faced
little woman stood frozen by the hearth, jaw agape,
eyes wide, a withered hand clutching a wooden spoon.
One glance at Lachlan spurred her to life, and she
threw down the spoon and darted forward. Lachlan
pivoted and strode toward a narrow, twisting staircase
that led to the upper loft.

Catching sight of Lachlan's grim expression, the old
woman shrieked, "Och, nay, milord, dinna go up there,
I beg ye." She grasped his powerful shoulder, dug her
clawlike fingers in his greatcoat, then clung like a
dried-up thistle. "Please, dinna!"

A thump sounded overhead. Lachlan's booted foot reached the rickety wooden stairway; then he pelted up. The old woman fell back, weeping and wailing. Fiona brushed past her, then bustled up the stair behind Lachlan. A shout went up over her head; then she heard a woman's shriek.

Fiona popped up into the loft, then skidded to a halt. Light trickled in from one grimy window, the slanted ceiling made it nearly impossible to stand, and a rough wooden bedstead filled the icy chamber. On the bed knelt Sorcha, stark naked except for a tattered patchwork quilt clutched to her breasts. Her long black hair was snarled, her dark eyes were cloudy with sleep, and her jaw hung nearly to her collarbone. Crouched beside her was a brawny, fair-skinned young man with blond hair so pale it was nearly white. The blacksmith, Fiona presumed.

Lachlan towered over the bed, bent to avoid the low ceiling, then grabbed the smith's bulging bicep and yanked him from beneath the quilt. Fiona blushed and dropped her gaze. Sorcha wasn't the only one as naked as the cold, hard truth. Taking a deep breath, she darted a peek at the smith's privates, then stifled a giggle. *Mon Dieu,* and the cold truth wasn't the only thing that was hard!

"L-Lachlan, let me explain," Sorcha gasped. " 'Tis all a mistake—" Her voice rose shrilly as Lachlan shoved the smith back onto the bed.

"Cover yourself," Lachlan said, voice low and velvet-soft. Fiona shrank from the steely menace in his tone. Sorcha had no such qualms. She flung herself across the bed and latched on to Lachlan's shoulder.

"Lachlan, please—"

He peeled away her fingers one at a time, then stepped back and glared down his aristocratic nose.

With an expression of vaguely disgusted amusement, he turned to the cowering smith. "I ask ye only one thing, Murdo. Do ye ken that Sorcha is carryin'?"

Murdo's prominent Adam's apple bobbed; he ducked his head, and his milk-white skin went scarlet. "Aye, milord. B-but how did ye ken? Sorcha told me no one had heard the news 'cept her *athair.*"

Lachlan folded his arms across his chest and continued to glare like an autocratic schoolmaster. "And I take it ye sired the bairn?"

Murdo looked confused, then eagerly nodded his head. "Och, aye, milord. Sure and I am the *athair.* Sorcha said—"

Sorcha shrieked and flew at poor Murdo, teeth bared, claws drawn. "Ye great, daft sod! Ye've ruined everythin'—"

"Sweetin', what's amiss? Ye swore the bairn was mine. Ye promised ye'd lain wi' no other mon but me!" Murdo ducked and raised his arms to ward off his lover's blows. The quilt slipped off Sorcha's nude form, and Fiona got an eyeful of what Lachlan—and Murdo as well, it seemed—had been enjoying all fall.

Fiona's gaze flew to Lachlan's handsome face. To her astonishment, his lips twitched up at the corners. Quickly, his features smoothed into a stern mask, but she detected a ghost of amusement in his silvery eyes.

He flicked a wintry glance at his former mistress. "Tell me the truth, Sorcha. The bairn is Murdo's, isn't it?" He waved a hand at Murdo's head, and Fiona decided that the muscular young man might pass for an albino. "Ye might as weel make a clean breast o' it while ye've got the chance, for likely when the bairn is born, he'll have skin and hair as white as his father's. What will ye do then?"

Sorcha snatched up the quilt and covered herself. Murdo's puzzled frown melted into halting comprehension. He poked a finger into his lover's shoulder. " 'Ere, now. What's this? Were ye tryin' to pass the bairn off as Maclean's?"

"Oh, shut up!" Sorcha shrieked.

Lachlan tossed Fiona a quick wink, then folded his arms and gazed speculatively into the middle distance beyond Sorcha's tangled hair. "Madam, ye ken I'm a mon who prides himself on his devotion to logic over emotion, and if I were to deduce anything, I'd say that your father put ye up to this. Angus despises me. Doubtless he thought it a rare joke to trick me into rearin' a smithy's bastard." He arched a brow. "Would that be correct?"

Sorcha jumped up, yanked the quilt from the bed and wrapped it around her curvaceous form. Murdo squawked and scrambled to cover his goose-pimpled nakedness. "Aye, ye're right, ye bloody, suspicious, pryin' bastard," Sorcha hissed. "Me da told me to lie to ye. He wanted to see me weel set up in the castle, no' bogged down in a sty like this, scrubbin' me clothes in the burn and livin' on tatties and porritch."

"Oy, that's enough, ye grumplin' fishwife!" Murdo bolted up, white cheeks flushed, green eyes flashing. "Ye didna think yourself so fine when ye were pantin' to bed me." He lunged and caught Sorcha by the hair, giving Fiona a startling display of rounded white buttocks and dangling red ballocks. "I'll no' stand for this. I'll no' be made a cuckhold—"

Lachlan grasped the smith's bulky shoulder and spun him around. "Haud yer wheest, Murdo. All lassies are daft when they're wi' child. It doesna mean they dinna care for ye." He tossed the smith a between-us-men wink. "Sorcha's just been addled by her father's sour spirit. But ye'll no' let a bandy-legged goat like Angus Beattie keep ye from true love, now will ye." It was a statement, not a question.

Murdo hung his head. "Nay. But I dinna like this lyin'—"

"Nor do I," Lachlan cut in. "But 'tis a husband's job to steer his wife on the right course, aye?"

The smith's head shot up. "Ye mean ye'll consent to me weddin' her? Ye dinna want her for yourself?"

"It'll be a sacrifice." Lachlan's face was as serious as a saint's. "But sure and ye've a better claim to her than I. Ye've a fine son comin', and he'll need his *athair's* name."

Sorcha pouted and flounced down on the bed. Lachlan reached in the pocket of his greatcoat, then tossed Murdo a silver coin. "Here. Me best wishes to ye on your impendin' nuptials." He elbowed the smith in the ribs. "One piece o' advice. Toss the old mon out, and dinna let Sorcha out o' your sight."

With a roguish smile, he turned and caught Fiona's elbow with strong, warm fingers. "This way, madam. I'll no' have ye gogglin' at Murdo's privates a moment longer. 'Tis likely ye're makin' comparisons, aye?"

Fiona smothered a smile and allowed Lachlan to escort her outside. His dazzling dimples never wavered, and his gray eyes sparkled like the morning sun.

After they had walked a few hundred yards beyond the huddle of crofts, she realized they weren't floundering back through the snow toward the castle, but were heading toward the sea cliffs. She stopped, panting. "Lachlan? This isn't the way back."

He gazed down at her with elaborate patience. "Ye said ye wanted help findin' Sir Hector's treasure. So, much against me better judgment, that's what I'm doin'."

"But the map said we would find the treasure under the stairs, not out here in the middle of nowhere. You read me the Gaelic yourself." She untied her shawl, flung open her cloak, undid the three horn buttons at the top of her bodice, then plunged her gloved hand between linen shift and whale-bone stay. With the clumsiness of frozen fingers, she caught hold of the folded piece of parchment on which Sir Hector had penned a rough map on a winter evening long ago. She tugged it out, unfolded it and flourished it under Lachlan's long nose.

"Th-there," she said, teeth chattering. "Look. It says *na staidhreachan.* 'Under the stairs.' " She pointed to a splotched, clumsily inked zigzag that could have been a staircase, a snake, or a row of pointed teeth. Floating incongruously above it was a winged creature with a forked tail and the head of either a horse or a pig. As Sir Hector had been no artist, Fiona could hardly tell which.

"Aye, *na staidhreachan* means stairs, but Sir Hector didna mean the stairs in Castle Taigh. He meant The Dragon's Stairs. That's why he drew that peculiar creature." Lachlan chuckled, then turned and strode toward the sea cliffs. "It looks more like a dog to me, but I'm sure he meant it to be a dragon."

Fiona dashed forward. Snow went over the top of her boot and slid like an icy tongue down her ankle. "What Dragon's Stairs? What are you talking about?"

Lachlan called back over his shoulder, "Better keep up, lass. Ye dinna want me to get to the treasure first. I might no' share."

Back at Murdo's cottage, Sorcha spat out a curse, then clawed her linen shift down over her snarled hair.

Murdo sprawled back on the ticking mattress, offering her a prime view of his engorged erection. " 'Ere, sweetin'. Come back to bed. I forgive ye." He waggled his narrow hips; his penis bobbed awkwardly. "Big Murdo wants ye, lass. Canna ye see? He's callin' ye—"

"Och, for Christ's sake, shut up!" Sorcha yanked on worsted wool stockings, then rammed her feet into heavy leather boots. "Ye'll get a tumble when I've paid back that arrogant, gray-eyed bastard and his mealy-mouthed cook, and no' a moment sooner."

Murdo closed his fist over his member. "Dinna be daft. Ye canna tangle wi' the laird and expect to get away—"

"I can do what I damn weel please." She wriggled into a rust-colored homespun skirt, then knotted the ties around her swollen belly. Och, only three months gone, and already puffed up like a guinea fowl! And for what? To birth a blacksmith's brat. "I'll remind ye that Lachlan Maclean's the laird no longer. Duncan Campbell is—"

She halted. Suddenly, a brilliant plan blossomed full-blown into her mind. She dashed to the grimy window, wiped a clean patch with her sleeve, then peered out. Lachlan and Fiona stood in the snow a hundred yards away, in the direction of the sea cliffs, studying a wee scrap of paper as intently as if it were the Holy Grail.

Och, what could be so fascinating about a piece of paper? Sorcha sat back on her heels and frowned. Her da had spent many a night eavesdropping on the French bitch and her crotchety old mother-in-law, and he had vowed that they were after some sort of fortune. Could the paper have something to do with that? Was it some sort of will, perhaps? Or a letter of credit? She had heard of such things; but she couldn't read, and she doubted she would recognize either one.

She gave a tiny shrug. What good was speculating? One fact was clear, and that was the reality she must act on: Duncan Campbell hated Lachlan, and he would love nothing more than to cut his proud, haughty rival down to size.

Elated energy surged through her; she wrapped a fringed shawl around her hair, then yanked her scarlet cloak from the bedpost. She would tell Duncan that Lachlan had fathered her child, and he would force Lachlan to marry her. Och, 'twas perfect! Duncan would see his enemy wed to a peasant, and she would be mistress of the castle. She would spend the rest of her life living in the lap of luxury, not cleaning up after the likes of Murdo.

She tossed her lover a baleful glance. He smiled hopefully and stroked his manhood. "Come, lass, show us some kindness."

Sorcha gave a snort, then took one last peek out the window. Lachlan had grasped the bitch's elbow and was hustling her through the snow toward the sea. As Fiona stumbled in a pillowy drift, Sorcha saw the curious scrap of paper fly unheeded from the pocket of her cloak, then land beneath a gorse bush. Curiosity goaded her, and instantly she decided to snatch up the scrap on her way to the castle. Perhaps Duncan Campbell would read it and tell her what it was. If it pointed to something valuable, well, that would give him all the more incentive to help her.

With a superior smile, she turned, then sailed to the stairway. "Best whack off, Murdo. Ye'll be beddin' me no more—for I *will* be Lachlan's wife."

Twenty-one

Lachlan cast an expert eye at the lowering clouds, then took Fiona's hand and gently tried to encourage her to increase her laggard pace. It had taken them an hour to reach the narrow path at the top of the sea cliffs, then skirt along the edge of the windswept fields in a wide, southeasterly arc that had brought them outside the walls of Castle Taigh. As they had trudged through the heavy snow, the morning sun had surrendered its glory to the darkness of low, leaden clouds. The wind had risen, and now it buffeted in from the pewter-colored sea, chopping whitecaps on the water and flinging spray halfway up the ice-rimed cliffs.

"Please hurry, lass," he said, scanning the grim castle walls for signs of life. "This blasted snow's made it too difficult to ride, so if Duncan has sent for the sheriff, likely he'll come around to our side of the Isle by sea. That means he'll be landin' below and comin' up the sea stairs. We canna take the risk o' him seein' us."

Fiona gave a theatrical sigh and increased her pace; he bit back a smile. Och, who said the French were soft? She had kept up with his long stride like a seasoned soldier. But that must be her Scottish blood.

A fierce blast of wind howled around the castle wall. It clawed Fiona's shawl from her head, then sailed it over the cliffs, where it floated down into the thundering water. Her dazzling Titian hair flew around her and momentarily blocked her line of sight. She clutched his arm, then stumbled against his chest.

"Mon Dieu," she gasped. "Th-that could have been one of us."

Lachlan tightened his arms around her. Och, she felt so fragile, like a wee, trapped bird whose heart raced beneath his fingers. He brushed his chin across the satiny crown of her hair, then stroked his hands down the curve of her spine and instinctively molded her to him. St. Ninian, what manner of fool was he, to ache for this beautiful enchantress despite her lies and schemes? He gave a rueful smile, then settled her hips tight against his manhood. Sure and he wasn't thinking with his brain just now, so 'twas no surprise that he should act the fool.

Fiona cleared her throat, then fixed him with a pointed violet gaze. "I didn't mean for you to rescue me so, ah . . . vehemently, monsieur."

Her voice was serene, with just a touch of irony. Lachlan's heart gave a painful contraction, and for a moment he allowed himself to drink in the sensual curve of her lower lip, the haunting length of her dark lashes, the tiny gold flecks in her amethyst eyes. Those eyes were like a tranquil, midsummer sea at twilight, shot through with indigo and the sun's last golden rays.

He set her away from him, then sketched a mock bow. "I beg your pardon, madam. Blame it on me impetuous Scottish blood."

Fiona arched a delicate brow. "Impetuous, monsieur? I'd have styled you as cool and watchful, rather like a skilled and cunning hunter."

He turned to study the icy stone stairs. Cool, was he? Och, if she only knew the half of it! Likely her proper Catholic sensibilities would succumb to the va-

pors if confronted with the scorching lasciviousness of
his thoughts. His manhood gave a longing throb. With
a rueful smile, he held out his hand. "Give me the
map, lass. This is the spot. Ye'll see from Sir Hector's
drawin' that he meant this particular stretch of coast,
where the castle promontory takes a bold outward jut."

Fiona rummaged around in the pocket of her cloak,
and Lachlan reflected that the promontory wasn't the
only Maclean possession taking a bold outward jut.
Surreptitiously, he rearranged his randy flesh, then
glanced up. Fiona's wind-reddened cheeks had gone
alarmingly pale. "What's wrong?" he asked.

She swayed, then gazed up into his eyes, shock evident in every line of her face. "The map," she whispered. "I-I can't find it."

"What?"

She flushed, then glanced around, violet eyes panicked. "I must have dropped it somewhere on the path.
I stumbled so many times, and the drifts—"

"Dropped it!" Lachlan bellowed. "Ye dropped the
one thing that will lead us to the Macleans' lost and
only treasure?" His accent thickened furiously, and she
blanched. He clenched his eyes shut, gritted his teeth
hard, then clamped an iron control over his thunderous
Scottish temper. He inhaled several long, slow breaths
that froze his nasal passages. His lips twitched at the
corners. The curse of the Macleans, that temper of
his—though likely Fiona would say his curse was
pride, or stubbornness. He opened his eyes and found
her staring up at him, looking for all the world like a
paralyzed rabbit cornered by a snarling wolf. His lips
curved; to his astonishment, he realized he was smiling. He gave himself a stern shake, then scowled.

Her chin trembled. "Lachlan, I'm so sorry. I don't
know how it happened—"

He pressed a finger to her lips. "Hush, lass. The treasure is in the sea cave beneath those stairs. I havena been in there for nigh onto twenty years, but it's no' that big. I'll just search 'til I find it, aye?"

"*You'll* search?"

"Surely ye dinna think I'm lettin' ye down those icy stairs?"

Fiona met his eyes. Even with her wild, flame-red hair billowing behind her in the gusting wind, she managed to look unruffled. "I dug the map out of that filthy old stuffed boar, I figured out what the treasure is, and *I'm* going to find it."

"Nay, lass. 'Tis dangerous. I'll no' let ye risk life and limb—"

"Why?"

Her question was calm and entirely logical, and it managed to irritate him beyond the bounds of all reason. He opened his mouth to thunder, *Because I said so, that's why!* At that instant, the wind dropped, and he heard the sound of voices drifting from the inland side of the castle. He scanned Fiona's face, but she didn't seem to have heard them. He clasped her elbow. "All right. But we'd best get down those steps before snow falls." Or before Duncan and the sheriff hunted him down like a wild animal. Or before he swept his bewitching housekeeper into his arms and made an utter fool of himself.

Quickly, he followed her through the powdery snow, his hand protectively on her seaward shoulder. Thank God the snow wasn't deep here, for the implacable wind had whisked it toward the castle, leaving only a dusting of white atop the cliffs. It gritted beneath their boots, then swirled away, leaving no trace of their passing.

At the top of the sea stairs, the first pelting ice crystals bit into his frozen cheeks. He hated this type of snow: sharp, stinging, like tiny demon teeth. It reminded him of Culloden and of all the misery that had transpired there. He caught Fiona's waist, then stepped around in front of her. "Let me go first, *mo cridhe*. These steps are wicked slick even in summer. If ye slip, I'll break your fall."

"What if you slip?"

He didn't register the question, only the startling fact that he had called her *mo cridhe*. His heart. Och, St. Ninian.

He started down the narrow stairs. "Walk like this," he directed, keeping his voice firm and calm. "Step sideways, one foot at a time, and lean into the cliff. 'Twill keep your balance away from the sea."

Inch by inch, foot by foot, they picked their way down the stairs toward the crashing water. Generations ago, each narrow step had been hewn into solid granite by an industrious Maclean laird nicknamed The Dragon. According to Lachlan's late grandfather, the Dragon had been too cheap to pay a toll to cross his neighbor's property. The road to Mull's harbor had long since fallen into Maclean hands, but The Dragon's sea stairs had proved invaluable, for nowhere else on the Macleans' rocky slice of coast could a man land a boat. Over the years, the sea stairs had allowed Lachlan's family to export crops, to travel with ease and swiftness, and to amass a fortune by smuggling Virginia tobacco, French brandy, Spanish amontillado, East Indian spices, and West Indian sugar beneath the doltish noses of British duty officers.

Glazed with ice as clear and brittle as glass, the black cliff glistened in the gray light. At the foot of the stairs, gray-green waves smashed on the jagged rocks, then churned back out to sea with a thunderous, sucking sound. Strands of rockweed, as long and brown as a dead woman's hair, swirled in the receding water. Lachlan stiffened. The undertow around these cliffs was lethal; over the years, more than a few of his kin and tenants had drowned after a careless misstep.

Suddenly, frigid spray leaped up and splattered Lachlan's cheek; he gasped in shock. Behind him, Fiona cried out. Then she slithered down the slick, sharp stairs and crashed into him. For a split second, he swayed at the edge of the steps; below, the churning green sea waited to drag them both down to a sure and awful death. Then he lunged toward the cliff. His shoulder struck Fiona and pinned her to the rock. He heard the air *whoosh* from her lungs, felt her arms clutch his neck.

He heard the crash and suck of the sea, heard the mournful whistle of the wind around the cliff, heard Fiona's ragged attempt to breathe. Muttering an oath, he got both feet under him on what he prayed was not glare ice, then started to ease into a standing position. Fiona clung to him as if she were drowning.

"You . . . you saved my life," she murmured, voice so low he barely could hear her. "Oh, *mon cher,* you saved my life."

Sudden, wild emotion surged through him. He couldn't speak, so he buried his nose in the warm, sweet curve of her neck. Desperately, he inhaled the scent of her, all fresh herbs and sun-warmed French fields. Her hair whipped across his cheek like fiery silk; then her lips slanted against his. With a low groan, he captured her mouth and kissed her with raw, hungry passion—passion sparked by peril, fanned by threat, fed by the heart flame of unquenchable love.

When he raised his head, wet snowflakes swirled about them, mantling Fiona's auburn curls with a lacy veil of white. She gazed up through lowered lashes, then melted against him. He was about to tell her he loved her, had always loved her, when she gasped, then struggled beneath him, eyes wide and startled.

She squirmed into a sitting position, back pressed into a crevasse, eyes staring at a point beyond his shoulder, off the edge of the cliff and forty feet above the crashing waves. Her cheeks went ashen, then flushed a feverish red.

"What is it, *mo cridhe?*" He caught her gloved hand, then chafed it. Och, she looked as if she had seen a ghost. "Are ye all right?"

Her eyes skittered to his face, and she swallowed hard. "We've got to get down to the treasure. Now."

"Nay, lass. 'Tis too dangerous. We're goin' back up." Nothing was worth the risk of losing her.

She scrambled to her feet and stared past him. Just for an instant, from the corner of his eye, he thought he saw something—a figure? a shadow?—in the swirling snow.

She raised her chin. *"Non,* monsieur. We're going down, before it's too late."

Lachlan considered throwing her over his shoulder like a sack of oats and lugging her up the stairs to safety, but her eyes held an urgency that barreled its way into his mind. Fiona was thoroughly practical; she wouldn't make such a headstrong demand unless there was an excellent reason behind it.

He cocked his head and studied her trembling lips. "What did ye see just then?"

"N-nothing, monsieur. 'Twas merely the wind—a trick of the snow."

With a rueful shake of the head, he turned and started down the icy steps. "As ye wish, madam. But perhaps there is a ghost on these cliffs after all."

A few minutes later, they reached the looming jumble of boulders at the edge of the sea. Ice covered every surface, frozen and refrozen until it resembled spun sugar. Icicles jutted like fangs from the jagged cliff, salt spray and snowflakes wet their cheeks, and the roar and wash of the waves was deafening. Lachlan beckoned Fiona forward; then they thunked along a plank boardwalk that stretched between the rocks and the base of the cliff. The walkway ended in a long oak ramp that was bolted to the cliff, then descended at a sharp angle over the rocks and into open water. At the end of the ramp, a rectangular wooden platform floated atop empty whisky barrels lashed together with leather straps. Moored to the float was a small shallop, sails furled to the mast.

" 'Tis low tide," Lachlan yelled. "That's why the boat ramp is so steep. As the tide comes in, 'twill rise 'til it's nearly level."

Fiona eyed the structure dubiously. "What happens in a storm?"

Lachlan lifted her down onto a tussock of rockweed; then they clambered over slippery stones and ducked beneath the ramp. "We're on the leeward side o' the Isle." He jutted his chin toward the smudged gray outline of the mainland. "The Sound of Mull is fairly protected, but even so, I have to replace the bloody thing aboot once a year."

Fiona wrinkled her nose. "Not very economical."

Lachlan caught her hand, and they edged around a towering rock, then stepped into a small, protected crevasse between two jutting flanks of the cliff. At once, the wind died, and the deafening roar of waves grew softer. Lachlan bent down, crawled under a rocky overhang, then pulled Fiona behind him.

"Welcome to The Dragon's Lair," he intoned.

Eyes wide, Fiona gazed around. Wavy, liquid light
filtered in through the narrow opening between the
rocks, then reflected off a broad pool that filled the
cave's far corner. Eons of water had worn away the
angular, grayish stone until the walls resembled an in-
verted staircase riddled with ledges and crevasses.
Water dripped rhythmically from the low, gray-rock
ceiling, and rough, wet gravel crunched beneath their
feet.

"Mon Dieu," she breathed, turning in a slow circle.
"I've never seen anything like it." She held out a
gloved hand; a droplet plopped on it. "It's almost
warm in here."

"We're far underground." Lachlan reached in his
pocket, then drew out a small tinderbox. "And that's
spring water, no' a tidal pool. 'Tis the same tempera-
ture year 'round." He opened the box, set it on a ledge,
and struck a flint to the fluff of tinder. When a spark
caught and flamed, he drew a stub of candle from his
pocket, then lit it and held it aloft. "Och, there are a
thousand wee crannies where Hector could have hidden the treasure. Where should we start?"

Fiona frowned—the same deep frown she had worn
when she held his hand on Culloden battlefield, seventeen years earlier. "We've got to hurry." She clenched
her eyes tight, then crossed herself. "St. Jude, hear our
prayer—"

"Who's St. Jude?"

"Patron saint of lost causes." She held up her hand.
"Hush. Wait." She tilted her head, then gazed at a spot
five feet above the pool as if listening to an unseen
voice. Suddenly the cave grew deathly cold; a chill
shot down Lachlan's spine.

"What is it?"

She flapped her hand at him, then grinned at the air

above the pool, bobbed a small curtsey and said, "Thank you, Sir Hector."

"What?"

She tossed him a triumphant smile. "I know where it is." Before he could question her over the logic and practicality of talking to thin air, she darted forward, snatched the candle from his hand, then approached the pool.

"Look how clear it is," she marveled, holding the candle over the water so its flickering light shone down through the crystalline depths. Small stones—gray flecked with black, brown spotted with rust, white shot with gray—glittered at the bottom of the pool like rough natural jewels. "And the water's not that deep."

She thrust the candle into his hand, stripped off her gloves, caught up her skirts, then splashed down into the water. It closed over her boots and surged up to her knee garters. *"Mon Dieu!"* she gasped.

"Are ye daft?" Lachlan bellowed. He jumped in, and a loud splash echoed off the dripping rock walls. The water was frigid, though still far warmer than the sea. He caught his breath, then reached for her.

She eluded his grasp, then waded forward, skirts slogging against the gleaming, light-dappled water. "Here it is!" She flashed him a joyous grin, then leaned forward and plunged her arm into the pool.

Her prize surged to the surface with a splash and a cascade of shimmering water. The guttering candle-light caught the water droplets, then refracted off a plate-sized clan badge of solid, gleaming gold. Glittering diamonds, rubies and emeralds studded the engraved motto, and two rampant lions with sparkling emerald eyes and roaring ruby mouths curved around the circular edges as if fearlessly stalking their prey.

"Virtue Mine Honor," Fiona said, reading his clan's

motto. She smiled demurely and held it out to him. "In my heart I've always known this should be yours, monsieur. The saying might not fit, but those stalking lions are the perfect match for your proud hunter's soul."

Lachlan shook his head, too thunderstruck to speak. Och, St. Ninian, he never truly had believed Fiona's wild tale of hidden treasure. If truth be known, he had thought her mad and in need of humoring. He had hoped, of course, but he had been sure his hopes were as crazy as she.

He ran a hand over his eyes and blocked out the glittering bauble. The golden badge had adorned the shoulder of every Maclean chieftain since the 1300s, but how could it ever be truly his? 'Twas too late for him to take his place as chieftain. Too much time had passed, and too many lies had caught him in a foul trap of his own wretched making.

"Mon Dieu, this must be worth thousands of pounds." Fiona tilted the badge toward the candlelight, appraising the heavy gold and flashing jewels with the shrewd air of a French shopkeeper. She glanced up and caught his eye. "But it's worth more than that to you, *n'est-ce pas?* Its value lies in the power it bestows."

Suddenly he heard the scrape of boots on rock. Something blocked the light streaming in from outside the cave; then Fiona paled. She screamed, "Lachlan, watch out!"

He spun. The water slowed his momentum and the candle lurched from his grasp, but for a split second he saw the brawny hulk of Duncan's henchman. Peter jumped into the water, hands raised, clutching a wooden club. There was a deafening splash; Lachlan lunged sideways. He heard a sickening, bone-crunching *thwack!,* and everything went black.

Twenty-two

Lachlan's unconscious body pitched forward and landed with a splash in the icy water. Still clutching the clan badge, Fiona shrieked and dove toward him as his head slipped beneath the surface. Lachlan's assailant slammed his boot into Lachlan's back, pinning him facedown at the bottom of the pool.

"No, you'll kill him!" Fiona lunged at the man, then plowed her shoulder into his stomach, knocking him off balance and eliciting a string of furious Cockney curses. Before she could regain her footing, the man's arms closed around her waist; he lifted her half out of the water, then shook her.

"The badge," he snarled. "Give it to us, bitch."

Fiona squirmed frantically, then smashed her heel into the man's shin. He grunted and dropped her into the freezing water. Fiona flung the badge at him, hitting him squarely in the chest. "Here, take it! It's not worth dying for!"

She plunged beneath the water, her hands closed around Lachlan's muscular arm, and she tugged upward, frantic to save him before he drowned. Lachlan's head broke the surface with a splash, his solid weight lolled against her, and she staggered, flailing for purchase on the slick stones.

Their attacker leaped onto a dry rock ledge, then ran

toward the mouth of the cave. He paused, once again blocking the light. "Ye moight's well leave 'im. 'E's out cold, and the tide's comin' in fast. A bird the loikes of ye'll never get a heavy bloke loike 'im up them icy stairs." He tucked the clan badge in his belt, and perverse triumph spread across his broad face. "The guvnor fancies ye to warm his cockles, and so do I." He sniggered nastily, then held out a filthy hand. "He wants me to save ye, ducks, and I will—if ye swear to be me special pet."

Rage—hot, glorious, strengthening rage—surged through Fiona's body. "Oh! *Vous êtes un cochon dégoûtant.* I'd sooner drown than lay with a pig like you—or with a rat like Duncan Campbell." She braced under Lachlan's weight, freed a hand, then thrust up her middle finger. "He's a thief and he can go to hell!"

Duncan's henchman glowered, then scrambled through the narrow cave entrance. "Suit yourself," he called over his shoulder, voice echoing through the watery gloom. Then he was gone.

All Fiona's righteous rage left her like a shot; she felt cold, hopeless, frightened and alone. "Holy Mary, Mother of God," she muttered, dragging Lachlan's unwieldy body toward the dry cave floor, "be with us now and in our hour of—"

" 'Ods ballocks! Are ye still natterin' to that popish virgin? Now there was an unlucky lass—havin' to birth and raise a bairn without any o' the merriment leadin' up to it."

Fiona gasped; then relief barreled through her. "Oh, *merci, mon Dieu!* I never thought I'd be so happy to hear from a dead person in my life." She swallowed, then glanced around the dank cave. "Sir Hector? Where are you?"

There was a splashing and churning at the far end of the pool. Then, like mist rising from the surface of the water, Sir Hector appeared. "Now, this is a fine kettle of fish," he grumbled, sounding not the least bit worried by her dire straits. "Where's your knight in shinin' armor now, lass?" He swirled toward her, then hovered with morbid curiosity a few feet above Lachlan's head. " 'Ods nigs, if I were a bettin' mon, I'd bet ye wish ye'd stayed in France and married the Comte du Maine right about now."

A blast of chill air wafted over Fiona's shivering flesh; she pulled Lachlan's body to dry land, then struggled to free him from his waterlogged greatcoat. "You are a betting man, or at least you were." She dropped her own sodden cloak to the gravel. "And I've told you forty times, the comte had syphilis and spots."

Sir Hector swarmed in front of her. "Now I suppose ye'll tell me ye'd rather marry for *love*"—his gruff voice bit sarcasm into the word—"than for money. 'Ods bodkins, what a nitwit. To think I wasted all that time teachin' ye Rousseau—"

"Hush!" The greatcoat peeled away, and Fiona eased Lachlan to the gravel floor. Then she spun, wet skirts slapping about her ankles, and cocked her ear toward the entrance to the cave. "The tide's coming in fast—I can hear it. Good St. Brendan, we're about to drown, and all you can do is complain that I didn't make a good philosopher!" She balled her hands into fists, then lunged forward and swiped at the ghost's vaporous form. "What's the matter with you!"

Sir Hector shrieked and darted back. "Are ye mad, lass? Ye canna touch a ghost."

"Why not?"

"Well, er . . ." Sir Hector looked perplexed, then swirled agitatedly about. "Och, tripe and ballocks! Are ye goin' to wake that strappin' haunch o' beef ye've bedded, or no'?"

"Shut up and I will." Fiona flung herself down beside Lachlan, then stroked his cold, wet cheek. His long lashes fluttered, and her heart leaped into her mouth. She heard a slapping noise, then stared frantically at the mouth of the cave. Had that been sea spray splashing between the rocks?

A picture of injured dignity, the ghost drew himself up, then huffed away to a granite ledge. "Weel." Sniff. "Before I shut up, I have one last thing to say—"

A wave boomed outside the cave, and pebbles rattled in the receding undertow. *"Mon Dieu,* we're going to drown!" she cried. "I'll be meeting you on your own terms soon enough. Can't it wait 'til then?"

Another wave thundered into the cliffs. Fiona glanced back at the ledge; the ghost was gone. "Where are you?" she wailed, desperately chafing Lachlan's icy hand.

No reply.

"Oh, St. Joseph, this is it." She crossed herself. Did it hurt to drown? *Mon Dieu,* why did every passage to a better existence cause pain? "Obviously, God is a Catholic," she muttered.

Then, as clearly as if he still perched on the cave's stone ledge, she heard Sir Hector's voice in her mind: *God's no' a Catholic, lass. He canna stand all that incense. Nor does He want ye bargin' around heaven just yet. His nerves are no' ready for that sharp tongue o' yours.*

"I'm not the only one around here with a sharp tongue," she snapped.

"Lass." Lachlan's eyes flicked open; then he coughed with great, hacking spasms. "Am I alive or am I dead?"

"Oh, *merci mon Dieu,* you're alive." Fiona's heart contracted; then she leaned forward and smoothed her fingers over the austere lines of his face. "I was so worried—"

Another waved crashed against the rocks, and sluggish white foam dripped over the bottom of the cave entrance. "Lachlan, get up." She scrambled to her feet. "The tide's coming in. If we don't get out of here this instant, we'll be trapped."

Lachlan's brows slammed together; then he struggled up and saw the swirl of foamy water. "Good St. Ninian." He reached the cave mouth with one long stride, looked out, then motioned her forward. "It's no' too late. The flank o' the cliff is protectin' us from most o' the waves." He leaned out and pointed. "We can wade across to that rock. It's no' that deep, but—"

"But?"

He turned, scowling fiercely. "For the water to have poured in here, back in the fold o' the cliff, it must already be coverin' the rocks on the other side."

She bit her lip. "I-I don't understand."

"Remember when we stepped off the boardwalk, then ducked under the boat ramp?"

"*Oui.*"

"Weel, our cut-through may already be under water. There's no way to tell 'til we've gotten around that big rock. Now take off your skirt."

"What? Are you mad?"

He grabbed her waist, spun her around, then began untying the sodden laces at her waist. "If ye're wearin' that and get caught by a wave, ye'll be sucked down in a heartbeat." The ties came away; then the garment dropped about her ankles, leaving her in her knee-length linen shift, shoes, stockings, garters and bodice. She stood there opening and closing her mouth like a hooked sturgeon.

Lachlan slanted her a wink, then tapped her jaw

closed. "Best close your mouth, *mo cridhe*. Ye dinna want water gettin' in."

A frigid current of air licked the back of Fiona's wet calves, then slipped beneath her shift to some very private spots. She wrapped her arms about her ribs. "But I c-can't be seen like th-this! It's n-not p-proper." St. Anthony, her teeth already were clacking like castanets. What would happen if she got drenched?

Lachlan's grim expression turned positively murderous. He caught her arm, then shoved her up to the mouth of the cave. "I'm sorry for your sensibilities, *mo cridhe,* but bein' seen in your shift is a hell o' a lot better than drownin'." He clapped a strong hand on the top of her head, then pushed her down. "Now get on your belly and crawl out o' here."

Fiona considered arguing, but at that moment a gigantic wave crashed over the rock that protected the cave, and icy seawater cascaded into the tide pool below them. Spray slapped her face, stinging her eyes and washing away the last of her modesty. Clenching her teeth, she squatted down, ducked under the rough, dripping rock, then crawled forward on hands and knees. Grit ground into her palms, knife-sharp pieces of rock tore her knees, and water seeped through the thin linen of her shift, chilling her to numbness. She could hear Lachlan crawling along behind her, muttering Gaelic curses, and she breathed a quick prayer for the dignity of a properly covered bottom.

Then she was out. She eased down onto a rounded rock, then gasped as icy water swirled halfway up her shins. Instantly, the rock wobbled, and she reeled forward, flailing like a madwoman, leather shoes scrabbling for purchase on the algae-covered stones.

"Go!" Lachlan ordered.

Fiona's feet went numb; she plunged forward, letting

momentum carry her toward the jagged rock that blocked their view of the boat ramp and sea stairs. She smashed into it, breaking fingernails and nearly knocking the breath from her lungs. Lachlan plowed into her, pinning her to the rough granite; then she felt him ease up to his full height and peer over the edge of the rock. He went utterly still and spat out a curse, then ran hands that were surprisingly warm down over her arms.

" 'Tis under water—the spot we need to cross."

Fiona felt a sob well up in her lungs. She bit her lip and ordered herself not to cry. "W-what are we going to do?"

Lachlan didn't answer right away, and after a moment she realized he was watching the movement of the waves, timing the flooding crash against the rocks, then the sucking drag as the water returned to sea. Suddenly he grabbed her waist and lifted her. "Put your feet on the rock, *mo cridhe*. Then let yourself down on the other side. There should be a ledge where ye can stand."

Fiona opened her mouth to protest, but he already had her halfway over the craggy outcrop. She scrabbled down the other side, granite tearing into her palms and buttocks, then teetered on a flat ledge covered in reddish brown rockweed that squeaked and popped as Lachlan lowered himself beside her. He wrapped his arms around her and caught her to the reassuring strength of his chest.

"Listen," he ordered, lips cold and wet against her ear. "Watch the waves. If ye dash forward when the water is almost at its ebb, ye should reach the boat ramp when it's as shallow as possible. Ye'll have to grasp the bottom o' the ramp, take a deep breath, duck under, then feel your way across to the other beam.

Duck under that, pop up, get your footin', then scramble up on the boardwalk. If ye time it right, another wave will flood in right then. Its force should push ye forward, out o' the water and up onto the walkway."

Fiona's eyes wouldn't blink; instead, they stared in fascinated horror at the waves. Each successive breaker slammed into the cliff with the force of a thunderclap; boiling white foam geysered fifteen feet into the snowy air; clinging fingers of rockweed trailed in the roiling surf; then everything sucked back out to sea with awesome force. She tried to swallow, but her throat had gone dry. Which would be worse? Being smashed onto the brutal rocks, or being dragged down by the freezing, inexorable current?

Lachlan lowered his head and stared into her eyes, every taut line of his expression burning with intensity. "I'll go first. Watch me. Do exactly what I do. I'll be there to pull ye out if anythin' happens."

"No, I—"

She heard the chattering, sluicing, dragging sound of the outgoing waves. Before she could stop him, Lachlan charged through the swirling surf toward the boat ramp. Awestruck, she watched his lithe, powerful form barreling through the water with astonishing grace. As he predicted, he reached the ramp when the water reached its lowest ebb. Quickly, he ducked under.

Fiona dug her fists into her heaving stomach and prayed with all her might. Surely he should be up by now. She couldn't see him. Something was wrong! Quick as thought, she glanced out to sea, where the next wall of water was heaving in, gathering power, rearing up in a frigid green wall of force. She clenched her eyes shut and tried to scream, but no sound came.

Then she saw him on the other side of the ramp,

lunging toward the boardwalk. He caught it with a large, tanned hand, then heaved up so the edge of the weathered planks caught him in the stomach. He flung one long leg onto the walkway just as a breaker slammed into the cliff. As he had predicted, its force shoved him to safety.

Instantly, he was on his feet, turning and calling to her. She clung to the craggy rock, paralyzed with cold and fear. Lachlan bellowed to catch her attention, cupping his hand to his dripping face and shouting, "Go! Now!" She watched the outgoing wave with fascinated horror, then realized it was at its ebb.

She couldn't do it; she couldn't! The current was too wild, the water too icy. She would be washed away, then sucked down to a watery grave.

Then she heard Sir Hector's voice. *God doesna want ye bargin' around heaven just yet. His nerves are no' ready for that sharp tongue o' yours.*

She raised her chin. Well. If she couldn't trust a ghost on the subject of death, whom could she trust? Taking a deep breath, she launched herself off the rock.

Her first impression was that her feet were leaden blocks of ice. Only leaden blocks couldn't hurt, and agonizing pain, like the slash of a thousand icy knives, tore up her calves. She staggered and slogged forward, flailing like a clumsy gosling trying to fly. Then she slammed into the solid wetness of the wooden boat ramp. Grabbing the splintery beam with both hands, she uttered a silent prayer, dragged in a lungful of air, then ducked beneath the churning seawater.

The cold hit her like a fist; instantly, the air *whooshed* from her lungs. Her body spasmed with shock. She couldn't think, couldn't move. She felt herself begin to gasp. She would drown. No! She couldn't drown. Not today.

Gathering all her strength, she clawed her way along the rough planks until she felt the solid heft of the second beam. Instinctively, she ducked beneath it, then shot up. She broke the surface with a rush, gasping with long, ragged, involuntary sobs. Frigid salty water sluiced down over her face, stinging her eyes, filling her mouth. Then Lachlan shouted her name.

She staggered forward. Jagged rocks cut her feet; she smashed her knee against a boulder and fell, jamming her wrist with agonizing force. Then, by some miracle, she reached the boardwalk. Lachlan's warm hands, iron-hard and sure, curved under her armpits, then hauled her, kicking and spluttering, to safety.

She collapsed onto the planks, shivering with great, wracking spasms. Lachlan dragged her to her feet. "Come on. We've got to get ye inside before ye freeze."

She wanted to choke, "Too late," but her chattering teeth wouldn't allow it. A glacial blast of air smashed into her; instantly, her linen shift froze to her skin. Then Lachlan scooped her up and cradled her to his chest as if she were a little girl. Hot tears scalded her cheeks, and her body went limp against him.

As Lachlan turned and dashed through the swirling snow, she thought she heard Sir Hector say, *Now there's a knight in shining armor.*

But perhaps it was only the wind.

Twenty-three

Fiona shivered and huddled close to the crackling kitchen fire, then tucked her gloriously dry skirt around her legs. *Mon Dieu,* would she ever be warm again? The roaring blaze and a cupful of brandy hadn't made a dent in the bitter chill that had burrowed into her bones, and for an instant she longed for the cloying, oppressive heat of Paris in August.

Fergus gave a pitying whine, then buried his grizzled head in her lap, as if to offer what warmth he could give.

"Merci, mon cher," she crooned, fondling the dog's silky ears.

Outside the tall kitchen windows, fat snowflakes pelted down, burying the dead herbs in the garden and topping the castle walls with a thick frosting of white. Dull gray clouds suffocated the sloping land, and the wind howled like a banshee through the empty courtyard. She snuggled closer to Fergus, then shivered once more. *Mon Dieu,* Lachlan must be made of iron to have gone out again in this weather.

She sighed, then rubbed the wolfhound's bony brow. At least Lachlan was wearing warm, dry clothes, thanks to Rinalda. The cunning old healer had hobbled to their aid the moment they had sneaked back into the castle through a long-forgotten smugglers' passageway that led from the castle walls to the cellar. With a no-nonsense air that must have served her well as Lachlan's nanny, Rinalda had ordered them to remain below stairs while she fetched dry clothes and ascertained the whereabouts of Duncan Campbell.

When she returned, Lachlan explained to both of them that he must leave the island at once. "This weather may keep the sheriff off for a few hours, but it won't keep him away forever. And I dinna fancy bein' tossed in the tollbooth on a charge o' stealin'—even if it *is* more or less the truth." He raked a hand through his ice-tangled hair, then tossed Fiona a wink.

Fiona ducked behind an oaken cask of ale to strip off her frozen clothes. "But how will you get away?"

"I'll sail."

She stopped toweling her hair, then popped up over the rim of the cask. "You'd risk that sea again? Are you mad?"

"I think we've already established that I am. May we move along now?" Lachlan yanked off his ice-covered boots, then slung them behind a rack of dusty wine bottles.

"Haud ye wheest, the pair o' ye." Rinalda hobbled across the packed dirt floor, then stood in the light of a lantern that hung from a low brick arch. Fiona noted that she was using the polished mahogany cane Lachlan had given her. "Squabblin' like six pups over a single teat, ye are—and all this after ye coulda drowned." She prodded Lachlan with the tip of her cane. "Now hurry out o' them wet things. Campbell will be ringin' for his dinner soon. That's your best chance to get out o' here unseen."

Fiona tugged thick woolen stockings up to her bluish knees. "Rinalda, be practical. Where will he go? What will he do?"

"Och, and to think a canny lass like ye—" Rinalda halted abruptly, then yanked a bottle of Burgundy from the rack. "I've been studyin' on it. When that schemin' Sorcha came to see Campbell a few hours ago, natterin' aboot a treasure map, I listened at the door and heard what was at stake." She turned, planted her withered fists on her hips, then glared into the shadows where Lachlan was changing clothes. " 'Tis time to make your stand, lad."

Lachlan snorted. "I would if ye'd give me time to button me breeks."

"Ye're chieftain now, but ye'll need two things if ye plan to take your rightful place and help the clan. Otherwise ye'll have nothin' but an empty title."

Fiona tied the laces of her leather stomacher. "The first is money."

"I ken that," Lachlan called testily. "That's what the badge is for, *if* I can get it back."

"The second is Taigh Samhraidh," Rinalda said.

Lachlan strode from the alcove, glowering and looking every inch the bloodthirsty Highland warrior. "Good St. Ninian, woman! Are ye daft? Campbell will never relinquish this place."

Rinalda slanted him a sly smile. "He may have to." She plunged a hand down her rust-wool bodice, then drew out a letter. "I lifted this from Campbell's room. 'Tis a letter from a London goldsmith—"

Lachlan snatched up the letter, scanned it, then read it again more slowly. The austere lines of his face melted into a dazzling smile. "Och, I canna believe it," he cried, tossing the letter into the air, then catching it with two deft fingers.

Fiona sailed around the corner of the cask. "What is it?"

Lachlan's eyes blazed like diamonds set in silver,

and hard, masculine dimples bracketed the corners of his mouth. " 'Tis a final notice from Campbell's sole creditor. It seems the bloody fool—Campbell, no' the creditor—had the brainstorm of consolidatin' his debts. Evidently he borrowed an enormous sum from this"—he glanced at the letter—"Silas Green, then paid off everyone he owed. Now Green is callin' in the note. He says if Campbell canna pay in a fortnight, he'll take the item Campbell used as collateral."

Fiona frowned. "Which is?"

Lachlan flashed her a smile that was positively wolfish. "Taigh Samhraidh."

Recalling the incredible scene that had unfolded in the moldering cellar, Fiona suppressed a wriggle of excitement, then jumped up and stood with her back to the fire. She longed to shout, to sing, to thank God, the saints and the Holy Mother, but she couldn't. There was still too much that could go wrong, that had gone wrong. She closed her eyes and forced herself to review their plan.

First, they had to steal back the clan badge without alerting Campbell to the fact that they hadn't succumbed to a watery grave. Fiona crossed herself, then whispered to Fergus, "But 'tis really not stealing, since the badge rightfully belongs to Lachlan." Unfortunately, they could hardly march up and snatch the badge from beneath Campbell's nose and, as yet, Lachlan had offered no alternative plan.

Then they had to cross the Sound of Mull and make their way to London, likely with the sheriff hot on their trail, bent on arresting Lachlan for thievery. Fiona pursed her lips and wondered if the sheriff would call what Campbell had ordered done to them a crime. Fergus whined.

"*Oui,* you're right," Fiona said. "The sheriff would never believe us."

Suddenly, worry and remorse swamped her, and she slumped down on the wooden settle. *Mon Dieu,* what was the use of making plans? She had ruined any final chance she had of winning Lachlan's love. Stubbornly, she had insisted on going with him to London so they could offer the badge to Silas Green in exchange for the mortgage on Taigh Samhraidh. Lachlan had blustered and paced beneath the cellar's low brick arches and refused point blank until she reminded him that Campbell had designs on her virtue. Then she had made a serious tactical error.

"Oh, Fergus." She gazed sadly at the dog. "Sir Hector is right about my sharp tongue. And where were my wits?"

Thoughtlessly, she had insisted that she and Maeve had a vested financial interest in the clan badge and therefore couldn't let it out of their sight. " 'Tis our only surety against the future," she had told Lachlan in her practical French shopkeeper's voice. "If Monsieur Green cooperates, you'll get Taigh Samhraidh, but what will Maeve and I get?"

For a long, tense moment, Lachlan's silver eyes blazed into hers; then he dropped into a mocking bow. "Your pardon, madam. I must remind myself that you were raised in the cynical and self-interested French court, where the surface is often at odds with the substance." His voice was deadly soft, and his Highland burr had vanished, replaced by the clipped, sterling tones of the British aristocracy. His eyes never left hers, and the muscle in his cheek began to twitch. "I told you once before that you are like a cat, madam,

because you always make sure you land on your feet."
Then he snatched up the cloak Rinalda proffered and
flung it over his shoulders.

Fiona stood rooted to the cellar floor, appalled that
Lachlan could think she was selfish. She was only
looking out for Maeve, who had loved and cared for
her since she was sixteen years old. As he strode toward the secret passageway, she smoothed her expression into deceptive calmness. "Where are you going?"

"Ye said ye must look out for Madam Maclean's
best interest." His voice dripped sarcasm, and his *r*'s
rolled like a breaking sea. "So I'm goin' to fetch her."
He whirled, cloak flaring about him like raven's wings,
then ducked through the hidden door.

Mortification flushed Fiona's cheeks, and she attempted to swallow the ache in her throat. Then Rinalda had stumped up through the dank, drafty
shadows and peered into her face. "Och, lassie. Dinna
mind him. He's got a temper like poison, but he always
gets over it."

Fiona blinked at the dusty casks of ale. Poison. What
had Rinalda once told her about poison?

She squealed and grabbed the old crone's arms. "Rinalda! I've got it. I know how we can get the clan
badge."

Now as she thought on her rash plan, Fiona bit her
lip, then leaned forward and applied the poker to the
blazing fire. Sparks shot up the chimney, and Fergus
skittered out of her way. " 'Tis a good plan, but will it
work?" she muttered, glancing anxiously at the kitchen
clock. Rinalda had served dinner to Campbell and his
henchman nearly an hour ago.

The door to the back hallway swung open, and Rinalda hobbled in, accompanied by an icy draft. She carried a small tray covered with a silver dome, which the servants used to keep meals warm during the long trek from kitchen to dining room.

Fiona flew forward. "Did it work?"

With a flourish, Rinalda whipped the dome from the tray. On it, atop Duncan's dirty dinner plate, lay the gold clan badge, jewels twinkling faintly in the fire-light. "Of course it did, lassie." She cackled, showing a crescent of toothless pink gums. "Didna I tell ye I've more skill with herbs than the Frenchies? When I doctor a mon's food, he doesna taste it."

Fiona glanced dubiously at the congealed remains of rabbit stew. "But Campbell and his man are only sleeping, *oui?*"

"Like bears. They should wake in two or three hours—"

The courtyard door burst open, then banged against the wall. Lachlan barged in, accompanied by Maeve, a swirl of snowflakes and a blast of freezing wind. "We just saw the sheriff on the high road," he barked. He crossed the room in two long strides, then loomed over Fiona.

Her jaw dropped. *Mon Dieu,* she sometimes forgot what a giant Lachlan was. He grabbed her shoulders, silver eyes blazing. "I must leave at once. Since I dinna have the clan badge, there's no point in ye comin'—"

Fiona pressed a finger to his sculpted lips, then reached behind her, where Rinalda stood clutching the tray. "Here you are, monsieur." She slanted him an airy smile, then tossed him the badge as if it were a ripe peach. "That should buy our coach fare to London, *n'est-ce pas?*"

Twenty-four

Fiona rubbed a gloved knuckle on her temple and silently entreated St. Christopher, who watched over weary travelers, to let them find a suitable inn as soon as possible, for they had at last reached the outskirts of London. She opened her eyes to find her mother-in-law watching her with a rather cynical air and reflected that only yesterday Maeve had made cutting comments about St. Christopher's efficacy.

Mais certainement, it had been a dreadful journey. To Fiona's astonishment, crossing the Sound of Mull in a snowstorm had been the least of their travails, for Lachlan had proved to be an expert sailor. Rinalda and wee Hugh had accompanied them to the mainland; then the old nanny had taken the babe with her to visit a friend, a healer who possessed a cottage on the banks of Loch Linnhe.

Non, it hadn't been bad weather or fear of arrest that had soured Fiona to the joys of travel; it had been the interminable trip by public conveyance.

At the coaching inn in Edinburgh, eight people had crammed into a rickety vehicle intended to seat four—not including the driver, but counting the poor souls whose ill luck it was to ride on top with the coachman. The carriage seemed to have been built before the advent of springs, the granite-hard seats were devoid of any padding save itchy brown horsehair, and the coach stopped only three times a day, which meant Fiona perpetually felt thirsty—for why drink if it only caused difficulties?

She and her fellow passengers had been subjected to a series of lice-infested hovels that claimed to be inns, and Fiona hadn't slept for several nights, thanks to Maeve's snoring. Worst of all, for days she had been required to ride backward over appallingly rutted roads. Maeve knew that riding backward made Fiona nauseated, but she had refused to take turns, as had the two garrulous, opinionated ladies who were crammed in beside her.

Fiona sighed, then folded her gloved hands in her lap, for there was nowhere else to put them. She was squashed between a fat squire who had sweated all the way from Edinburgh despite the frigid weather, and Lachlan's iron-hard shoulder. Touching Lachlan should have been a pleasure, for he cut a stunning figure in snug fawn breeks, tall leather boots, blue broadcloth coat, snowy linen shirt, and, of course, his dashing black traveling cloak. But—Fiona sighed and stared out the window—Lachlan hadn't spoken three words to her the entire journey. She had tried everything to thaw his icy reserve; everything had failed. He looked through her as if she didn't exist and kept his cold, austere face averted from her at all times.

Fiona scowled at her mother-in-law, who arched a knowing brow. Lachlan, of course, had been dazzlingly polite to Maeve, treating her with a disarming combination of grave respect and rakish courtliness. Maeve, who had been determined to despise her dead husband's successor, had been won over in all of two hours.

Their coach rattled over a rough patch of cobblestones, and Fiona rubbed her fingers across the sharp vertical line between her brows. She had a dreadful headache, brought on by the reek of unwashed bodies and the earsplitting clatter of iron-bound wheels over potholes. The racket had gotten steadily louder as they penetrated deeper into the city, and now Fiona heard the calls of a scissors grinder and a flower girl adding to the din.

She peered out the dirty window and decided they must have entered a commercial district. The shop fronts had grown more ornate, the cacophony of creaking carriages and shouting pedestrians had grown louder, and myriad barrows and slap-dash wooden stands lined the streets, purveying everything from fried fish to baked apples.

Fiona's stomach grumbled loudly, and Lachlan's mouth twitched up at the corners. St. Hilda, she would kill for a baked apple right now, and she didn't care who knew it. Just then they clattered past a shop with wide glass windows and a carved gold and red sign that proclaimed, Chez Pierre, Patisserie.

"Oh, look!" she cried. "A real French patisserie, right here in London. Oh, I'd love to stop. Lachlan, can you ask the driver?"

Every head in the carriage swiveled to stare at her. Maeve's peaked gray brows arched higher, and the fat, sweating squire snuffled with laughter. Lachlan gazed down at her with wintry gray eyes, his expression a mask of bland politeness.

She felt her cheeks grow hot, then slumped back in her seat. As she tried to avoid Maeve's disapproving look, her gaze fell on Lachlan's threadbare carpetbag, which held the bejeweled Maclean clan badge. A ripple of anxiety eddied down her spine. Would they be able to sell it to Silas Green?

Suddenly, a brilliant idea began to form in her tired brain.

The carriage drew up before a cozy-looking half-timbered inn. Fiona sat up and breathed a silent prayer of thanks to St. Christopher that they had reached their destination at last. Now she could have a warm bath, hot tea and red wine. The clan badge—and her idea—could wait until tomorrow.

A ragged, blue-gray cloud of smoke drifted above the raucous crowd, obscuring the ceiling's massive, blackened oak beams and cracked white plaster. Long trestle tables, pockmarked with candle burns, dagger gouges and a velvety black filth built up over two centuries of hard use, stretched down the center of the tavern, where drunken tradesmen sat cheek-by-jowl with red-coated soldiers, apprentices, draymen, actors, scullions, and a colorful assortment of prostitutes.

Fiona couldn't stop staring at the ladies of the evening. In France, prostitutes had seemed to fall into two categories: either beautiful, exquisitely dressed courtesans who glided like graceful swans through the highest society, or filthy, disease-ridden streetwalkers who were likely to pick a man's pocket or slit his throat after providing a moment's illicit pleasure down some back alley. Or so Harry had told her.

She peered over the railing that separated their mezzanine alcove from the hurly-burly below.

"Ye best stop gawkin', missy." Maeve signaled for another glass of Rhenish, then settled her broad hips more comfortably on their wooden bench. "I said 'twas proper for ladies to sit up here, out o' sight from pryin' eyes. I did no' say ladies should have pryin' eyes."

Fiona flicked her mother-in-law a half-hearted

smile. St. Genevieve, was it a sin to wish she had been allowed to go downstairs into the lively tavern with Lachlan? *He* certainly seemed to be enjoying his pipe and whisky, the off-key wail of the fiddle—and the attentions of a petite, curvaceous brunette whose bodice was cut so low Fiona could see the tops of her nipples even from this distance.

Maeve followed her line of sight, then gave a disapproving snort. "Will ye look at that brazen slut? I vow, give her another minute and she'll have those greedy hands o' hers in Lachlan's breeks." She elbowed Fiona, then jerked her chin at the intimate tableau unfolding before them. "Ye canna trust hussies like that. A farthin' tumble's no' good enough for them. Och, nay. Before ye know it, they want to be set up in a house in St. Johns Wood wi' a carriage and a maid."

Fiona bit her lip, then took another gulp of thin, bitter Burgundy. *Mon Dieu,* Lachlan was smiling down at the voluptuous brunette as though she were *gateau au chocolat* and he was starving. Then, to her utter horror, the wench reached out and slid her beringed hand over the manly bulge in Lachlan's breeks. Furious jealousy and raw, shrieking pain jolted through her like an electrical shock. She choked on her wine.

"Will ye look at that!" Maeve gulped her Rhenish, then glanced from one end of the tavern to the other, as if seeking confirmation of the outrage they both had witnessed. She turned and scowled at Fiona. "I'm telling ye, missy, ye're playing wi' fire. I ken there's something between ye and Lachlan—"

Fiona struggled for breath. "I don't know what you—"

"Och, stop. Dinna play innocent wi' me. If ye want to bed Lachlan Maclean, ye have me blessing. I didna like to see ye fight, but I thought a wee bit o' trouble between ye' might be a good idea. A little salt to add piquancy to the sweet." She grabbed Fiona's elbow and lowered her lips to her ears. "But ye're playin' wi' fire. We need that mon's protection, and we need his money. So ye better get down off your high horse and patch things up before that predatory little pussycat down below gets her claws—"

"Will you please stop!" Fiona leaped to her feet, jostling the table and spilling her wine. "I can't stand any more! I've tried to do what you want, to be who you want, but you cannot keep changing course like this. First you despise Lachlan, then you flutter over him like a doting aunt—" Tears clogged her throat, and she dug her nails into her palms. Oh, *mon Dieu*, she wanted to throttle that little slut down below. How dare she touch Lachlan that way!

Maeve gaped up at her, astonished. Then she stared out over the noisy, smoke-filled tavern. Woodenly, she raised her glass and swallowed a mouthful of wine. Then she set the glass on the table and turned, gray eyes boring into Fiona's as if they were the Grand Inquisitor's. "Ye're in love wi' him, aren't ye?"

Fiona blinked rapidly, determined not to cry. Below her, Lachlan whispered something in the brunette's ear, sending her into a fit of giggles. Fiona's throat closed up, and she crumpled onto the bench, her horrified gaze never leaving Lachlan.

Maeve dug a handkerchief from the pocket of her black-serge skirt. "Here. Ye dinna have to answer. I can see it in your eyes." She shook her head, snatched up her glass, then stared at Lachlan. "I should have known. Och, Hector would be appalled at me lack o' sensitivity."

Fiona sniffed into the handkerchief, then smothered a watery smile. Sir Hector had thought his wife many things, but sensitive hadn't made even the bottom of the list.

Without turning, Maeve said, "Tell me, lass, were Hector and I too hard on ye? I ken he was always tryin' to cram that idiotic philosophy o' his down your throat, and I'll admit that I wanted ye to be safe and happy." Her wide, mobile mouth thinned sardonically. "The Catholic Church and the king of France don't look too kindly on miracle workers who hear voices, ye ken. Look what happened to Joan of Arc."

Numbly, Fiona stared at Maeve's thick gray coronet of braids. She hadn't spoken of Fiona's strange gift in years—not since Fiona had sworn that she would never, ever reveal it. Utterly confused, she pressed the square of cambric to her dripping nose and inhaled the scent of stale roses, feminine perspiration and coconut bonbons—the inimitable aroma she would always associate with her mother-in-law.

She dropped her hands in her lap and smiled wanly. "Oh, *ma mère,* I just wanted to please you. I feel as if you and Sir Hector were the only real parents I ever had. I never knew my birth parents, and my adoptive parents were so . . . so *disapproving.*"

"And Hector and I weren't?"

A shrill peal of laughter drowned out Fiona's reply. She and Maeve turned just as the brunette streetwalker climbed onto Lachlan's lap. At the same instant, Lachlan glanced up and met Fiona's gaze. He arched a languid, mocking brow, and his ice-gray eyes blazed a fierce, masculine challenge.

"That's it." Maeve slammed her palms down on the grubby table. "Do ye love that arrogant rogue or no'?"

Fiona swallowed the bile in her throat. Lachlan shifted the wench off his lap with a playful pat on her bottom. Then he stood, tall, lithe and powerful, towering head-and-shoulders above the roistering crowd. A wrought-iron oil lamp hung mere inches above his head, and his chestnut hair waved loose down his back, gleaming russet in the golden light. With torturous yearning, her eyes traced the angle of his jaw, then devoured his sensual mouth and tanned cheeks, scored now with an arrogant smile. She memorized his peaked brows and chiseled cheekbones, the laugh lines at the corners of his eyes, and his long, elegant nose. *Mon Dieu,* how she loved his haughty glares down that knife-straight nose.

She dropped her gaze, then glanced up at Maeve from beneath wet, trembling lashes.

Maeve patted her hand and smiled shrewdly. "I thought so. Now go tell him."

"What?"

Maeve jerked her chin at Lachlan's broad back. "He's leavin', and the wench is goin' wi' him. Now go after him and do what ye have to do. Tell him ye talk to saints, tell him ye were kicked out o' a convent, tell him ye see ghosts, for all I care. Just go tell him ye love him."

With skirts flapping around her ankles and her stomach giving sickening little leaps, Fiona paced the worn plank floor of the inn's only private bedchamber. *Mon Dieu,* she was mad, mad! And what on earth had possessed her to gain entrance to Lachlan's quarters? Minutes earlier she had bribed a maid to let her into the slope-ceilinged room, for she had decided to have things out with her arrogant employer once and for all, and she hardly could do that in the cramped quarters she shared with Maeve. Now she was beginning to think better of her rash behavior.

Good St. Genevieve, whatever had happened to her modest widow's decorum? She stifled a bitter snort. Jealousy, that's what. *Mon Dieu,* she never knew how jealousy could burn like acid to one's heart.

She strode to the tiny window under the eaves and peered out over the fog-shrouded streets of London. It was well past midnight, and she ached for sleep; but her swirling emotions wouldn't allow it. What if Lachlan had gone with the prostitute? Or worse, what if he should bring her back here? Good St. Valentine, what would she do then? Sick, torturing panic barreled through her; then she caught a glimpse of her stricken face in the wavy window glass and ordered herself to calm down. This was ridiculous; she was behaving like an idiot.

Exhaustion lapped at her body like chill North Sea waves. She felt weak and shivery and—*c'est vrai*—half out of her wits for want of sleep. Her weary, tear-strained eyes settled on Lachlan's low-poster bed. Surely he wouldn't be back for hours, if at all. No doubt he was snoring, replete and smug, in the prostitute's bedroom, darn his heartless, lecherous hide!

Fiona perched on the lumpy ticking mattress, then woodenly inspected the brown-wool blanket for bedbugs. Finding none, she heaved a sigh and lay down. *Mon Dieu,* how heavenly it would be to snatch even a few moments of sleep without Maeve snoring in her ear.

Laughter drifted up from the taproom below; then a footfall sounded outside the bedchamber door. She scrambled up. Slowly, the door swung open, and Lachlan stood on the threshold, silhouetted by the hallway candlelight. A faint shadow of stubble covered his hard cheeks, lines of exhaustion creased the corners of his eyes, and his clothes reeked of tobacco smoke and cheap gardenia perfume. His black brows lifted in mild surprise; then he stepped into the room, closed the door and sketched a nonchalant bow.

"Good evening, madam. To what do I owe this honor? Here to haggle a bit more over your share o' the treasure?" His eyes fastened on her breasts, and he smiled, teeth white and wolfish in the murky shadows.

Fiona ordered her galloping heart to still, then frowned. Even from here she could smell the whisky on his breath. *"Non,* monsieur. I . . ."* Mon Dieu,* what should she tell him? "I, er . . . thought you would be sleeping elsewhere this evening. Madam Maclean snores dreadfully, so I thought I would avail myself of your chamber. I . . . I'm terribly tired. . . ." St. Benedict, that excuse sounded lame even to her ears.

Lachlan's brows lifted. "And where did ye think I'd be sleepin'? With that light o' love downstairs?" She blushed and looked away; he chuckled and swayed closer. "Och, that wouldna be jealousy heatin' those bonnie cheeks o' yours, now would it?"

"Non, monsieur. I have no right to be jealous over you."

"Och, too bad. I'd rather hoped ye had." A quick note of regret underscored his teasing tone, then vanished.

Her head shot up. "Was that *petit tableau* downstairs for my benefit?"

He tossed her a rakish smile, but his eyes had hardened to ice. "Now why would I want to make ye jealous? Ye made it quite clear ye only care for me money, aye? Sure and logical, practical lassies like ye dinna get jealous."

He stepped closer, smiling seductively, and her heart gave a shriek of agony. *Mon Dieu,* why was she torturing herself this way? He was merely toying with her. He didn't care; he never had cared.

"You make me sound like a heartless machine, monsieur."

"Perhaps ye are." His voice was a taunting growl, and he lowered his head until their lips were a finger's breadth apart. She smelled the whisky on his breath, felt the masculine heat of his body.

She wouldn't flinch. "I'm not, I swear it. You . . . you just misunderstood me." His mouth hardened, and he started back. Quick as thought, her hand flew out and tangled in his long, tousled hair. It slipped like dark silk through her fingers. "Lachlan, why have you been so cold? Why have you rejected me?"

Startlement shot across his handsome face; then he caught her shoulders, eyes blazing with silver fire. "Do ye think I've wanted to reject ye?" His whisper burned like quicklime across her mind, across her heart. "Do ye ken what I've felt, sittin' beside ye all the way from Scotland, watchin' ye fall asleep on me shoulder, seein' ye cold and weary and lookin' like ye'd never again find happiness or peace?" He inhaled sharply and clasped her face between his callused palms. "I didna want to reject ye, I wanted to love ye"—his voice grew bitter, hoarse—"but I'll never, *never* give me heart to a schemin', lyin'—"

She clapped her hand over his mouth and whispered, "But don't you know how much I love you?"

Keening silence stretched between them until she thought she must scream, lash out, anything to break the agonizing tension. Lachlan's eyes scorched into hers with violent intensity; then he jerked her to her feet and crushed her to him. The burning curve of his erection pressed against her belly; she felt the despair coursing through him, sensed the rage that fueled his need. To her astonishment, her hurt and confusion vanished, drowned by a surging riptide of desire that swept away everything but the need to love this man, to feel the wetness of his mouth on her nipples, to welcome the heat and thrust of his manhood against her womb.

"Ye canna love me," he rasped, raking his teeth across her throat. "If ye kent all the mistakes I've made, all the sins I've committed, all the hurts I've caused—och, ye'd turn away that beautiful, tranquil face, and I'd no' see love, but scorn in your eyes."

He roughly cupped her breast; then his fingers spiraled over her nipple, and he rolled the erect point between thumb and forefinger, pinching until mingled pain and lust arrowed through her. His lips closed over hers, his tongue thrust into her mouth, and he teased her with expert kisses that grew more and more savage.

"But for tonight I dinna care," he muttered. "Tonight I will love ye, *mo cridhe*. I'll love ye, or I'll die."

Swiftly, he undid the laces at her bodice and flung it to the floor, then caressed her breasts through the linen of her chemise and kissed his way down between them. Her knees buckled, and she collapsed against him. With lips never leaving hers, he lifted her off her feet, then lowered her to the bed. The hard bed pressed her buttocks, and a wild sensation of freedom, of liberation, of raw, primal womanhood shot through her. With a joyous laugh she kicked off her skirt and flung her arms above her head into the lumpy, musty pillow.

"Ye really must stop laughin' when I make love to ye, *mo cridhe*." Lachlan arched a stern brow, then dropped to his knees and tore open his breeks; a button zinged across the room. "It tends to put me off me stride."

His enormous penis jutted from its confines, hot and

thick and erect. He reached for her hand, then closed her damp fingers around his manhood and gripped, hard. "Stroke me," he growled. "Feel how much I want ye, how much I need ye." She squeezed and caressed, moving up and down, glorying in the feel of him, in the heat and life surging beneath his flesh. He was an iron bar sheathed in velvet.

"Dinna stop," he sighed. Suddenly his head fell back, and he groaned, half laughing, "Och, nay, stop, stop. If ye dinna, I'll spill me seed like a green lad."

Love and pure, savage need overwhelmed her, and she wrapped her legs around his narrow waist, then urged him between her thighs. The silky slick crown of him rubbed against her wet folds; she moaned and writhed against him.

He gave a roguish chuckle, then silked his work-roughened palms across her belly. "Och, and are ye still plannin' to be a nun, *mo cridhe?*" He slipped three long fingers between her thighs, then deftly rubbed her woman's nub until she begged for release.

"Lachlan. Please. Love me, take me. Now." Molten heat crashed over her in shuddering, tantalizing waves, bringing her closer, closer, yet never there.

She dug her nails into his naked buttocks. He leaned forward, captured her mouth, eased the crown of his penis inside her, then plunged home. She gasped at the slick, hot surge of his iron-and-velvet flesh deep inside her. With a ragged cry, he clamped his hands to her hips, then violently thrust forward, again and again.

"Ride me, use me," he moaned against her mouth. His tongue suckled hers—swift, wild, urgent—then he ground into her with slow, deliberate thrusts of barely controlled power.

Fiona's nipples burned against the crisp hair on his chest, and she shuddered, moaned, writhed against him. He plunged his tongue deeper into her mouth, mimicking the rhythm of his hips, then dragged her lower lip between his teeth. She felt a sharp nip of pain; then a whole new world of sensation cascaded through her flesh and pooled between her thighs. She groaned, arched her back, twisted her head to the side.

Lachlan murmured his approval. "Come wi' me, *mo cridhe.*"

She felt herself gather, tighten, focus. Her arms and legs twined around him and she ground against his hardness. She stopped breathing, stopped thinking— then she exploded in a glorious burst of sensation, a shattering wave of ecstasy.

"Och, Christ—I love ye, *mo cridhe.*" His cry was hoarse, broken, revelatory. "I love ye more than me own life."

He plunged deep inside her, then groaned long and low. He pulsed, shuddered, released, then melted down into her arms. After several gasping, dazzled moments, they drifted together into blissful, sated sleep.

"Sure and ye've warmed me up now, *mo cridhe.*" Lachlan turned his head and glanced a kiss on Fiona's tangled hair. " 'Tis a pity we didna do this after sloggin' around in that freezin' sea water."

They lay snuggled deep in the musty ticking mattress, with the blanket, which Fiona fervently hoped was bedbug free, tucked tight around them. Her head rested against his broad shoulder, and his fingers stroked her bare thigh, sending little thrills of pleasure through her limp body. She pressed her womanhood against the hardness of his thigh and inhaled the musky scent of their lovemaking, then curled her toes over the luscious carnality of it all.

"Now who's the practical one, eh?" She nuzzled his stubbly cheek, then lay back, smiling and stretching like a contented cat. *"C'est vrai,* I've been too rational in the past, but no more. You've convinced me. 'Tis much more fun to feel, *n'est-ce pas?"*

"Aye." The skin around his eyes crinkled rakishly; then he kissed her nose and traced his finger over her mouth, which was exquisitely swollen with the passion of their kisses. "Nay, these are no' the lips o' a dried-up nun. I'm afraid ye'll never make it in a convent, *mo cridhe."*

Frowning, Fiona sat up and gazed into his passion-dark eyes. Her belly clenched, and her pulse raced; but she hardened her resolve. The time had come. She *had* to tell him the truth. After all, wasn't confession good for the soul? "Lachlan? May I tell you something?"

He cocked his head. "Ye sound serious. Is somethin' wrong?"

"Well, it depends on how you look at it." She cleared her throat and attempted to smooth her face into its customary tranquil lines. "Have I ever told you I was expelled from the convent of the Ursulines because I predicted someone's death?"

When Fiona finished her tale, Lachlan rolled onto his elbow and appraised her with a swift, raking gaze. Although the room was nearly dark, her fiery hair gleamed like polished copper, and her eyes shone like serene amethyst pools in the cool dawn light. His brows knit. Sure and she didn't look mad, although her behavior certainly could be classed as odd upon occasion.

"Lass." He toyed with a strand of her silken hair,

thrilling to its softness beneath his fingers. "Ye dinna really believe ye can see and talk to ghosts, aye?"

She scowled and pushed away from him. "You don't believe me?"

Uneasiness slithered down his spine. "Weel . . . ye do seem to have a rare talent for healin'." He smiled ruefully, then held up his twisted hand to prove his point. "And I did see ye rouse that pup—but sure and 'tis as ye said. Poor wee Lazarus was only stunned, aye?"

Her level gaze never left his, but it seemed as if a curtain whisked down over her violet eyes, darkening them to a shade both icy and remote. *"Eh bien, comme vous souhaitez.* Perhaps all this passion has addled my wits." She tossed him a brittle little smile. "Sir Hector always said love ruined the mind—*while* he was alive, of course."

Lachlan cupped her cheek in his hand, suddenly ashamed for being so callous. "Fiona, lass. I didna mean—"

She pouted sullenly, then sat up, reached for his black traveling cape and wrapped it around her luscious nakedness. After several long minutes, she spoke. "Whether you believe me or not, I've told you the truth. Now I expect the same from you. And I'm not giving your blasted clan badge back to you 'til you've told me everything."

He gave a startled snort. "What?"

"You heard me, monsieur." Her voice was direct and no-nonsense, definitely the French shopkeeper's tone now. He had heard her speak just this way to inn-keepers all across England, haggling over the price of their rooms. "I've taken the badge—"

"Ye did what?"

"Bellow away, monsieur. It won't do a bit of good.

I've hidden the badge in a safe place, and you're not getting it back until you tell me about your brothers, Catriona, why you fought for the British—everything." Her tone softened, and she clasped his hand, her eyes warm and beseeching. "Oh, *mon cher,* you cannot hide the truth forever. *Ce n'est plus nécessaire.*"

Lachlan clenched his jaw and dragged several labored breaths through pinched nostrils. The wee lunatic had stolen his clan badge! Good St. Ninian, he ought to thrash her bonnie arse 'til she begged for mercy! His manhood throbbed at the mere thought. "Madam, do ye have any idea what the English penalty for throttlin' one's lover might be?" His tone was frigid, scathing.

Fiona arched a tranquil brow. "Well, in France, monsieur, it would be considered a *crime passionnel,* and you would be let off with a fine of fifty livres."

Lachlan blinked. Och, there she sat—cool tone, level gaze, with just the faintest spark of mischief in her calm violet eyes. He scrubbed his hands down over his face, then threw back his head and laughed. "Ye're irresistible, *mo cridhe.* Och, heaven help the mon who ever tries to stand up to ye." He reached up and pulled her down beside him. "Ye want the truth, aye?" She nodded, and he leaned back against the musty pillow. Then, stroking her hair the way one might stroke a cat, he began his tale.

Twenty-five

"As ye ken, *mo cridhe,* Sir Hector and the Maclean clan supported Charles Edward Stuart, Scotland's own Bonnie Prince Charlie, in his fight to regain the British throne from that usurping Hanoverian, George II." Lachlan snorted. "Bonnie Charlie was, but no' terribly bright. His early victories over the English at Falkirk and Prestonpans had gone to his head, ye ken, and he wouldna listen to his advisers. O' course, they weren't perfect, but they did care for the Highlanders—which is more than I could say for the prince."

He scowled, leaned back against the pillow and folded his arms across his chest. Och, he had buried his feelings about the past for so long that he hardly remembered how things had started—or how he had felt all those years ago. Where to begin?

"Madam Maclean's probably told ye that me wife Catriona was a Campbell, and half English into the bargain," he said. "We married young. I wish I could say it had been arranged by our parents, but it wasna so."

Fiona's naked body stiffened beside him. "You loved her, then?"

He raked an irritable hand through his hair. "I didna ken what real love meant back then. I suppose I did, or perhaps I was just taken by Catriona's beauty." He paused, avoiding Fiona's direct gaze. "Ye've seen her portrait, but it doesna do her justice. The looks are the same—she was tall and slender, verra blonde and pale, like a faery princess. But no artist could capture her true nature." He gave a harsh laugh. "She was too good at hidin' it. Och, I'd been married to her for a year before I saw her true colors, so how could I expect a stranger to have unmasked her?

"At first she pretended to love me, but a few weeks after the weddin', me *athair* died and I became laird. Then Catriona changed. The power o' her station seemed to go to her head, and she became cruel, mockin', cunnin'. Then her brother Duncan came to stay with us. They were twins, ye ken, and she hated to be parted from him, even to spend time wi' her husband." He halted, shocked by the bitterness in his tone.

"Duncan and I never were friends, and before long I grew to despise him. He'd fallen into a burn as a child and broke his leg, and because Catriona had been too little to rescue him, he blamed her for his lameness. Guilt's a prime weapon, and he manipulated Catriona somethin' fierce. She'd do whatever he wanted, no matter how . . . perverse."

All at once something became clear in his mind, and he paused and mulled it over. "It was as if we were all playin' a game, wi' the person who was more loved holdin' all the power. Catriona loved Duncan, so he manipulated her. I loved Catriona, so she manipulated me—until I finally saw what was goin' on, that is."

A swift, staggering shaft of rage stabbed through him, leaving him shaken and stunned. St. Ninian, how could he still feel such fury, after having felt nothing for so long? Och, one thing was certain: he never could tell Fiona the complete truth about Duncan and Catriona, for he couldn't face it himself. How did one admit that one's wife had committed incest?

He sat up and flung back the bedclothes. "I was a fool. For months after Prince Charlie landed in Scotland and most o' me clan joined up with his army, I tried to appease Catriona. Duncan and the Campbells supported the English, and whenever me brothers chivied me to fight for Prince Charlie, I'd reply that I couldna bring grief to me wife by fightin' against her blood. I'd remain neutral. I thought it the best course anyway, as I didna see how the Prince had a prayer of winnin' against the might of King George and the Duke of Cumberland. My duty was to protect Taigh Samhraidh and its people, and I wouldna see them starve while I marched off with the prince."

He fell silent as pale dawn light filled the chilly room. After a moment, Fiona tucked the blankets back around his waist.

"You mustn't catch a chill," she murmured.

"But Catriona wasna satisfied with that," he said, staring blankly out the lightening window. "Och, nay. She would have me fight *for* the English. Duncan couldna march or bear arms because o' his crippled leg, so I must go in his place. I refused, but after a time, 'twas as if events took on a life o' their own.

"First, me brother Diarmid declared for the prince." Lachlan clenched his eyes shut, reliving his last, wretched quarrel with his impossibly handsome, impossibly arrogant brother. "He'd been miserable since me marriage to Catriona, I suspect because he'd fallen in love wi' her, too." He shook his head, then smiled mirthlessly. "Jamie, the youngest, longed to join the Jacobites as weel, but I made him stay home and help wi' the estate. He hated me for it—as much as Jamie could ever hate anyone."

He took a deep breath. " 'Twas early April, 1746, when Diarmid and me old friend Hugh Rankin—poor dead Maire's brother-in-law—returned to Taigh Samhraidh with news. Hugh had fought victoriously with Prince Charlie since Falkirk, but things had changed. The English army had taken the offensive and was chasin' the prince back to Inverness. The prince's Highlanders were exhausted, starvin', disillusioned . . . and many had deserted to tend their land and plant a crop before their bairns starved.

"Hugh came to beg me to join the army. In strictest confidence, he told me that Prince Charlie was plannin' a surprise attack for the night o' April 15, the Duke of Cumberland's birthday—no doubt assuming that the English would be drunk from celebratin' their leader's birth. The Highlanders were bold, courageous warriors, but they kent the value o' surprise. They also kent that the duke's troops outnumbered them four to one. They were desperate. They needed every man. So against me better judgment, I told Hugh that Jamie and I would go to Inverness to fight for the prince.

"At that moment, Catriona burst into the room. She was cryin', near hysterical. She ordered Hugh, Diarmid and Jamie out, then shrieked at me, sayin' I was an evil, betrayin' whoreson who wished her and her brother dead. I explained that fightin' honorably with me clan and brothers hardly constituted an attack on her, but she wasna in her right mind. We argued all the way to our bedchamber. Finally she flung out that she was carryin' and that if I fought against the Campbells, I'd be killin' me own bairn's relatives. I was so stunned I left her alone. What could I say after that? I wouldna fight against me brothers, and she didna want me fightin' against hers."

Lachlan halted, then fisted his hands until his nails

dug into his palms. "I kent by then that I no longer loved her, but I wanted a son somethin' desperate—an heir to carry on after me, to protect our people. It must have showed in me eyes, and by revealin' that emotion, I handed Catriona the weapon she needed."

"What did she do?" Fiona asked in a wary tone.

Lachlan clenched his jaw and ordered his thundering pulse to slow. When he thought he could trust his voice, he said, "Hours later, Rinalda came to me, half out o' her wits. She'd been readyin' me wife for bed when Catriona suddenly dashed a basin of water over her nightshift, then ran out o' the castle in the direction o' the cliffs.

" 'Ye must go after her—she's stark out o' her mind,' Rinalda cried. 'She said she'd kill the bairn.'

"I raced from the castle and found Catriona on the sea cliffs. 'Twas black as pitch and bitterly cold. Catriona's wet shift had frozen to her skin, but she held her ground, shivering in the wind seventy feet above jagged rocks and crashin' sea. I held out me hand to her, but she laughed like a crazed thing and shoved me away.

" 'Promise me!' she shrieked. 'Promise me ye'll fight wi' the Campbells and the English, or so help me, I'll jump. I'll dash meself to bits right in front o' ye. Oh, I ken ye dinna care for me, but what aboot your son? Will ye let your blood die because o' your own bad choices?' "

Lachlan buried his head in his hands. "What could I say?" he asked, appalled by the hoarseness of his voice. "I couldna let me wife and child die. So I agreed. I said I'd fight for the English."

The room grew lighter, and he heard the first bustling sounds of city life drifting up from the London streets. Hooves and wagon wheels clattered on the cobblestones, milk pails rattled, scullions chattered, and a vendor called, "Bridies, bridies! Hot and tidy! Full o' meat, treat to eat!"

Fiona snuggled close, then wrapped her soft body around him. "You don't have to tell me any more—"

"Nay, I want to." And to his astonishment, he did. Suddenly he felt a surge of energy, as if he had been released from life imprisonment in a cold, dark and lonely cell into fresh air and sunshine. Words bubbled up, and he hardly could speak fast enough, so urgent was his need to explain.

"The next mornin', Hugh, Jamie and Diarmid left to join the prince, cursin' me all the way. After they left, Catriona fitted me up in the Campbell plaid, crest and badge. 'Tis how warriors mark friend and foe on the battlefield, ye ken. Against me better judgment, I left Angus Beattie in charge o' the estate, then took me leave o' Catriona and the servants. I'd thought Duncan would be there, gloatin' that I'd given in, but he'd ridden off somewhere on business.

"Weel, *mo cridhe,* I hardly need tell ye about Culloden, as ye saw the horrible aftermath yourself. The Duke of Cumberland had been warned o' the surprise attack, and his army—the army I joined—had more than enough time to ready for the fight. The Highlanders lined up like cattle for the slaughter that snowy April dawn, and slaughter it was. The British were hale and dressed in bold scarlet uniforms, wi' their cavalry mounted on fine horseflesh. And the weapons! Och, ye never saw the like. Scores o' cannon and shinin' new muskets. I still shudder to think o' it."

He ground to a halt. He forgot Fiona and the inn and the homely sounds of a London morning. Suddenly he was back there, facing death.

* * *

Lachlan couldn't see through the billowing smoke. The British cannon exploded behind him, shaking the earth and thundering in his ear. A ball shrieked past his head, and he plunged to the ground, then rolled through the icy mud, trying to escape a hail of lead from the Highlanders' guns. A piercing, inhuman scream knifed through the driving sleet. He struggled up. Och, St. Ninian, the English had hit Prince Charlie's horse! The poor creature squealed and plunged, its white flanks streaked with foam and blood.

Grapeshot whined to his left, and three redcoats fell, their blood gouting up in bright scarlet streams, pumping in time to their cries. Another cannon thundered, and Lachlan dove to the ground, then crawled backward until he hit something. He turned and met the ravaged gaze of a corpse. One side of the soldier's skull had been blown away, and his gray brains oozed out, mingling with the blood on the muddy ground.

A hoarse Gaelic roar tore the air, and the MacIntosh clan broke and ran, racing straight into the English cannon. Plaids swirled, claymores glinted, dirks flashed, pistols cracked. The Highlanders were charging!

Lachlan lunged to his feet. He couldn't do this. He couldn't fight against his kin, his clan, his brothers. He couldn't betray his blood and heritage.

He jerked his claymore from its sheath and plunged straight into the Highland ranks, then turned and charged with them. Desperately, he looked about him as he hacked at English limbs. Where were Jamie, Diarmid, Hugh, Uncle Alexander, Sir Hector Maclean? He had to find them, join them, fight at their side. Nothing was more important than that. Nothing.

Suddenly, a burly Highlander raised his sword and charged at Lachlan, a blood-curdling scream tearing from his mouth. Horrible realization dawned, and Lachlan swallowed a curse. Good St. Ninian, he was wearing Campbell regalia. He was likely to be killed long before he found his brothers.

There was another *boom,* and all went black.

Lachlan woke to find the Highlander on top of him. Warm blood trickled down Lachlan's cheek, and he tasted it, slick and coppery, in his mouth. Was it the man's or his own? He grunted and tried to shift his fallen comrade's body. His nostrils flared. St. Ninian, what was that horrible smell? With a groan, he sat up and tried to push the corpse away, but his wrists ended in a twisted mass of blood. He could feel nothing. Och, good Christ, he had lost his hands!

In desperation, he kicked at the corpse, then noted with dull horror that his thigh was gashed open like a gutted deer. He dragged his gaze from the ragged wound and, for the first time, really looked at the Highlander's body. His stomach heaved. The cannon had ripped the man in two, splattering blood and entrails across Lachlan's face and chest.

He collapsed back in the icy mud. Then, bit by slow, agonized bit, he felt his life begin to drain from him. The battlefield transmogrified into a nightmare of mindless screams, biting sleet, choking smoke. A squealing, riderless horse bucked through a hail of grapeshot. Another MacIntosh warrior staggered past, blood geysering from the shredded flesh that had been his throat. Ragged cries rose around Lachlan like the screams of the damned.

Then there was another explosion, followed by a shower of hot lead. Killing pain lanced his ears, stabbed his brain, shredded his reason. Hands pressed to his skull, he cried a prayer for forgiveness, then blacked out.

* * *

Lachlan's stomach roiled, and a scalding tear squeezed under his lid. He clenched his jaw and ordered himself to forget, *forget!* He never should have allowed himself to remember, to feel. Fiona cradled his head on her bare breasts, and he buried his face in her soft, warm flesh. Och, how could he let her see him like this?

"I remember finding you," she murmured, stroking his cheek with heartbreaking tenderness. "At first I thought you were my father, although *c'est vrai*, I knew in my heart you weren't. But something in you called to me. It was as if you were the only person truly alive on that battlefield."

He gazed into her beautiful violet eyes. "What called to ye?

"Your kind heart."

He drew a ragged breath, then swallowed the tears clogging his throat. St. Ninian, he had been right all those years ago. He had thought the fey, red-haired lass holding him in her arms on Culloden battlefield had been an angel. "And ye are," he murmured.

"*Pardon, monsieur?*"

"Nothing."

She struggled up, baring her voluptuous, rose-tipped breasts to the cold air. Instantly her nipples hardened, and he felt a surge in his loins. She laughed. "Wipe that lustful look off your face, monsieur. We're not done here." She planted her hands on the lush curve of her hips, then pinned him with a mock-stern gaze. "Why on earth, if you actually did cross the line and fight with the Jacobites, have you let all those vile rumors stand for all these years? *Mon Dieu,* even your own brothers don't know the truth! What in the name of St. Francis were you—"

He clapped a gentle hand over her mouth. "Och, ye French are a feisty lot, aye?"

"I'm not French."

"If ye'll hush a moment, I'll tell ye." He took a deep breath and collected his thoughts. "After ye came along like a ministerin' angel and your mother dragged ye off the battlefield, I passed out. Hours later I woke in the back o' a wagon filled with wounded English soldiers. Me mind was so addled it took me a while to piece things together, but finally I realized the duke's men never kent I'd defected. They saw me Campbell plaid and badge and hauled me off to their field hospital.

"For weeks I suffered a wicked fever, half out o' me mind and ravin' like a lunatic. When I finally came to me senses, I was back at Taigh Samhraidh. Duncan, who didna ken I'd joined the Jacobites, gave me the"— he quirked his fingers like quotation marks—"happy news that Prince Charles Edward Stuart was bein' hounded across Scotland and that the Jacobite cause was dead."

Lachlan swallowed and stared up at the ceiling, blinking back tears of rage and frustration. "I asked to see me wife, and Duncan went pale. 'Tis the first and last time I've ever seen him show genuine human feelin'. He finally choked out that she was dead—an abortion gone wrong. She thought I was dyin', and wanted to be free o' every tie to me. Without the bairn, she would be a rich widow and could devote her life to Duncan." He ground to a halt, nearly sick with bitterness and disgust. Och, aye—Catriona had been more than eager to resume her perverse relationship with her brother.

"I wept, then exploded wi' rage. I ordered Duncan off Taigh Samhraidh, only to be told it was now his as reward for faithful service, since—aside from me—the Maclean clan had fought against the king. I demanded to see me brothers, only to be told they'd been judged guilty o' treason and banished to the Colonies—another reason I never would be allowed to keep Taigh Samhraidh."

Fiona slipped her hand in his, but he barreled on, bent on purging his soul. "I *ached* to kill Duncan and go after me brothers, but one thing stopped me. As I lay ill, Duncan spent hours regalin' me wi' the horrors the survivin' Jacobite clans had suffered. Crops and homes burned, animals slaughtered, women raped and bayoneted, lads too small even to handle a *sgain dhu* hanged. Thousands o' people were starvin' and dyin' o' the wretched diseases that feed on poverty. Only the clans that had been loyal to the crown were spared. And that's what stopped me from slittin' Duncan's throat.

"He believed that I was a Loyalist." Lachlan threw back his head and laughed with bitter harshness. "In a bizarre fit o' generosity, no doubt fueled by guilt over Catriona, he offered to let me stay on as steward. He admitted he kent nothing aboot running the estate. That lazy fool Angus Beattie had been drivin' it into the ground, and Duncan intimated it would go badly for me former tenants if I refused.

"Instantly, I saw it. I was the only thing standin' between the remnants of me clan and their complete destruction. By keepin' me mouth shut and livin' a lie, I could protect them."

He raked a hand through his hair. "Och, for years it's haunted me. How much o' me decision was for me own good, and how much was for theirs? Should I have spit in Duncan's face, sworn me allegiance to poor, defeated Prince Charlie, and been banished to America like me brothers?" He glared at Fiona, brows lowered in a fierce scowl. "Weel?"

Fiona's calm gaze never wavered. She didn't reply for a long moment; then she tilted her delicate chin and said, "You've held your clan together, haven't you?"

"Aye."

"Your people are clothed, fed, safe, healthy and relatively prosperous?"

"Weel, for the most part. Ye ken the problems wi' the roofs and drains, and the Rankins dyin' o' the consumption—"

"Are they the only one's who've died?"

"Aye, but—"

"And how many Highlanders outside your clan have died? Those who've not had a protector like you?" Fiona's voice quavered with emotion.

He dropped his gaze. "Tens of thousands, lassie. Ye ken that." As it always did when he contemplated the cruel fate of the Highland Scots, a bitter wave of anguish washed over him. But beneath it, like a grain of gold at the bottom of an ocean, lay a glimmer of hope. His people, at least, had been spared.

Fiona smiled rather pointedly. "Then, you've answered your own question, haven't you?"

Lachlan's mouth quirked. "Why do I have the feelin' I've just been interrogated by Socrates?"

"And you've spent years searching for your brothers, haven't you? To make sure they were all right? And you offered to send them money."

"Aye, and a lot o' good it's done me." He slumped down on the musty pillow. "As a good Catholic, *mo cridhe,* surely ye ken what Christ says. Ye canna buy forgiveness."

Twenty-six

"Oh, *non, non.* One of the *palmiers, s'il vous plait. Oui,* that one." Fiona accepted the deliciously flaky, sugar-sprinkled pastry, held it to her nose, inhaled in an ecstasy of sensual delight, then bit down. She closed her eyes and sighed. *"Oh, c'est merveilleux!"*

Pierre Mercier, who owned the patisserie Chez Pierre, grinned and slapped his floury palms together. "It is my 'onor to serve you, *madame.* The English—*hunh!* No taste, no palate, no *reconnaissance.*" He drew a silver tray of *babas au rhum* from behind his tall glass counter, then presented it with a flourish. "Tell me what you think of these, madam. The texture is *un peu grossier, peut-être?*"

Fiona plucked one of the small turban-shaped cakes from the tray, then cast an anxious eye at the inn across the street. Yesterday, during the commotion of arrival, Lachlan had left his carpetbag in her care. The instant his back was turned, she had snatched the carefully wrapped clan badge from among his meager belongings, then hurried across the street to the patisserie, just minutes before it closed.

Upon meeting a fellow countrywoman—one who had been employed in a Parisian patisserie, no less!—Pierre Mercier had welcomed her with open arms. They had fallen into an hour's discussion of glace and gateau, of cinnamon and of marzipan, at the end of which Monsieur Mercier had been only to happy to hide a small, wrapped parcel of hers in his kitchen.

Fiona's teeth sank into the rum-soaked cake; then she smiled, simultaneously savoring the confection and the memory of Lachlan's furious expression when he realized she had stolen his property. Her heart contracted, her knees melted like butter in a skillet, and she sank onto a stool. *Mon Dieu*, it seemed she had stolen more than Lachlan's precious badge. She swallowed and shut her eyes, suddenly awash with joy and love. Holy St. Valentine, she had stolen his heart—just as he had stolen hers.

"Merci, merci," she whispered, not minding if the pastry chef thought her thanks were intended for him, not for God and the saints.

She curled her toes in her sturdy boots, then licked crumbs from her fingers. After she and Lachlan had made love once more in the bright morning sun, she had left him shaving in his room, then dashed over to the patisserie for fresh, buttery croissants—and the clan badge. Lachlan had kept up his end of their bargain, after all. She dimpled. He deserved his reward.

Pierre appraised her flushed cheeks, then shot her a knowing Gallic smile. *"C'est bon, n'est ce pas? Mais rien ne vaut amour."*

Nothing is better than love. What would Sir Hector say to that? She turned the thought over in her mind, then stood and reached for her basket. In it, the priceless clan badge rested under a pile of croissants. *"C'est vrai,"* she murmured. *"C'est vrai."*

Suddenly a shout went up on the street. Fiona and Pierre exchanged startled glances and hustled to the window. A crowd had formed outside the inn, and six tall, red-coated dragoons were jostling through the tavern door.

"Isn't it rather early for soldiers to be patronizing a tavern?" Fiona asked.

"I 'ave seen this before, madam." Pierre shook his balding head disapprovingly. "It appears they 'ave come to arrest some unlucky soul."

Apprehension gripped Fiona's belly. Suddenly, her gaze fell on a familiar, hunched figure standing safely out of the soldiers' way. "No!" she gasped. She thrust the basket at Pierre. "Hide this. Give it to no one but me." Then she dashed through the door and flew across the street.

The soldiers had disappeared into the tavern, and a muffled shout echoed from inside the half-timbered structure. The crowd milled about, poking one another in the ribs and calling odds on the likelihood of the unlucky thief escaping the law.

"Monsieur!" Fiona cried, heart thundering into her throat.

Duncan Campbell looked up, a supercilious smile on his ferretlike face. Fiona stumbled to a halt before him; he shifted his crutch out of her way and inclined his head. "Madam Fraser," he drawled, "I'm glad you've decided to join me at last. It seems His Majesty's dragoons are about to capture a jewel thief—and I'm sure *you* wouldn't want to be implicated in such a crime."

Fiona dug her nails into her damp palms and gaped at Duncan's arrogant expression. Her mind whirled; she felt as if she were trapped in a maelstrom of shock and dismay and would drown at any moment. "H-how did you find us?" she croaked.

Duncan flicked dust from his green-velvet traveling cloak. "Lud, 'twas easy as following a fox through fresh snow. When that blundering sheriff found Maclean gone, I suspected what was afoot. When I discovered that the clan badge and my letter from Silas Green had disappeared—well, my dear, it didn't take a fortune-teller to predict that Maclean was flying to London in hopes of outwitting me." He took her elbow, then surveyed her bosom with a predatory leer. "Imagine my delight when an innkeeper along the London road described a towering Highlander with a crippled hand traveling with a red-haired French beauty—"

"Campbell! I'll see ye in hell for this!"

Duncan and Fiona swung about just as the soldiers dragged a wildly struggling Lachlan through the tavern door. He was barefoot, clad only in breeks and a full-sleeved linen shirt. A flush stained his tanned cheeks, and his furious silver eyes seared across the crowd, then incinerated Duncan's foppish nonchalance. Fiona watched in horror as one of the soldiers slammed the butt of his musket into Lachlan's flat belly. Lachlan doubled over; then the soldier grasped the Highlander's long, unbound hair and smashed the side of his face into the tavern's stone wall.

"Stop!" Fiona shrieked. She started to bolt forward, but Duncan grabbed her arm and yanked her to a halt.

"Forget that arrogant fool," he hissed, sour breath hot against Fiona's cheek. "He'll rot away in Newgate while I settle my debts and gain a place at court—all thanks to a certain valuable piece of jewelry."

Fiona stared across the cobbled street as the king's soldiers dragged Lachlan's limp body into an enclosed carriage. Blood trickled from a lurid gash high on his cheekbone, and his head lolled back liked a dead man's. Two red-coated officers slammed and bolted the carriage door, then signaled to the coachman; the horses lurched forward, and iron-rimmed wheels rattled over the cobblestones. After a few moments, the goggling, chattering crowd of draymen, laundresses and shopkeepers trailed away.

The last of the six soldiers appeared in the tavern doorway. Catching sight of Duncan, the man frowned, then strode smartly across the street, saber swinging at his side. He halted and fixed his impassive gaze at a point above Duncan's curled and powdered wig. "Your pardon, sir. My men and I have searched the criminal's chamber, and there's no sign of the, er . . ."—his eyes flicked to Fiona, then looked straight ahead—"the item you seek."

Fiona's paralyzed brain jolted to life. They hadn't found the badge! With her thoughts racing wildly, she shook Duncan's hand from her arm and spun to face him. Surely they couldn't hold Lachlan without evidence. But what could she do? How could she throw Duncan off the scent? And dear God in heaven, where was Maeve?

Suddenly, her addled wits registered that Duncan had made no mention of Sir Hector's widow. Did he know Maeve was with them? Did it matter? Oh, *Mon Dieu*. She resisted the urge to cross herself, breathed a silent prayer, and said, "Monsieur, I-I think you know that I have, ah . . . a certain attachment to Lachlan Maclean. I would not see him hurt for anything in this world."

Duncan stopped glowering at the rod-backed soldier, then appraised her with shrewd interest. "What are you saying, madam?"

She looked down at her boots, then darted him a tremulous glance from beneath lowered lashes. "P-perhaps we can come to an agreement, monsieur."

"About what?" Duncan's voice cracked like a whip; Fiona forced herself not to flinch.

"Am I mistaken in my belief that you"—she knotted her hands in her skirt and contrived to blush—"have an interest in me?"

"And if I do?"

She raised her eyes and fixed him with a limpid gaze. "I know where Monsieur Maclean has hidden the clan badge. I would do anything to save him from prison. If you promise me you'll drop all charges and have him released, I'll bring you the badge—"

"And what's to stop me from having you arrested as an accessory to his crime? I'm sure a few hours among the sodomites and cutthroats of Newgate would make you spill what you know."

Swallowing the bile in her throat, Fiona leaned forward, pressed her breast against Duncan's shoulder and whispered, "But you wouldn't be able to bed me in prison, monsieur." Her pulse lurched, and for a horrible moment she thought she might faint. St. Benedict, she was taking a risk, but she could think of no other way to save Lachlan.

For an instant, she thought a blush ghosted across Duncan's pocked skin; then he waved the soldier out of earshot, grasped her upper arm and dragged her against him. Lust flared behind his glittering blue gaze, and to her dismay, she felt the jut of his manhood against her belly. "I wouldn't count on that," he hissed. "But, for the sake of argument, let us say I prefer to sample your charms in the comfort of my chambers instead of the filth of Newgate."

She fluttered her lashes as if surrendering to his virility. "Then, monsieur, I would make you this offer. Order Monsieur Maclean's release. Let me go fetch the badge from its hiding place. I'll come to your lodgings, and we will, ah . . . make our exchange."

Duncan shifted his weight on his crutch and flushed.

"Do you think I'm a fool, madam? Why in God's name would I let you out of my sight? For all I know you'll take the badge and disappear back to France."

She gazed blankly into Duncan's ratty face. How could she convince him? She couldn't let him come with her, or all would be lost. At last she nodded. "I see your point, monsieur, but I swear that I will come to you. If you wish, you may wait until I arrive with the badge before you order Lachlan's release." She clutched his hand and at last allowed her true feelings to shine through her eyes. "You know I'm in love with Lachlan. I never would gamble with his life." She lowered her voice to a pleading, helpless tone. "You hold all the cards, monsieur. You hold me in your power."

A smug expression crawled across Duncan's face, and he puffed up like a ruffled grouse. Fiona bit back a jaded smile. She had learned many truths during her years in France; among them, that men were incapable of resisting an appeal to their vanity.

He hobbled back a step, then flourished his arm in a clumsy bow. "Madam, I accept your terms. In two hours—"

"Please, make it three. I cannot retrieve the badge that quickly."

"In three hours, then, I'll expect to see you and the clan badge at my lodgings. Number Two Whitham Crescent, near Green Park." He motioned to the soldier, then tossed the man a gold coin along with a meaningful look. "And if you don't arrive . . . Well, madam, men die in Newgate all the time."

"Ma mère!" Fiona pelted along the inn's upstairs hall, pleading with God and the saints that her mother-in-law would be awake and unharmed. She flung open

the door to their chamber, then nearly collapsed with relief. Maeve sat at a rickety table, holding a quill pen and scratching away at a piece of paper. "Oh, *Dieu merci*," Fiona breathed, slamming the door and slumping against it.

Maeve cast her a stern glare, then sanded the paper and stood. "There ye are, missy. Stop gogglin' and get your cloak. We've got to get out o' here at once."

"Then you know what happened?"

"Ken what happened? I'm the one who had to stand here and watch while some lick-spittle lobsterback pawed through me belongin's." She made a *humph*ing noise, then caught up her cloak and gloves.

"They . . . they didn't realize who you were?"

"Nay, thank the good God." She strode to the door, black-wool skirts swirling about her sturdy ankles. "They took Lachlan. Ye saw that, didn't ye?" Fiona nodded, perilously close to tears. Maeve patted a hand to Fiona's cheek. "Buck up, lass. All's no' lost. For some reason, they didna find the badge." She smiled, and her broad face softened indulgently. "I can't imagine where that strappin' charmer hid it, but—"

"He didn't hide it—I did!" Fiona blurted, unaccountably irritated. *Mon Dieu,* Maeve's doting aboutface on the subject of Lachlan was beginning to wear on her like a tight boot.

Maeve's peaked gray brows flew up. "Where in God's name is it?"

"Next door. But never mind that. We've got to fetch it and think of some way to get Lachlan out of prison. We've got less than three hours—"

Maeve grabbed Fiona's arm and hustled her from the room. "I've already thought o' that. We're goin' to the king—"

"What?"

They clattered down the stairs, and Maeve thrust the folded paper under Fiona's nose. "I've written a message to John Stuart, Earl of Bute. He's no longer prime minister, but he's a Scot and he's an old friend o' mine. He should have enough sense to hear us out. He kens that Sir Hector was one o' the staunchest, most powerful leaders o' the Jacobite cause. As Sir Hector's widow, I've told him that I must meet wi' him immediately."

"But why would a former prime minister of England take the time—"

"Because I'm tellin' him that we're newly arrived from France and that I have grave news. Prince Charles Edward Stuart is secretly returnin' to England to rally the Jacobites. He's plannin' another attempt on the throne."

Fiona halted. "But that's preposterous."

"Why? Charles did just that in 1750 and in 1753. Why wouldna he try it again?"

"But you know 'tis not true."

Maeve chuckled and prodded Fiona into the street. "Ye ken that, and I ken that. But Bute doesna ken it."

Twenty-seven

Fiona clenched her quivering stomach muscles and sat straighter on her delicate gilt chair. Long afternoon shadows slanted across the gleaming parquetry floor, adding a red-gold sheen to the polished wood. Ruby-damask draperies muffled what little sound drifted in through the windows, and intricate needlepoint tapestries in shades of scarlet, rust and maroon hung on the mahogany-paneled walls.

Fiona shivered. Sitting in this quiet antechamber, waiting to see George III, King of Great Britain and Ireland, Elector of Hanover and Duke of Brunswick-Luneburg, was like sitting in a lion's hungry mouth.

It had been hours since they had met with John Stuart, Earl of Bute. That unpopular statesman had been only too happy to dump the vexing possibility of another Rising in the lap of his successor, the arrogant and favor-currying George Grenville. In truth, Bute hardly had questioned his old friend Madam Maclean's story, so anxious was he to muddy the political waters swirling about his rival.

Fiona's mouth quirked in a sardonic smile. It seemed things weren't so different in France and England, after all.

Maeve cast her a quelling glare, then nodded toward the door. Two tall, silent footmen with admirably muscular calves, delicate powdered wigs and shiny garnet-satin livery stood at the chamber entrance, though whether to spy on them or prevent them from escaping, Fiona couldn't say. Her gaze wandered from the footmen to her mother-in-law. *Mon Dieu,* Maeve didn't seem ruffled in the least. In truth, Fiona had gained a whole new appreciation for the venerable lady, for Maeve had proved an astonishing diplomat while spinning their tale for Bute, then repeating it to Grenville. Like the most skillful of courtiers, she had hit just the right balance between flattery and haughtiness while using her wits to bend the truth to her advantage. To Fiona's surprise, her tactics had worked, and they now awaited their audience with the king.

Suddenly, she heard shouting in the outside passageway. "The king! The king!"

The footmen snapped to attention, then bowed at the waist as the tall mahogany doors flew open. Maeve and Fiona leaped to their feet, then sank into curtseys so low Fiona's curls brushed the lustrous floor. Two sets of gentlemen's shoes one buckled with silver, one with gold—halted in front of her nose.

George Grenville said, "Your Majesty, may I present Madam Maclean and her daughter-in-law."

"Come, come. You may rise."

The king's voice sounded hale and hearty, but Fiona detected an odd undercurrent in his tone. She straightened and fixed her eyes on a point six inches to the right of the king's shoulder, for it was an unpardonable impertinence to look a monarch in the face.

From her peripheral vision, she saw that George III was tall, well built, young and surprisingly handsome—if one's taste ran to bulging blue eyes, a large German nose, sensitive lips and pale skin. He wore an intricate powdered wig with the hair combed back in a ribbon and sausage curls at the side; a royal blue satin frock coat with turned-back sleeves lined in cloth of gold; a red-damask waistcoat that almost matched the chamber's draperies; white-satin breeks tied with gold ribbon at the knees; and pristine white-silk stockings.

He glanced at Fiona and blinked, then waved a manicured hand at Maeve. Lace floated at his cuffs. "You have news of that bloody Young Pretender? Come, come. Let's have it."

Maeve smiled airily, as if conversing with a gardener, then spoke in perfect British tones. "In truth, Your Majesty, I must confess that what Grenville has told you is a fabrication. I am happy to report that Charles Stuart is in Italy—penniless and likely drunk. He has no plans to travel to London, and from all accounts, including my own personal observation, he has given up all thought of ever again making another attempt on Your Majesty's throne."

The red rays of sunset slanted like ghostly fingers across the room, and the air echoed with silence. At last Grenville's mellifluous tones broke the astonished stillness. "Your Majesty, I must solicit your most humble pardon. These ladies came to me under Bute's auspices. Based on their intimacy with him and with the Jacobite exiles in France, I accepted his assurances that their story was true. I assure you, I had no idea—"

The king held up a hand. "Silence." He peered down into Maeve's ruddy face. "Madam, what would possess you to seek and audience with us, then recant your wild and inflammatory tale? Are you mad?"

The hair lifted at Fiona's nape. Again that peculiar tone in the king's voice—a thrill, a recognition, an excitement, rather like the tone Pierre Mercier had used when he had asked Fiona, "Are you French?"

Then she heard a familiar, gruff Scottish burr in her

ear. *Och, lassie. And to think this mincin' booby is king in place o' our own bonnie prince! He's losin' his reason, ye ken.* She stifled a gasp and clenched her hands into fists; Sir Hector's voice grumbled on. *I'm tellin' ye, 'tis true. He's been depressed. He suffered a fit last month—all thrashin' and slobberin'. Only his leeches and body servant ken it—and his wife, o' course. Och, she's a great comfort to him, but 'tis no' enough. He'll die ravin'. Mark me words.*

Fiona dragged her attention back to the conversation. To her amazement, Maeve had launched into the real reason they had inveigled their way into the king's presence.

"Your Majesty, you know that my husband fought against your grandfather during the last Rising. We were forced into exile, as would be expected. We lost everything, and my husband died in poverty, a sad and broken man. He paid the price for his beliefs, and that's as it should be. But I don't believe that my daughter-in-law, who was a wee child at the time, or that I should continue to suffer over male foolishness we didn't condone and couldn't control. I've never held political beliefs, Your Majesty. I've just been a wife."

She spoke so rapidly the king wasn't able to interrupt. A look of befuddlement slipped over his patrician features, and he stared at her as if she had three heads.

"I didn't know what I could do to convince you that I had washed my hands of the Jacobites long ago," Maeve said, "and that I wanted your pardon. Then something happened, and I got an idea." She paused and lowered her voice to a dramatic whisper. "Right now, falsely accused and thrown in Newgate, is a loyal Scotsman who fought for the British during the Rising."

Fiona's head swiveled. She had come to Scotland to find the truth, and she had. Lachlan had not turned against his blood. Instead, he had fought bravely for his clan, then put the best interests of his people in front of his own desires. Did Maeve still believe he had betrayed his clan and fought for the British? Or was she perpetuating a lie in order to help him? *Mon Dieu,* what a tangled web.

"Of what is this man accused?" The king's voice hinted at no little irritation.

"Of thievery, Your Majesty." Maeve jutted out her chin. "But he is no thief. He is a caring steward of the land." Then she launched into a colorful explanation about Duncan Campbell, Taigh Samhraidh, Maire Rankin, and the two hundred pounds taken from the estate to repair the tumbledown crofts.

That caught the king's interest. He threw himself into a gilt chair and crossed his long legs, ankle over knee. "This Maclean is a farmer, what?"

Suddenly, Fiona remembered Lachlan's disparaging comments about the king, whom he had called Farmer George because of the monarch's well-publicized fondness for the royal estates at Richmond and Windsor. Before Maeve could reply, Fiona bobbed a curtsy and said, "He is, Your Majesty—and a fine one at that. Monsieur Maclean is most interested in all the latest agricultural improvements, and he's made any number of innovations. . . ."

Her voice trailed off. The king was staring at her as if she were a mouse who had addressed a lion. A dull red suffused his pale cheeks, and his blue eyes seemed to bulge even further. "Madam, may we deduce from your accent that you are French?" he asked. She nodded, too flustered to explain. He smoothed the lace at his cuffs, then tossed her an off-kilter smile. "Then, we will conclude that your manners are not as they should be."

All at once, she caught an ominous flash of light hovering around the king's body, all muddy brown and dark-blue, like ink spilled into a churning puddle. Inside the light, she saw an old man—alone, blind, mad and dying. She froze, hand halfway to her mouth. *Mon Dieu*, Sir Hector was right! George III would one day be a hopeless lunatic.

The king smiled, oblivious to her distress. "Now, since you seem to like to chatter, you'll tell us about this man's innovations, what?"

Fiona clenched her eyes shut. St. Francis, she knew nothing of farming. She desperately trawled her memory for anything agricultural, but came up empty. Then, outside in the corridor, she heard yelping from the queen's renowned pack of Cavalier King Charles spaniels.

Inspiration struck. "Your Majesty, I was raised in Paris, and I am no countrywoman, but I can tell you that Monsieur Maclean has bred the most marvelous hunting dogs. They are completely new. No one has ever seen the like. Such heart, such intelligence, such beauty." She smiled six inches to the left of the king's shoulder. "May one inquire if His Majesty enjoys hunting?"

"Ah! Who doesn't!" The king slapped his thigh and gave a hearty laugh. "Just last week we shot thirty ducks at Richmond. Lost half of 'em, too, blast it all. No way to retrieve them out of that demmed cold river."

"Then, if I may be so bold, please allow me to say that Your Majesty must meet Monsieur Maclean. His dogs are a miracle. They will leap into the iciest water, retrieve the heaviest bird and return it as if it had never been touched. They are large, heavy-coated, sweet-faced and"—she smiled at the king's shimmering cuffs and knee ribbons—"they are the color of pure, spun gold."

George III seemed ready to discuss dogs and hunting for the rest of the afternoon, but George Grenville interrupted. "Forgive me, but may I remind Your Majesty that this Maclean is a Scot? Even if he fought for your royal grandfather, his clan did not. Madam Maclean freely admits his estate was confiscated and given to this, ah . . . Duncan Campbell. That being the case, it was a crime for him to have pilfered two hundred pounds from the estate, no matter how noble his motive." Grenville's voice practically dripped sarcasm.

The king scowled. "We did not ask your opinion, sirrah! From the sound of things, this Campbell is bent on running a fine estate into the ground. He's mortgaged it to the hilt and cannot pay his debts. What kind of gentleman . . . what kind of landowner is that?" He snorted, then turned. "Ladies, we are most anxious to see these marvelous hunting dogs. If we have this Maclean fellow released, is there any way for him to return Campbell's two hundred pounds?"

Fiona and Maeve exchanged glances. They had agreed on the way to Lord Bute's residence that they wouldn't mention the clan badge or that Lachlan was now chieftain of Clan Maclean. The whole Highland clan system was supposed to have been wiped out after the Rising, and the mere idea of its existence was anathema to the German Hanovers.

Suddenly, Fiona could take no more dissembling. There was a reason she hadn't made a good courtier or a facile philosopher: sometimes, one had to reveal the truth.

"Your Majesty, there is a way to settle this matter," she replied. "Monsieur Maclean can return the money he, ah . . . borrowed, and he can pay off the lien against

Taigh Samhraidh. But if he does so, 'tis critical that the estate legally be returned to him, and to his future heirs."

The king's pale brow furrowed. "Madam, I appreciate that this Maclean was loyal to the Crown, but do you understand the controversy that will arise if word gets 'round that we restored his estate after his kin and clan fought against our grandfather?"

Fiona dropped her gaze and swallowed. Maeve was right. What use was revealing all if all was destroyed? *Mon Dieu,* she hated this. All her life she had been told to hide her true self for fear of the consequences. Then, when at last she had found the courage to tell Lachlan about her strange gift, he hadn't even believed her.

For a split second, his handsome, laughing face flashed through her mind. Lachlan was the greatest nobleman she had ever known, and he had lived a lie for years. To him, telling the unvarnished truth had not been nobler than helping the people he loved.

She clenched her eyes shut, suddenly remembering a saying that Sir Hector—pragmatic curmudgeon *extraordinaire*—had tried to drum into her skull for years. *Pure truth is like a rough diamond, lass. Its greatest value is revealed only when one has the sense to cut and polish it.*

The king cleared his throat. "Madam, we asked you a question."

She curtseyed. "Your Majesty, if you will order Lachlan Maclean released and brought here to the palace along with Duncan Campbell, I think we can sort everything out." She fixed the king with a level gaze and smoothed her face into tranquillity. "Oh, and I'll need to send a message to Monsieur Pierre Mercier."

Twenty-eight

"I declare, His Majesty is quite, quite mad!" Queen Charlotte deftly flicked open her ivory-boned fan and used it to block her conversation from the prying eyes of George Grenville. She leaned closer to John Stuart, Earl of Bute, and hissed in her thick German accent, "What must he be thinking? To meet with these ragtag nobodies, these . . . these Jacobite troublemakers? Upon my soul, this must be some scheme of Grenville's. *You,* my dear Bute, would never so misstep."

Fiona glanced down at her travel-stained black-wool skirts and pretended she couldn't hear the queen's remarks. *Mon Dieu,* Queen Charlotte was right. She and Maeve looked like ragamuffins compared to the royals, their courtiers and the present and former prime minister. Why, even the footmen possessed a greater air of *élan.*

She plastered a serene smile to her face and pretended to admire the elegant private drawing room to which she and Maeve had been escorted. Everywhere she looked there were magnificent gilded pier glasses, muted pink Aubusson carpets garlanded with roses and ribbons, graceful china figurines, gilt-framed portraits and gleaming Chippendale tables and chairs. Rose-colored silk draperies had been drawn to block the cold winter's night, and fires popped and crackled in the twin white-marble fireplaces.

At the far end of the drawing room, the king sat in intent discussion with Duncan Campbell, who had arrived moments earlier in response to the royal summons. A flickering glow from dozens of beeswax candles shimmered on the rose damask upholstery and polished mahogany tables—and glinted in Duncan's furious blue eyes. Fiona suppressed a shiver, then prayed for mercy. Duncan clearly was doing his best to convince the king that she and Maeve were dangerous lunatics, and likely he was succeeding.

"I beg your pardon, madam."

Fiona looked up to find George Grenville at her elbow. He bowed gracefully, and she was startled to see a shrewd and wary kindness in his wide-set blue eyes. "You appeared distressed just now, madam," he said in a velvet-smooth voice. "May I be so bold as to hazard that you overheard the queen's remarks?"

"I, ah . . . yes. I did." Fiona cocked her head and studied the statesman before her. He was dressed soberly, if expensively, with a severe white-linen stock and a coat and breeks of black velvet. His powdered wig was thick and tightly curled, adding width to his long oval face, and unlike most courtiers, he wore neither patches nor face powder. Bute had wasted little time in the carriage en route to the palace before disparaging Grenville for unwise political choices, particularly in regard to taxation. But Fiona sensed the prime minister was more eager for approval than power.

She gestured to the chair beside her. "Please, sir. Do sit down."

As he sat, Grenville whispered, "I understand you

are from France, madam. Are you at all acquainted with the political situation in England right now?"

"Non, monsieur."

Grenville look gratified at having fresh clay to mold. "You know that the war with France in the Colonies is at an end?"

"Oui, monsieur. The loss of Quebec and Montreal was greeted with great distress in Paris, as was the death of le Marquis de Montcalm. He was a courageous soldier."

Grenville cleared his throat. "Yes, well. Be that as it may, the war has nearly bankrupted the government. The last thing His Majesty and Parliament need at this time is more trouble in the Highlands."

"But, monsieur, as Madam Maclean told the king, Charles Stuart has no plan—"

"Yes, yes, I know. But the Highlands remain recalcitrant. Smuggling is rampant, the Crown duty officers seem incapable of collecting taxes on Scots whisky, and British peers who were granted estates after the Rising report that their tenants are not capable of meeting their rents, let alone turning a profit."

Fiona kept her gaze fixed on Grenville's eyes. "Monsieur, if that is true, your government has no one to blame but itself. Why should the Scots labor for Englishmen, who do nothing but oppress them? If you see Scotland as a source of much-needed revenue, you should let the people have more control over their lives."

"Madam, I quite agree. A wise government knows how to enforce with temper, or to conciliate with dignity."

Fiona clasped his forearm. "Then will you help me? The best way to secure loyalty and prosperity in the Western Isles is to return Taigh Samhraidh—"

The drawing-room door swung open. "Your Majesty, Lachlan Maclean."

Fiona looked up; Queen Charlotte screamed; the king and his courtiers leaped to their feet. "Good God!" cried Grenville. "Surely that man can't be alive!"

Fiona sat frozen to her chair as two stout footmen carried Lachlan into the room. He sagged unconscious between them, arms clutched over their shoulders. Blood had crusted over a deep gash in his cheek, his lip was split and swollen, a purple bruise had distorted one side of his face, and his nose appeared to have been broken yet again. Blood dripped from it onto the Aubusson rug, adding dark-red blooms to the elegant floral design.

"Lachlan! What have they done?" She bolted forward, then reached him as the footmen lowered him onto a gilt settee. She pressed her hand to his feverish cheek, instantly feeling the faint flicker of life beneath her palm. *"Dieu merci,* he's not dead."

Blood thundered in her ears, and her hands shook as she ran her fingers over the break in his nose—his long, elegant nose. She bent to press her ear to his chest, and her gaze fell on his crippled hand. Someone had smashed it beyond recognition as a human appendage.

She stood, then whirled. The king and queen, Maeve, Duncan, Grenville and Bute clustered behind her; a ring of gaping, silk-clad courtiers hovered behind them. She stabbed a finger at Duncan. "You! You did this—"

"Madam, I assure you, I never touched the man." Duncan held up two smooth, manicured hands to prove his claim. "Surely you don't expect a lame man—"

Fiona lunged forward and grabbed the frogged la-pels of his coat. "You ordered it! I saw you pay those soldiers to beat Lachlan. You wanted him dead and out of the way!" She shook Duncan, nearly jostling him off his crutch. "You'll never get the clan badge—"

"Madam."

Fiona halted, stunned by the musket crack of authority in the king's voice.

"That will be enough," he snapped. "This is not a bear pit, and you will comport yourself like a lady when you are in our presence." He peered over her shoulder at Lachlan's crumpled form, then frowned in aggravation. "Demme, this is a mess."

Fiona pushed away from Duncan, then sank into a trembling curtsey. "Please, Your Majesty, have you a court physician? This man is grievously injured. I . . . I fear there are ribs broken, and his head . . ."

George III waved his hand at a footman. "Send for Carstairs at once." The footman hurried toward the door, and the painted and powdered courtiers broke into a chorus of murmurs and giggles. The king silenced them with a glare, then took Fiona's hand and patted it. "Madam, our physician does not live with us at court. We fear it may be some little time before he arrives."

"Carstairs?" Bute interjected. "John Carstairs? Since when is he Your Majesty's physician?"

The queen dragged her blue-marble gaze from Lachlan's wounds, then briskly fanned her pale cheeks. "Since our last lying in, sir. He is most advanced, most modern, yet still so entertaining. During our travail, he distracted us from the pain with folk tales from the Scottish Highlands."

"But his family are Jacobites," Bute protested. "Surely you know that?"

The courtiers' murmurs grew louder; Fiona stifled a

groan of despair, then sank onto the settee beside Lachlan. Good St. Joseph, she wanted to scream! The man she loved was dying, and all these men cared about was cold-hearted politics.

Tripe and ballocks. What do ye expect, lassie? For them to be wipin' Lachlan's arrogant arse?

Fiona pressed a hand to her galloping heart. There was no mistaking Sir Hector's gruff Highland burr. She stared around the room, wildly searching for the grumbling ghost. Had anyone else heard him? *Non.* The queen was fanning herself with haughty little flicks, the king was scowling at Bute, and the courtiers still hovered and murmured like a swarm of perfumed bees. She clenched her eyes shut, then stroked Lachlan's fevered cheek.

Suddenly she felt Sir Hector at her shoulder, so close she shivered from the blast of frigid air that always accompanied him. His voice rumbled through her mind like distant thunder.

Och, for a wench wi' the second sight, schooled in all the tenets o' reason and logic, ye're the thickest, blindest creature I've ever kent. That bloody Sassenach doctor wilna get here in time. So if ye want that brazen cocksman ye've fallen love wi' to survive, then ye'll have to save him yourself.

She crossed herself and murmured, "St. Joseph, help me."

"What was that, my dear?" The king leaned closer, then shuddered as he brushed near Sir Hector's unseen form. "Brrrrr. I say, 'tis cold in here. Like walking into a tomb, what?"

Fiona dragged Lachlan into a sitting position, then cradled his face to hers. Their features meshed, cheekbone to cheekbone, and she trailed her fingers through his matted hair, then found a gash at the base of his skull. It was bleeding, and a brilliant stream trickled down his neck and stained his white shirt with rivulets of scarlet. Tentatively, she pressed her fingers to his torn flesh.

Gather your courage, lass. Sir Hector's voice blustered through her mind. *Ye canna save him 'til ye find the strength.*

Fiona blinked back tears and nearly screamed from the excruciating tension shrieking along her nerves. That was easy for Sir Hector to say; he was already dead. He didn't have to suffer the consequences. He didn't have to fear being accused of witchcraft or heresy—or plain old madness. She wiped a sweaty palm across her brow. Good St. Joan, even if she could heal Lachlan's wounds in front of king, queen and courtiers, how would she ever explain it?

"Poor man," a woman cooed. "Perhaps 'twould be kindest to put him out of his misery."

Behind Fiona, the queen and her courtiers fell to discussing Lachlan as if he were a downed racehorse.

"I heard that one of the cooks is skilled with herbs. Perhaps a poultice?"

"A poultice? Lud! Next you'll have Gypsies chanting over him. This is the age of reason, not superstition."

Queen Charlotte swept closer, and Fiona caught the scent of orange water and face powder that hung about her satin skirts like a physical presence. "Carstairs declares one must heal the soul along with the body," the queen said. "Oh, he had so many fine tales!" She spun about and rapped her husband's arm with her fan. "Liebchen, did you know that in medieval times the common folk believed a king could heal by touch alone? 'Twas said the monarch's healing power came from God, as did his sovereignty."

George III snorted, but looked vaguely pleased. Again Fiona caught an odd frisson of imbalance about him, as if he were a dog that had been stricken with madness, but did not yet show it.

An elegant, acid voice hissed from the back of the room. "King's touch, eh? *That* would be something to see—and I vow, 'twould settle the Jacobites once and for all."

"Enough!" John Bute roared. " 'Tis no laughing matter. A man's dying here, and those bloody Jacobites still cause unrest in this country."

Fiona gnawed her lip, then clenched her fists 'til her nails dug into her palms. King's touch. *Mon Dieu*, could an old Highland legend provide the cover she needed? She uttered a silent prayer, then extended Lachlan's limp, bloody hand toward the king. "Your Majesty," she whispered, "will you help him?"

The king blinked owlishly. "What's that, my dear?"

"Please, Your Majesty." She lowered her lashes and blushed. "I'm very religious—and very superstitious. If the doctor will not arrive in time, it would be such a kindness to me if you would lay your royal hand upon Monsieur Maclean. It . . . it could do no harm, and perhaps 'twould do some good."

The king stared at her for a long, uncomprehending moment. Then he nervously settled his satin frock coat into a more flattering line and waved his arm at the crowd. "Out. All of you, out. We wish to be alone with this lady."

Queen Charlotte gaped. "But, *liebchen*—"

"Lady, you will do as we command."

The queen blushed, then took Bute's arm and swept toward the door. The courtiers groused and protested, then trailed slowly from the room, the king's footmen nipping at their heels like busy Highland sheepdogs.

Fiona noticed that Maeve, Duncan and Grenville had stayed behind. She bowed her head. *"Merci,* Your Majesty. I know 'tis foolish to be so superstitious—"

"Nonsense. Nonsense! 'Tis clear to us that you love this man, madam. And one should not judge what is done out of love, what?" He edged closer to the settee, looking flushed and embarrassed, yet curiously eager. He cleared his throat, straightened his shoulders, then, with a regal flourish, laid his beringed hand on Lachlan's damp brow.

Fiona closed her eyes and silently began to pray, then surreptitiously pressed her fingertips to the wound at the base of Lachlan's skull. At first she felt nothing but a dull, blank, colorless void. She took a deep breath, then whispered, "Lachlan? Will you come back to us, *mo cridhe?"*

Suddenly she felt delicious warmth and the unmistakable liquid shimmer of life beneath his ragged scalp. Then another sensation tingled through her fingertips, and excitement shot like quicksilver through her veins. This feeling wasn't coming from Lachlan; it was radiating out from her, out from her very soul.

She clenched her eyes tight, and energy surged through her arm. She went still, then forced herself to focus, to open as a conduit for the glorious golden surge of light. Lachlan stirred, and she caught a fleeting mental image of summer fields and heather and the tang of salt sea air. *Mon Dieu,* she could nearly taste that air: strong, vibrant, thrumming with the muted and joyous hymn of life that lay just below the hearing of human ears. She smiled. *Most* human ears.

She took a deep breath and let herself relax. Then she hovered a few inches above Lachlan's bluish lips and whispered, "Come back to us, *mo cridhe."*

Lachlan's lids fluttered. Above her, Fiona heard the

king gasp. Lachlan mumbled in Gaelic; then his eyes flew open. The king jumped back; Fiona snatched her hands from Lachlan's wound.

The bleeding had stopped.

"Lass," Lachlan croaked. He grasped her shoulder and shakily hauled himself upright. "Are ye an angel?" His silvery eyes cleared; then he swayed forward and coughed with great, hacking spasms. "Och, am I alive or am I dead?"

Fiona's vision blurred, and she realized hot tears were trickling down her cheeks. She leaned forward and smoothed her fingers over the agitated lines of his face. Better that he not know the truth. She cupped his bruised cheeks in her hands, then slowly, tenderly kissed his mouth. " 'Tis I. Fiona. Not an angel."

Lachlan chuckled weakly. "Aye. Angels canna kiss like that." With trembling fingers, he wiped away her tears, then pressed his lips to her forehead and kissed her as tenderly as one might bless a child.

"By Jove!" Grenville exclaimed. "It worked."

She turned as Grenville stepped forward, Maeve close on his heels. He caught Fiona's eye, and for a split second, she thought she saw him wink. Then he flourished his arm in a courtly bow, and Maeve sank into a deep curtsy before the king.

"Your Majesty," Grenville intoned. "I am astonished, sir, astonished. And I am humbled. Why, I scarce know what to say." He straightened and patted his wig, as if the wonderment of what he had just witnessed had gone to his head. Again, Fiona caught a shrewd flash of perception in his wide-set eyes. "I have always known of His Majesty's divine right to the throne of Britain, but when word of this gets out—"

The king held up a pale, trembling hand in a gesture of deprecating modesty. "Enough, sirrah. 'Tis nothing

We'll not speak of it again." He slanted Fiona an uncertain gaze, and his cheeks flushed. She smiled and nodded, then curtseyed deeply.

"*Merci,* Your Majesty," she murmured. "*Merci.* Your power humbles and overwhelms me."

Duncan Campbell stumped forward. "Oh, this is preposterous." The scar on his cheek pulsed angrily, and livid red spots rode high on his angular cheeks. "Your Majesty, this is some type of trick designed to gull and flatter you. Why, I doubt Maclean was seriously injured—"

"How dare you?" Maeve whirled and glared as if Duncan were a rabid dog. "How dare you speak thus to the king?" She jutted out her chin, then nervously wiped her palms down over her black skirts. Fiona smothered a smile. Maeve had never been nervous a moment in her life.

"His Majesty just healed this man," Maeve snapped. "He snatched him from the jaws of death. We all saw it with our own eyes." She stepped before the king, and her keen gray eyes filled with shimmering tears. Fiona gaped. *Mon Dieu,* Maeve didn't need Lachlan's financial support—she could make a fine living on the stage.

"Your Majesty," Maeve pleaded, "God has just worked a miracle through your royal touch. Please, sir, I beg you. Don't send Mr. Maclean back to prison."

The king frowned. "Madam, you make too much of this. And we cannot set aside the law of the land on a whim. If Maclean stole money from Duncan Campbell, it must be repaid." He turned to Fiona. "Madam, you told us earlier that there is a means to settle this debt."

"*Oui,* monsieur," Fiona replied. She darted across the room, where a small, covered basket rested unheeded beneath a gilt chair. She snatched the basket up, then ran back to the king. With an air of great drama, she flipped open the lid, then drew out the jeweled clan badge. The heavily engraved gold gleamed in the candlelight, and the emeralds in the lions' eyes flared like green fire. Grenville gasped, and the king's brows shot up.

"This belonged to Sir Hector Maclean," she said quickly, so Duncan wouldn't cut her off. "It has belonged to his family for centuries. Now, since he is Sir Hector's sole heir, it rightfully belongs to Lachlan Maclean." She shot Duncan a scathing glance. *"That* man stole it from him. He planned to sell it, pay off the lien on Taigh Samhraidh, then use the balance of the funds to purchase a title, so he could take his *place"*—her voice oozed sarcasm—"among the peerage."

The king looked at Duncan with the expression usually reserved for finding a dead fly in one's soup. "Is this true, sirrah?"

Duncan's anxious gaze darted between Fiona and the king. "Your Majesty, I fought for your grandfather, and I own a mighty estate in the Isles. Surely I deserve a title—"

"Ye deserve nothin'," Lachlan hissed. He staggered to his feet, gray eyes glittering with fever. "Ye're a thief—a schemin', graspin'—"

Duncan lurched forward, teeth bared in a furious grimace.

"Stop." Hands raised, Grenville stepped between them, then bowed to the king. "Your Majesty, I beg you to settle this matter before these gentlemen come to blows."

Duncan scowled like a petulant child. "Your Majesty, the Duke of Cumberland saw to it that I was given Taigh Samhraidh for loyal service to Your Majesty's grandfather. That badge came with the estate. It had been hidden there—"

"Hidden by my husband!" Maeve cried. "And he left everything he owned to Lachlan Maclean."

Duncan planted his crutch in front of the king, then grasped the royal sleeve. "That badge is mine. Taigh Samhraidh is mine. You *must* proclaim me rightful laird."

The drawing room fell silent. A livid tide of red washed over the king's cheeks, and he glared at Duncan as if he wished to pluck him off like an engorged louse.

Then Lachlan stepped forward. With a wry, teasing smile, he grasped Duncan's arm and lifted it from the king's. "Och, ye wee, hot-headed *turach,* didna your fine London friends ever teach ye to show respect for the king?" He arched a roguish brow and rolled his *r*'s like loaded dice.

Fiona caught her breath. Although George III was a tall man, Lachlan towered over him, and standing there in his filthy suede breeks and bloodstained linen shirt, he resembled nothing so much as a wild Scottish highwayman.

"I beg you to forgive Campbell, Your Majesty." Lachlan's words were respectful and his accent was that of an exquisitely educated British peer, but his tone was light and bantering. "We Scots are a primitive, stubborn lot and often inclined to forget our drawing-room manners." Then he made a leg and flourished his arm in a bow of stunning masculine grace.

Fiona's heart contracted. *Mon Dieu,* never had Lachlan looked more dangerously handsome, more lethally powerful, than at this moment. Something flickered in George III's cold blue eyes. Respect? Regret? Admiration? Her skin tightened.

Suddenly, the king's gaze darted toward the corner of the room. His cheeks went ashen, and his jaw sagged. Fiona glanced over her shoulder, then froze. In the distant, fire-shot shadows of the chamber stood a Highlander in full battle regalia. His tartan kilt stirred about his knees as if blown by an unseen wind. A dagger was thrust in his black-leather belt, a sheathed sword hung at his side, and the carved hilt of a *sgian dhu* jutted from the top of one wool stocking. A full plaid crossed his broad chest and was pinned to his shoulder with the gold Maclean clan badge. Half of his face was painted blue, in a barbaric pattern designed to strike fear in Sassenach hearts. His hands clasped a claymore that was nearly as tall as Fiona.

Listen to me, George Hanover. Sir Hector's voice was hoarse, spectral, fiercely bitter. George III's flesh seemed to sag on his bones; he turned as pale as death.

"What is it?" Lachlan asked. He quizzically tilted his head, glanced from Fiona to the king, then followed the direction of their paralyzed gazes. Maeve and Duncan did the same, then exchanged puzzled glances. Clearly, none of them saw or heard a thing.

In life I was Prince Charlie's mon, but in death, I am God's. Sir Hector touched the jeweled badge pinned over his heart. *George Hanover, heed me now. Unless ye wish to wander in Purgatory for an eternity alongside me vengeful soul, ye'll do what ye ken is right.*

Then Sir Hector Maclean sheathed his claymore and disappeared.

George III expelled his breath in a long, tremulous gasp, then sank onto the settee. He closed his eyes for several long moments, then opened them and quickly motioned Lachlan and Fiona forward. He plucked the clan badge from Fiona's hands and held it out to Lachlan. "Sir, we present you with your rightful inheri tance, and we return the estate known as Taigh Sam-hraidh into your expert care." He swallowed and looked as if he was about to faint. "Have you anything to say?"

"Aye, Your Majesty." Lachlan caught Fiona around the waist, then pulled her against his chest. "Would I be too much the wild Highlander if I kiss this lady in front of ye?" The skin crinkled around his eyes, and his lips quirked in a devilish smile. "After all, Your Majesty, she is me betrothed—and a treasure beyond price."

Twenty-nine

It was Christmas Day, and the great hall of Castle Taigh fairly rang with festive merriment. Shiny holly garlands were looped above the doorways, and mistletoe wreathed the stuffed boar's head, dripped from the elk's antlers, and hung from the massive wrought-iron chandeliers, where the wax drippings from dozens of candles nestled among the plant's white berries. A fire roared in the carved stone hearth, and pine boughs had been tossed over the oak logs to add their pop, crack and spice to the fragrant air.

Fiona drew a quavering breath, then smiled. She had slaved alongside the servants day and night to ready the hall for her wedding. The carved-oak refectory table had been polished to a high sheen, the stone floor had been scoured, and the stained-glass windows had been scrubbed until they shone like jewels. Now, to her great joy, not a hint of dank, miserable cold remained. Indeed, the table all but groaned under the weight of braided and glazed sweet breads, mincemeat pies, plum pudding, roast goose, venison pasties, congealed salmon, potted eels, apple tarts, pickles, dates, almonds and a three-tiered *gateau au chocolat* iced with snowy white frosting and studded with red and green heart- and holly-shaped marzipan.

She stepped back from the oak railing of the minstrel's gallery, then wiped her damps palms down over her skirt. She hadn't wanted to take the time to order a new gown in London, so she was to be married in a dress sewn here on the Isle from lavender-blue velvet presented as a gift from Two-Pack Ian. Lachlan had insisted upon that particular fabric, suavely declaring that it matched the tranquillity of the twilight sea and the serene violet of her eyes.

A blush warmed her cheeks. *Mon Dieu,* what a charming rogue—and where was he, anyway? Their guests had arrived over an hour ago, and the hall below was packed with tenants, kin, dignitaries and neighbors. All had sampled freely from the punchbowls of spiced wine and the casks of fresh, sweet ale, and now they laughed, roared, danced and pummeled each other in an excess of holiday glee.

She leaned her elbows on the gallery rail and smiled. The tenants, especially, had reason to be happy. Lachlan's first move, now that he had been restored to his rightful position as laird, had been to slash the crofters' rent and begin improvements to the worst of the cottages. Indeed, he spent most evenings with his gold-rimmed spectacles propped on his long, elegant nose, poring over outlandish plans to rotate crops and crossbreed his sheep with some herd in Italy renowned for spectacular wool. But, to Fiona's astonishment, he had not publicly announced that he now was chieftain of Clan Maclean.

"Och, lass, 'tis no' somethin' a mon just up and forces on folk," he had said when she questioned him. "After all that's happened since Culloden, I canna expect things to be as they once were." His wide-set eyes had grown distant, and she had known he was thinking of his brothers in America.

A fiddler struck up a sprightly rendition of "The

Holly and the Ivy," and below in the hall, the guests began to stamp their feet. Fergus and Lazarus, who were freshly bathed and wore red ribbons on their collars, began to bark. Suddenly, a shout went up, and the Lord of Misrule and a ragtag band of musicians joined the celebration. The costumed players danced, piped and fiddled their way around the candlelit room, heralding the appearance of the Yule log—a chunk of wood gaily decorated with holly, ivy and mistletoe. With elaborate ceremony and many bawdy jests, the Lord of Misrule placed the log in the fireplace, then lit it to welcome the Christmas season. Then the musicians and a bagpiper began a heart-stirring reel.

"Come down, Madam Fraser." The Lord of Misrule tilted back his head and beckoned to her with a black-gloved hand. "There's someone here who verra much wants to dance wi' ye."

Fiona frowned and peered down at the laughing crowd. The Lord of Misrule was dressed in a gold-and-purple court jester's costume, with a black mask over his tanned and chiseled features. Because she was standing above him, she hadn't noticed his unusual height. Her lips twitched. *Non,* it couldn't be.

"Weel, then," the jester called. "If ye'll no' come down, I'll come up."

In a flash, she heard footsteps pounding on the carved spiral staircase that twisted up to the gallery. Then the Lord of Misrule towered over her. She clasped her hands behind her back and leaned against the railing. "Lachlan? Is that you?"

He bowed extravagantly. "Guilty as charged—and a mon sore stricken wi' love for your beauteous face and sensitive heart." He tore off his mask, then whisked her into the sheltering warmth of his arms. His silvery eyes glinted like the stars in the winter sky, and his dark hair brushed against her cheek with the startling intimacy of a kiss.

"Och, *mo cridhe*," he murmured, tenderly kissing the tip of her nose. "Will ye hear these words from a mon who's been a fool? I love ye, lass, and I have since the first moment I saw ye. I was just too stubborn and proud to admit it." His arms tightened around her until she thought her ribs would snap. "Ye're so fine, so good. I thought ye'd never look at a mon like me, who's made so many mistakes—"

He lowered his lips to hers, and his kisses no longer were tender. His sweet, whisky-scented tongue thrust deep into her mouth, and he claimed her, marked her, made her his for all time.

Barking, cheering and stamping of feet dragged them back to their senses. Fiona stepped into the shadows and blushed. "I . . . I didn't realize they could see us. *Mon Dieu*, they must think I'm a brazen hussy."

Lachlan chuckled, teeth glinting wolfish and white. "Weel now, we'd best mend that impression wi' a proper weddin', aye?" He smiled deep into her eyes and held out his hand—his crippled hand. It was nearly useless now, for Duncan's henchmen had smashed each long, tanned finger with the butt of a musket. The king's physicians had set the delicate bones, but they hadn't healed properly.

She caught his hand, then pressed it to her lips. "Oh, my darling, darling heart. I love you so much. It hurts me to see you like this." Tears welled in her eyes, and Lachlan scowled like a black-hearted highwayman. "I-I don't mean that 'tis unattractive," she added hastily. One by one, she kissed each twisted finger. "Nothing about you could be unattractive, ever. I mean I can't stand to see your . . . your . . ."

"Wounded pride?" Lachlan offered with a rueful

smile. "Nay, lass. That's long gone." He held up his mangled hand, then turned it so that the candlelight fell on it.

"Lachlan?" she whispered. "You know I can heal it, don't you?"

He studied his hand nonchalantly, as if it were a curiosity of mild and passing interest. Then he met her gaze, and his warm silver eyes seared to her heart. "Aye, I ken it, lass. I've kent since that day on Culloden battlefield." His voice quavered and grew hoarse, revealing the depth of his emotion. "But in truth, *mo cridhe,* I dinna want ye to heal me hand— ever. 'Tis a symbol to me now. It reminds me that ye love me as I am."

Fiona's heart gave a great exultant leap of joy, and she threw her arms around his neck. Oh, she loved this man! She wanted to be part of him, one flesh for all eternity. She raised her mouth to his, and their souls melted together in a kiss of mutual forgiveness and understanding.

There was a clatter on the spiral staircase. Lachlan and Fiona stepped apart; then Rinalda hobbled up beside them. "Och, lad," she cried, poking her shiny mahogany cane at Lachlan's costumed shins. "Get ye out o' that gaudy rig and in your proper garb. We've a weddin' to hold."

Lachlan slanted Fiona a rakish wink, then swiftly kissed her cheek. "When next I kiss ye, lass, we'll be mon and wife—and I, for one, canna wait for the honeymoon." Then he spun and disappeared down the stairs.

Fiona started to follow, but Rinalda caught her arm. "Wait ye, lass. There's somethin' I wanted to say before ye become the laird's wife."

Fiona peered through the shadows, caught by the

urgent tone in the old crone's voice. Her heart began to pound. "What is it?"

"Och, dinna sound so spooked, lassie. 'Tis good news." Rinalda grinned, revealing glistening false teeth. Fiona smiled. Clearly this wedding was important to Rinalda if she had taken the trouble to put in her dentures. "Ye ken I've the second sight, aye?"

Fiona nodded.

"And ye've mentioned before aboot tryin' to find your real parents."

Fiona's stomach clenched. "You . . . you haven't found them, have you?"

Rinalda shook her head, and the lace lappets on her cap slapped against her withered cheeks. "Nay, lassie. I wish I had, but it proved beyond me power. Perhaps 'twasn't *meant* for me to find out." Her tone was almost comically heavy with portent.

Fiona pressed a hand to her waist. "Then what did you find?"

"Weel, when I went to the mainland wi' ye, ye'll recall that I took Maire Rankin's bairn and visited an old friend—a healer, like me, who lives near Loch Linnhe. I'd recalled a tale she told me once, and I wanted to hear it again." Rinalda sank onto a stool. "Ye've heard o' the *daoine stith,* aye? The little people?"

Fiona nodded.

"Weel, folk aboot here believe the *daoine stith* crave a human bairn for their own. 'Tis said if a lass be unlucky, or has done somethin' to offend, the little people will come in the night, snatch away her bairn and put a faerie child—a changeling—in its place. But *daoine stith* canna thrive with human folk. They're sickly babies, prone to cryin' and wastin' away. So, ever' once and again, a mother will be forced to abandon her changeling child, for 'tis no' human and canna be raised as such."

"W-what are you saying?"

Rinalda laid her birdlike claw over Fiona's hand. "Me friend recalled such a thing happenin' nigh onto twenty-four years ago. A drover found a bairn—a wee lassie—left alone on a hill near the loch in the middle o' the night. He and his wife took the babe in, but they already had six bairns o' their own, so a young couple livin' nearby who couldna have children adopted the lass. A fair, violet-eyed thing she was, wi' flame red hair. Perhaps she just needed love, for she survived weel enough after that."

Fiona stared into Rinalda's rheumy eyes. "The young couple were Deirdre and Ian Fraser." Rinalda nodded, and Fiona bent forward, then pressed her hands to her cheeks. *C'est vrai*, she hadn't needed the healer's confirmation; she had known all along.

"Mon Dieu, my mother was right. I really am a changeling." Wild laughter erupted inside her, then burst from her throat. "I can't believe it. Good St. Winifred, Lachlan will love this!" Her voice rose hysterically.

Rinalda whacked Fiona's shin with the cane. "Get ahold o' yourself. Surely an educated, rational lass like ye doesna believe in faeries and selkies."

Fiona dragged a trembling hand down over her face, then wiped away her tears. Oh, what did it matter? Did one truly have to divide life into an all or nothing scheme—science or superstition, reason or emotion, body or spirit? She gazed down on the great hall, where the minister from the kirk was herding the guests into some sense of order. She stood, then tugged the neck of her bodice a fraction lower. Perhaps it was time she stopped listening to others and started listening to her heart.

* * *

Fiona stood at the end of the great hall, beside the minister and in front of the stained-glass window of Matthew, Mark, Luke and John. She smiled up at the saints, then whispered a silent prayer of thanks to God and the Holy Mother. She didn't cross herself, as the dour Calvinist parson likely would faint if he suspected her Papist faith.

The expectant guests began to murmur and turn toward the far end of the hall. Fiona resisted the urge to stand on tiptoe and crane her neck along with them.

" 'Tis The Maclean!" a man shouted. "The Maclean!"

Fiona's heart lurched. Surely not. *Surely* Sir Hector wouldn't appear here, at her wedding—

The crowd parted, and Lachlan stood before her. His gaze locked onto hers, and he broke into a dazzling smile. It was like looking into the sun, for his silver eyes shone with teasing, rakish merriment—and with pure, soul-shattering love.

Only then did she take in his appearance. Her jaw dropped. If she lived to be a hundred, she would never see a man more stunning than Lachlan Ailm Adair Maclean, for he stood before her in full Highland regalia.

He strode forward, and his blue-and-green Maclean tartan kilt swung gracefully about his knees. It was belted to his narrow hips by a black-leather strap, and a badger-fur sporran brushed his powerful thighs. The jeweled hilt of his *sgian dhu* glittered from the top of one white stocking, and his black-leather shoes were buckled with silver. His full plaid crossed his broad chest and was pinned at the shoulder with a circular silver brooch, for the gold clan badge had been sold to settle the debts of the past. His wide shoulders strained under a black-velvet jacket, and a lace jabot accentuated the courtly effect of his snowy linen shirt. With braids at his temples and a dirk in his belt, Lachlan was the image of a powerful clan chieftain.

He reached her side, then tapped her jaw shut with one long finger. "Best close your mouth, *mo cridhe.* Ye dinna want flies gettin' in."

The minister cleared his throat and whispered, "Sir, you court danger. You know wearing the kilt and plaid is illegal, and the sheriff is one of the guests."

Lachlan winked. "Aye, I ken. I borrowed this wretched collar from him." He rolled his *r*'s wickedly and tugged a finger between lace jabot and tanned neck, grimacing dramatically all the while. "Shall we get this show on the road? Me bride is eager to start the honeymoon."

The minister caught up his worn leather bible and opened his mouth to begin the marriage service.

"Wait," a gruff voice boomed through the crowd, "ye canna marry them!"

Lachlan, Fiona and the minister turned as one, and Angus Beattie stepped forward. The room tilted and grew hot, the faces around Fiona turned fuzzy and gray, and a tingling roar crashed through her ears. Holy St. Genevieve, this couldn't be happening. Sorcha's father had come to stop Lachlan from marrying her. Oh, *mon Dieu,* what if he already was married? What if Sorcha—

Her knees buckled.

"Lass, dinna faint," Lachlan ground out. "Ye're too practical to have the vapors." He pulled her against him, then rounded on Angus. "What's this all aboot, Beattie?"

Angus bobbed his grizzled head, then patted a callused hand down over his hair as if smoothing it into place. "I . . . I beg your pardon, me laird. But I couldna see ye married this way. No' when things need to be set aright."

Fiona's mouth went dry. She couldn't hear it, couldn't hear that Lachlan would never be hers.

Angus knelt in front of Lachlan, then bowed his head and held out a dagger. The hilt was plain horn, worn from generations of hard use. "I am Angus Domnhil Beattie, o' Taigh Samhraidh," he said. "And I come to honor The Maclean. *Cean-cinnidh,* I am your mon. Ye are me chieftain."

A great cheer went up. "The Maclean! The Maclean!"

Fiona pushed against Lachlan's broad chest and tried to look up into his face; she could feel his heart thundering beneath her palm. "What is that about?" she hissed beneath the crowd's joyful cheers.

Lachlan drew himself up to his full height, then slanted a silver-eyed glare down his long, aristocratic nose. "Madam, those are the ancient words o' homage that a Highland Scot pays to the chief o' his clan." His pronouncement was undermined by the beguiling glint of mischief in his eyes. "Now—are *ye* ready to swear your obedience likewise?"

She pinned him with a calm, level gaze and contemplated telling him that a changeling obeyed no one but herself. Then she dimpled and demurely lowered her lashes. "Of course, monsieur."

Lachlan chuckled and took her hand. The crowd stilled, and the minister opened his prayer book; then his resonant voice rang through the great hall.

"Dearly beloved. . . ."

Epilogue

Castle Taigh, Isle of Mull
1769

Lachlan lounged against the terrace's carved stone rail and smiled. Before him, smooth emerald lawns stretched away to the sea, and the warm July air was sweet with the scent of pink apothecary roses, which Fiona had planted five years earlier to celebrate the birth of their son. The afternoon had started to wane and soft golden sunlight added a tranquil beauty to the white-swathed tea tables and the silks and muslins of the ladies' graceful gowns.

A light breeze stirred his hair; he brushed a strand from his eyes and smiled. He was forty-three years old today, and along with a touch of silver at his temples he had achieved everything a man possibly could want.

"Well, Lachlan. I must say you're looking very pleased with yourself."

He turned and smiled as his brother Diarmid strolled toward him across the flagstones. Diarmid was dressed soberly but expensively in deep blue broadcloth, and his aquamarine eyes were startling against his black hair and tanned skin. Looking every inch the prosperous Virginia planter, he stood beside Lachlan and gazed out over the birthday guests.

"May I take it that the complacent smile on your face has something to do with your outrageous good fortune?" Diarmid's Highland accent had been all but obliterated by a cultured Colonial drawl. He arched a wry black brow, and rakish dimples scored his cheeks. "I must say, Fiona is nearly as beautiful as Lucy."

"Och, and dinna be forgettin' me own bonny Clemency, or I'll be forced to call ye out." Jamie Maclean strode up the steps to the terrace and joined his two older brothers. His myriad responsibilities as the most powerful shipbuilder in the Province of Maine hadn't dimmed his teasing charm or the roguish glint in his eyes, and Lachlan's four-year-old daughter, Maeve, had fallen in love with him at first sight.

Jamie tossed back a cup of whisky-laced punch, then leaned his elbows on the parapet and gazed across the lawn at his wife and children. Clemency Maclean was showing Jamie's tall, coltish daughter Elizabeth and their impish, redheaded son Alexander the herbs that grew in the kitchen garden, and her lustrous raven hair streamed loose beneath a wide-brimmed straw hat.

Lachlan grinned. Fiona and the utterly unconventional Clemency had adored each other on sight. He turned and elbowed Jamie in the ribs. "Young Elizabeth told me that Clemency once was accused o' witchcraft. Is it true?"

"Aye."

Diarmid gave a snort of laughter. "That explains a lot. Sure and it would take a sorceress to tame our Jamie."

Jamie cuffed his brother's shoulder, but his warm indigo gaze never left the ivory curve of Clemency's cheek.

"Daddy! Daddy, watch us!"

Diarmid's twin daughters, Emma and Celia, bar-

reled across the manicured grass. "Hugh taught us how
to do a somersault!" Celia squealed, thrusting a finger
at Lachlan's ward, who had been raised in the castle as
a member of Lachlan's family since the death of Maire
Rankin. Beside him stood Lachlan and Fiona's son
Ian, the young Master of Mull and future chieftain of
Clan Maclean.

Hugh gave the rambunctious little girls an encourag-
ing nod. Instantly, the twins dropped to their knees and
flipped over in a flurry of muslin skirts and eyelet
petticoats. Their mother, Lucy Maclean, strolled up behind them, laughing.

"Up, you two urchins. Now take a bow. A Gypsy
always knows how to add drama to the show." To dem-
onstrate, Lucy doffed her pert straw hat, then flourished it gallantly before her and offered the men a
theatrical bow. Her black eyes sparkled with merriment
as her daughters mimicked her perfectly.

"Your turn now, Maeve." Lucy turned with a swirl
of canary-silk skirts, then looked about as if baffled.
"Maeve! Where are you, luv?" She waved to Fiona,
who had just wheeled Rinalda out onto the terrace in a
cunning chair with wheels, which Lachlan had devised
when the old healer no longer could walk. "Fiona—
have you seen your daughter? She was with us just a
moment ago."

Jamie straightened. "Och, but Maeve's a bonny lass.
Sure and she takes after her mother, aye?" He slanted
Lachlan a roguish glance. "How ever did ye pick her
name, though? Maeve is Irish, no' Scots."

Lachlan's lips curved into a gentle smile. Och, he
owed so much to the first Maeve Maclean, who had
died a year ago in Paris, in a fashionable town house a
few blocks from the convent of the Ursulines—which,
to his relief, Fiona never again had expressed a desire

to enter. It had been Maeve who had written to Diarmid and Jamie, explaining the truth about what Lachlan had done and exactly why he had done it. She had insisted, as the widow of Sir Hector Maclean, that the two stubborn colonials put aside their grievances and give Lachlan the love and respect due him as their eldest brother and chieftain. Jamie and Diarmid eventually had capitulated, and a lively correspondence had sprung up between the old world and the new. To Lachlan's great joy, Fiona had arranged this surprise reunion in honor of his birthday.

His smile faded. This was the first time Diarmid and Jamie had returned to Scotland since Culloden. In truth, they shouldn't be here at all, for they had been banished for life and forbidden to return—not that the law had ever stopped a Maclean.

He met Jamie's indigo gaze. "I named me daughter for Sir Hector's widow. I owe her a debt I can never repay, for she brought me Fiona, and she brought the three of us together once more—"

His voice grew hoarse. He cleared his throat, then looked out over the castle walls to the endless cobalt sea. Soon, his brothers and their families would return across that sea to America. Perhaps he would never see them again, for relations between Britain and her Colonies were as unstable as a keg of gunpowder: one spark, and there would be explosion, then conflagration.

Fiona glided up beside him, then touched his arm. He looked down at her, and instantly all his worries for the future faded away like frost beneath the rays of the sun. Motherhood had deepened her air of serenity, and while her eyes still were the shade of the twilight sea and her hair still gleamed like dancing flame, one thing about her had changed. After the birth of their son Ian,

she no longer could summon her ability to see spirit
talk to saints and heal with touch alone. To Lachlan
astonishment, his fey wife didn't miss her uncann
powers one whit.

"I have children, a home and the love of a man lik
no other," she said when he had remarked on it. "O
course, I *will* miss Sir Hector. . . ." She had fixe
Lachlan with a level violet gaze, then twined her arm
around his neck and kissed him deeply. "But it seem
a fair trade to me."

Now her pale, beautiful brow was furrowed, and sh
wore one of her famous frowns. "Lachlan, Maeve wa
playing with Ian and Hugh all afternoon. Now she
disappeared. Lucy's gone to search the castle—"

"I know where Maeve is, Aunt Fiona."

Fiona and Lachlan swiveled. Jamie's daughter Eliza
beth stood before them, twisting her nail-bitten finger
in her skirt. Lachlan felt a quick pang of tendernes
Although Elizabeth was suffering through an awkwa
adolescence, her Titian hair and cobalt eyes clearl
marked her as Jamie's daughter—and promised tha
one day she would be a stunning beauty.

Elizabeth blushed beneath her freckles, then m
Lachlan's questioning eyes. "I saw her running towar
the path to the sea cliffs just a few minutes ago, whe
you all were watching the twins. I said she shouldn
go there alone, but she said she was meeting her gran
father, and he would look after her."

"Her grandfather?" Fiona's nails dug into Lachlan
arms, and the color drained from her cheeks. "Eliza
beth, are you sure that's what she said?"

"Y-yes, ma'am."

Speechless, Lachlan stared down at his wife, su
that the stricken look in her eyes mirrored his ow
thunderstruck expression.

Jamie put his arm around Elizabeth, then tapped her on the nose. "What nonsense is this, ye wee toe-rag? Ye ken your grandfather Maclean died long before ye and Maeve were born—"

Fiona whirled, caught up her lavender-muslin skirts and pelted down the terrace steps.

"Fiona, wait!" Lachlan bit back an oath, then strode after her. Och, this was nothing but a bit of foolishness. Sure and Elizabeth took after her father, who was a wee bit overfond of jokes and teasing.

He rounded the corner of the castle wall, then halted. Fifty yards away, Maeve—his loving, fey, solemn-eyed daughter—stood at the edge of the sea cliffs, seventy feet above the jagged rocks and frigid, crashing surf that had drowned many a Maclean before her. His heart stopped.

Fiona gasped and raced forward, hair tumbling loose from its pins. Lachlan opened his mouth to shout Maeve's name, then stopped. What if he startled her? What if she stumbled, lost her footing, fell? Och, St. Ninian, she was only four years old. She was his heart, his wee redheaded lassie. She was so like her mother, and, oh, dear God in heaven, he couldn't lose her, *wouldn't* lose her.

He bolted forward. Maeve squatted down, plucked a green thistle, then held it up as if offering it to someone. She smiled up into the crystalline air, dimpling like a cherub. At that moment, Fiona reached her, grabbed her arm and yanked her back from the brink of the cliffs. Maeve opened her mouth and began to howl.

"Here, lassie, what's all this? Och, now, haud yer wheest." Lachlan reached his wife and child, flung his arm around Fiona's trembling shoulder, then hustled them away from the cliffs. Fiona looked as if she might faint, so he lifted Maeve into his arms. "Hush, lassie. Ye're too big to cry."

Maeve stopped howling, then sniffed theatrically and pinned him with an aggrieved glare. "M-mummy scared me."

"Holy Mary and all the saints!" Fiona cried. "Maeve Genevieve Maclean, I've told you a thousand times to stay away from those cliffs! You could have fallen. You could have been killed—"

"But I wasn't," Maeve blurted, pouting mightily. "I was safe. Grampa wouldn't let me fall."

Lachlan dragged in a breath and struggled to hold his temper. "Wheest, lassie. Both your grandfathers are dead—"

"Not Sir Hector. He's standing right over there." Maeve squirmed from Lachlan's arms, then thrust a defiant finger at a spot near the edge of the cliff. Lachlan and Fiona spun and stared. Lachlan saw nothing but azure sky, rough granite and swaying green stalks of grass and thistle, with the sapphire sea and the blurred gray bulk of the mainland beyond. He cast Fiona a startled glance. Could it be?

She met his gaze, violet eyes wide and astonished. He cocked a questioning brow; she bit her lip and shook her head. Apparently, she had seen nothing.

They turned and gazed down at their daughter. Tears clung to her long dark lashes, and her pouting lower lip trembled. Fiona sank to her knees and wrapped Maeve in her arms. "It's all right, *ma chère.* We believe you." She held the child away from her and smiled into her eyes. "Sir Hector is quite a character, isn't he?"

Maeve sniffed and nodded.

Fiona leaned forward and pressed a kiss to her brow. "Oh, *ma chère.* Your gift is a treasure. Cherish it and keep it safe. Not everyone can see with the heart, you know. But you do. And so does your father."

Fiona smiled up at him, then stood with lithe grace. Lachlan caught his breath, then gently drew her into his arms. "I love ye," he murmured, voice hoarse with overwhelming emotion.

"I know." She smiled deep into his eyes, then raised her mouth to his.

Lachlan's lids fluttered shut, and he lost himself in the magic of her kiss. Och, until the day he died, he never would grasp that such pure and perfect love could exist in this world. 'Twas a rare treasure, indeed.

Put a Little Romance in Your Life With

Betina Krahn